CLASSIC
CLASSROOM CLANGERS

Compiled by
VIN SHANLEY

ROBSON BOOKS

This edition published in Great Britain in 2004 by Robson Books,
The Chrysalis Building, Bramley Road, London W10 6SP

An imprint of **Chrysalis** Books Group plc

British Library Cataloguing in Publication Data
A catalogue record for this title is available from the
British Library

ISBN 1 86105 333 9

Typeset by SX Composing DTP, Rayleigh, Essex
Printed and bound in Great Britain by
Creative Print & Design (Wales), Ebbw Vale

CLASSIC
CLASSROOM
CLANGERS

The Author

Vin Shanley lives in Billingham, Stockton-on-Tees, where, from 1985 until 1995, he was headteacher at St Michael's Comprehensive School. Since then, he has enjoyed success with two best sellers, *Classroom Clangers* and *Football Shorts*. He has also written four Assembly/ PSE books designed for secondary schools, and is in the process of completing Volume V of the *Essential Assemblies and PSE For All* series.

This book is dedicated to all teachers and school personnel, without whose commitment our children and grandchildren would not prosper as they do.

Contents

Introduction

It is comforting when even the greatest and the famous make gaffes. The difference between them and us more humble folk is that their howlers are captured, more often than not, on video or radio recordings. Most of them, thankfully, have the grace to laugh at themselves and we, for our part, appreciate that "there, but for the grace of God, go I". We laugh not at them, but with them. And so, before we launch into a catalogue of clangers from the world of education, let us enjoy some others from the world of the famous – and sometimes from the not-so-famous . . .

When Ronald Reagan was telling the world that the United States had much to offer the Third World, he made the following error nine times in a speech: "The United States has much to offer the Third World War."

Richard Nixon, attending Charles De Gaulle's funeral: "This is a great day for France."

Entertainer and comedian, Michael Barrymore, compering *Quiz Show:* "So, Carol, you're a housewife and a mother. And have you got any children?"

Jim Siebal, Mayor of St Paul, Minnesota: "I'm not indecisive. Am I indecisive?"

Decca Records executive to the Beatles in 1962: "You'll never make it – four-man groups are out. Go back to Liverpool!"

Samantha Fox, singer/model: "I've got ten pairs of training shoes – one for each day of the week."

In education the gaffes fall thick and fast, and thanks are due to those teachers who have provided such gems as the following, and the hundreds which appear in this book...

Q: Use "judicious" in a sentence.
A: Hands that *do dishes* can be soft as your face, with Mild Green Fairy Liquid.
Q: Who was it who did not like the return of the Prodigal Son?
A: The fatted calf.
Q: What is artificial respiration commonly known as?
A: The kiss of death.
Q: What is the treatment for a badly bleeding nose?
A: Circumcision.
Q: Use "unaware" in a sentence.
A: "Unaware" means your vest and your pants.

So, without further ado, let's read the gaffes from the wise and the not-so-...

1

The Curriculum

We all have our memories of favourite subjects at school which usually spring from an empathy we had with a kindly teacher or a facility for a subject which, by the grace of God, was naturally bestowed upon us. That is not to say that our proficiency in that discipline protects us against dropping clangers.

Who can forget the report on TV of a certain American senator, promoting "Spelling Week" in a school, who displayed his skills at the blackboard by putting an "e" at the end of potato?

Yes, even the best of us can slip up, and the more important and self-opinionated the person dropping the clanger, the more enjoyable it is for those who witness it.

Certain subjects are more popular than others. English, history and geography, for example, figure largely, mainly because pupils can always write something and rarely reach an impasse – unlike maths or a Greek translation, in which a dead end as final as the summit of Everest can rapidly be reached.

Still, it must brighten up the day of the marginalised

classics teacher when this type of letter appears in a national newspaper . . .

As a normal wife and mother, I have found Latin immensely helpful in every way. *(Letter in Daily Mail)*

Careers

When it comes to a choice of career, there are those who have no doubt in their minds about what they want to do, especially after sampling certain jobs through "work experience", which one pupil described as "the start of adultery life".

After attending James Hawes Funeral Parlour for his "work experience", school leaver Trevor Newman, 16, said: "I participated in a cremation, visited a mortuary, and was shown a body. It was great. What's more, if they take me on, I'll never be out of a job." *(Waltham Forest Guardian)*

I want to be a butcher because I like meating people.

Q: List the careers you are considering.
A: I want to be a pote.

I would like to be a braim surgian.

Punctuation can make all the difference . . .

Student desires post; domesticated, fond of cooking children.

Extracts from work experience application forms handed in . . .

Wish: To end all the killing in the world.
Hobbies: Hunting and fishing.

Q: Are you a natural born British subject?
A: No – by Cæsarian section.
Q: Length of residence in Britain *(if applicable)*
A: 26 ft.

One school leaver was applying for a brickwork course. Under the title "Examinations to date" were four columns. "Subject", "Grade" and "Date" were neatly completed for his five exam passes. But under the fourth heading, "Board", was written: "Yes I was", "lots", "not so much", "no" and "yes, very much".

Others know what they want to do but don't get the chance . . .

Arriving at Messrs Trimmings of Castleford to start her first day's work, Miss Alison Knaggs, who has been unemployed since leaving school two years ago, was told that she was redundant. "I did not have time to take off my coat," she said, "but a spokesman for the firm said he understood how I felt."

Man, honest. Will take anything.

Some get no sympathy . . .

Delia Morrison has been barred from her parents' home because she married a grave-digger. Her mother, 55-year-old Mrs Gladys Peat, of Geneva Drive, Darlington, Co. Durham, said yesterday: "We have never felt so ashamed in our lives. If we had known what he was we would have thrown him out long ago." *(Sunday Express)*

... while others get all the sympathy ...

Henry, aged 20, whose godparents include the Duchess of Gloucester and the Duke of Kent, is a jazz drummer who went to Eton. "But he's been on the dole lately," said Bunty. "Which is a bit sad when he's so close to the Queen." *(News of the World)*

Some are in no doubt as to what should happen or should not ...

Mrs Dimmock deplored the fact that young people no longer went into private service. She thought that, apart from the pleasant relationship that existed between employer and employee, the servant picked up a far better accent. *(Worthing Gazette)*

"Do you gents want something to drink?", though said in a perfectly friendly manner, was not, in my view, the right way for a wine waiter to address First Class passengers. *(Sunday Times)*

Others have no idea what is happening ...

A 19-year-old girl told a Canterbury court today that she was getting married on Saturday but did not know her fiancé's job. Asked by the clerk for her fiancé's occupation, she replied: "I have never asked him. I know he goes out each day." *(Evening Standard)*

But there are plenty of good careers on offer – aren't there?

DENIS HEALEY COMMUNITY CENTRE: Foundry Mill Street, Seacroft, Leeds 14. PART-TIME CLEANER – £24,551 per hour. *(Leeds City Council Dept of Education)*

DO YOU SCRATCH your bottom while taking a bath? Have it re-glazed by the professional. *(Edinburgh Advertiser)*

Tired of cleaning yourself? Let me do it.

FOLDERS FOR SALE: Stock up and save. Limit: one.

PURLER Tornado would train girl to ride wall of death; good knitter preferable. *(Southend Standard)*

SINGLE GIRL GROOM REQUIRED TO WORK UNDER STUD GROOM. Able to ride/exercise.

URGENTLY WANTED BY MACHINE TOOL FACTORY. Male parts handlers. Box 132.

WANTED 50 girls for stripping machine operators in factory.

WANTED Unmarried girls to pick fresh fruit and produce at night.

And others not so good . . .

WANTED . . . EDIBLE OIL TECHNOLOGIST *(The Observer)*

HELP WANTED Man wanted to handle dynamite. Must be able to travel unexpectedly. *(Daily News, Newfoundland)*

> **URGENTLY REQUIRED — Pump Attendant**
> PART-TIME — 126 hrs week
> *Apply:* Whittlesey Motors Ltd
> EASTREA ROAD, WHITTLESEY,
> PETERBOROUGH

(Peterborough Evening Telegraph)

WANTED Smart Young Man for butcher's. Able to cut, skewer and serve a customer. *(Local paper)*

Woman wants cleaning three days a week. *(Guardian)*

WANTED Chambermaid in rectory. Love in, £475 a month.

MORTGAGE RESEARCHERS Required for prestigious offices in Hamilton Square. To work with small friendly professional team. Flexible shits 5 pm-9 pm. Excellent hourly rate, plus bonuses. Due to expansion, immediate positions. *(London Advertiser)*

TOILET CLEANER required 5-8 pm, Mon-Fri in Kew, Richmond. Good rates of pay. Must be able to ride a bicycle. Please call Hazel Nish on . . . *(Hatford Tribune)*

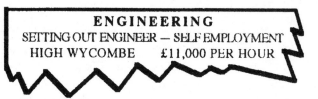

ENGINEERING
SETTING OUT ENGINEER — SELF EMPLOYMENT
HIGH WYCOMBE   £11,000 PER HOUR

(Hertfordshire's "Job Opportunities")

YOGA INSTRUCTOR
PERMANENT POSITION
You must have minimum level 3 standard combined with excellent customer service skills and the ability to work unsupervised.

(Sheffield Star)

WANTED IMMEDIATELY A woman for boiling down. Apply Blake Potted Meat Company *(New Zealand newspaper)*

WANTED Women, Evening Shift, 5.30 to 9.30, for backwashing, regilling, and tophat minding. *(Bradford Telegraph and Argus)*

Unexpected vacancy for a knife-thrower's assistant. Rehearsals start immediately. Apply in writing to Black Horse Lodge, Linford, Milton Keynes. *(Bedfordshire Times)*

The Royal Navy is sometimes called the senile service.

To help new graduates into the world of work, a New York research firm asked personnel executives at 200 leading companies to describe the worst gaffes they had witnessed in the interview room. Here are some of the replies . . .

One candidate arranged for a pizza to be delivered to my office during the lunch-hour interview I had arranged with him. I asked him not to eat it until later.

When I mentioned that we had gone to the same school, he immediately stood up and began to belt out the school anthem.

On the phone I asked the candidate to bring his CV and a couple of references. He arrived with his CV and two people.'

When I asked the candidate to give a good example of the organisational skills she was boasting about, she said she was proud of her ability to pack her suitcase "real neat" for her vacations.

I once had a candidate who actually showed up for an interview during the summer wearing a bathing suit. She said she didn't think I'd mind.

One candidate couldn't answer any of my questions because he had just had major dental work.

English

A class had been asked to write an essay on "The funniest thing I ever saw". The lazy boy of the class sat dreaming away while the other boys were busy writing. Soon his teacher went up to his desk to see his effort. It ran as follows: "The funniest thing I ever saw was too funny for words."

Essay "on a ceremony you have witnessed": "When the wedding was over the bridegroom clasped his loved one tight in his arms, while the little organ began to swell and fill the room."

Transparent is something you can see through – like a keyhole.

Q: What is a young horse called?
A: A clot.

I met Miss Enid Blyton, whose books for children have sold 40,000,000 copies, and asked her how she works. "Some writers plan chapters and work things out in advance," she said. "I just sit down and open the sluice gates and it just pours through." *(Daily Express)*

We do feel that an improvement with her English language would help her if she is to persue a career in banking. *(Work experience report)*

On day three of the term, September 1998, after the "Literacy Hour" had been introduced into primary schools, a ten-year-old enthusiastically enquired: "Sir, when are we going to do that 'leprosy hour'?"

How can the French expect to attract our tourist trade? This year, at five different French hotels, the tap marked "C" turned out to be "H". *(Letter in Evening Chronicle)*

I really felt sacred as I waited for the dentist.

Rusty, a pony owned by a 16-year-old grammar school girl, Elizabeth Millbank, of East Street, Blandford, Dorset, is terrified by fireworks. So, on 5 November, she will sit with him and read Shakespeare aloud. *(Daily Mail)*

Barbarians are little metal balls you put in wheels to make them run smoothly.

"What is 'wanderlust'?" was a question put to senior girls at a Southend school. One girl replied: "It is what people go on cruises for."

Dear Mrs — J. has not learnt the lines for English as I don't think he needs to learn about Shackespear. Something else would of been better. I should think they

want to learn proper English first. *(Letter from a parent to a Dorset teacher)*

Q: Name one book written by Thomas Hardy.
A: Tess of the Dormobiles.

A census is where everybody in the house has to be filled in.

The judge said that he had been living off the immortal earnings of his wife.

The answer to the following question makes it clear that the little lad knew that the word "frugal" had something to do with saving . . .

Q: Show that you know the exact meaning of "frugal" by writing a short paragraph including the word.
A: A beautiful princess was at the top of a tall tower. She saw a handsome prince riding by. "Frugal me, frugal me," cried the beautiful princess. So the handsome prince climbed the tall tower and he frugalled her and they lived happily ever after.

Last night it was so cold when I got in from school, I switched on the emotion heater and had a hot bath.

To scotch something means to drown your sorrows in whisky.

The little lad asked the school for a copy of *She Stoops to Conga.*

Q: Use the word "foul" in a sentence.
A: My dad took all the family to Birtsmorton Water Foul Sanctuary on Sunday.

A buttress is the wife of a butler.

Q: What is the plural of potato?
A: Turnip.

A deaf mute is a dead dog.

Q: Give the opposite of "filly".
A: Empty.

Hogmanay is another type of wood.

A rudder is what you milk a cow with.

Never look a gift horse in the ear.

Heroine is a hard drug which is addictive.

Q: Who was Robinson Crusoe?
A: A famous singer.

Q: What is a brassière?
A: Something you warm your hands on.

Q: What's a suspended sentence?
A: Where the man gets hanged.

Q: Write a word which describes a man who keeps on despite all difficulties?
A: Passionate.

The girl insisted on riding side-salad.

Another tragic thing in our family was my brother.

The boys earned some money by cleaning widows.

Schools without capital punishment are rather boring. Without capital punishment nobody pays any attention.

On *The Highwayman*: They gagged Bess and tied her to a narrow bed. From this we know that she was a virgin because she still had a narrow bed.

On *Dulce Et Decorum Est*: You can imagine the misery he must have felt, being alive one day and dead the next.

Excerpt from *Lady Macbeth's Diary*: "Macbeth will kill him tonight. It's a shame really; he struck me as a nice man."

Shakespeare wrote tragedies, comedies and hysterectomies, all in Islamic petameter.

Most of Shakespeare's plays are terrible tragedies.

An example of a heroic couplet are Romeo and Juliet.

Romeo's wish was to be laid by Juliet.

Miguel Cervantes wrote *Donkey Hote*.

John Milton wrote *Paradise Lost*. Then his wife died and he wrote *Paradise Regained*.

Q: How did Odysseus trick the Cyclops?
A: He told him that his name was Norman.

McAnulty's Yellow Line
Coach Tours and Private Hire
"Les Miserable"
Point Theatre, Dublin
Limited Number of Tickets available

(Newry Reporter)

As I approached the house, I saw a man mowing the lawn with a small child.

My family condescended from Wealdstone.

There was the pupil who thought Shakespeare came from Arabia.

Her father was a civil serpent.

As he walked through the room he heard the sound of heavy breeding.

The heroine has to be like Julius Caesar's wife – all things to all men.

Complete the following: "A stitch in time . . ."
". . . is worth it because you don't have to buy a new jumper."

Complete the following: "A rolling stone gathers . . ."
". . . a fair bit of speed."

The vicar was wearing his cossack.

My dad has an infinity with birds.

It seems the man was a blank clerk.

I put my foot on a sharp tack which made my foot howl with pain.

Q: Explain the circumstances in which this quote from Macbeth was made: "I heard the owls scream and the crickets cry."
A: Macbeth was on his way to murder Duncan when he heard the call of nature.

Teacher: Josh [six-year-old] – What do you do when you come to a full stop?
Josh: Er . . . You get off, Miss.

Q: What form of verse best describes 'Mary Had A Little Lamb' and 'Little Jack Horner'?
A: Mercenary rhymes.

A goblet is a male turkey.

Q: Use the word "tackle" in a sentence.
A: A tack'll make you sore if you sit on it.

All sentences are either simple or confound.

Rhythm is a horse trotting on a road.

The Royal Wedding was a whore inspiring event.

He spent his days in prison sewing children's balls together.

The octopus wrapped his testicles round the diver and strangled him.

Correctly English in 100 Days – East Asian book title.

If you ever come within a mile of our house, will you stop there all night?

Q: Use the word "denial" in a sentence.
A: Cleopatra lived on Denial.

For his comfort the roadman has a brassière which is very nice on a cold day.

Horoscopes

Due to unforeseen circumstances we are unable to bring you horoscopes this edition!

(The Journal of Yarm & District)

A 1982 circular from the Joint Matriculation Board Examinations Council announced ...

It has been decided to modify the format of the English Literature (Advanced) Paper I. In future, in order to avoid

any possibility of confusion, section B will consist of essay questions on the plays of Shakespaere.

A teacher from a school in the south of England told the story of the occasion when a colleague in the English Department invited an eminent French poet to give a talk to his second-year class. For 40 minutes the guest gave an interesting discourse. At the end, he offered to answer pupils' questions. There was a pause before one young boy plucked up the courage. "Sir," he asked respectfully. "How much did your trainers cost?"

Q: Name a famous "Willy".
A: Willy the Poo.

Q: Give the opposite of woe.
A: Giddyup.

. . . they were married and lived happily even after.

(Malvern Gazette and Ledbury Reporter)

WANTED Man to take care of cow that does not smoke or drink. *(Herald)*

WANTED A domesticated lady to live with an elderly lady to hell with cooking and housework. *(Agency magazine)*

Work for the Lord. The pay isn't good, but the retirement benefits are out of this World. *(Church bulletin board).*

Monotony means being married to the same person all of your life.

And what of English around the world . . .?

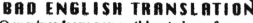

BAD ENGLISH TRANSLATIONS
Our wines leave you nothing to hope for
— In a Swiss restaurant
**Because of a big rush we will execute
customers in strict rotation**
— In a Rhodes tailor shop
Teeth extracted by latest Methodists
— Outside Hong Kong dentists
Would you like to ride on your own ass?
— Thailand donkey ride
Specialist in women and other diseases
— In a Rome doctor's office
Special today — No Ice-Cream
— In a Swiss mountain inn

I've said goodbye to boyhood – now I'm looking forward to my adultery.

Still, even the greatest can make mistakes . . .

Jane Austen from *Northanger Abbey*: Such was Catherine Morland at ten. At fifteen appearances were mending; she began to cut her hair and long for balls.

Man jailed after restaurant row

Indian staff terrified as he demands italian food

(Evening Express)

Charles Dickens from *Little Dorrit:* No public business of any kind could possibly be done at any time, without the acquiescence of the Circumlocution Office. Its finger was in the largest public pie, and in the smallest public tart.

From *The Last of the Valerii:* Next after that slow-coming, slow-going smile of her lover, it was the rusty complexion of his patrimonial marbles that she most prized.

Russell Ash and Brian Lake have located some unusual British titles in their Bizarre Books *(Pavilion)* . . .

Peculiar Pastimes

Teach Yourself Alcoholism, by Glatt Meier (EUP, 1975)

How to Pick Pockets: A Treatise on the Fundamental Principle, Theory and Practice of Picking Pockets, by Eddie Joseph (Vampire Press, 1946)

The Great Pantyhose Crafts Book, by Ed & Stevie Baldwin (Western Publishing Co., 1962)

Build Your Own Hindenberg, by Alan Rose (Putnam, 1983)

Hand Grenade Throwing as a College Sport, by Lewis Omer (Spalding & Bros, 1918)

Books to Make the Heart Sink

The Romance of Cement, by the Portland Cement Company (Liverpool & Knight, 1926)

I Was a Kamikaze, by Ryuji Nagatsuke (Aberlard-Schuman, 1973)

The Wit of Prince Philip, by HRH Prince Philip (Leslie Frewin, 1953)

The Sunny Side of Bereavement, by Rev. Charles E. Cooledge (Gorham Press)

Premature Burial and How It May Be Prevented, by William Tebb & Edward Perry Vollum (Sonneschein, 1986)

Do-It-Yourself Coffins: For Pets and People, by Dale Power (Schiffer, 1997)

Specialised Subjects

Truncheons: Their Romance and Reality, by Erland Fenn Clark (Herbert Jenkins, 1935)

American Bottom Archaeology, by Charles John Bareis & James Warren Porter (University of Illinois Press, 1983)

Whippings and Lashings, by The Girl Guide Association (1977)

Inappropriate Authors

Oh! Sex Education, by Mary Breasted (Praeger, 1970)

Motorcycling For Beginners, by Geoff Carless (EP Publishing 1980)

Death in Early America, by Margaret Coffin (E P Dutton, New York, 1976)

Vasectomy: Male Sterilising, by Paul J. Gillette (Paperback Library, New York, 1972)

Medicine

The Complete Guide to Selling Your Organs, Body Fluids, Bodily Functions, and Being a Human Guinea Pig, by Jim Hogshire (Loompanics, 1992)

The Romance of Leprosy, by E. Mackerchar (Lepers Mission, 1949)

What You Didn't Know About France

A local food speciality of Provence is a quack monsieur.

Small cafés in France are good for eating snakes.

We saw a girl in our hotel with frogs' legs.

Many Frenchmen wear berries on their heads.

French children drink bowels of hot chocolate.

In France, school is compulsive from the age of six.

At Chateaudun, if you want to go for a long walk, you can walk along the river Loire.

Fish are soled in Brittany.

A past President of France was called Guillotine.

On French motorways they have toll-boobs.

Fruits de mer are fruits of the sea, eg coconuts and pineapples.

Fruits de mer are cockles and wenches.

The French have a two hour dinner break because they find it more fascinating than us.

When driving in France, it is very easy to get confused – so don't forget to drive on the left.

In France the whine is much cheaper.

At the citadel in Boulogne, we saw the spot where the Unknown Worrier rested.

Prices are high on the Eiffel Tower.

If crossing the Channel by car, you have to book a fairy.

Grapes are pressed and they excrete their juice.

Beaujolais Nouveau is a health food.

Cabernet d'Anjou and Saumur are French political parties.

The Arc de Triomphe is famous for the forbidden soldier who is buried on top of the arch.

At the Arc de Triomphe, you can see the infernal flame.

The Arc de Triomphe is the biggest horse race in France.

I had a sandwich and a white café au lait.

You get information from the French Tourist Bored.

We visited Notre Dam.

Quasimodo made the bell at Notre Dame.

La mère works in the town hall.

The religious event which takes place when a French boy or girl reaches the age of 13 is: circumcision or castration.

Parasites are the inhabitants of Paris.

Literal translations . . .
Est-il parti, ma tante? Is there a party, my aunt?

Sacré Coeur. Holy Dog.

La raison du plus fort est toujours la meilleure. The biggest raisins are always the best.

La pauvre femme tourna vers . . . The poor woman turned green . . .

Un grand garçon à lunettes. A big lunatic boy.

J'ai grand faim. I have a big wife.

Beurre. Cold.

Pas de deux. Father of twins.

Coup de grace. Lawn mower.

Avez-vous des timbres? Have you any wood?

Je voudrais une fiche. I would like a cod.

Est-ce qu'il y a un bon bistro ici, s'il vous plaît? Could you pass the gravy here, please?

La brasserie est grande et bonne. The brassière is large but good.

Je voudrais prendre pour mon petit déjeuner un oeuf a la coque dur. I would like to have for my breakfast a hard cock's egg.

Voulez-vous poisson hors-d'oeuvre? Do you want fish or duvre?

Le chef vous propose. The chef would like to marry you.

Je voudrais une bouteille de vin rouge. I would like a bottle of rough wine.

Je voudrais louer une bicyclette. I need a bike to get to the toilet.

Sommes-nous bien sur la route pour Paris? Do we pass the Somme on the way to Paris?

General Knowledge

Give an example of the following . . .

An occupation where you need a torch.
A: A burglar.

A dangerous race.
A: The Vikings.

Some famous brothers.
A: Bonnie and Clyde.

A part of the body beginning with "N".
A: Knee.

Something you put on walls.
A: Roofs.

Something that floats in the bath.
A: Water.

A famous Royal.
A: Mail.

Something in the garden which is green.
A: The shed.

Something slippery.
A: A conman.

A food that can be brown or white.
A: Potatoes.

A famous Scotsman.
A: Jock.

Something you do in the bathroom.
A: Decorate.

A song with "moon" in the title.
A: Blue Suede Moon.

A famous bridge.
A: Bridge Over Troubled Water.

A bird with a long neck.
A: Naomi Campbell.

Something you open other than a door.
A: Your bowels.

When the court is assembled the judges come out of the robbing-room.

Q: What is the currency used in Denmark?
A: The Denmark.

Remembrance Day is on a Sunday, for the First and Second World Wars. Thousands of popsies are sold in the streets.

The Royal Prerogative is the little dog the Queen goes around with.

Q: What do the letters HRH stand for?
A: Duke of Edinburgh.

Q: How does the law define "actual bodily harm"?
A: It means actually harming someone's body.

Q: What should you do if you get obscene telephone calls?
A: Ask the operator to stop them.

Q: Name a paint which protects wood.
A: Brown.

Q: How do prescription drugs vary from over-the-counter drugs?
A: Some drugs have a more lusting effect.

Q: Why are some farmers in favour of fox hunting?
A: Because it gives them the chance of dressing up.

Q: Who would you expect to see with a mortar board?
A: A bricklayer's mate who has to keep the bricklayer in bricks.

Q: What is anthropology the study of?
A: Ants.

People have to pass MOT tests every 12000 miles.

Q: What do the letters "MW" mean on a radio?
A: It must not be used on top of a microwave.

Q: What is an exporter?
A: Somebody who used to have a job carrying cases at railway stations.

Q: What do you get from the pine tree?
A: Pineapples.

Q: What are steroids?
A: Things for keeping the carpet on the stairs.

Pupil: Miss, what's Huntingdon's Chorea?
Teacher: It's a hereditary disease which is quite common in isolated communities where they're so interbred.
Pupil: Do they have a lot of bread shops there, then, Miss?

If you have no money, you could try the porn brokers.

Q: Why does a surgeon wear a mask when he performs an operation?
A: So if he messes it up the patient won't know who did it.

Aristotle Onassis was a Greek shitting typoon.

Slogan by pupil devising an anti-smoking poster . . .

GIVE UP SMOKING – NO BUTTS

Geography

European errors . . .

The steamer sailed from Dieppe to Newheaven.

Q: Which is the nearest port to Dover?
A: Calais – unless you go by aeroplane.

The advantage of living on an island is that you get the spray from the sea.

Q: Name a Spanish holiday resort.
A: El Dorado

Nobody goes to Lloret de Mar anymore. It's too crowded.

Today, Rome is full of fallen arches.

The Mediterranean and the Red Sea are connected by the sewage canal.

Q: What is the capital of Spain?
A: "S".

Lancashire and Cheshire exam question: "On the outline map of England and Wales provided, shade in the Highlands of Scotland."

American absurdities . . .

Q: How are buildings in San Francisco built to be safe from earthquakes?
A: The buildings don't quite touch the ground.

Some parts of the Grand Canyon are a mile deep and two miles high.

Difficulties facing the American farmers of the Mid-West are draughts and incests.

General geographical gaffes . . .

Q: What is the major export of Brazil?
A: Brazil nuts – but only at Christmas.

To make rubber you cut the bark off a hyena tree. The rubber is then smoked.

The climate of the Sahara is such that the inhabitants have

to live elsewhere.

Q: What is the correct name for the method of providing water for crops in dry areas?
A: Irritation.

Tea-bushes sometimes grow to 20 feet tall, but as the women are only five feet, they have their tops cut off.

Q: Write down what you know of Red China.
A: It looks nice on a white tablecloth.

The cold at the North Pole is so great that the towns are not inhabited there.

An Eskimo lives on a kind of leather called blubber.

Q: What are "glaciers"?
A: People who fix windows when they're broken.

Q: What is the Equator?
A: It is a menagerie lion running around the Earth through Africa.

GREENLAND VOLCANO IN ERUPTION by arrangement with *The Times* *(The Scotsman)*

Q: Name the five continents.
A: a, e, i, o, u.

British blunders ...

Cooler in the South, warmer in the South is the seven-day forecast of the *Sunday Express* weather experts. *(Sunday Express)*

Sheffield is in a valley in Yorkshire slopping up the side of the moorland.

Q: What is the best way to protect crops from storms?
A: By planting trees. A 60ft tree can break wind from 300 yards.

Q: Name a cow that gives a lot of milk.
A: Daisy.

Q: Give an area of low population density.
A: Graveyard.

Manchester is one of the densest cities.

During the strikes under Margaret Thatcher, the coal industry was nearly destroyed when the miners were driven into the ground.

Crewe is the biggest conjunction in England.

The Zulus lived in mud huts and used to have rough mating on the floors.

And parents will do even more than can be expected to give their offspring a place in life ...

Seeking to improve her young son's poor knowledge of geography, a Norfolk reader persuaded him to take up stamp collecting. Only two weeks later, she had striking proof of how wise she had been. "Where is Spain?" she asked him. Without hesitation he replied: "Five pages after Portugal."

(Overheard) I cannot believe it. That geography project has

to be handed in tomorrow. I feel really sorry for Mam – it'll take her ages.

History

Ancient, and not so ancient, history . . .

The world began millions of years ago with little orgasms crawling around it.

Ancient Egypt was inhabited by Mummies who wrote in hydraulics.

The Egyptians built the pyramids in the shape of a huge rectangular cube.

The Greeks were lazy people because they worshipped idles.

The Greeks were highly sculptured people.

The Greeks had myths. A myth is a female moth.

Socrates died of an overdose of wedlock.

In the Olympic games, the reward to the victor was a coral wreath.

Q: What is the name given in Greek mythology to the creature that was half man and half animal?
A: Buffalo Bill.

The government of Athens was democratic because the people took the law into their own hands.

The Punic Wars were fought between the Romans and the Carthage Indians.

1st pupil: What's Carthage, anyway?
2nd pupil: You know – it's that stuff in your bones.
3rd pupil: Don't be silly – that's carnage.

Sparta protested, saying that all the cities' fornications in Greece should be dismantled.

Julius Caesar extinguished himself on the battlefields of Gaul.

Brutus stabbed Caesar. Dying, he gasped out: "Tee, hee, Brutus."

At Roman banquets the Romans wore garlics in their hair.

The Romans were called Romans because they never stayed in one place for very long.

The artichoke was an ancient instrument of torture.

Because of the good roads in Rome, Christianity travelled faster than ever before.

King Arthur lived in the age of shivery with brave knights on prancing horses and beautiful women.

King Harold mustarded his troops before the Battle of Hastings.

Year 8 were watching a video on the Norman Conquest and the commentator referred to William the Conqueror, adding "also known as William the Bastard". One of the lads asked the teacher: "Sir, what's a bastard?"

"A bastard," said the stoical teacher, "is when a child is born to a couple who are not married."

Another little lad, as proud as Punch, announced to the class: "Hey, Sir, I'm one of them, then."

Magna Carta provided that no free man could be hanged twice for the same offence.

In midevil times most people were alliterate.

During this time, people put on morality plays about ghosts, goblins, virgins and other mythical creatures.

Q: What does "impregnable" mean?
A: It means that you cannot have babies.

William Tell invented the telephone.

William Tell shot an arrow through an apple while standing on his son's head.

Martin Luther was a German pheasant.

Martin Luther was excommunicated by a bull and nailed to the door at Wittenburg Cathedral.

Protestants disliked the smell of incest in the Catholic Church.

It was Donatello's interest in the female nude which made him the father of the Renaissance.

Q: What was Leonardo da Vinci's major claim to fame?
A: Sailing the *Mona Lisa* round the world.

Christopher Columbus was a great navigator who discovered America while cursing about the Atlantic.

Columbus' ships were called the *Nina*, the *Pinta* and the *Santa Fe*.

Henry VIII always had difficulty getting Catherine of Aragon pregnant.

Some of Henry VIII's wives were – Chattering of Aragon, Amber Lin, Jane Saymore, Ann of Cloves and Catherine Purr.

From the womb of Henry VIII protestantism was born.

Q: What stood Henry VIII apart from all other English Kings?
A: He was the fattest human being of all time.

Queen Elizabeth was the "Virgin Queen". When she exposed herself before her troops, they all cheered.

And Sir Francis Drake said: "Let the *Armada* wait. My bowels cannot."

Queen Elizabeth knitted Sir Walter Raleigh a cardigan.

Mary, Queen of Scots, married the Dolphin of France.

Children were born every year in the 18th century.

Q: Explain the importance of Wat Tyler.
A: Wat Tyler is a magazine for bathroom fixture handymen.

America was discovered by Colombo.

Later, the Pilgrims crossed the ocean, and this was called the Pilgrim's Progress. The winter of 1620 was a hard one for the settlers. Many people died and many babies were born. Captain John Smith was responsible for all this.

American Indians used to live, and some still do, in a reservoir.

Q: What were the three major causes of the American Civil War?
A: (a) Indians, (b) Hot weather, (c) Arguing.

Finally the American colonists won the war and no longer had to pay for taxis.

Benjamin Franklin died in 1790 and is still dead.

Abraham Lincoln was born in a log cabin that he built with his own hands.

On the night of 14 April 1865, Lincoln went to the theatre and got shot in his seat.

Under the constitution of the United States the people enjoyed the right to bare arms.

The watchwords of the French Revolution were Liberty, Equality, Maternity.

All through the French Revolution the women of France knitted and they dropped a stitch every time a head fell into the gelatine.

Napoleon wanted an heir to inherit his power but since Josephine was a baroness, she couldn't have any children.

Jacques Cartier, while searching for the North West Passage, stumbled across the great St Lawrence River and mapped it.

Queen Victoria was the longest Queen.

Queen Victoria sat on the thorn for 63 years.

Queen Victoria was a moral woman who practised virtue. Her death was the final event which ended her reign.

Wellington's nickname was "Ironpants".

Q: Name two of the key figures in the Industrial Revolution. *A:* Margaret Thatcher and Arthur Scargill.

In the nineteenth century, people stopped reproducing by hand and started reproducing by machine.

Cyrus McCormick invented the McCormick raper, which did the work of a hundred men.

The invention of the steamboat caused a network of rivers to spring up.

Florence Nightingale was a woman from a very early age.

Victorian ladies had thrills around their bottoms.

Charles Darwin was a naturalist who wrote *The Organ of the Species*.

Karl Marx became one of the Marx Brothers.

The First World War ushered in a new era in the anals of human history.

Universal suffrage was when the whole world suffered.

Q: With what do you connect the name Baden-Powell?
A: You connect it with a hyphen.

When Vesuvius erupted, there were floods of molten lager flowing down the mountainside.

Q: Name a great man of this century.
A: Martian Luther King.

Anne Frank hid in an attic for two years so the Romans couldn't get her.

The Russian Revolution was an uprising from the bottom.

Another important invention was the circulation of the blood.

Q: Describe what life was like in the trenches during the First World War.
A: It was OK when soldiers sang songs like "Anyone Who Had A Heart" to keep their spirits up.

When the soldiers went to battle in 1914 they had no idea what they were letting themselves in for. They thought it would be just like they saw on the telly with the British always beating the Germans and like the cowboys always beating the Indians.

The year 1936 was fairly uneventful. George V died and Edward VIII abdicated. The Crystal Palace burned down. Benny Goodman launched the swing era. The prophesied end of the world proved less nigh than anticipated. But perhaps the event with the greatest long-term significance was the staging of the first Hotel and Catering Exhibition at Olympia. *(Natural Gas magazine)*

Hitler was a madman, and this was his fatal floor.

Asked "What was the wartime Black Market?" in an Eden Camp History Theme Museum questionnaire, one pupil wrote: "For most people, the Black Market meant a little fiddle with the woman who owned the corner shop."

One way to settle the Middle East problem would be for the Jews and Arabs to sit down together and settle this like good Christians.

Q: What is Britain's highest award for valour in war?
A: Nelson's Column.

Home Economics

It has never been the same since they stopped cooking at school . . .

Q: Name a chicken dish with spices.
A: Chicken in Harpic.

Q: Chow mein is a popular Chinese dish. Name some others.
A: Kebabs and also chips with curry sauce.

Q: For how long would you boil a size 3 egg?
A: For no longer than four hours.

And how you do it throws up some novel methods . . .

My old uncle has an unusual pulse beat – sixty to the minute. Without the help of a clock, he can time accurately eggs boiling for three minutes, rounds of boxing and the two minutes' silence on Armistice Day. *(Letter in Illustrated)*

And . . .

Sir, The hymn "Onward Christian Soldiers", sung to the right tune and in a not-too-brisk tempo, makes a very good egg timer. If you put the egg into boiling water and sing all five verses and the chorus, the egg will be just right when you come to "Amen". *(Letter in the Daily Telegraph, 1983)*

Q: How would you keep milk from going sour?
A: Leave it in the cow.

A vegetarian is a horse doctor.

Then add the milk and the butter and rub the mixture well into the floor. *(Cookery book)*

Due to copy error, we regret that the Surprise Apple Sweet Potato recipe in the October issue was incomplete. Please add: 4 cups of mashed potatoes and 3 large apples. *(Cannery publication)*

At the end of the school's two hour itinerary, refreshments were provided by Ready-Mix Concrete Ltd. *(Eastwood and Kimberley Advertiser)*

Keeping all food under cover is the first step towards ridding the house of aunts.

To prevent tears when peeling onions, either bite on a slice of bread or work under a running tap and breathe through the mouth.

An oyster is a fish built like a nut.

A gripe is a ripe grape.

School's Daily Specials include select offerings of beef, foul, fresh vegetables, salads, quiche.

A number of stories have emerged about certain star footballers' lack of culinary awareness . . .

One reporter, who refused to divulge the name of the England international concerned, recounted sitting next to him at the Professional Footballers' Awards. The waitress asked him whether he would care for the "fish hors d'oeuvre". He replied: "You had better give me the d'oeuvre – the fish plays havoc with my stomach."

On another occasion, a footballer asked for "café au lait, please – and would you make it white".

And can it be true that one, when asked if he would like a prawn cocktail, replied: "No thanks, I'll have a drink with my main meal."

. . . and, asked whether he liked scampi, responded:

"Yeah, I love all Walt Disney's films."

One story, which is true, at least according to ex-international, Chris Waddle, concerns his friend Gazza. Apparently, on a pre-season tour of New Zealand, when the two were colleagues at Newcastle, Gazza came down late for breakfast at the team's hotel. "What can I get you?" asked the waitress. "I'll have a full English breakfast," replied Gazza. "I'm sorry," said the waitress, "but I'm afraid we've run out of bacon." "What?" exclaimed Gazza. "40 million sheep and no bacon?"

When the late and great Matt Busby joined the Forces during the Second World War, the recruiting sergeant asked him his occupation. "Footballer," replied Matt in his strong Scottish accent. When he was posted to his new unit, he found out that he had been registered as a "food boiler".

West Ham and England striker Ian Wright when asked during one of his first TV interviewing slots, "What's your favourite 'haute cuisine'?", responded, "Hot food."

But back to food . . .

Q: Give an example of unacceptable food hygiene.
A: If you find a bird dropping on a table – it's not all right to eat it.

Q: What rights do you have if you are sold out-of-date food?
A: You have the right to see the manager and bring it up in his office.

Q: If a person is feeling ill, why is it not a good idea for them to be serving food.

A: Because it is dangerous for deceased people to carry hot food.

Miss, you know it says on the work-sheet that I have to clean the cooker inside and out? Well, I've tried, but it is too heavy for me to get it into the playground.

If you want to be a cookery teacher you must spend a lot of time cooking yourself.

Q: What is rhubarb?
A: A kind of celery gone bloodshot.

Husk fresh corn; spread ears lightly with peanut butter. Place on grill, turning until done – about 10 minutes. Or let everyone grill his own ears, using long skewers to do so.

Marinade the steak in the sauce for at least two hours, then cook under a hot grill, basting with the sauce at frequent intervals. Alternatively, pour off sauce after marinading, heat separately, and let your guests pour it over themselves.

This packet of ready-made pastry will make enough for four persons or twelve tarts.

And other aspects of home economics . . .

Miss, I can't find the invisible thread.

Q: What's a bidet?
A: It's a thing that keeps you warm in bed.

Freelance eggs are more natural than battery-produced ones.

When buying cutting-out shears, consider – "Do they succumb to my needs?"

The mail order protection scheme is not being able to try underwear on because it is unhygienic.

Diets are for those who are thick and tired of it.

Now that preservatives have been introduced, the life expectancy of food is much longer.

If teeth are not cleaned, plague is the result.

And babies . . .

To avoid accidents always keep your hair in a net and never have a baby in the kitchen.

Q: How can parents help when a child wakes in the night suffering from breathing difficulties?
A: Make them inhale a steam kettle.

Q: What is the purpose of a placenta?
A: It's a place where you leave children when you do your shopping.

The first thing the doctor has to do when the baby is born is he has to cut the biblical cord.

If the baby does not thrive on fresh milk then it should be boiled.

When my Mam had the baby, she told my Dad to phone for the ambulance when the contraptions were 10 minutes apart.

Pregnant women get sudden urges for things like pomigranits.

And sorry . . . wrong order:

RETRACTION The "Greek Special" is a huge 18 inch pizza and not a huge 18 inch penis, as described in an ad. Blondie's Pizza would like to apologize for any confusion Friday's ad may have caused. *(Daily Californian)*

Maths

Sky reporter speaking with a young supporter outside Elland Road before a Leeds United v Manchester United League match:

Reporter: Who's going to win tonight, then?
Little lad: Leeds.
Reporter: And who's going to score?
Little lad: Lee Sharpe.
Reporter: How long have you supported Leeds, then?
Little lad: (Pause) Er . . . six years.
Reporter: And how old are you?
Little lad: Four.

Q: Does anyone know what a ratio is?
A: Please, Miss, I think he's a sailor.

Q: If a single ticket costs £26.48, how much does a return ticket cost?
A: Twice as much as that.

Q: How would you share 20p between four men?
A: I wouldn't because it's hardly worth it.

Q: If six boys and five girls want to go to the farm for their outing, how many would that be altogether?
A: All of them, Miss.

When one class was asked to draw two lines of symmetry, one pupil drew two lines of gravestones.

A circle is a round straight line with a hole in the middle.

A Year 6 Maths SAT test posed the question: If one can of Coke and a bag of popcorn costs £1.45 and the Coke cost 90p, how much does the popcorn cost? Give reasons for your answer.
A: 60p – because that is what my Mam pays when she goes to the pictures on a Saturday night.

Teacher: Right, Tommy. A mother has five children and only four potatoes to share among them. If she wanted to give each child an equal share, how would she do it?
Tommy: Mash them, Miss.

If you asked six friends to name the commonest bird in Britain, the odds are that nine out of ten would say the sparrow. *(Weekend)*

I have been informed that the school bus companies will be getting 12 new drivers – 5 men and 4 women. *(Parent's newsletter)*

30,000 pigeons were released, filling the air with the flutter of a million wings.

Music

The following commentary was heard and recorded from a BBC *Music and Movement* programme for children: "We are going to play a hiding and finding game. Now, are your balls high up or are they low down? Close your eyes a minute and dance around, and look for them. Are they high up? Or are they low down? If you have found your balls, toss them over your shoulder and play with them."

While on the subject of innocence . . .

The little girl had just visited a local comprehensive school to watch a musical play. "Which school was it?" asked her mother. "Oh, it was that Catholic school – the Immaculate Contraption."

Mrs Nightingale of Swallow Street has reopened her music school. Phone Robin for appointment. *(Eastern Province Herald)*

What is it about string musicians which cause problems . . . ?

Nero was a cruel tyrant who would torture his poor subjects by playing the fiddle to them.

He clearly fitted into the same category as the following musician . . .

"What do you think of the violinist?" George Bernard Shaw was once asked by one of his students.
"He reminds me of Paderewski," replied Shaw.
"But Paderewski is not a violinist."
"And neither is this gentleman."

The Old Malthouse School has just produced a short history which includes some memories at random, such as that of the music master who said his favourite instrument was the viola because so few boys played it. *(The Old Malthouse Mag)*

The new automatic couplings fitted to the organ at Hyde public school will enable Mr R*** to change his combinations without moving his feet. *(Hyde Old Boys' Magazine)*

A tangerine is one of the smallest members of the percussion family.

A folk-singer is someone who sings through his nose by ear.

The music teacher stopped the orchestra for the umpteenth time and addressed the drummer: "George, I don't expect you to be with us all the time, but I would greatly appreciate it if you would be good enough to keep in touch now and again."

The story is told that, as a courageous but not gifted boy called Rodney sang "Danny Boy" at the Christmas school panto, a lady in the audience began to cry uncontrollably. "Are you Irish?" asked the usher. "No," replied the lady. "I'm his singing teacher."

The western side play Country and Western, the Scottish play the Gay Gordons. Where would we be without music?

Beethoven wrote music even though he was deaf. He was so deaf he wrote loud music.

Mozart was a child orgy.

Mozart lived until the end of his life.

Her singing was mutiny on the High Cs.

Wagner wrote music which is better than it sounds.

Ten musicians from the Western Orchestral Society – incorporating the Bournemouth Sympathy Orchestra and Bournemouth Sinfonietta – are to lose their jobs. *(Daily Telegraph)*

Beethoven was a great composer. He wrote many works. He also had a large family and used to practise on the spinster upstairs.

Q: For what was Stradivarius famous?
A: For discovering the upper layer of the atmosphere.

Q: Why is one of the composer Handel's best known

works called "The Water Music"?
A: Because he lived on an island.

Sign on Music Department entrance – **Bach After Lunch**.

An orchestra has a man called a conductor who stands out in front with a piece of paper which tells him what music the orchestra is playing.

But as we all know, conductors are too clever and perceptive merely to do that – or are they?

On his first day in charge, the story is told of the new conductor addressing the orchestra: "From now on, things are going to be different around here. Everyone will be expected to be on time and work long hours."

Displeased with this, the tympanist beat on the drums: "BOOM, BOOM-BOOM BOOM."

"All right," said the conductor. "Who did that?"

The 150 members of the Queensland Flute Guild were asked not to wear backless dresses at the Brisbane Conservatorium of Music concert. "Please wear high-back dresses," pleaded their president, James Carson. Asked why, he said: "We want to pin sheet music on their backs. They can come frontless, but not backless." *(Sheffield Star)*

"LEONORE" – ONLY OPERA BEETHOVEN WROTE ON MONDAY EVENING *(San Antonio Express, Texas)*

Peter Henly, the winner of the Cassel Silver Medal for the best boy musician in the school, will play a corset solo during the concert. *(East Kent Mercury)*

A CORRECTION: In a caption in last night's *Evening*

Gazette, Dorothy Duffney, conductor of the Cleveland Musical Society, was described as Mrs Vera Beadle. She is, of course, Mrs K. Atkinson, of Hartburn Lane, Stockton. *(Evening Gazette)*

Nature Study

In winter bullfinches are best fed on bacon rinds and great tits like coconuts.

A kangaroo keeps its baby in its porch.

A cuckoo is a bird which lays other birds' eggs in its own nest and viva voce.

Australia's animals include the kangaroo and the Coca-Cola bear.

Fish swim about in shawls.

An Australian dog is called a dingy.

In cold weather Eskimos turn their skins inside out to trap the heat.

The camel is the sheep of the desert.

A lion is a tiger with black and white dots.

Q: What is the essential difference between an annual and a bi-annual plant?
A: An annual is the name given to a plant which dies every year. Bi-annuals only die once.

Q: What is a Kiwi?

A: A type of polish.

Q: What would you find in an orchard?
A: Flowers.

Q: What's the obvious advantage of camels holding lots of water?
A: They rarely go to the toilet.

And some unusual questions . . .

What do unicorns eat?

Do camels have to be licensed in India?

Is it legal to keep an octopus in a private house?

A quorum is a place to keep fish in.

An artist specialising in marine paintings of storms at sea had some of his work exhibited at St Ives. A schoolgirl who studied the paintings and was then introduced to the artist exclaimed with deep sympathy: "You really do have terrible luck with the weather."

Q: What has four legs and flies?
A: A dead horse.

Q: How might it be possible to stop a nosebleed?
A: Put the nose much lower than the body until the heart stops.

Q: What should you do if a dog bites you?
A: Put the dog away for several days. If it has not recovered, then kill it.

I think some dogs ought to be compulsorily castrated. They should not be allowed to increase willy-nilly.

Religious Education

The Old Testament can cause some confusion . . .

The first book of the Bible is Guinessis.

The first pair ate the first apple.

Cain, one of the sons of Adam and Eve, asked: "Am I my brother's son?"

In the Old Testament, but not in the New, it's an I for an I."

Teacher to eight-year-old: "George, what name did God give the first man?"
George: "Adam, Miss."
Teacher: "And the first lady?"
George: "Did he call her Madam, Miss?"

Noah built an ark, which the animals come on to in pears.

Goliath was a bit bigger than a telephone box.

The last book in the Bible is the Epilogue.

"Moses was found floating on the River Trent."

Moses went up on Mount Cyanide to get the Ten Commandments. He died before he ever reached Canada.

Moses came down from Mount Sinai with the tabloids.

Moses led the Hebrew slaves to the Red Sea, where they made unleavened bread which is bread without any ingredients.

Solomon, one of David's sons, had 300 wives and 700 porcupines.

Jacob, son of Isaac, stole his brother's birthmark.

One of Jacob's sons, Joseph, gave refuse to the Israelites.

The Jews were a proud people and throughout history they had trouble with the unsympathetic Genitals.

As can the New Testament . . .

Jesus was born in Bethlehem, at the age of 32, I think.

Jesus was caught preying.

Jesus walked along the road to Jerusalem with his 12 decibels.

Jesus was erased from the dead.

The Jews were disappointed with Jesus because He was not that kinder leader.

. . . and it turned out to be the Good Smartin.

Q: What were Jesus' final words to the Apostles at the Last Supper?
A: Who's going to do the washing up then?

The kingdom of God is wherever you would like it to be. It has no bounders.

The Sunday School teacher asked a little girl if she knew who Matthew was. The answer was no. The teacher then asked if she knew who John was. Again the answer was no. Finally the teacher asked if she knew who Peter was. She answered: "I think he was a rabbit."

Q: Was it lawful to buy or sell on the Sabbath Day?
A: Buy.

And a general idea of religious practices and beliefs . . .

Almost every church in England had an authorised virgin tied to the pulpit.

We are always getting the Geneva Witnesses knocking on our door.

On Whit Sunday all the disciples had a touch of wind in the Upper Room.

St Patrick chased all the bad snacks out of Ireland.

Q: Who is the patron saint of travellers?
A: St Pancras.

Humidity is the distinctively Christian virtue.

The epistles were the wives of the apostles.

Jesus was born by supernatural contraception.

Jesus healed people with very bad illnesses, like the Widow of Nairn's son – he was so ill he was dead.

Q: What was the name of the saint who looked after all the birds and the animals?
A: It was Francis of Onassis.

Our Lady and all the angels have lilos on their heads.

Last weekend, the Bishop came to our school and turned some of the Sisters into Mothers in a short, but very interesting, ceremony.

The Pope, at this time, was inflammable.

The little Scottish girl was asked what was the safest way of crossing the road. Her answer: "By the presbyterian crossing."

Q: Give an example of a "white lie".
A: My library book was overdue once and I said that I couldn't get down there through the flue.

Q: Describe two of the projects CAFOD supports in the Third World. Explain how they help to serve those suffering from poverty.
A: CAFOD supports places like Bosnia. They try and give people food. Also in places like Euthanasia people are dying every day.

Q: Complete the following: 'Those who live by the sword . . .
A: . . . will get shot by those who don't.

From a 1998 GCSE Religious Education examination paper: Suffering may raise a problem for religious believers, but thanks to the ingenuity of the Bible, most things can be explained – and when they can't, RE teachers may make something up.

Q: Many people are reluctant to share what they have. Suggest reasons for this.
A: Because some people are greedy and want everything.

People like this should be shot.

Some people think of heaven as all fluffy clouds and no sex.

Although I'm a Methodist, and therefore not a Christian, I believe in God.

People who do wrong are always paid out by God, but I wish he'd hurry up about it.

A seven-year-old insisted on telling his teacher what he thought the Commandment "Thou shalt not commit adultery" meant. "Miss, it means that you shouldn't put water with the milk."

Q: Name two hymns to the Blessed Virgin.
A: 1. Hail Holy Queen 2. Mary Had A Little Lamb

A young gentile pupil visiting a Jewish school asked one of the sixth-formers if the glasses he was wearing were special ones that you needed to read Hebrew.

Sister Eulalia was sitting meditating at her window when she saw, from her first-floor room, an obviously dejected and depressed "gentleman of the road" sitting on the convent wall with his head in his hands. Taking pity on him, she folded £5 into a note with the words "Don't Despair – Sister Eulalia" written on it. She then threw it towards him where it landed at his feet.
    The next day, Sister Eulalia was told that a man was at the door, insisting on seeing her. She found the stranger of yesterday waiting. Without a word he handed her some money. "What's this?" she asked. "It's your £50. Don't Despair came in at 10 to 1."

Irreligion is one of the great faiths of the world.

Monks sleep in dormitories and sometimes lay brothers.

Evening Subject: "What is Hell like?" Come and hear our new organ. *(St James's Boarding School's Sunday Service)*

NOTE: In some of our copies the article "The Power of the Papacy" described the Pope as "His Satanic Majesty"; this should read "the Roman Antichrist". *(Protestant Telegraph)*

Science

A twelve-year-old girl's school essay on "The Opposite Sex" is reported to have included the sentence: "I do not think much of the opposite sex because when I want to do anything they want to do the opposite."

Conversation was about the flight of the American space shuttle and the four-year-old daughter, who had been listening in, was asked if she knew what space was. "Yes," she replied immediately, "a place in the car park."

The light passes into the eye through the lens and is focused on the rectum.

Germans are so small that there may be as many as one billion, seven hundred million of them in a drop of water.

Nitrogen is not found in Ireland because it is not found in a free state.

One of the wonders of modern science is bringing a dead body back to life through artificial insemination.

Water is composed of two gins, oxygin and hydrogin.

Blood flows down one leg and up the other.

Germinate: To become a naturalised German.

Vacuum: A large empty space where the Pope lives.

Gravity was invented by Isaac Walton. It is chiefly noticeable in Autumn when apples are falling off the trees.

Comotose is when you get dead feet, like when you get frostbite.

Q: What is the difference between lightning and electricity?

A: We do not have to pay for lightning.

Q: What safety advice would you give to somebody working with acids and reactive materials?
A: BE CAREFUL!

Heli Bop comet has been visible at night to the naked since January.

Pure water must contain hydrogen because oxygen would float away if it was not for hydrogen.

Q: What is Charles Darwin best known for?
A: His book – *The Origin of the Speeches*.

Q: Why do you think it is important for houses to have windows?
A: It gives you a chance to see burglars before they can get in.

Q: What changes happen to your body as you age?
A: When you get old, so do your bowels and you can get intercontinental.

The blood flows through the alimentary canal into the abdominal canopy.

The cow has a pulse as well as anybody else.

Q: What is an animal with a backbone called?
A: A vibrator.
And . . .

TARANTULA – When a scientist dies in agony with his head swollen to twice its normal size and his hand grown claw-like, only Matt, the young town doctor, is suspicious. *(Review in Lincolnshire Free Press)*

Overheard – In the Playground and Elsewhere

Well, why don't you like lads wiv 'airy ear'oles then?

1st girl: Jimmy walked me home from the shops last night. I don't like him much.
2nd girl: Neither do I – he's only after one thing.
1st girl: Yes, I know, he's always cadging yer fags.

1st girl: I've just been to *Evita*.
2nd girl: You don't look very brown.

1st boy: Did you have a good holiday in Spain?
2nd boy: Yeah – it was great.
1st boy: Was the flight OK?
2nd boy: Yeah – but I was glad to get back on terracotta.

I wonder how much deeper the ocean would be without sponges?

Honk if you love peace and quiet.

Small boy: Daddy, why are we going here? *Father:* To get away from your mother.

Woman to small boy: Take your cap off, Patrick, so that the wind can blow the dandruff from your hair.

Dad to son on beach: Now tell Daddy where you buried the keys.

Boy: You're not normal.
Girl: Yes I am. I've always been normal.
Boy: No, you're not. As long as I've known you, you've never been normal.
Girl: Yes I am. My mam and dad are normal too – it's our Joanne who has to use shampoo for greasy hair.

1st girl: I have a set of silk undies. They're lovely, but they cost a lot.
2nd girl: I have a silk nightie.
1st girl: That's nice. I could never afford anything like that.
2nd girl: I didn't buy it. My sister gave it to me. She bought it for her honeymoon and never wore it.

Overheard in grocery store . . .

Patron: Are they twins?
Wife: Yes.
Patron: Are they both yours?

Two young teenagers were discussing the time, in the future, when they might get married. "I'm not having any of this woman's lib stuff," the lad declared firmly. "I'm going to be the boss and you'll do as I say." Then he added: "Would that be all right with you?"

"Mary, where is Utopia?"
"I'm not sure, but I think it's in the Mediterranean."

1st little girl: The angel said Mary was going to have a baby and she had one the next day.
2nd little girl: Don't be silly – it takes a year.

Little girl: Is it true that when you die you go to Devon?

1st girl: I have to go to the hospital to visit my granny tonight.
2nd girl: What's the matter with her?
1st girl: I'm not sure really, but my mam says it's a serious operation – something about a hysterical rectum.

Q: How can he remember all that?
A: He's got a pornographic memory.

And you have no idea how difficult it is, actually, to get a budgerigar out of a treacle tart.

One boy to another: "I had one up my trouser leg last year."

I don't like the play, but I've got the best bit. I have to say: "Bubble, bubble, toilet trouble."

1st student: You would get bored watching Olivier play Hamlet.
2nd student: Well, I don't like football – especially foreign teams.

Overheard in Rimini: "Hey, Mam, they've even got pizzas in Italy."

A mother and small son were walking past the statue of David in Rome and the mother was saying to him: "No, George, you should know – Big Ben is a clock."

Two lads having an argument in the playground – one said to the other: "Hey, don't fly off at a tangerine."

On a bus passing a cinema . . .

First girl: I don't fancy that, do you?
Second girl: What's that then?
First girl: Going to see that Richard the 'undreth and eleventh.

1st boy: We went to Bamburgh Sands on Saturday.
2nd boy: Was it nice?
1st boy: Well, there's miles and miles of sand. Did you know they filmed part of *Lawrence of Olivier* there?

I wish I could have had her legs – on her they're such a waste.

If I had a figure like 'ers, I'd walk on me hands.

I wish my backside was as flat as his.

We went to Blenheim Palace. The grounds were lovely and were designed by Capability Smith.

It was a Catholic school's governors' meeting where the new parish priest had not met fellow-governors, one of whom was a nun in charge of the convent. The chairman introduced them thus: "Father, you haven't met Mother, have you?"

Overheard at a football match: "Come on, Our Lady of the Most Holy Rosary, get stuck in."

Pupil welcoming guests: "Can I take your clothes off?"

Overheard in playground: "Well, her dad's the head-teacher, she's bound to get RIP treatment."

1st boy: Hey, Sean, what's that on your cheek?
2nd boy: It's a birthmark.
1st boy: Really. How long have you had it?

In restaurant . . .

Mother to waiter: Could I take what my son has not eaten, which is most of his dinner, home for the dog?
Three-year-old: We don't have a dog, Mammy.

Girl: My mam had to go to see about her bad back yesterday.
Teacher: Is it any better?
Girl: Yes, a lot. She said the psychopath was very good.

My granny is in hospital for an operation on a detached retinue.

What he lacks in intelligence, he makes up for in stupidity.

He is very clever but sometimes he lets his brains go to his head.

Why did your mam name the baby John? Every Tom, Dick and Harry is called John.

"Our George is going to court today."
"Why – what's he done?"
"Nothing, he's been called as a witness for the prostitution."

A girl, explaining why her father, a philosophy PhD, can't give medical advice: "He's a doctor, but not the kind that does anyone any good."

In a restaurant where there was a kids' ball pool (an area filled with plastic balls), a little girl ran up to her father and exclaimed: "Daddy, I've just kissed Jason in the balls."

An elder sister talking to her little brother going into church:
Sister: They won't allow you to talk, you know.
Little brother: Who won't?
Sister: The Hushers.

Teacher: The hike will be over ten miles long.
Little lad: Does that mean we'll need long walking socks, Miss?

Then there's always the comic . . .

Father to little boy of five or six: "If you don't stop whining, Margaret Thatcher will come and get you."

At the zoo where some small boys were looking up at a giraffe: "Bloomin' heck, hasn't he got a long way to wee."

Overheard in classroom: "My dad's the second best fighter in the town – whenever he has a fight he always comes second."

One man confiding to another: "When it came to education, my father wanted me to have all the opportunities he never had. He sent me to a girls' school."

1st teacher: How is it that you know so much about plants?
2nd teacher: Well, when my husband died, I buried myself in the garden.

As a child I had every toy my father wanted.

And where do they get them from?

First little boy: I like goldfish.
Second little boy: So do I, but when you're swimming among them, they suck yer arms.

"I've got a very soft spot for our headteacher," said the obviously irate young lady. "A swamp."

I'm really mad – that really has got my dandruff up.

1st boy: When I was in Spain, I nearly got stung by one of those huge jellyfish.
2nd boy: You mean the Portuguese menopause?

Just look at your fingers. They're filthy. Suck them – go on – suck them.

Her mam used to take her to the school bus every morning and meet her off it again at night. She still doesn't know how she got pregnant.

The scene is the top of a bus where a little girl is sucking a lolly and now and again rubbing it on the fur coat of the lady in front of her. Her mother said: "Don't do that, you'll get hairs all over your lolly."

The class of seven-year-olds were learning the difference between "sh-" and "ch-", aided by pictures of ships and churches. One perceptive little girl politely pointed out: "Please, Miss – this rule doesn't work all the time, does it?" "Yes it does, Charlotte," insisted her teacher.

"Do you enjoy Kipling?"
"Don't know – never been kippled."

3

Children

Children are not everyone's favourite people. It could be that some are resented because they are too clever by half than the adults with whom they associate. Parents who feel this way will enjoy the definition of a precocious child as one who took his nose apart to see what made it run. In fact, some parents show a positive aversion to them even when they care for them themselves.

Prince Philip, himself a father of four, said in October that the population problem could be solved if unwanted children were not born. And, he claimed, most children after the second were not wanted. *(Sun)*

Most of us parents know that, in order to keep down the price of school lunches, meat in some dishes is being partly or wholly replaced by protein made from soya beans. But what about the Cambridgeshire school which is offering its pupils fried codpieces? *(New Public Service)*

I've often wondered what little brothers were for. *(John McEnroe after beating Patrick)*

I don't play with my children. I can't tolerate whingers. *(Chris Eubank on family life)*

You wouldn't believe it, but the same kids who are eating you out of house and home are never there. *(Hal Roache)*

Insanity is hereditary. You get it from your kids. *(Graffiti, London, 1979)*

My mother loved children – she would have given anything if I'd been one. *(Groucho Marx)*

I think I was popular with my teachers . . . on Saturdays and Sundays. *(Eric Morecambe)*

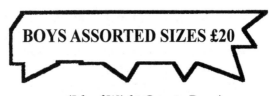

BOYS ASSORTED SIZES £20

(Isle of Wight County Press)

He didn't like children. He finished his drink with a silent toast to Herod. *(Kingsley Amis)*

One in four children are the result of undersired pregnancies. *(Scanorama magazine)*

The more I see of children, the more I like dogs.

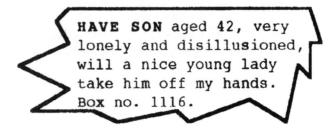

HAVE SON aged 42, very lonely and disillusioned, will a nice young lady take him off my hands. Box no. 1116.

(Wellington Star, Taunton)

The kidnappers took me to Jersey, bound and gagged, and my parents finally realised that I'd been kidnapped and they snapped into action . . . They rented out my room. *(Woody Allen)*

Ah, the patter of little feet around the house. There's nothing like having a midget for a butler. *(W. C. Fields)*

I love children . . . parboiled. *(W. C. Fields)*

Boys will be boys – and so will a lot of middle-aged men.

Of course children brighten up a home. They never turn the lights off.

MENU
Fish and Chips – £3.50; 1 Piece Fish – £2.70
Chips & Peas – £1.50; Children – £1.00
(Bridlington Restaurant)

A 12-year-old boy was shot dead by a sentry on duty outside a fort in Lisbon. The sentry reported that the boy ignored his challenge in the dark. Army officials last night carried out a reconstruction of the events. A civilian, Carlos Chaves, aged 33, played the role of the boy. He too was shot dead. *(Newcastle Evening Chronicle)*

A doctor has compiled a list of poisons which children may drink at home. *(Ottawa Journal)*

Whether you like them or not, there can be no argument that sometimes children can come out with comments and views which add to the brightness of the day. They can show a remarkable innocence and a commonsense view of situations which can evade and reduce to guffaws and hilarity the most hardened critics and observers of life.

In church for the first time, the little boy watched, wide-eyed, as the choir, all in white surplices, filed in. With wonder in his voice he whispered: "Are all those people going to get their hair cut?"

Teacher Gillian Freeman tells the following story . . .

On playground duty, I was approached by a pair of outraged five-year-olds who told me that their friend Stephen was eating worms. I hotfooted it over to the suspect, who was standing suspiciously close to the flower bed.

"Stephen, are you eating worms?" I demanded.

"No, Mrs Freeman," he replied indignantly.

I was greatly relieved, as I was unsure what sanctions should follow worm eating. Would a trip to the office for First Aid be needed, or maybe even an emergency emetic?

"Good. It isn't very nice to eat worms, is it, Stephen?"

"No, Mrs Freeman," he answered. "That's why I was only sucking them."

The children Mrs Hall had taken to the local fire station had thoroughly enjoyed their field trip and the firefighters were enjoying answering the questions. "Could you please tell me," asked a six-year-old, "how you get back up the pole?"

A teacher was taking a group of pupils around Stonehenge when one of them said: "Miss, I was here three years ago and it hasn't changed much."

Jack Benny was very proud of the fact that a school in his home town of Waukegan, Illinois, was named after him, and used to return to speak to the children when in the neighbourhood. His speech concluded on one occasion, he

asked if there were any questions. "Mr Benny," one young pupil asked, "why did they name you after our school?"

The school team was about to be selected for the annual area swimming gala. All pupils in Years 3 to 6 were asked to stay behind after assembly for a meeting, when non-swimmers were then told they could go. Emma, a recent recruit to the school, burst into tears. After she had calmed down, she was asked the reason for the outburst: "I don't want to go. I really like this school." *(Steve Harrison)*

Q: What seven-letter word has three "u"s in it?
A: I really don't know, but it must be unusual. *(Henry O. Dormann)*

In 1983 on the tour of New Zealand and Australia, the Prince and Princess of Wales approached a group of young children in South Australia on one of their "walkabouts". The nearest child was patted on the head by Princess Diana. "Why aren't you at school today?" she enquired. "I've been sent home with head lice," replied the boy.

A small boy in a junior class was contentedly making a meal of some chewing-gum. Following an age-old school custom, his teacher commanded the offender to leave his seat and deposit the delicacy in the waste-paper basket. Peter emerged from his seat but on reaching the basket stood still and looked very much perturbed. Asked to explain, he answered pathetically: "I'll cop it, Miss, when I get home – my brother only lent me it for the afternoon."

Cheap. Electric guitar and powerful amplifier. Phone 536478. If boy answers please ring off and call later. *(Basingstoke)*

The teacher at a Durham school was becoming more and more irritated by Thomas who was continually sniffing. When she could stand it no longer she asked him: "Thomas, do you have a handkerchief?" Thomas replied: "Yes, Miss. Would you like to borrow it?"

Last night I was feeling very thirsty so I went downstairs for a drink of water. My mammy and daddy were lying on the carpet in front of the gas fire with nothing on – sunbathing. *(Little boy writing in his diary)*

The three-year-old told the childminder that her grandad had gone away in an aeroplane to Oil. It was only when her mother had come to collect her it was clarified that he had gone on his holidays to Greece.

Little girl: Mammy, how do the Spice Girls learn all the words to their songs?
Mother: Well, just like you learn all the words to your nursery rhymes.
Little girl: Oh, do they sit cross-legged on the carpet?

Q: What do you think is the best aspect of school meals?
A: Teachers have to suffer too.

Teacher: If all the good people in the world were red and all the bad people were green, what colour would you be?
Little girl: Miss, I think I'd be streaky.

When my son was eight years old he came home from school and announced he was in love, adding: "But I can't marry her. She's a Roman Catholic and I'm a prostitute." *(Letter in the Sunday Sun)*

A Fife teacher asked her class if any of them had been to Turkey. "Yes," one replied, "but we pronounce it 'Tor-kee'."

The school hall was full of children, staff, helpers and governors. The pantomime began. Soon the time came for Jack to go to market with the cow. He met "the baddie", who tricked him. If Jack could answer three questions, he would keep his mother's cow and get some money.

"What is your favourite colour?"

"Easy," said Jack. "Green."

"What is the capital of France?"

As quick as a flash, a voice piped up from among the six-year-old class at the back of the hall. "F – it's F," he shouted. "The capital of France is F. I know because I can spell it."

A class of six-year-olds had been learning about the "magic 'e'" ("win" becomes "wine", "tub" becomes "tube" . . .). The class had also had head lice. One of the pupils told his mother as she treated his hair not to worry as he could change his "nit" to "nite" with the magic "e".

Then there are those who are too clever by half . . .

Young scientist's rocket kit for sale, used once only. Also good home for only white mouse in neighbourhood which knows what it's like from 50ft up. *(San Francisco News)*

Little girl in her first year at secondary school to mother: Did you see my French teacher?

Mother: Miss Daneuve – yes, she was very nice.

Little girl: She's not a Miss, she's a Madam.

Prodigy – a child who plays the piano when he ought to be in bed.

And there are those who claim unhappy and poverty-stricken childhoods ...

Eric: When I was eight I ran away with a circus.
Ernie: Really?
Eric: Yes. Then when I was nine, they made me bring it back again. *(Eric Morecambe and Ernie Wise)*

Ernie: I had a pretty tough childhood myself, you know. At the age of five I was left an orphan.
Eric: That's ridiculous! What could a five-year-old do with an orphan? *(Eric Morecambe and Ernie Wise)*

There are those who like to recall their impoverished background, remembering the days when they took their fish-paste sandwiches to school wrapped up in the waxed paper of Mother's Pride.

Heads will recollect at retirement celebrations such fictional observations about the retiree as ...

He was so poor that one day his mam gave him a button and told him to nip next door to Mrs Bate's and ask her if she would put a shirt on it.

He was so poor he couldn't afford shoes – he set the boot studs into his feet.

One day he went to school with the sole of his boot hanging off. He met the head who took a bundle of notes secured with an elastic band from his pocket and gave him the elastic band to stop his sole flapping.

And what about Granny and Grandad ...?

A grandmother is a lady who has no children of her own. She likes other people's little girls.

A grandfather is a man grandmother. He goes for walks with the boys and they talk about fishing, and tractors and things like that.

Grandmas don't have to do anything but be there.

They're old, so they shouldn't play or run. It is enough if they drive us to the market where the fairground is and have plenty of change in their pockets, or if they take us for walks, they should slow down past things like pretty leaves and caterpillars.

Usually they are fat but not too fat to tie our shoelaces.

Usually they wear glasses and funny underwear. They can take their teeth and gums out.

Everybody should try to have one, especially if they don't have a television, because grandmothers are the only grownups who have got the time.

4

Things They Thought They Heard

Thanks to a number of factors – the limited vocabulary of small youngsters, indistinct and poorly articulated speech and the mixture of music with lyrics amongst them – children can easily put their own interpretations on the spoken word, as these examples show . . .

There is a phrase in the Beatles' song "Lucy In The Sky With Diamonds" which goes ". . . the girl with kaleidoscope eyes". A young pupil was convinced it went ". . . the girl with colitis goes by".

A young boy called his teddy bear "Gladly" because of the line from the hymn which sounds like: "Gladly, my cross-eyed bear . . ." (Gladly, my cross I bear . . .)

Our Father, chart in heaven, hullo how be you then?

Our Father, who aren't in heaven, hello, what's your name?

Our Father, who art in heaven, Harold be thy name.

Our Father, who art in heaven, how d'you know my name?

. . . and lead us not into Penn Station.

A little girl returned home to tell her mam that her elder sister would be late. She had been selected as a prostitute for the netball team.

All things bright and beautiful, All teachers great and small.

Surely good Mrs Murphy shall follow me all the days of my life. (Surely goodness and mercy shall follow me . . .)

Blessed art thou a monk's women. (Blessed art thou amongst women.)

A whale in a manger.

The Russians revolted and overthrew Nicholas II who was bizarre. (. . . who was the Tsar.)

Mrs Gulliver, from Barnard Castle, County Durham, recalls a story told to her by an elderly friend. When, as a schoolgirl, her friend, fellow classmates and teacher had to sing the National Anthem, she was always puzzled by the phrase "send him victorious". She asked her teacher whether the King really liked plums because she had only greengages in her garden and could she send them some of them rather than Victorias.

It ordipends on what you think.

I have unopened mind about that.

Every sentence and the name of God must begin with a caterpillar.

While shepherds washed their socks by night . . .

Jesus said to His disciples: "Follow Me and I will make you vicious old men."

I know that my reindeer liveth. (. . . Redeemer liveth.)

Hail! Thou that art highly-flavoured. (. . . highly favoured.)

Rachel will have to work hard next term if she is to be sure of a GCSE in June. A lot of his mistakes are due to carelessness.

A Hampshire reader insists that under "Headmaster's Comments" in her nine-year-old son's report are the words: "Unimaginative but reliable. Would make a good parent."

This boy listens in school with the flawless dignity of the dead.

 Not a very good set of reports, but don't take too much notice of them – two of them, I know, were written by tired men.

COMMENT: (DO TAKE THIS OPPORTUNITY FOR EXPRESSING ANY CONCERNS YOU MAY HAVE . . .) I think I can do better if he tries.

To be charitable, let us say it was a Freudian slip when a Sussex teacher wrote on a pupil's report that his "excuses are always interesting and varied. I am, however, running out of patients."

Alan is producing his best work . . . alas.

George has told me he wants to pass his exams badly – I can assure you he is going the right way about it.

Thomas's handwriting is so bad we cannot tell if he can spell or not.

William is very intelligent but his handwriting is atrocious. Would make a good doctor.

Bernard's idea of hard work is sharpening his pencil and putting his books away.

I can only hope that should Charles ever have children, they give him the same experience that as a child he has given me!

Regan writes well, spells well and has a fertile imagination which, unfortunately, is sometimes matched by an overuse of earthy language.

Jenny is a clever girl and wants to go into bonking.

His work is as sloppy as a soup sandwich.

I received David's report and agree with you that he is bone idle. I don't know why it is – I think he takes after his mother whose father used to say as a child she had swallowed a teaspoon and hasn't stirred since.

5

Letters

The majority of letters arriving in schools from parents are usually excuses or explanations for a situation which has happened, or is going to happen . . .

Dear Sir/Miss . . .

✗ Please excuse John from school today as his father's ill and the pig has to be fed.

✓ I have some good and bad news for you. First of all, the good news – I will be taking my son away on Friday. Now the bad news – he will return in time for school on Monday.

Maryann was absent December 11-16, because she had a fever, sore throat, headache and upset stomach. Her sister was also sick, fever and sore throat, her brother had a low grade fever and ached all over. I wasn't the best either, sore throat and fever. There must be something going around, her father even got hot last night.

Sorry Kevin was late but me and my husband rather overdone it this morning.

John will be off until Friday. He has a cole slaw on his top lip.

You remember all the nose bleeds George has been having and made him stay off school? Well, the doctor is having him taken into hospital to have his nose circumcised. So that should be the end of his problem.

Sorry Mary wasn't at school yesterday but she had dire rear.

My son is under a doctor's care and should not take P.E. today. Please execute him.

Fiona will not be in school tomorrow. In the morning she is having a bath, then we are going to the hairdresser's and then to a dinner-dance at the club until 11.30 pm. I hope this is all right.

Sorry Anne was absent from school but she had an ulster in her throat.

Even though Jane left early for the bus, she had to come back with her stomach.

Elizabeth has been absent because her mother has had twins. I can assure you it will not happen again.

I am sorry that my son is late in handing in his homework. Yesterday morning when he had to hand it in, he had to go to hospital with his foot. He has brought it with him this morning.

I am asking you not to use corporal punishment on George. We never do except in self-defence.

John was off with information of the lungs.

I have kept Kevin off school because the doctor says he has slipped his dick.

Jennifer will not attend school for the next few weeks as we are going on holiday. I hope this does not interfere with your plans for industrial action or anything.

Dear School: Please excuse John being absent on Jan. 28, 29, 30, 31, 32, and also 33.

Joanne won't be in school for a few days because she's got trouble with her eye. The doctor thinks it's a misplaced rectum.

I'm sorry Ernie has not been to school all week, but we had a week last week I can tell you. On Monday, our Ernie broke his collar-bone and ended up in hospital; on Tuesday, Auntie Florrie collapsed and died at the club; and on Friday, I won £10 on the bingo. Isn't it funny how things always seem to happen in threes?

Brian was absent from school because he went to his grandmother's funeral. He stayed the night at his cousin's and he didn't come home on Tuesday because he had a hangover from drinking too much at the party afterwards.

Sorry Victor could not attend school yesterday as we had no sugar for his breakfast cup of tea.

Emily was not in school yesterday because my brain was disengaged. I thought it was half term.

Please excuse Jimmy for being. It was his father's fault.

Some parents seem to believe anything . . .

Angela did not come home till gone 11.30 last night, and I can't think where she'd got to but when she came in she was covered from head to foot with straw.

Guy couldn't come back to school yesterday as his mother was ill. There is no way he went to see *Grease*.

It was true what Harry told you. He was in the fish and chip shop when some of your pupils came in and battered him.

I was amazed that Kirk obtained an 'A' for his Home Economics – even the dog would not eat the scones he brought home.

Billy wasn't in school this morning because he looked after me when I went to get my eternity allowance.

Please send me a form for free dinners for children at reduced prices.

My daughter was absent yesterday because she was tired. She spent a weekend with the Marines.

My husband will not be able to come to the parents' meeting this afternoon because as you know he is in prison. He is not very happy with Richard's report and wants him to be disciplined.

Thank you for your letter on the arrangements for Entrance Appeals. We shall waste no time in reading it.

I'm pleased you are keeping Moira in detention. I think it will have a sanitary effect on her.

Very sorry Sharon has been absent again but she is very poorly with flu – could you please see that she is raped up warm at breaktime.

I kept Michael off school for his breathing again as he never gets any sleep with it when it comes on.

Ernest has been off school for two days according to his eye, which he hurt playing football.

Darren was of school with what I thought was appendersitis but it wasent He was loaded with wind and he hadent been going to the toilet regular the doctor give him medersing to take which give him diharrea But I had my daughter of with spots and the doctror told me to keep her away from other people. Anyway Darren came out in the same spots as his brother did I don't know what they were but I think it was a form of chicken pos spots. Thats why he never returned to school he is better now though.

Jonathan was late for school because 2 gerbils escaped behind the washer.

Rebecca could not come to school today because she has been bothered by very close veins.

Paul was absent on Friday before they broke up because I slept in. Somebody took out the fuse of the main box which is outside the front door and none of us woke up till I looked at my watch at 10.20. Even Lee my youngest son didn't go to school till 12.45 after dinner.

Chris will be absent today and probably tomorrow. As he was walking to school it was snowing and he had his head down and walked into a lamp-post. He has a bruised head.

We had to take Michael to the hospital last night after he fell off his bike and hit his head. Fortunately, when they X-rayed it they found nothing. He will be back tomorrow.

Please excuse Samantha having a shower, being how she is. Being how you are yourself sometimes, you will understand how she is.

Please excuse Josie for being absent yesterday. She was in bed with gramps.

Letter from school to new parents: "At the beginning of each school year we assign pupils to specific lockers. We expect them to remain in the lockers to which they are assigned . . ."

Parents who consider that the behaviour of pupils is unacceptable and uncivil should see the headteacher.

Letter in a Norfolk school magazine . . .

Dear Editor,
I was very distressed to read in your Spring issue a note
recording the death of Walter Brown. Of all the Old Boys
I knew, he was undoubtedly the one I most admired. I
cannot believe he is no longer with us.
Yours sincerely, Walter Brown.

6

Sex

Schools are doing a valiant job in Personal and Social Education in attempting to cultivate in their pupils a sense of responsibility and morality in matters of sexual relationships. It is a task avoided by so many parents who, quite rightly, wish their offspring to be virtuous and decorous while being unwilling or unable to inform them themselves. Unable, perhaps, is the operative word if this letter is anything to go by.

Why all this fuss about sex education in schools? I am sixteen and I taught my mother about reproduction, using the correct biological terms. The present generation of parents cannot tell their children how they came to be born because they do not know. *(Letter in Daily Mirror)*

Perhaps the following observer thought schools should get down to the fundamentals in the Creative Design module . . .

"Too often biology is used in schools as a vehicle for sex education," declared Dr Gilbert Russell, Education Secretary of the Church of England Moral Welfare Council, in Bristol yesterday. *(Western Daily Press and Bristol Mirror)*

Shocking sight

I must add my voice to those who object to the naked bathers on the eastern section of Eastney beach.

Walking with my five-year-old granddaughter I was quite shocked at, and needless to say un-prepared for, the sight of naked male bodies sprawled across the shingle.

Quite obviously, they delighted in showing off their private parts and, my granddaughter being of an impressionable age, I had to tell her these men were fishing with special rods.

It is surely about time the police made a concerted effort to rid this beautiful part of the south coast of these wanton exhibitionists.

Mengham Road
Hayling Island

(The News, Southampton)

And perhaps schools are not always blessed with suitable teachers of the subject ...

A schoolmistress said at Ilford County Court last Wednesday that she did not like seeing men's short underwear on a clothes-line, and also objected to seeing men's pyjamas hanging in an "indiscreet" way on the line. It caused her embarrassment to see them. *(Ilford Guardian)*

And not everybody benefits from school-based explanations ...

Mike Harding once said: "When I was at school, the books on sex gave me a terrible inferiority complex."

But these textbooks could have interesting additions . . .

Graffiti – next to heading "SEX APPEAL" was written "Please give generously"!

And certainly the need for sex education is there, judging from the following . . .

A student undergoing a word-association test was asked why a snowstorm put him in mind of sex. He replied frankly: "Because everything does."

A teacher at a school in Buckinghamshire asked which of the senior boys would like to be present at the birth of any children they might have after they were married. One would not commit himself. Pressed for his opinion, he finally said: "Well, Miss, it depends if I know the girl very well."

Q: How important are elections to a democratic society?
A: Sex can only happen when a male gets an election.

And you must always be careful what you say and what you write . . .

A biology teacher was handing out sheets to a Year 11 class on sexual reproduction and enquired: "Right – has anyone still not got their 'Male Reproductive Organs'?"

Humans need to reproduce to continue the specious.

The pill is easy to use and very useful for an eager woman.

Q: From what may men in their fifties suffer?
A: The manopause.

Q: State one change in boys at puberty.
A: Their vice deepens.

Male mammals have eternal sexual organs.

My sister's expecting a baby, and I don't know if I'm going to be an uncle or an aunt.

My father told me all about the birds and the bees. The liar – I went steady with a woodpecker till I was twenty-one. *(Bob Hope)*

I got this black eye fighting for my girlfriend's honour. She would insist on keeping it.

Anne Boleyn: Not tonight, darling. I've got a headache.
Henry VIII: We'll soon fix that!

Boys and girls develop in different places.

Twins are two things which come together unexpectedly.

He had been eating tomatoes and drinking milk, and the woman may have mistaken this as an offer of sex. It was not, he said. *(Rhodesia Herald)*

A sex line caller complained to Trading Standards. After dialling an 0891 number from an advertisement entitled "Hear Me Moan", the caller was played a tape of a woman nagging her husband for failing to do jobs around the house. Consumer Watchdogs in Dorset refused to look into the complaint, saying: "He got what he deserved." *(Gloucester Citizen)*

Police arrived quickly, to find Mr Melchett hanging by his fingertips from the back wall. He had run out of the house when the owner, Paul Finch, returned home un-expectedly and, spotting an intruder in the garden, had dialled 999. What Mr Finch did not know was that Mr Melchett had been visiting Mrs Finch and, hearing the front door open, had climbed out of the rear window. But the back wall was 8 feet high and Mr Melchett had been unable to get his leg over. *(Barnsley Chronicle)*

The money will not be going directly into the prostitutes' pockets, but will be used to encourage them to lead a better life. We will be training them for new positions in hotels. *(Daily Telegraph)*

Police called to arrest a naked man on the platform at Piccadilly Station released their suspect after he produced a valid rail ticket. *(Manchester Evening News)*

For seven and a half years I've worked alongside President Reagan. We've had triumphs. Made some mistakes. We've had some sex . . . uh . . . setbacks. *(George Bush)*

In her statement the girl said that he had put his hand on her chest and a guinea pig which she had under her jumper had bitten him. *(Cannock Advertiser)*

It is comforting to know that our MPs are trying to instil a bit of morality . . .

BRAZIER'S ANGER AT SEX TOYS

MP Julian Brazier is getting hot under the collar about a scheme to issue sex aid at Family Planning Clinics across the Country. The Chairman of the Conservative Family Campaign is angry that vibrators are being handed out willy nilly on the National Health. *(Canterbury Times)*

But in America ...

Walter Mondale: George Bush doesn't have the manhood to apologize.
Bush: Well, on the manhood thing, I'll put mine up against his any time.

7

Parents

It is amazing how much the body figures, in some shape or form, with parents.

7th August 1915: On the bus the other day a woman with a baby sat opposite, the baby bawled, and the woman at once began to unlace herself, exposing a large, red bosom, which she swung into the baby's face. The infant, however, continued to cry and the woman said: "Come on now, there's a good boy – if you don't I shall give it to the gentleman opposite." *(The Journal of a Disappointed Man, W.N.P. Barbellion)*

And on the same theme . . .

Stockport Research Interest Group. Wednesday, January 28, 7pm, School of Nursing. Stepping Hill Hospital. Speaker Anne Thompson: "Why don't women breast feed? Cheese and wine party follows."

At an annual dinner for parents, a woman eventually turned to the gentleman next to her who had not stopped talking all evening and said: "The story of your pelvis has fascinated me throughout dinner, but I think I should point out that I am a Doctor of Chemistry."

The mother had always said, whenever any of her three children received a knock on the head or knee, "Gentle, gentle, it will be all right." As a result knocks in the family become known as "gentles". One day Dad had fallen from a step ladder, landed on his knees and skinned them. The next day as he sat waiting in a crowded shopping centre for the family, the four-year-old ran up and jumped on his knee, in the process catching his injured knee-caps. As he winced, audibly and visibly, the little girl shouted back to her mother: "Oh dear, Mammy, I think I've hurt Daddy's 'gentles'." Passers-by were greatly amused.

My husband and I had just put our children to bed when we heard sobbing coming from three-year-old Eric's room. Rushing to his side, we found that he had accidentally swallowed a penny and was sure he was going to die.

Desperate to calm him down, my husband palmed a penny from his pocket and pretended to pull it from Eric's ear. Eric was delighted. He snatched the coin from my husband's hand, swallowed it and demanded cheerfully: "Go on, Dad – do it again!"

There are the proud parents . . .

Comment by proud mother at a parents' consultation evening: "I keep telling him – if he sticks in and gets these GCSEs, then the world's his lobster."

Two mothers were talking about a recent fancy dress party outside a primary school in Leeds:
Q: Did your little daughter enjoy herself?
A: Oh, yes, she looked lovely. We dressed her up in one of those Japanese commodes.

"Alan broke his leg in two places a month ago at nursery school – we don't know how!" his father laughed. *(Slough Observer)*

There are the troublesome . . .

Dad volunteered to babysit one night so Mum could have an evening out. At bedtime, he sent the youngsters upstairs to bed and settled down to read the newspapers. One child kept creeping down the stairs, but Dad kept sending him back. At 9.00 pm the doorbell rang. It was the next door neighbour, Mrs Smith, asking whether her son was there. The father brusquely replied: "No". Just then a little head appeared over the bannister and a voice shouted: "I'm here, Mam, but he won't let me go home."

At the court hearing following the junior school football match, the mother said she was not very abusive, but she did call Mr — "a monkey-faced, button-eyed old g-t". *(Liverpool Echo)*

You really do no good by constantly scalding a child. *(Women's magazine)*

Headteacher: I am very sorry that your son was picked upon and punched in the ordeal.
Mother: He wasn't. He was punched right in the stomach and kicked where it hurts.

Parental expressions every child should know even though they only lead to irritability and resentment . . .

Some day you'll thank me.
I don't want to hear any more about it.
When I was your age . . .
You don't know when you are well off.

We had to eat what we were given.
We would never have dared say that to our parents.
We had to be in by nine o'clock.
I wish that I had had the opportunities you have.
We had to be happy with two days at Blackpool for our holidays.
We were happy with a tangerine and a few nuts for Christmas.
As long as you live in my house . . .
How many times have I told you . . .?
This is hurting me more than it's hurting you - apropos of which reassurance . . .

Father, chancing to chastise
His indignant daughter Sue,
Said: "I hope you realise
That this hurts me more than you."
Susan ceased to roar;
"If that's really true," said she,
"I can stand a good deal more;
Pray go on, and don't mind me."
(Harry Graham, Ruthless Rhymes 1899)

Children can be equally irritable when they come out with such bons mots to parents as . . .

This is the 1990s, you know!
Times have changed since the First World War.
All my friends can . . ./have . . .

Parental odds and ends . . .

I have found that the best way to give advice to your children is to find out what they want and then advise them to do it. *(Harry S. Truman)*

Doctor: I don't like the look of your husband.
Wife: I don't, either, but he's good to the children.

Parent: John hasn't arrived back home.
Headteacher: Didn't he tell you? He's gone to see *Dr Zhivago* today.
Parent: What's the matter with him now, then?

Mother: Did you enjoy your visit to the zoo with Daddy today?
Eight-year-old: Yes and so did Daddy – especially when one of the animals came in at 20-1.

A teacher asked her class of eight-year-olds to write about their personal heroes. One little girl brought her essay home and showed it to her parents. Her father was flattered to discover that his daughter had chosen him. "Why did you pick me?" he asked expectantly. "Because I couldn't spell 'Schwarzenegger,'" the little girl replied.

8

Newspapers

MAGGIE SOLD! An autographed photo of Margaret Thatcher fetched £1.60 at a school auction sale in Oyne, Aberdeenshire. A box of haddock raised £8. *(Sunday Mail)*

CORRECTION – Due to a printing error, a story in last week's *Gazette* referred to school athletics coach Billy Hodgkins as an "old waster". This should, of course, have read "old master". We apologise to Mr Hodgkins for any embarrassment this has caused.

A talk on guide dogs for the blind will be given at Brazeley Library, Cedar Avenue, Horwich, on Monday at 7.30 pm The talk will be given by Mrs Wooff. *(Bolton Journal)*

But Alderman Rita Ubriaco criticized the motion, saying the objection was similar to a recent action by the nearby Dryden Board of Education ". . . who damned *Lord of the Flies* because they thought it had to do with men's trousers." *(Montreal Gazette)*

(Pictured left) 17-year-old Lynda Stuart from Barbados, photographed at home in Cobham with her pet dog, who has been chosen as head pupil of Westminster School. *(The Lady)*

Museums enable people to explore collections for inspiration, learing and enjoyment. *(British Association of Friends of Museums newsletter)*

Owing to a transcription error, an article in Saturday's *Independent* on page 9 on Irish premier Charles Haughey mistakenly read "A man of immense rudeness". This was intended to read "A man of great shrewdness". *(Independent)*

Dudley's Head of Schools said: "Last month we had a special in-service course on bullying for members of school staffs." *(County Express, Stourbridge)*

Written around the edge of my son's "I am 2" badge taken from a birthday card are the words "Unsuitable for children under 3 years of age". *(Jane Fallows, Gordonvale, Queensland)*

Redbridge Borough Council is to prosecute a school in its district after its kitchens were found to be overrun with cockroaches. The Council decided to take action when the cockroaches were still found in the kitchens three weeks after they had received a warning. *(Grauniad)*

Academy-award-winning documentary in which Jacques d'Amboise, principal dancer of the New York City Ballet, leads a thousand children in his annual gaga performance. *(Bradford Telegraph and Argus)*

There are also the universities, in which it is estimated that one person in 1150 is educated. *(Northumberland newspaper)*

The current *Radio Times* has an interview about exams with John Mann, secretary of the Schools Council, which quotes him as saying: "It is not very satisfactory to divide kids into sheep and goats . . ."

A remittance prince? While the British press speculates that **Prince Andrew** is being sent to Lakefield College School to help Canada through a constitutional crisis, our sources tell us that the real reaxon for the prince's being sent to Cannadda in midterm is that heb xng bi& ng $!((prondi iic454- % BNOThb;t cppty whhhhhhenn e9090 ()() whch isssn't too sprising to those who know the boy's private interests. *(Toronto Sun)*

An urgent investigation has been launched by Solihull Council after a local schoolgirl was involved in a freak accident this week. Keeley Carter, aged 11, fell from stairs at Kinghurst Junior School, North Solihull, impaling her mouth on a 6ft wooden steak, at Monday lunchtime. *(Solihull News)*

Extra money for spending on schools means that no child in a York school needs to go outside to the toilet. In some cases after waiting for nearly 100 years! Phew – that's a relief. *(Labour Party leaflet)*

Football Club helps stab tragedy children
(Northern Echo)

• LABOUR ROSE

NEWS FROM THE CITY OF
YORK LABOUR PARTY

THOUGHT FOR TODAY: The whle wrod is in a state of chassis – Sean O'Casey *(The Rising Nepal)*

Madam – I am writing in response to the article on last week's front page of the *Standard* about proposals for a professional creche facility to be launched in the old hospital records office and cottages. As a parent of teenagers I am very aware and concerned about the needs of gangsters in the town at present. From the mid to late teens there is nowhere for them to go in the evenings as a drop-in facility other than pubs. *(Wilts & Glos. Standard)*

All the children in the picture were born after Mrs — and her husband parted in 1930. Altogether she has had eighteen children – fourteen of them, she says, by various fathers. Mrs — says: "It has been a hard job bringing them up. But I am proud of my family. I neither smoke nor go to the cinema. My only relaxation is the radio." *(Sunday Pictorial)*

A bovine bingo game is being staged on the school playing fields on Sunday. A cow will be brought to the field, and where she makes her first deposit will be the lucky spot. The winner gets 25 per cent of the proceeds up to £100, and lots of pats on the back. *(St Albans Review & Express)*

Names of town, district council chairmen and their vices released *(Malawi Daily Times)*

A school spokesman said: "He will be sorely missed at the Rectory, most of all perhaps for his wife's counsel and considerate nature, for which countless staff, parents and pupils had cause to be grateful." *(Richmond and Twickenham Star)*

Much-travelled Royal Marine: Since leaving Cottage Grove (St Luke's) School, in 1942, Sergeant James Robert Newman (49) considers he has had a full and exciting wife. *(Hants Telegraph)*

Emma Duncan, of Lancaster Girls' Grammar School, passed four A-Levels in her recent exams, not ½ as was printed last week. *(S. Blyth, Cumberland News)*

What is dyselxia? *(Nursery World)*

Meetings

● DYSLEXIA: Occupational Therapist at Alder Hey Hospital Wendy Smith will be addressing the Liverpool Dyselxia Association on Wednesday at Liverpool Hope University College.

(Liverpool Echo)

An interesting address on "The National Care of the Child" by Miss Palmer was much appreciated by all, and Mrs Lever in a short address made an appeal for the use of the humane killer. *(Berkshire newspaper)*

In last week's notebook under the heading "What's in a name?" the name of a Honolulu councillor was misspelt as Mr Kekoalaulionapalihauliulio David Kaapuawaokamehaheha. This should have read: Mr

Kekoalauliionapalihauliulio David Kaapuawaokame-haheha. *(Municipal Journal)*

The tutors also complain of the many sixth-form candidates who appear at interviews in open-neck shirts and whose aplications fomrs abound in spelling mistake. *(Daily Telegraph)*

The parents say they are not concerned with the rights and wrongs of the teachers' dispute – only with the welfare of the chicken. *(Newcastle Evening Chronicle)*

The Misses Doris, Agnes and Vivian Smith are spending several days at the home of their mother, Mrs W.L. Lawrence. This is the first time that the community has had the pleasure of seeing the Smith girls in the altogether at one time. *(Sydney Daily News)*

He is the son of the ancient principal of our college who, behind his thick glasses, hid a heart of gold. *(Courrier de Saône et Loire)*

Embarrassed BBC Television officials admitted last night that their exclusive film of the Loch Ness Monster was, in fact, a duck. *(Daily Telegraph)*

DID YOU KNOW . . .? The first Boy Scout troop in Vermont was organised in Vermont. *(Middlebury Independent)*

Daventry Development Committee are looking for two pretty girls to show off their expansion regions. *(Northampton Chronicle and Echo)*

Crash courses are available for those wishing to learn to drive very quickly. *(Eastbourne Gazette)*

A colleague was tuned to a provincial radio station. The disc jockey introduced a record for a listener "who's 111 today". *[Pause]* "Sorry. That's not 111. He's ill."

Once again I felt that there is no more creative and health-giving activity for the young than the preservation, resuscitation and running of a railway worked by steam locomotives. *(Letter from the Master of a Cambridge college in The Times)*

In our report last week of Davison School PTA Fête we referred to Mr Ron Marshall as being the late organiser. This should have read fête organiser. We apologise for the error. *(Worthing Gazette)*

FULLY FURNISHED HOUSE – 3 kitchens, 2 bathrooms, 3 toilets. Suitable students. £30 per student per wee. *(Express and Echo, Exeter)*

If they could save children from dying before the age of one, there would be a better prospect of them reaching to adolescence. *(South London newspaper)*

LUCKY CARETAKER
WAS STABBED THREE TIMES

PUPILS CUT
TO EASE CROWDING

. . . and the second seminar will be on the unorganised conference . . . er . . . I'm sorry – the UN organised conference.

The computer class for nudists, 50-strong, consists of housewives, teachers, doctors, engineers and office workers. Dr R. J. Gibson, club secretary, explained that it is being started partly because the weather is not always suitable for badminton. *(Sunday Citizen)*

Sandhurst captain-coach Ron Best made it 105 girls for the season yesterday, when he booted 13 goals against Kennington. *(Bendigo Advertiser, Australia)*

A foreign teacher nicknamed "Mr Wortical", who was sacked from a primary school because his spoken English and grammar were said to be below standard, had been adjudged "not goon enough to teach in primary schools" before he took the post, it was revealed yesterday. *(Daily Telegraph)*

The birth rate declined, in the period 1972-1978, from 20.82 per thousand people to 15.98. A main cause of all this is the difficulty of making ends meet. *(Observer)*

All he asked was a fireside chair and a couple of good boobs. *(Cape Times)*

Presbyterian crossing facilities outside the school have been championed by the councillor.

The production at St Clare's was beautifully moved and staged. Gropings were splendid and moves were well thought out.

Sister Gillian's "bust clinic" referred to last month was, of course, a "busy clinic".

The annual Christmas party at the Ashley Street School was hell yesterday afternoon. *(Springfield newspaper)*

I know Sir Peter Parker hasn't forgotten me. I remember him at the dancing class as a girl of 14. *(London Evening Standard)*

The shooting of the cadet force was excellent. The shooting of the sergeant major was especially satisfactory. *(Daily Express)*

John Harkes going to Sheffield, Wednesday. *(New York Post)*

9pm Broadcast on behalf of the Conservative Party. 10pm They Think It's All Over. *(Independent)*

Water levels are low. Why not fill up the reservoirs from the mains? *(Letter in the Poole Daily Echo)*

The age limit for Girl Guides was formerly 18 years, but now by general request it has now been raised to 81 years. *(Local newspaper)*

WOMAN HURT WHILE COOKING HER HUSBAND'S BREAKFAST IN A HORRIBLE MANNER *(Texas newspaper)*

The little children are more outgoing than the adults. They have all made genuine friends here and we have no problems at all – well, only one. The smallest were not used to wearing knickers. *(Daily Telegraph)*

Princess — on her way to school. She attends a co-educational establishment at which are a number of other children. *(Daily Telegraph)*

We apologise for the error in last week's paper in which we stated that Mr Arnold Dogbody was a defective in the police force. This was a typographical error. We meant, of course, that Mr Dogbody is a detective in the police farce and we are sorry for any embarrassment caused. *(Ely Standard)*

The British legal system is the best in the World. Each case is tried with scrupulous fairness and justice is not only done, it is seen to be done. There are no inflexible rules: the law is elastic. *(US college magazine)*

Overcome by gas while taking a shower, she owed her life to the watchfulness of the caretaker. *(Cheshire Weekly)*

MISS FRIAN, FORMER PRINCIPAL, UNVEILS BUST AT DEDICATION CEREMONY *(Catchgate College magazine)*

The Mayor was visiting the school with his bitter half. *(Consett Times)*

Widower, 50s, teacher, C of E, own home, wishes to meet

widow for fiendship. *(Express and Star, Wolverhampton)*

The report was signed by five faulty members of the University. *(Herald & Post)*

Mr Okum, the chairman of Governors, lives with his wife, his childhood sweetheart, and three sons in Chalmonte. *(Bury Advertiser)*

The all-girl orchestra were rather weak in the bras section. *(Slough Times)*

A village teacher in Spain turned his horse upside down in a frantic search for a missing lottery ticket while villagers waited outside for news. *(Daily Telegraph)*

She is now a language teacher but was a former dental nurse of Finnish extraction. *(Mail on Sunday)*

I took my eight-year-old to the Doctor, a Dutchman, when she had flu. He asked her how she felt. "I'm all clogged up," she replied. *(Letter in Durham Advertiser)*

During the school match, Meads was kicked on the head, and had to have three stitches put in the cut. Kirkpatrick broke his nose early in the match. Villepreux played most of the game with two ribs broken. Many others were hurt. Some of the injuries were deliberately inflicted. These deeds made unpleasant watching. But, taken as a whole, this was not a game that got out of hand. *(Guardian)*

The thirteen pupils were able to see the hospital's special baby car unit. *(Thurrock Gazette)*

HORSE GIRL SUSPENDED BY HEAD *(Daily Telegraph)*

It was decided in the redevelopment that, at the centre of the college, Copcastle Square would be made into a rotunda with a doomed roof. *(Bury Evening Telegraph)*

IRAQI HEAD SEEKS ARMS *(Newspaper headline)*

(Needham Market newsletter)

9

Adverts

Significant mis-spellings can make a major difference . . .

From *The Times Educational Supplement . . .*

APPOINTMENT OF
FIRST
HEADMASTER
THE INGLISH SCHOOL—ESTEPONA
An Educational Cooperative and Trust
(approved by the Spanish Government)
Estepona (Malaga), Spain

And from the *South China Morning Post . . .*

SMITH CORONA

Introducing The Spell-Right III™
Electronic Dicitonary

GREAT YARMOUTH OPEN BOWELS FESTIVAL –
Great Yarmouth Bowling Greens, Marine Parade
(What's On, When and Where – East Anglia)

Teachers – Why not Explore France on a Horse? – Village
Gits, Self Catering or Full Board *(Horse & Pony)*

Wendy House – suitable for 3-4 year-old. Good condition
– very turdy *(Evening Gazette)*

Technician Required For De Brus School . . . Good
interpersonal and communicatino skills would be an
advantage.

Garden refuge collected.

And if they really meant what they said . . .

Advert in the Western Gazette . . .

FRIENDS' ACADEMY, Locust Valley, Long Island, Co-
educational, with special opportunities for boys. *(Friend's
Intelligencer)*

The Indian Express is proud to announce . . .

Artificial Limbs
Centre has
new head
Express News Service

And a good camping opportunity in Southport . . .

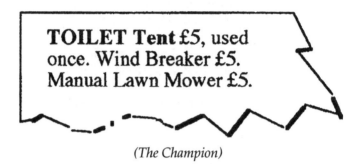

TOILET Tent £5, used once. Wind Breaker £5. Manual Lawn Mower £5.

(The Champion)

While Camera Weekly issues an unusual invitation . . .

74 Diary: where to shoot kids singing carols in a courtyard and the best guide to photogenic country walks

. . . and as for the Korean Weekly . . . !

대영여행사

Dai Young Travel

Dialectical Materialist and elderly mother require housekeeper. *(Daily Worker)*

THREE GIRLS, navy school skirts, age 11 years. £10 the lot. *(Lancaster Grauniad)*

10.50 [FILM] LAP DANCER (Arthur Egell, 1995) Erotic drama – starring Elizabeth Wagner as a woman who turns to lap dancing to make ends meet. *89578976*
12.15 NFL American Football

Children's Branded Trainers
(adidas)

Large selection of Ladies
aerobic wear
(adidas/puma)

Children's Branded Bottoms
from £12

(Ukay Clothing – Norfolk Citizen)

NORTHWOOD PREPARATORY SCHOOL (MOOR PARK) – LUNCHTIME PLAY SUPERVISOR for our 408 year old boys. Please tel. Mrs Hampel on . . .

TYPING * SHORTHAND * AUDIO-TYPING. Learn with a qualified tutor. Morning sessions 9.15am-12.15pm. Beginners, refreshers or nature students. *(Whitstable Extra)*

THE HITE REPORT ON MALE SEXUALITY (September: £12 [cased]; £9.95 [limp])

Advert from The Times Educational Supplement . . .

Wanted Head of Junior School . . . Roll is largely Muslim. Strong Church of England links and a regular communicant preferred.

Our FREE teachers' educational package is very suggestive indeed. *(Advertising flyer for canal boat trips around Birmingham)*

And then there are the courses on offer . . .

Girls and Boys in School – The course is intended for headmasters, deputy headmasters and other staff. *(Details of equal opportunities course offered under the Council of Europe teacher bursary scheme)*

Exams. Learn the principles of success in studying and passing exams. One day course. *(Wirral Globe)*

South Glamorgan Institute for Higher Education, Cardiff, is offering Degree in Dietetics (four-year Sandwich Course).

BEBE CAR DUPLA TANDEM PRAM and all accessories £150, Britax Rocker Bye £15, plus Walker £15, and baby £5. *(Herald and Post)*

Six Faces of Wine
CHALFONT'S COUNTY SECONDARY SCHOOL
NICOL ROAD. Weds 7.45–9.15pm 6 fortnightly
meetings 12 January 1983. Ms P Drinkwater

Spotted in Buckinghamshire WEA Brochure . . .

Rentokil Pest Control Division wish St Theresa's Prep School another 40 pest-free years. *(The Universe)*

NORTHFIELD GARDEN PARTY – 17 JULY, 2.00-5.00. STALLS – GAMES – MUSIC – COMPETITIONS. NB Bring an umbrella! No toilet facilities provided.

BURROWS BOOKSHOP – Visit us for a wide choice of Summer reading. Holiday and Leisure Guides. Children's books to keep them abused in the holidays, and lots, lots more. *(The Ely Crier)*

Extract from the South China Morning Post . . .

From the program of a forthcoming Royal College of Physicians' conference on the medical effects of alcohol:

- 9.20:   Effects of alcohol on the heart
- 9.50:   Alcohol and the heart
- 10.20: Alcohol and the nervous system
- 11.20: Effects of alcohol on the gastrointestinal system
- 10.10: Nutrition and alcohol
- 12.40: Bar open

Intelligent young European lady wanted for interesting and responsible work. Typing useful but not essential.

Must be proper good at grammer and spelling. *(Handscodt Bugle and Advertiser)*

Sign in School Cafeteria in Worcester: "Shoes are required to eat in the cafeteria." Underneath was written: "Socks can eat wherever they want."

10

Notices

Notices, which in recent years have proliferated almost as much as circulars, and intrude upon our lives from street to stretcher, frequently give conflicting messages . . .

ANY PERSON NOT PUTTING LITTER INTO THIS BASKET WILL BE LIABLE TO A FINE OF £5 *(But, Sir, I haven't got any litter!)*

DOGS MUST BE CARRIED ON THE ESCALATORS *(And what if I don't have a dog?)*

SCHOOL OF THE SISTERS OF CHARITY *– NO PARKING – NO TURNING*

PLEASE DO NOT LOCK THE DOOR AS WE HAVE LOST THE KEY

✓ Please do not feed the ducks. If you have any suitable food, please give it to the teachers on duty.

BELL OUT OF USE – PLEASE USE KNOCKERS

SWIMMING POOL – PEDESTRIANS ONLY

The spare key to the First Aid Room is available in the First Aid Room. *(Sign in Kent school)*

PLEASE TAKE A TRAY (*And what happened when Jimmy tried to walk out the door with one under his arm?*)

CHILDREN FOUND STRAYING WILL BE TAKEN TO THE LION HOUSE (*Notice at Kyo Zoo*)

Year 7 are saving aluminium cans, bottles and other items to be recycled. Proceeds will be used to cripple children.

Assistant Cook Required For St Anselm's Secondary School (No Objection to Sex)

Mrs Kearney would be grateful for anything you want to get rid of for the Christmas fayre on Thursday evening. Why not come and bring your parents?

TOILET OUT OF ORDER. PLEASE USE FLOOR BELOW.

You are invited to take advantage of the chambermaid. (*Japanese hotel*)

Visitors are expected to complain at the office between the hours of 9 and 11 a.m. daily. (*Athens hotel*)

And when a single letter, or phrase, can make such a difference . . .

A seven-pound baby boy arrived last night *to frighten* the lives of Mr and Mrs Caswell.

Congratulations to Alan and his wife Amy on the *girth* of their first child.

The senior choir invites any member of the school who enjoys *signing* to join the choir.

The head will be away for the rest of the week. ***Massages*** can be given to his secretary.

Mrs Thomas Jennings' classes for children of pre-kindergarten age will be resumed on Mondays, Wednesdays and Fridays, from 9 to 12 o'clock. A slight ***smack*** will be served at about 10.30. *(Connecticut paper)*

The Low Self Esteem Group will meet Thursday at 12.30 pm. Please use the back door.

Year 9 will be presenting Shakespeare's *Hamlet* in the main hall at 7 pm tonight. All staff are invited to attend this tragedy.

Mr and Mrs John Bowley, both teachers, are the parents of their child, a daughter born at Windsor Hospital on August 15th.

Lost in school yesterday – tan leather wallet, containing photographs, personal cuttings, and £50. Finder may keep photographs, clippings and the wallet, but the owner has a personal attachment to the money.

FOR SALE: an antique desk suitable for lady with thick legs and large drawers.

11

Further Education

Students attending Chichester College of Further Education have been advised to sing "God Save The Queen" while frying bacon. Mrs Ivy Davey, their instructress, said: "'God Save The Queen' has a running time of about two minutes – just right for each side of a rasher."

En route to give a lecture in Cleveland, Lancelot Dillger pulled out of his driveway and drove straight into a delivery van. With his car incapacitated, Dillger borrowed his father's, but in hurrying to get to the lecture hall he took a corner too fast and crashed into a truck. Dillger finally arrived to give his lecture, in a taxi. His topic for the evening was "Safe Driving".

Paul Norris's girlfriend could be a very lucky lady. For 20-year-old Dorset Institute of Higher Education banking student Paul has just won £30, and he may spend some of the money on her. *(Bournemouth Evening Echo)*

Students who marry during their course will not be permitted to remain in college. Further, students who are already married must either live with their husbands or make other arrangements with the Dean. *(Syllabus of an Ohio College)*

Britain's 100,000 undergraduates and students returning from vacation this month will be told not to deal with fellow students selling shirts, jewellery and other finery to earn extra cash. But insurance selling at universities and colleges will be allowed because it is considered "enterprising". *(Daily Telegraph)*

Domestic staff in one of Aberdeen University's halls of residence may refuse to work overtime again after a serious incident involving a Brussels sprout last year. *(Gaudie, Aberdeen)*

Three years after she presented a thesis showing that elderly people moved their legs with greater speed when they were in a hurry and reduced the speed of their legs when they were not in a hurry, Miss Stina Fjeleer-Modic, of the Royal University, Stockholm, has submitted a research project on the consumption of cooked meats. Interviewed at her home in Flassturm, Miss Fjeleer-Modic said: "During my investigation I ate 4,756 pork chops in restaurants, canteens, private houses, army barracks, three Institutes for the Insane, and a prison. My study has shown that it is undesirable for a chop to be more than two centimetres thick or to remain in a utensil for more than three minutes after frying."

Some recent PhD theses . . .

The Concept of Social Rage in the Old Testament and the Ancient Near East *(Michigan)*

Homosexual Tendencies in Seagulls *(California)*

Suicide amongst Eskimos in Alaska *(Alaska)*

The Gnome and Its Uses in Certain Old English Poems *(Oxford)*

The Leg Muscles of the Adult Honey Bee *(London)*

The Correct Alignment of Various Fixtures in the Bathroom *(Stockholm)*

Recent Commissions from the government-funded Economic and Social Research Council . . .

Family, friendship and neighbourhood among rural Finns *(1 year: £8,049)*

The development of crying in infancy and its effects on the mother *(3 years: £35,632)*

The social organisation of long-distance traders in Libya *(3 years: £18,962)*

Exchange rates in late mediaeval Europe *(1 year: £5,130)*

Judging the probability of future events *(2 years: £19,686)*

The culture of drinking in an English community *(1 year: £21,040)*

Patients' comprehension of doctors' instructions *(3 years: £11,650)*

Scientists at the University of Pittsburgh researched into how plump women could lose weight after the menopause. It took four years of hard graft, rigorously studying the body fat and cholesterol of 500 volunteers. The conclusion they came to was that a better diet and more exercise would probably do the trick.

According to the National Institute for Healthcare Research in Maryland, when one person hurts another, "forgiveness causes restorations in relationship closeness".

Astonishingly, researchers at the University of Iowa found that youngsters do more exercise if their parents work out in the gym and that they are more likely to smoke if their mothers or fathers smoke.

Professor: Here you see the skull of a chimpanzee – a very rare specimen. There are only two in the country – one is in the National Museum, and I have the other.

Revd William A. Spooner's classic spoonerism telling a student to leave his class for non-attendance and lighting fires:

Sir, you have tasted two whole worms; you have hissed all my mystery lectures and been caught fighting a liar in the quad. You will leave Oxford by the next town drain.

Chelsea College of Physical Education in Eastbourne is recovering with eight broken ribs in a clinic at Sierre in the Rhone Valley. *(Evening Standard)*

One of Princeton University's (USA) best-loved traditions is the Nude Olympics, an event which takes place after the first snowfall. About 350 second-year undergraduates gather at midnight to run naked through the quad, apart from boots and scarves, and emboldened by the demon drink.

CHEATS (INC.) PROSPER: Toronto, 16 December – The old custom of cheating in university essays has become big business in the United States. Last year companies selling essays made about $550,000, and now they are

planning to expand into Canada. One company is training men to manage offices in Toronto, Montreal, and Vancouver, and another is installing a free telephone system for students to order essays from anywhere in North America.

Essays produced under non-examination conditions generally count in North American universities towards a final degree, and education officials say that, if the practice of buying essays is allowed to continue, a college degree will become increasingly less credible as a certification of academic competence.

In the United States last year, the leading essay houses sold more than 10,000 papers. Mr Bill Carmody, who runs the oldest and largest such firm, International Termpapers Incorporated, has built a file of more than 80,000 essays. He has a staff of over four hundred freelance writers who write for a fee of £1 a page. Mr Carmody sells copies for £2 a page. *(Guardian)*

12

Headteachers

It is not easy to be a successful headteacher. Targeted as the "whipping" boys, or girls, of disgruntled staff, governors, Local Education bureaucrats, and OFSTED inspectors, they plough a lonely furrow. Few achieve – though many think they do – majority support within their schools as they attempt to keep as many balls in the air at once, without being kicked in them too frequently. It is only in the period of an OFSTED inspection, when there is unity against the common enemy, and during the relief and euphoria of staff immediately following such a trauma, that the headteacher enjoys temporary respite from belligerent members of the school community.

Is it any wonder then that so many lose concentration and drop howlers, appear miserable, bad tempered or merely insane. The story is told of a particularly depressed head visiting his doctor and being told: "You urgently need a holiday – might I suggest Lourdes?"

Perhaps he's the one who failed to take the advice given, and appeared in a Manchester paper under the heading . . .

DEAD HEAD ON STAFF 25 YEARS

Or maybe he was the one who earned this slot in the Birmingham Post . . .

Tom Brown, 73, a former comprehensive school head-teacher, abandoned his broken-down Skoda on the M5 and took a bus and a train back to his home in Tewkesbury, Gloucestershire – 70 miles away – where, five hours later, police informed him that he had left his 84-year-old wife, Catherine, in the car. Mr Brown said: "I told her not to worry, and set off for the nearest village. I suppose I must have got confused."

And "confused" seems to have been an apt description of the following . . .

At a PTA Annual Meeting, one unfortunate head had the misfortune to utter: "As head of the school I am, of course, the shepherd of the flock. I see our deputy head, Mr Cochrane, as the little crook on the staff." *(Daily Telegraph)*

Headteacher: There is clearly a problem with discipline on the buses . . . Mr White and myself have been disgusting together . . . er . . . discussing . . . sorry about that! *(Parent-teacher meeting)*

The headteacher apologised to the parents because the treacherous winter weather had produced dangerous slippery conditions on the school drive and walkways. Financial constraints had meant that remedial action could not be taken. He informed them that the deputy headteacher responsible for the school budget was gritting his teeth in the circumstances. *(Cleveland school's PTA meeting)*

Mr E. G. Winterton, headmaster, would not comment on the threat. However, he did say: "Some children have been behaving very childishly." *(Doncaster Post)*

Many years ago, Lord Altrincham visited the local grammar school at Chipping Sodbury to present the prizes, and in his introductory speech the head began: "How pleased we are that our Lord has come down today . . ."

And in similar vein . . .

Lord Halifax, the former British ambassador to the United States, once visited a college in Fort Worth, Texas, and addressed the students. The principal introduced him without any problem right up to his closing remark. Then he said: "When the speech is over, if anyone wants to ask questions, the Lord will provide the answers."

The headteacher of a Surrey school once started his assembly with the words: "Today I shall be talking about a 'New Cantament Testicle' – sorry . . . er . . . sorry about that . . . I mean a 'New Testament Canticle'."

The story is told of a headteacher from Buxton who went to pay his condolences to the wife of a retired former colleague who, at an advanced age, had died. As they talked, he put his arm around her shoulders and then supported her twice when her knees buckled. When this happened a third time, the woman looked him in the eye and said: "For God's sake, will you let me kneel down and say a prayer."

The headteacher emerged from his office one morning and announced angrily: "There's just one thing that makes me really mad – bad manners and mathematical incompetence."

A headteacher in Bolton, commenting on the school

league tables in which his school came bottom, with 8% in English and science and 0% in maths, said: "Standards are improving in all four subjects."

Headteacher to staff: There is no point in being pessimistic. It wouldn't work anyway.

Headteacher at prize giving: Once again the Ornithological Society got us off to a flying start.

From "The Teacher" . . .

My sister, a headteacher, lives in a rather remote part of the country and has a breakdown garage next to her house. One morning she answered the phone and heard a voice say: "Can you tell me if there is a Mr Fog there?"

Looking out of her window she saw a man standing at the garage. "Hold on," she said. "There's someone outside. I'll go and ask him his name." With that she dashed outside, asked the man his name and returned to the phone. "Sorry, he isn't Mr Fog," she said.

"Madam," said the voice, "This is the weather centre. We had an agreement with your husband that I would occasionally phone to see what the weather was like in your area. Is there a mist or fog?"

Headmasters can be omnipotent in their little spheres of influence. As Winston Churchill remarked: "Headteachers have powers at their disposal with which prime ministers have never yet been invested."

A headteacher clambered into bed in the middle of winter. "God, your feet are cold," exclaimed his wife. "How many times have I told you," he retorted, "that when we are in bed you can call me 'George'."

Some heads can be pretty miserable, short-tempered or political . . .

My husband and I are shortly to attend an important public dinner, and I understand we shall be seated side by side. He is rather a taciturn man and I feel we shall sit in silence throughout the meal which will look as if we are not on good terms, whereas we are happily married but not in the habit of making conversation to each other. *(Letter in Woman and Home)*

Surrey's County Education Officer is to look into parents' allegations that an infants' school headmaster assaulted a boy with his artificial leg for turning the wrong way in a Maypole dance. *(Times Educational Supplement)*

You haven't been as much an audience as a challenge – and I have to tell you – you won!

. . . of the Association on Alcoholism to speak at the school. He is an excellent speaker and will probably be willing to have a "quick one" with some of us after the evening is over.

The new head was holding his first staff meeting: "I want you all to feel free and speak your mind. I don't want any yes-men around me. I want everybody to give their opinion – even if it does cost you your job."

Note to staff at girls' public school from the headteacher: "Lazy girls should be jogged into action by the news that the Duchess of Kent is doing her own nails."

They say life begins at forty – but so does lumbago, bad eyesight, arthritis, and the habit of telling the same story three times to the same person.

Shortly after his arrival in a new parish, the vicar was asked to conduct the funeral service of a retired headteacher. In the service he announced: "I'm sorry that I cannot pay tribute to the deceased as I did not know him. But if any of you would like to say a few words, please feel free to do so."

There was complete silence. "Now don't be shy," continued the vicar. "I'm sure some of you would like to say a kindly word about your friend." Finally a voice from the back muttered: "His brother was worse."

Some advice for would-be headteachers . . .

If you can keep your head while all around are losing theirs, then you clearly don't understand the situation.

Be thankful for your problems, for if they were fewer, someone with less ability would have your job.

If you're not big enough to stand criticism, then you're too small to be praised.

No matter what goes wrong, there is always somebody who knew it would.

Forgive your enemies but never forget their names.

The most knocking is done by those who can't ring the bell.

Speak when you're angry and you'll make the best speech you will ever regret.

A headteacher laughs at his Chair of Governors' jokes not because they are clever, but because *he* is.

Speeches are like babies: Easy to conceive, but hard to deliver.

A meeting is an event at which the minutes are kept and the hours are lost.

A chairman who can smile when things go wrong has found someone to blame it on.

When someone says he is laying all his cards on the table – count them.

A man would do nothing if he waited until he could do it so well that no-one could find fault with it.

The more you say, the less people remember.

Never leave school angry – stay back and fight.

Live every day as if it's your last – and one day, you'll be right.

Always be lenient – sometimes lean one way and sometimes the other.

Rule A: The headteacher is never wrong.
Rule B: If anyone discovers he is wrong, refer to Rule A.

Extracts from heads' speeches ...

Do you know what it means to go home from school each night to a woman who will give you a little love, a little affection, a little tenderness? To go in and be given a large gin and tonic and then a meal fit for a king? I'll tell you what it means – it means you're in the wrong bloody house! That's what it means.

I'm pleased myself and my wife have found one of the secrets of a long marriage. We take time to go to a nice restaurant or a cosy pub twice a week. A warm corner, subdued lights, soft music, and dancing. She goes on a Tuesday – me on a Friday.

Last year after the inspection we were poised on the edge of a precipice. This year, thank God, we have taken a great leap forward.

Head commenting on burst pipes which flooded some classrooms: "This is the worst disaster since I was appointed."

I will put down my foot with a strong hand.

Father Taylor will now lead us in a few words of silent prayer.

I'm looking for four lads who are quick at picking up music – Right, move that piano over there!

Head to staff: "You are to stand by the fire doors. When I ring the fire alarm, you will allow nobody to leave, explaining it is not a fire – it is just a nuclear attack."

Piece of information from the headteacher of a West Country school at the annual PTA dinner: "As in previous years the evening will conclude with a formal toast to the new president. The champagne will be provided by the retiring president, drunk as usual at midnight."

At another PTA annual dinner, the head's wife was chatting away to the parents on her table about how, as a young girl, before she was married, she was very innocent and naïve. She said: "I didn't even know what a homosexual was until I met my husband."

Headteacher at PTA Annual General Meeting: "Mr Carroll has been elected and has accepted the office of Chairman. We could not get a better man."

Perhaps what heads need for stress is the following, which appeared in a 1920s American chemists' circular ...

BLANKS NERVE TONIC – drives away nervy symptoms, gives power to brain and body.
LEAVES BEHIND – irritability, indigestion, rheumatism, neuralgia, hysteria, etc.

13

Teachers

The perception the public used to have of the teaching profession as highly respected members of the community has declined rapidly over the years. Changing social outlooks and "mores" have caused their status to plummet and hurtle down the "awe league" along with vicars, priests, doctors and solicitors – to name but a few previously revered occupations. Some of them do little to enhance the profession's reputation . . .

MAN BARKS AT DOG, FINED £5 – Mr Claude Wilson, aged 34, of Benfleet, Essex, a teacher who barked at an Alsatian after it barked at him and had a scuffle with its owner, was fined £5 with £5 costs by Rochford magistrates yesterday. *(The Times)*

Sir, I am a teacher and as such do not like wasting time when I am watching TV. I always like to do something else – at the same time I do foot, finger and eye exercises. I shrug my shoulders and roll my head round and round. During the World Cup, whenever the players took a corner or there was an injury I went down on my back to do a few tummy exercises and circle my legs round in the air. *(Letter in Daily Mail)*

HMI criticized the fact that pupils were not allowed to speak in class. When they wanted to attract the teacher's attention they had to wave a small flag. *(The Times Educational Supplement)*

This is a good teaching film . . . No high or low church bias . . . That is left for the teacher to put in. *(Dawn Trust Films, 1949 catalogue)*

In 1967, Thomas Litz, a teacher in Switzerland, set aside homework, which he marked but forgot to return. It was only in 1988, while sorting through old papers that he came across the exercises. One of the pupils now taught with Thomas at the same school and finally had his work returned after 21 years.

Sometimes what they say can damage their reputations . . .

Whenever I open my mouth, some fool speaks.

This optional subject is compulsory.

Trace events up to Henry VIII.

Draw a Roman soldier you know.

Teacher's instructions on how to use Pritt Stick: "Take off the top and push up the bottom."

Children will not be able to skate on frozen water unless it has been passed by the headteacher.

If you can't keep quiet, shut up!

I want to hear it so quiet that we can hear a mouse dropping.

We must be more tolerant of one another and respect the fact that people have their own opinions, beliefs, likes in music, etc . . . Grigor – get that earring out now!

All right, everybody, line up alphabetically according to height.

Mr Evans, a teacher, claimed the light was green but he was found guilty of failing to obey traffic lights and was fined £100. Mrs Rose Evans told the magistrates the light was blue. She was given an eye test.

My wife, a teacher like myself, left me recently because of my 20-year addiction to gambling. Is there anything that I can do to win her back? *(Letter to the Daily Mail)*

Teachers, however, remain one of the most dedicated of professions and are still prepared to expand their charges' experiences by taking them on trips, which are always stressful . . .

Sir, Last Saturday I took a group of boarders at the prep school where I am housemaster to a football match between Maidenhead United and Ruislip Manor.

On the way to the game the boys were asking me how I chose their Saturday night video. I told them that I took note of the film's classification and tried to avoid bad language, violence and nudity.

We stood behind one of the goals; in the first minute the goalkeeper dropped the ball and uttered an expletive that echoed around the ground.

In the fifth minute, the right winger was scythed to the ground by a vicious tackle that left him writhing in agony. However, I felt pretty sure that my third "video worry" would not occur – then halfway through the second half, a streaker danced across the pitch.

Circular to Exmouth schools . . .

Nine people were bitten by donkeys on Bridlington Sands, 172 were stung by jellyfish and another 13 were bitten by dogs. These are just a few of the 2,186 cases handled by First Aid posts on the town's beaches. Only one casualty required hospital treatment – a male tourist from Holland who had to have a stick of rock removed.

Malcolm Laverty of Bury First School, Pulborough, took his class of ten-year-olds to the coast of North Wales to study a contrasting area of the country. Assembled outside the main gate of Conwy Castle, they were asked to suggest reasons why this particular site was chosen to build such a stronghold. Whilst some eyes glazed over, others surveyed the surrounding area and tried to imagine what it was like hundreds of years ago.

Edward finally raised his hand. "Sir, was it because it could be near the public lavatories?"

Sometimes a visit from a dignitary can be dangerous ...

The Bishop of the Diocese was visiting a Catholic junior school and asked one class of seven-year-olds some questions on religion. He ended up by asking: "Is there anything that God cannot do?" There was silence for a while until one little girl answered: "Please, Sir – Miss says that even God couldn't stop us talking."

But clearly there are some who think teachers are really daft ...

Win a weekend break for two at one of the Care Leisure luxury hotels in the New Forest *or* Take your class on a free visit to one of Central Southern England's leading visitor attractions.

Teachers can be very wise ...

Well done to the Birmingham teacher who, on receiving a letter from her bank manager saying it appeared she was overdrawn, wrote back to ask him to let her know when he was sure. *(Guardian)*

... and dedicated ...

Mr Thomas's teacher colleagues will be sorry to learn that he had an operation last Wednesday and had his leg removed. All being well he should be back on his feet, and back to his job in the classroom, by the end of November. *(Cobar Age, New South Wales)*

We wish him every happiness in his retirement. For over twenty-five years his learning and his wit have enriched the minds of all the boys to whom he taught English. It is true to say that as a teacher he was in a class by himself. *(Sussex school magazine)*

Still, some pupils do show respect . . .

After he had finished robbing her home, the burglar bent over his 81-year-old victim, gave her a kiss, and said: "You were always kind to me." Whereupon the retired Cleveland schoolmistress recognized the intruder as her favourite pupil from 1925, Fergus Wayne. On her positive identification, Fergus was subsequently charged with robbery.

Michael Lee, deputy head of The English Martyrs, Hartlepool, and one-time school team manager, tells the story of preparing his team for their local cup final . . .

We had recently not had a good run, and I decided to give a psychological pep-talk before the match. I told the centre forward to get out there and pretend that he was the best scorer in the North-East. I told the centre half to pretend he was the best defender, and so it continued with each player in the team. The message was positive – pretend you *are* the best. We lost 3-0. I was pacing the changing room, trying to figure out what to say when the big centre forward came in, walked up to me, put his arm around my shoulders and said: "Don't worry, sir – just *pretend* we won."

But what is the reality of teaching beyond the fantasy of what the government's spin doctors would have us believe . . .?

The story is told of the retired woman teacher who died and went up to heaven. St Peter told her that she must spend one day in hell and a second in heaven. Only then could she decide where she wished to stay permanently. She entered the lift and eventually she arrived in hell. It was beautiful – blue skies, wonderful views, golf courses, continental-style streets with umbrellas and wicker chairs. The teacher met some old friends and they had a chat and a "gastronomique" lunch. Afterwards she returned to heaven for her second day, when she spent the time with a couple of angels sitting on a cloud strumming a lyre and singing hymns. When St Peter appeared and asked her what choice she had made, she opted for hell. Down the teacher went on the long journey, and when the door opened she was astonished to see a barren landscape with rubbish everywhere. Her former colleagues were dressed in sackcloth and ashes, picking up garbage and looking totally miserable.

"I don't understand," she said. "What has happened?"

"Ah," Mephistopheles replied. "Yesterday was the interview. Now you're on the staff."

14

Christmas

Christmas, so very special for children, figures prominently in humorous stories of life at school.

The seven toddlers playing the dwarfs in St Joseph's Primary School pantomime in Washington, County Durham, were told to wear their Newcastle United shirts for the part. It was just too much for one of them, who defiantly arrived in his Sunderland top – and, no, he wasn't playing Dopey.

The teacher asked the class of seven-year-olds to name one of the animals in the stable with Jesus when he was born. "A whale, Miss," said George. "Why is that, then, George?" "Well, Miss," came the reply, "we're always singing 'A whale in a manger . . .'"

A seven-year-old boy was told that he was going to be in the Christmas play. A few minutes after he arrived home, the mother of the little lad telephoned the headteacher and said: "Jimmy has just arrived home and he tells me that we have to find a costume for him because he's in the school play and he is going to be a book." The headteacher thought for a moment and said: "No, no . . . he is going to be a page."

"Granny," said the six-year-old returning from school one December evening, "you wouldn't believe it, but we're doing one of those Nativity plays again this Christmas – and it's the same story as last time."

Santa was paying his Christmas visit to St Patrick's junior school and the following conversation took place:

"That's not Santa – that's Mr Joyce, our headteacher," said one little girl.

"No, Lucy. It just looks like Mr Joyce, but it isn't."

Little girl: "Yes it is Miss. Nobody else has got as big a nose as that."

A mother and her eight-year-old son stood in front of Tintoretto's painting of the Nativity. "What I cannot understand," said the boy, "is why Jesus wasn't born in a proper bed when his father was God." His mother explained patiently that Mary and Joseph were on a long journey, that there was no room at the inn and, anyway, they were very poor. "How can they have been very poor when they managed to get themselves painted by a famous painter?"

The teacher had never wanted to use Billy, often a disruptive influence, to entertain the parents in the intermission of the Christmas pantomime. Though he had been desperate to participate, he had been passed over for the more predictably well-behaved John and Sarah. Come the night of the panto, the teacher was obliged to turn to Billy for help when John and Sarah failed to turn up. "Up you get, then, Billy, and do the farmyard impressions you said you were good at." Billy got hold of the mike and confidently began: "Hey you, you little *****, get off that *****ing tractor!"

Overheard in playground ...

First girl: What can I get Rod for Christmas?
Second girl: Get him a nice book.
First girl: He's already got a book.

SIX MILLION DOLLAR MAN – £3. *(Notice on toy stall at school's Christmas fair)*

When Mary found out from the Angel Gabriel that she was going to be the mother of Jesus, she went off and sang the Magna Carta.

And they brought gifts of Gold, Frankenstein and Myrrh.

During the Christmas processional hymn, the heel of a girl chorister caught in a grating. Not wishing to hold up the ceremony, she marched on minus a shoe. Moved to chivalry, a male chorister following tried to pick up the shoe. Unfortunately the heel was stuck firmly in the grating, so again not wanting to hold up the procession, the chorister picked up the whole lot and continued up the nave. The officiating clergyman promptly fell into the hole. *(Ely Diocesan newsletter)*

GO MAD THIS WEEKEND – BUY SOME BEEF.

(Sign at restaurant where a North Yorkshire school staff held their festive meal)

And have you ever wondered where some of the children's toys end up ...?

"Youngsters think the toilet is a safe hiding place," said Derek Waites, a manager at Northumbrian Water's Stockton-on-Tees treatment works. "At Christmas we can

tell what the most popular presents were. Toys float through miles of sewers to our works. We've fished out quite a number of Action Men. We have even found a 12ft python. It gave one of our men a shock – he had gone to investigate a blockage and it landed on his head. Fortunately it was dead. False teeth are also found in sewage works at this time of year. Some people have too much to drink and lose them. One man rang up to ask if we had found them. He tried on a set we had fished out, but when he put them in, they weren't his."

Help can come in the most unusual of ways at Christmas . . .

Eric: My wife said the other day that I'd done absolutely nothing to help with the Christmas dinner. Absolutely nothing.
Ernie: What did you say?
Eric: I said, "What! Look at the turkey – I bought it, I've plucked it and I've stuffed it!"
Ernie: Good for you!
Eric: Now all she's got to do is kill it and put it in the oven.

15

Names

Sometimes the appropriate name appears to have been designed for the circumstances . . .

12.00 IT'S IN THE CLOSET,
IT'S UNDER THE BED. A
documentary about
vampires, werewolves,
and other such favourite
screen creepies.
12.25 NIGHT THOUGHTS
with the Revd Kenneth
Wolfe. Close
(Guardian)

He said both of the student's assailants were white, aged about 22, and one had a large "buzzard-like" nose. Witnesses should contact Mr Bird of Hornchurch CID. *(Romford Recorder)*

Adult education students at Brentwood, Essex, are taught woodwork by Mr Joiner, art by Mr Painter, seamanship by Mr Waterman and flower arranging by Miss Baskett. Belly dancing is taught by Miss Button.

The New Scientist has drawn scholars' attention to the *The British Journal of Urology*, by J. Splatt and D. Weedon; and also to the fact that there is W.I. Ball, an eye surgeon, and J. Lust, a New Zealand sex therapist.

Entry in the DEATHS column of the *Veterinary Record* . . . Dr P. J. Posthumus RGM writes – "Dr Peter Jacobus Posthumus, who died in August 1991, . . ."

Some people are given names they would never have chosen for themselves. A perusal of school registers from any large comprehensive school will reveal at least a couple of unusual names, and here are a few examples from County Durham . . .

Teresa Green, C. Lion, Brad Hall, R. Soul, Brian Olivers *(initials)*, Annette Kirton, Duncan Biscuit, Orson Carte, Sean A. Legg, Russell Sprout, A. Pratt, Walter Wall, Rose Berry, Eileen Dover.

The great-great-grandson of Carlos III of Spain, Don Alfonso de Borbon y Borbon (1866-1934), had 94 first names.

My Father, Albert Hall, was born in 1883 and ran away from home as a young boy. Asked his name by the recruiting sergeant, he said: 'Hall, Sir.' 'First name?' 'Er . . . Albert, Sir.' To which the sergeant replied: 'Now, you fellow, none of your clever stuff here.'"

The longest name appearing on a birth certificate is that of **Rhoshandiatellyneshiaunneveshenk**, of Beaumont, Texas.

Chris Freddi's *Book of Funny Names* includes a number of referees with unusual names for their chosen occupation:

Charlie Faultless, a Scottish referee from the 1950s, and Segar Richard B****** from the 1880s.

In 1997, GB Information compiled a list of the unfortunate, but genuine, names of individuals who must find the Christmas period particularly trying . . .

•17 Mary Christmases •4 Holly Berrys •2 J Christs •Sandra Claus, who lives in Yorkshire •3 Kings from Leyton Orient •2 Turkeys from London •5 Terry Tubbys from Birmingham •73 people in Britain called La La and 262 named Po, Dipsy and Tinky.

Why is it that in the world of entertainment, and especially among the musical fraternity, there is a penchant for "different" names? It must be hard enough to have to carry the burden of a successful parent without having to be additionally burdened with an outrageous name. Of the nine parents listed below, it is noticeable that all but one – Woody Allen – possesses a regular Christian name. Americans do appear to have an inclination for bestowing the most bizarre names on their offspring. One would have thought that, had these parents been serious in their choice of names for their children, they might, at least, have changed their own to reflect their madness . . .

Dandelion *(daughter of Keith Richards)*
Free *(son of Barbara Hershey)*
Satchel *(son of Woody Allen)*
Moon Unit *(daughter of Frank Zappa)*
Dweezil *(son of Frank Zappa)*
Rain *(daughter of Richard Pryor)*
Zowie *(son of David Bowie)*
Sage Moonbled *(son of Sylvester Stallone)*
God *(daughter of Grace Slick)*

Others are just not satisfied with the name they have been given . . .

The case was that of William David Coleman, aged 22 of Liverpool, who denied being in unlawful possession of a motor car, a suitcase, and a guitar, and obtaining a driving licence by giving a false name of William Peter Johaan Karl Amsberg von Hapsburg Schleswig Holenstein von Hanover Zu Amsterdam. *(Liverpool Echo)*

In the United States the determination to derive commercial or other benefit from being the last listing in the local telephone directory has resulted in self-given names starting with up to 9 "Z"s – an extreme example being "Zachary Zzzzzzzzzra" in the San Francisco book.

And coming together can be such fun . . .

BONE-MARROW: The engagement is announced between Joanne Louise, only daughter of Mr and Mrs D. Marrow, and Kevin James Bone, only son of Mr and Mrs J. Bone. *(Bury Times)*

Dr I.L.C. Sly and Miss N.J.E. Fox: The engagement is announced between Ian, younger son of the late Capt L.T. Sly and of Mrs A.G. Sly, of Canterbury, Kent, and Nikola, only daughter of Mr and Mrs N.E. Fox, of Great Bealings, Suffolk. *(Press and Journal)*

COLMAN-BALLS: The engagement is announced between TIMOTHY, son of Mr and Mrs B.P. Colman, of Fakenham Road, Drayton, and MARIE, daughter of Mr and Mrs R.E. Balls, of West End, Old Costessey. Love from both families. *(Eastern Evening News)*

And a different type of coming together . . .

The new teacher was going around the class asking names.

"And what is *your* name?" he asked the little lad.

"Alex," came the reply.

"Alex what?" asked the teacher.

". . .-ander," was the response.

Then some people make a right mess of it . . .

"Now, Muhammad, that's a popular Christian name, isn't it?" *(Interviewer of Muhammad Ali, 1980)*

The proud mother was so delighted with the way the doctor had eased her through her delivery she said she would like to name the boy after him. "What's your name, doctor?" she asked. "Clarence," he replied. For a moment the young mother was thoughtful, and then she said: "You don't have a middle name, do you?"

16

Would You Believe It?

AUSTIN ALLEGRO 1300. Taxed, MoT, radio. £395 ono.
Btn. 776155 after 6pm.
AUSTIN-Cyril. Forever in our thoughts. Ivy, Jim & family.
AUSTIN PRINCESS 2000 HL, 1979, Superb, low
mileage, history. £10,956. 673620. *(London Evening
Standard small ads)*

Spelling tests in English and French are to be demanded
in Parliament for officials responsible for British pass-
ports. The current passport contains a non-existent
French word and the visitor's passport misspells
'"Gibraltar". When an MP queried it with the Passport
Office, he was told: "Oh, really, have we? We spelt
Sweden wrong in the last issue." *(Daily Telegraph)*

Can anyone recommend school for boy 14, where
reincarnation is accepted and astrology understood?
(Advert in Daily Telegraph)

Court Report from *Reynolds News* . . .

Mr T. Belk, clerk to the Middlesbrough magistrates: Why
have you not sent your child to school regularly?
Mr J. T. Howlett: Because he has no boots.

Clerk: But you went to school without boots when you were young, did you not?
Parent: Yes, sir.
Clerk: Then why cannot your son do the same? It will not do him any harm.

Brighton Film Studios are making a Conservative propaganda film without a name. The public will not be allowed to see it. *(Brighton and Hove Gazette)*

How many of us at school realised that Perkin Warbeck was a figure in the Jewish World plot against Aryan sovereignty? *(Aristocracy, published by the Imperial Fascist League)*

Newport Council are holding an open day at their Telford Depot in Corporation Road on Wednesday 1 July. Among the attractions is a sewer jetting model display, a display of cesspit emptying plant and graffiti removal techniques. *(Newport Free Press)*

Renewal notices for three books from Lincoln City Library have come from the Saudi Arabian desert, where Mr Ronald Paing, a local schoolteacher, inadvertently took them on a nine months' stay in Mubbaraz. The books were treatises on central heating. *(Guardian)*

And now, just before *The Sinking of the Scharnhost*, attention all shipping. *(BBC Radio 4 continuity, 1984)*

The road leading to St Michael's School has been affected by severe flooding – traffic is reduced to a crawl. *(BBC Radio 2 traffic news, 1984)*

We are now going over to our reporter who accompanied the teachers' march on one leg. *(BBC News, 1981)*

There will be widespread fist and mog. *(Radio 4)*

More about that delay on British Rail Southern Region. We have our reporter on the line . . . *(Radio 4)*

Defending solicitor, Mr Richard Snow, suggested that Brother Finbarr, a teacher, was mistaken in identifying his client, as he had spoken to him through a row of runner beans. *(M. Rendall, Western Gazette)*

£12,000 worth of compact discs were stolen from Morecambe Library while a crime prevention exhibition was taking place in an adjoining room.

If all the pupils who fell asleep during assemblies were laid end to end, they would be much more comfortable.

There was the dyslexic ex-pupil who held up a bank with a gnu.

The school chaplain told the governors that an increased number of pupils were attending services and also reported that death watch beetle had been confirmed in the chapel.

Smoke alarm firm, CIG-arrête, has produced a vandal-proof alarm to be installed in school toilets to catch rule breakers. "This should *weed* out the offenders and gradually *filter* out the habit," says a spokesman.

A teacher in Thornaby village primary school, Cleveland, confiscated a white powder being passed around in tinfoil by an 11-year-old boy. A crime lab identified the powder as amphetamine sulphate (Speed or Whizz); the boy was interviewed by Cleveland police and suspended from school for 15 days. Five weeks later, the police admitted that "detailed analysis" showed the powder was sherbet, as the boy had insisted from the start.

When Middlesbrough Football Club were relegated at the end of the '96-'97 season from the Premiership, fifth formers at the prestigious St Michael's RC School in Billingham held what they described quite inadvertently as their "Going Down" dance at the team's Cellnet Stadium.

When newscaster Trevor McDonald launched his campaign to improve spoken English, he was interviewed on Radio 4. "What are you hoping to achieve?" asked Sue McGregor. "Well, Sue," responded Trevor. "The things I'm hoping to achieve is . . ." Ah, well.

IT'S RUBBER-LEGS ROBERTS. Did you go to school with Peter "Rubber-Legs" Roberts who, at the age of 15 in 1953, was a pupil at Rossington Secondary Modern School? Can anyone remember bullying Peter at school? If so, he would like to invite you to spend a weekend on his yacht in Cannes, and to discuss your problem. Peter bears no ill will to any of his school chums, sends them his best wishes for 1999, and hopes they are all keeping well. He also hopes his old school pals will reply to his letter through the *Villager. (From Doncaster's Villager, January 1999)*

17

Inspectors

OFSTED inspectors are one group of bureaucrats who are not highly regarded within the ranks of teachers. They tend to be seen as the instruments of ivory-towered mandarins who are detached from the real world of education. There exists a yawning gap of credibility between those who inspect and those who teach – a situation which has been described as "similar to surviving life as a foot-soldier in the trenches, where the strategists ten miles from the front have an unrealistic grand plan to win the war".

Hence the reason why sarcastic and contemptuous cracks and quips, examples of which follow, are circulating throughout staffrooms as teachers wreak secret revenge on these agents of depression and torture, the traffic wardens of the education world.

The judge addressed the witness in the box. "Now," said the judge, "you do understand that you have sworn to tell the truth, the whole truth and nothing but the truth?"

"Well," the witness replied, "I think I ought to tell you that by profession I am an OFSTED inspector."

Tony Blair in Cabinet: "There seem to be only two possible ways of solving this fiasco and constant changing in education. There is the miraculous and the practical. We can all kneel down and pray that God will intervene and solve the problems. That's the practical. The miraculous is that you, David *[Blunkett]*, and OFSTED sit down and discuss it sensibly with the teachers.

Question: What is the difference between a Rottweiler and an OFSTED inspector?

Answers . . .
You can have a Rottweiler put down.
A Rottweiler has only one face.
A Rottweiler doesn't smile just before it attacks.
A Rottweiler is less aggressive.

And others . . .
Q: How is an OFSTED inspector like a bank robber?
A: Once he's done the job he gets away as fast as he can.

Q: Why is an OFSTED inspector like a eunuch?
A: A eunuch knows what to do but cannot do it himself.

Q: What's the difference between a terrorist and an OFSTED inspector?
A: You can negotiate with a terrorist.

Q: What do you call a group of failed teachers?
A: An OFSTED team.

Q: Why is an OFSTED inspection like childbirth?
A: It takes months of preparation, is over in a short time, but the effects can last for life.

Q: What's the difference between an OFSTED inspector and a haddock?
A: One's wet and slippery and the other is a fish.

Q: How many OFSTED inspectors does it take to change a light bulb?
A: Ten. One to remove the bulb and the other nine to decide whether it should be replaced or put under special measures.
Alternative answer: One. The lay inspector is an electrician.

OR ...

How about six?

1 to change it
1 to read the plan on how to change it
1 to observe the changing
1 to write it up
1 to assess
and 1 who we are never quite sure why they are there, but it makes for an even number.

OR ...

We are unable to give you that information until the report is published.

There's only one f-in OFSTED
But that's quite enough for us.
But with no f-in lesson plans
There's one hell of an f-in fuss.

We tried to treat the lead inspector as a treasure – bury him with care and affection.

Q: Why are OFSTED inspectors like pigeons?
A: They should never be looked up to.

You can tell an OFSTED inspector, but you can't tell him much.

Q: How do OFSTED inspectors keep fit?
A: They jump to conclusions.

OFSTED inspector: Everybody hates me.
Wife: Don't be silly. Everybody hasn't met you yet.

Seven-year-old to visiting OFSTED Inspector: Our teacher has been very busy lately. He's marked all our books, which he never does, and he's put some pictures up on the walls.

The inspector was talking to a little girl, who informed him that she had heard her teacher talking to the headteacher, and she was so pleased the inspector had come. "Miss said your turning up today was all she needed."

The greatest number of schools attended by a pupil is 265, by American Wilma Williams from 1933-1943, when her parents were in show business.

The inspector was in a class of eight-year-olds in York. Robert was listening attentively as his teacher described Paris. "A beautiful city," she enthused, "with elegant buildings and fine old churches, art and pavement cafés. A romantic city. Have any of you ever been to Paris?" Robert had. "Robert, you lucky boy. When did you go? Last summer? With your parents? Oh, you lucky boy. Did you like it?" "Not really," said Robert. "It was full of dog s**t."

David Blunkett's faith in his saintly Chief Schools' Inspector appears to be shared by the Muslim Education

Co-ordinating Council, which advertised a speech by "Mr Christ Woodhead" at its forthcoming conference. *(Mail On Sunday)*

18

Administration

Sometimes one wonders whether those who have such an impact upon education – politicians, education officials and governors – read what they have written, or think before opening their mouths.

The following examples would seem to give some credence to this observation of Carl C. Byers: "An Education Committee – a group of the unfit appointed by the unwilling to do the unnecessary."

My purpose in writing to you is to notify you of the anticipated changes for the 1993/4 survey. To date there are no major changes expected, but should any occur we will write and let you know. *(Letter to all Chief Education Officers from Department for Education statistician)*

In the latest issue of *Professional Administration*, the official publication of the Institute of Chartered Secretaries and Administrators, the first article is headed: "Great educational expenditure has not produced the long-awaited economic expansion." It is signed by C. A. Horn, PhD, MSc, BSc (Econ), LLB MBIM, FCIS, FIWSP.

Labour councillors believe that including formal

academic qualifications in job advertisements leads to discrimination against people who done badly at school. *(Reading Chronicle)*

Sir Douglas denied that the relatively high level of public school and Oxbridge-educated people selected for high Civil Service grades was the result of any deliberate bias. There was a danger that the Civil Service might appear to be "perpetuating itself in its own image", but one explanation could be that talents were inherited and talented parents were wealthy enough to send their children to public schools. *(Guardian)*

After my marriage I taught a class of backward children in a county primary school. I feel I have the right kind of training and experience to understand your problems and represent you on the City Council. *(From an election address)*

The governing body vetoed the idea of extra litter bins being placed in the school ground because, they said, they would just attract more rubbish.

Safety experts say school bus passengers should be belted.

On Cleveland Radio there was a report about educational spending cuts in North Yorkshire. A spokesman stated: "As a result of cuts, the library project at Easingwold School will have to be shelved."

Mr Chairman, I move that all fire extinguishers be examined ten days before every fire. *(School governors' meeting)*

"I am not against comprehensive education but I want it within the grammar school framework," Councillor Stirrup explained.

"Women already hold too many of the best posts," declared Councillor W.H.S. Colbourn at yesterday's meeting of the Gloucester Education Committee. Councillor Colbourn said that if women were to be given all the best jobs men would soon be pushed out altogether and in a few generations human life would become extinct. *(Daily Herald)*

"The school is next to a graveyard, so what is wrong with building a funeral parlour?" Thus said Councillor Edwards: "Let's breathe a bit of life into the place." *(Hoylake and West Kirby News)*

The Mayor said he was a great animal lover, and he detested people who were cruel to animals. "It is bad enough with children, but when it comes to dumb animals it is terrible." *(Dorset County Chronicle)*

Council bosses have ordered teachers at a Derbyshire school to move a children's Wendy House because it doesn't have planning permission.

He urged that a pedestrian crossing should be installed. He knew the boys would not use the crossing, but if they put one there, then the Council's responsibility would end. *(Evening Standard)*

Mr Chairman, I have to tell you that I think this proposal to merge the two schools is completely phony with a capital F.

A councillor remarked at a teacher's interview that he had noticed from his application the candidate had attended a Physical Education College – when he had written "FE College".

Minister of Sport, Denis Howell, thinks we should start preparing for retirement from an early age. "It's as important as planning for a career," he claims. He says: "I believe we should start preparing people for retirement while they are still at secondary school, though people look at me as though I am mad when I say that." *(Evening Standard)*

Additionally, there is little doubt that, outside the core, the curricular guidelines will be far less specific, with the exception, perhaps, of technology, and Mr Baker's pet, history. But one can hardly expect sensitivity from a man who reads *The Charge of the Light Brigade* to a class of Russian children.

Others are merely thoughtless . . .

Mrs Jessie Kitchen, aged 71, of Dennis Close, Ashford, Middlesex, was given a canteen of cutlery by her employers, Surrey County Council, for 30 years' service [in school meals] – followed by a bill for £1.12 as part payment for the gift. The Council said her choice cost just over the £25 limit for 30 years' service, and she had to be charged the extra. *(Guardian)*

"I must admit that it was an awful moment," said Councillor Cherry Westburn, Chairwoman of the Raymeadow Education Committee. No sooner had Councillor Anthony Clarke finished reading his report on current teaching methods than Councillor Grey began to attack him, saying that his views were expensive and old-fashioned. In the middle of all this, Councillor Clarke went white and buried his face in his hands, whereupon Councillor Grey shouted: "I hope you are burying your head in shame!" But in fact Councillor Clarke was dying of a heart attack.

The full cost of the government-subsidised school dinner is about 49p, made up of 16p for food and 33p for administration. *(Daily Telegraph)*

GREAT SERVICE TO EDUCATION ...
Mr Eric Jones resigns from
County Committees *(Salisbury Journal)*

By the Same Author

Classroom Clangers *(Compiled in collaboration with John Golds)* [0 09 970451 X] Arrow Books, 1996
Essential Assemblies For All, Vol. I *(Original version)* [0 952 56671 0] Clarus Publications, 1996
Football Shorts [0 09 925643 6] Arrow Books, 1997
Essential Assemblies For All, Vol. II *(Original version)* [0 952 56672 9] Clarus Publications, 1997
Essential Assemblies and PSE For All, Vol. III [0 952 56673 7] Clarus Publications, 1998
Essential Assemblies and PSE For All, Vol. I/II *(Reformatted and combined, with PSE Supplement)* [9 952 56678 8] Clarus Publications, 1999
PSE Supplement to Essential Assemblies For All, Vol. I & II [0 952 56679 6] Clarus Publications, 1999
Essential Assemblies and PSE For All, Vol. IV [0 952 56674 5] Clarus Publications, 1999
Essential Assemblies for the Busy Headteacher (???), Vol. I [0 952 56676 1] Clarus Publications, 2000

All items available by mail order direct from Clarus Publications: 51 Kader Avenue, Acklam, Middlesbrough, Cleveland TS5 8NH. Telephone: 01642-897513; Fax: 01642-828924.

AUTHOR'S NOTE

Thanks to Juliet Burton, to everyone at Severn House and to Clare Yates for making this book possible. As ever, special thanks to Jess Knowles for keeping me sane. No thanks to Lulu the cat for jumping on my keyboard and engaging the numbers lock. It took me ages to find out why I appeared to be typing u77er n4n5en5e.

ONE

Charles Mendenhall let himself out of the house via the French windows and stepped into the soft evening air. It had been a hot June day, which was why he had waited until it was almost dark. Not that it mattered; there would be moonlight and starlight, and having lived at Woodlea House for over thirty years, he believed he could probably negotiate every shrub, tree, pond and path of the gardens blindfolded.

Jogging. It really was the most moronic thing to do. But quite addictive. Yes, it was moronic, repetitive, boring and extremely unsightly. After all, who would want to look at the blotchy legs of a flabby sixty-four-year-old puffing along the lanes? Which is where grounds of nearly four acres came in so handy. Charles Mendenhall would not be seen dead running around his neighbourhood in shorts, trainers and sweat-stained T-shirt, but there was no one to see him here in the evenings, except perhaps David, should he make an unannounced visit. He had bought the trainers and shorts and the step-counter thing he couldn't get to work two months earlier and for six weeks had just looked at them as they lay, neatly arranged, on a chair in his bedroom. He'd been too tired or too busy with other things; it had been raining or it had been patently too warm to run. The whole idea was stupid; he would look utterly ridiculous. Then one day he had realized he could just jog through the garden. Round and round the house. He felt silly for not having thought of it earlier.

The first time he had ventured out in his unfamiliar sports gear, brimming with good intentions to jog each day for at least half an hour, he had lasted five minutes and had to lean against the big oak for support, panting and heaving, wondering whether he was going to have a heart attack. He had gone to see his doctor who had examined him and told him that his heart was fine and exercise would not kill him. But even his doctor thought jogging was stupid. It could give you jogger's bladder, ruin your joints if you ran on hard surfaces, pump you full of car fumes if you did it near a road.

But how else were you supposed to lose the flab? He had been doing it for two weeks now, had lost four pounds and had become quite addicted to running. Looked forward to it. Always at dusk, always the same route.

Charles closed the door, took a deep breath of the summer-scented air and set off: across the terrace, on to the expanse of the large lawn, green fading to grey in the settling darkness, diagonally to the western edge, around the long flower bed, on to the stone-flagged path. Past the cool greenhouse, seven strides, past the heated greenhouse, eleven strides, across the circular scented garden with its curved benches, past the oaks, on to the small lawn with the statue of Hebe, along the eastern edge of the lily pond, down into the dell and the apple orchard, once around the double row of ancient unproductive trees, up the eight steps to the gravel path, his least favourite bit of the run, through the long borders and between the dark yews and so back on to the large lawn at its eastern end.

And around again: across the large lawn, past the green-houses, seven strides, eleven strides, across the scented garden. Charles slowed beside the three oaks, stopping by the edge of the small lawn. There was that strange feeling again. He had felt it the other day and it was just as strong as it had been then: the conviction that he was not alone in the garden. Trying to calm his breathing, he stood and looked back. The sensation had come to him in the scented garden, as though someone was running silently behind him. There was enough light left to see that there was no one in the circular garden, but the feeling that there was someone present besides himself was so strong it would not have surprised him to see a person sitting on one of the two benches. It was difficult for deer to get into the gardens unless someone left the rear gate open. *Someone* could only mean the gardeners or his own son, but when David did visit he showed little interest in the garden and even less in the woodland that lay beyond. He should check, of course. Deer had caused havoc in the gardens last time the gate had been left open.

His breath had calmed a little, but not completely, and he realized that anxiety had got hold of him, here, in the centre of his own realm. He turned and looked unhappily across to the statue of Hebe, a mere silhouette in darkness. It was late. One and a half turns round the garden would have to be enough tonight. He retreated from the statue as though it was a living threat and crossed the scented garden in a hurry, but he was loath to run now because the noise of his running steps would mask any other sounds. *Walk, don't run. Walk, don't run.* He retraced his steps: hot greenhouse, cool greenhouse, stone-flagged path. He sighed with relief when he reached the open space of the lawn and started jogging again, back towards the safety of the house.

Until he saw it. One side of the French windows stood open. Had he not closed it properly earlier? Fear crept up on him from the empty gardens behind and crawled towards him from the gaping darkness of the open door. *You forgot to close it, that's all.* Charles tried to convince himself of it, but there was nothing wrong with his memory; he could clearly see himself shutting the door, could hear in his mind the snick of the lock. Irresolute, he stood in starlight in the centre of the lawn. *The house is too big for you now that Yvonne is gone. You have become old and frightened, and you are jumping at shadows.* He forced himself to take calm breaths, straightened up and crossed the lawn to the offending French window. Cautiously, quietly, he slipped inside the drawing room, stood still and listened to the aching emptiness of the house. Never before had the stately ticking of the long-case clock sounded so loud in his ears. It took several minutes of listening for Charles to convince himself that he was alone in the house.

McLusky stepped out of the shop into the bright sunshine and experimentally stomped his brand-new black gentleman's umbrella on to the pavement. He held it in his right hand and walked a few paces, using it like a walking stick. Then he changed to the left hand and took a few more steps but failed to get the rhythm right. He felt foolish and decided to carry it instead. DI McLusky hated umbrellas even more than he hated rain. They were a nuisance when it was windy and an even greater nuisance to carry around when it wasn't raining at all. Which it was not, though heavy thundery showers had been forecast. Not that McLusky cared all that much about thundery showers or getting wet. He had bought it because Laura had pointed out to him only the other day, as they were getting drenched running from a restaurant to a nearby pub, that it was the man's job to keep his dinner date dry; that a bit of old-fashioned courtesy – and courtship – would not go amiss if he was serious about them getting back together. Which McLusky was: quite serious. Brolly-buying serious, even though he found the chivalrous-male routine a touch sexist.

He was on his way back to Albany Road police station through the pedestrianized part of Broadmead. It was busy and he was in danger of – and sometimes tempted to try – puncturing his fellow lunchtime shoppers with the metal point of his furled umbrella. There was a sudden commotion a few yards ahead of him: calls of protest and people moving quickly. Ahead he heard the prattling sound of a scooter engine. A young man on a black Benelli scooter had come up across the crowded pedestrian-only thoroughfare and was holding station, engine revving, in front of a men's clothes shop. The rider was wearing a full-face helmet and had his face obscured with a scarf. He was looking over his shoulder at the entrance to the clothes shop, which was wide open because of the heat. McLusky knew a getaway rider when he saw one. He sped up to get to the scooter. Just at that moment he heard a shout and a bareheaded teenager came running from the shop, holding a thick stack of men's designer shirts in front of him. He swung himself across the back seat of the scooter, hotly pursued by a male shop assistant. McLusky took two steps forward and jabbed his umbrella into the spokes of the rear wheel just as the rider sped off. It was a short journey: the engine whined and the scooter jerked forward but came to an almost immediate and sudden halt, unbalancing rider and pillion. Both fell to the ground and the scooter engine cut out. The pillion, still clutching the stolen shirts, fell heavily, hitting his head on the unforgiving pavement. The rider scrambled to his feet only to have them knocked from under him by

McLusky, while the shop assistant pounced on the pillion who had still not let go of the shirts and was bleeding over them from a split eyebrow.

'Sit on him!' called McLusky to the assistant, but the man was more interested in recovering the shirts and let go of the twisting, punching and kicking thief who took off down the road at a speed that suggested he might have achieved a cleaner getaway without a scooter. The scooter rider was also trying to punch his way out of McLusky's grip, but the detective inspector remembered much of his basic training and once he had hold of one of the man's arms the outcome of the struggle was predictable. The rider screamed in protest inside his helmet as McLusky bent the arm until the struggling stopped. He wrenched open the visor of the helmet but left the silk scarf that covered the suspect's face in place, not wanting to get bitten.

The rider was rolling his eyes, trying to get a look at his assailant. 'Let me go, you stupid wanker! I'll fucking kill you!'

'That's been tried before,' growled McLusky truthfully. 'I'm a police officer and you're under arrest.'

'What?!' he wailed, disbelief in his voice.

McLusky dropped a heavy knee into the man's back to make sure of him, rattled down the caution and thumbed his radio. Just then a uniformed police officer, guided there by the CCTV operators, arrived at the scene. It was PC Becks, whom McLusky knew well. The DI handed the still restless man over to him once Becks had cuffed him.

'I did caution him, Becky. The other one got away, I'm afraid.'

'No, he didn't; he ran straight into us. We were just around the corner getting out of the car and CCTV relayed that he was on his way. Pym has got him in the car. Let's have your helmet off, lad,' PC Becks said. The suspect tried to headbutt him with it so McLusky kicked him hard in the back of the knee, grabbed his cuffed wrists and forced him to the ground. This was unpopular with the man who started swearing incoherently.

'Thank you, sir,' said Becks.

'My pleasure. Charge him with robbery, reckless driving, resisting arrest and ruining my umbrella. The scooter will be stolen so charge him with that as well.'

The PC removed helmet and scarf from his prisoner. The driver looked no older than fourteen. 'And driving without a licence; he's far too young.'

Young, yes, thought McLusky, but he could see the hard lines of grown-up contempt in his face. The boy still hadn't quietened down when PC Becks marched him away and offered to introduce him to his new, improved pepper spray if he didn't cooperate.

McLusky tried half-heartedly to retrieve his umbrella but it was comprehensively mangled. 'Poor thing never lived long enough to see its first drop of rain,' he muttered and, leaving the scooter lying there, walked back to the umbrella shop to buy another one.

He made it back to Albany Road station without further incident. Still feeling foolish carrying it around but quite pleased with his lunchtime exploits, he strolled exaggeratedly across the CID room towards the kettle, swinging his umbrella in time.

DS Jack Sorbie looked up from his desk and eyed McLusky with distaste. He held the unshakeable conviction that his own low promotional prospects were entirely due to McLusky having been 'imported' from Southampton into Bristol CID. He burped quietly behind his hand, bringing back the taste of his lunchtime pints of cider, and looked studiously down at his computer screen when McLusky sauntered past him with a mug of coffee.

In his office McLusky leant the umbrella against a filing cabinet and then manoeuvred himself into the narrow space between his desk and the window. His office, which he suspected had been converted from a broom cupboard, was minute, possibly not large enough to open his umbrella in without knocking the collection of empty coffee mugs off the filing cabinets. Albany Road station was a cramped 1960s cube of a building near the harbour. It had never been modernized, which meant that the electric wiring was fragile, the plumbing was noisy and there was no air conditioning. Sometimes

McLusky heard unexplained rustling from inside the wall beside his desk, which he thought was either rats or the sound of cheap cement bricks crumbling. His office was a complete tip again. Files covered all the surfaces, including the floor. The small desk had barely enough room to accommodate the computer screen, keyboard and phone as well as the files and forms he had dumped on it. In winter his office was well-heated since the radiator under the window had been designed for a much larger room, but in summer it could get stifling in here. The window was wide open; it gave on to the service area at the back of the station and overlooked the backs of houses. He made room for his mug of coffee on the desk and turned on the plastic six-inch fan which started up with an annoying buzz and shook its head jerkily from side to side, making a squeaking sound at every jerk. Its airstream lifted the corners of files and papers and contributed to the impression of disorder on his desk.

He lifted the mug of economy instant towards his lips but was gripped by a sudden cough and splashed several forms with coffee while setting it back down. This cough was getting annoying; it had started over a month ago and he could not get rid of it. It was beginning to worry him, too. McLusky smoked – had smoked since his early teens – and he had now given up trying to give up since it always failed and cost him weeks of irritable misery. Once his cough subsided, he took a few sips of coffee and lit a cigarette, the latter strictly against regulations since the entire building was a no-smoking area. Perversely, smoking usually stopped his cough, as it did now.

He picked up the topmost form and shook a couple of drops of spilt coffee from it on to the carpet. It was the form that came with the memo informing him about his upcoming AFT. McLusky hated acronyms almost as much as the nonsense they usually stood for – in this case his Annual Fitness Test. This worried him as much as his cough. He had recently tried to cut down, luring himself away from cigarettes by eating sweets and chocolate bars. He had put on a stone and a half in a very short time. He had stopped eating chocolate now – almost as hard to quit as smoking, he had found – but the weight had stayed on. The AFT was looming closer; he'd never

manage to lose the weight in time. He pushed the form aside
only to reveal the next piece of bumf he had brought back
from the latest PIM he had attended. PIM stood for Performance
Improvement Meeting where they had talked at great length
about PPAF, the Policing Performance Assessment Framework,
and the paper he was staring at now was headed *The Changing
Face of PPAF*. It was so naff you could not make it up, yet
someone obviously had. Anything to avoid having to go out
there and catch criminals.

His apparent inability to come to grips with completing
paperwork on time or returning questionnaires by the required
deadline had been brought up by Superintendent Denkhaus at
his last PDR – Personal Development Review – where
McLusky had confessed that his stress levels rose dramatically
as soon as a questionnaire landed on his desk. They had
promptly sent him an SAF – a Stress Assessment Form – to
fill in, which amused him only long enough to drop it into the
bin. When they asked why he hadn't returned it, he pretended
not to have received it. They had sent him another one, which
added to McLusky's stress.

Some of these acronyms did not even make sense; it was
obvious that HOLMES – the Home Office Large Major Enquiry
System – had 'large' and 'major' squeezed into it purely to
spell the name of the famous detective, since there were no
'small' or 'minor' enquiry systems as far as he could tell.
WORMS stood for Warrant Management System, which surely
should be WARMS. McLusky sighed and pulled the Stress
Assessment Form towards him and started filling the blank
spaces with impatient, jabbing biro marks.

Selling up was out of the question. Yes, Woodlea House had
become too big with Yvonne dead and David, his less-than-
perfect son, visiting only when his business ventures needed
bailing out, but he could not imagine living anywhere else. It
was home. Could the strange feelings of unease he was
experiencing from time to time perhaps be a sign of old age?
Becoming fearful? He did not feel old yet – hell, he had just
taken up jogging and was already feeling the benefits. Maybe
he should talk to his doctor about it. Anxiety disorder, that

kind of thing. But he didn't want to start taking pills for bloody anxiety; that was ridiculous.

He stood on the veranda, the French windows closed firmly behind him. It was late again. A bit too late for his liking – he preferred a little more illumination for his evening run – but he had been working on his still life until the last light had drained from the sky. Perhaps he should give it a miss tonight.

No, that would be cowardly. It would be giving in to wishy-washy feelings of angst. Anyway, exercise, he had heard on Radio Four, was beneficial in cases of anxiety and depression. He performed a few half-hearted warm-up exercises, jogged on the spot for a moment, felt foolish doing it and set off. The moment his feet touched the springy lawn he felt better, full of purpose, and he fell into the familiar rhythm of running and breathing: monotonous, measured, meditative. He broke into a sweat almost immediately. Along the long flower border, on to the stone-flagged path. He was not sure why he wore a T-shirt at all – no one was going to see him – but he had never liked being bare-chested, except perhaps on a beach or a boat. And he hadn't been on a boat since . . . well, since that day in 1998. Past the cold greenhouse, seven strides, past the heated greenhouse, eleven strides. He felt vulnerable unless he was fully dressed; even these ridiculous shorts made him feel somehow exposed. He had never been a very physical person, much to Yvonne's regret. And David's, too – he hadn't been the football-kicking type of dad, to be sure. Through the scented garden and up towards the three oaks.

Charles slowed. It was even darker here close to the large trees and, damn it, here it was again – that anxious feeling – and it had caught him at almost exactly the same spot in his run. He had never checked the back gate. Why had he not made the effort? He would feel better now if he knew it was secure. In the light of day he had dismissed all his night-time fears, yet here was that feeling again. He had also meant to talk to the gardeners about the back gate, but the business of the day had driven it from his mind. He stopped running and jogged on the spot for a bit, then stood still altogether, trying to level his breathing. It was the same feeling, and he felt it in the same place – how odd – as though it was somehow bound up with the location. The anxiety sat in his stomach just below his solar plexus, but the impression that he was being watched he felt all over on his exposed skin. He took a few tentative steps forward under the dark canopy of the oak trees, then stopped again and looked back towards the lower scented garden where nothing moved. The thin sound of a crack, as from a twig snapping underfoot, reached his right ear, and he whirled around, looking up towards the circular lawn where the statue of Hebe stood unrecognizable, a black silhouette in the fading grey dusk. The crack had been quite close. Did twigs crack by themselves? It could be a badger. Badgers could dig their way into the garden even under the enclosing wall. He felt the desperate urge to turn back towards the house the way he had come. But no. He was not going to give in to childish feelings. Then quite a different thought struck him. What if he was going senile? Dementia? Whatever it was, he could not allow himself to be spooked in his own garden. He would go forward, not back; he would get past this anxiety and resume his run. He was still sweating. It was very warm and very still. Perhaps he would just walk the rest. Yes. He moved forward, tentatively, setting down each foot in turn quietly, towards the figure of Hebe. There were still crickets rasping in the grass around him. Another crack, this time behind him. He turned around. Under the three oaks, where he had halted a moment ago, stood a figure, completely dark, as though masked; not even the eyes were visible. The figure stood not twelve paces away in the deeper darkness under the trees.

'What . . . what are you doing here?' Mendenhall asked. His voice was not as firm as he would have liked. 'What do you want?' He received no answer. But somehow he knew what the figure wanted, instinctively, however absurd it might be. 'Why?' he whispered into the silence. The dark shape took three, four, five quick paces towards him, raised one arm and levelled a gun at him, the bright metal glinting in the starlight. He flinched back. The muzzle flash was blinding, the sharp bark of the shot shrill in his ears. The bullet ripped through his throat and unbalanced him. His hand flew up to the screaming wound and found gushing blood. The pain was hideous. He opened his mouth, perhaps to scream, but already could not find the strength. He felt the world fading from him, darker and darker still, weightless and hideously silent. He did not feel himself crumple to the ground where he lay still, did not hear the soft swish and bubble as his heart pumped his blood into the lawn.

TWO

McLusky gasped, then swallowed down the remark on his lips. He wanted to scream, '*How* much?' but felt he might descend into a parody of the outraged customer.

The man behind the desk was aware of it. 'You did say "whatever it takes" when you brought it in,' he reminded him. 'There was the bodywork, front panels, headlight, replacement bonnet and the respray. And you asked us to get it through the MOT while it was in and that took some welding and, of course, the new brakes. Satnav installed and one speaker replaced, oil change, valeting—'

'Yes, yes, I can read,' said McLusky who was holding the itemized bill and reaching for his credit card. The drawbacks of having bought an enormous twenty-year-old Mercedes were there in black and white.

The garage manager tried to cheer him. 'Your car should drive like new. Now it's been fully serviced, it should also do at least fifteen miles to the gallon again. If driven reasonably. It is a very fine example of an SEC and unless you drive it through a fence again, it should give you years of service and pleasure.'

Service and pleasure, thought McLusky as he handed over his card, sounded like some corporate logo. In his mind he tried it out above the Avon and Somerset Constabulary emblem and quickly dismissed it. Yes, the car looked as splendid as when he had bought it, if not better. He had foolishly fallen in love with the thing and handed it over to the garage like a wounded pet after he had used it as a battering ram to break down a rather substantial fence. Never mind; there was the possibility of compensation; his actions – highly commended – had after all saved a life. His bravery for confronting a gun-wielding killer unarmed and without his bullet-proof vest had also found favourable mention, although less charitable colleagues had called it stupidity. In retrospect, McLusky had to agree with them; he still relived the incident in his nightmares.

All thoughts of it disappeared, however, when he swung himself, several thousand pounds poorer, into the leather driving seat of his car. He patted the walnut dashboard, started the five-litre engine and, with a Stone Roses tape in the old-fashioned stereo, turned into the Fishponds Road and glided majestically through the morning traffic. He had his car back, it had passed its MOT, the ashtrays were empty and the cigarette lighter worked. He inhaled the fragrant smoke and tried to relax into the pleasure of driving, but the thought of his own bodywork having to pass an MOT soon spoilt it for him. He took a couple of greedy drags from his cigarette and dropped it half-smoked out of the window. He admonished himself in an imitation of Laura's voice – 'Filthy habit anyway, Liam' – yet he thought he could feel the unsmoked half of the cigarette like an amputated phantom limb.

In the Albany Road station car park he inserted the Mercedes into its designated parking space, patently designed for vehicles of lesser dimensions, wriggled with difficulty free of the car, then made his way inside. He checked his watch: ten past eleven. Clearly coffee time. He bought a cup of strong canteen coffee, covered it with the saucer to keep in the heat and balanced it up the stairs, acknowledging 'good mornings' without taking his eyes off the cup. Earlier he had bought Danish pastries from Rossi's, the Italian grocery above which he rented a flat from the Rossi family, and in his mind was already sinking his teeth into one of them when his mobile rang. He fished it from his jacket pocket and answered it.

It was DS Austin. 'Where are you, Liam?'

'Do not fret, I am here; ETA one minute. What's up?'

'Suspicious death and it's ours.'

'Typical.' McLusky put away his mobile and seconds later saw Austin in the flesh, standing at the top of the stairs.

DS James Austin, known to his friends as Jane, was a dark-haired Scotsman whose soft Edinburgh accent had mellowed even further by not having lived there for seventeen of his twenty-nine years on earth. McLusky often accused him of secretly working out in the gym, but Austin was simply young, fit and naturally athletic. His fiancée had made him give up smoking and he drank less in a week than the inspector did in a day. McLusky was breathing hard by the time he reached the CID floor. The lift was in fact working again, but only adventurous souls ever used it since the thing was half a century old and regularly got stuck between floors. 'What have we got, Jane? Tell me in my office.'

He squeezed himself behind his desk, uncovered the cup and set it on its saucer; he opened a drawer from which he withdrew the bag of pastries. Picking an apricot Danish for himself, he offered the remaining one to Austin who asked what it was and, on being told that it was custard, declined.

'Body found at the victim's home just outside Dundry. Large property. Victim identified as Charles Mendenhall, sixty-four.'

McLusky had fitted half his pastry into his mouth and only Austin could have interpreted his next utterance as 'Do we know him?'

'Nope.'

'Who found the body?'

'The gardeners.'

'*Ners*? Gard*ners*? It's that kind of place, is it?' He picked up his car keys and the remaining pastry. 'How can you not like custard? Everyone likes custard.'

They took McLusky's car. 'Nice around here. Some massive houses,' he said as he navigated along pleasant lanes, passing several large detached properties sitting impressively in their rural Somerset setting south-east of the city.

'Not much of a nightlife around here,' complained Austin.

'Do you and Eve do a lot of that?'

'Not really, no. Here it is: Woodlea.'

It would have been difficult to miss since a uniformed officer was guarding the wide-open wrought-iron gate to the property. It was PC Ellen Purkis who knew both of the detectives; she allowed herself a brief smile tailored in intensity to the sombre occasion and stepped back to allow them to pass. Purkis had been guarding the entrance for an hour. She was desperate to use the toilet and had been contemplating a quick dash into the hedgerow on the other side of the lane when the detectives arrived.

The drive towards the house was tarmacked, completely straight and lined on both sides with chestnut trees. The house was set back a hundred yards or so from the lane and the square forecourt was crowded with vehicles: vans, a red hatchback, police cars in bright livery, a police Land Rover, a forensics vehicle, the grey coroner's van and the pathologist's night-blue Jaguar, all standing in a line, bonnets pointing at the immense nineteenth-century building. The police Land Rover, which belonged to DSI Denkhaus, stood at the very right, blocking the wooden gates of the double garage. McLusky had an immediate impression of solid wealth. The house looked well maintained; all the windows sparkled in the sunlight, the planters near the door were crammed with well-tended plants. 'In the library with a candlestick,' he muttered as he parked his Mercedes at a wilful angle.

A pink-faced scene-of-crime technician in a blue scene suit was removing an aluminium case from the back of his van. 'In the garden behind the house,' he answered McLusky's question. He automatically handed the detectives two medium-sized suits to put on. 'I'll take you.'

'Cause of death?' McLusky asked.

'We're fairly certain it was a shooting.'

They rounded the east side of the house with the scene-suit material swishing synthetically as they walked. 'If it was a shooting, I'll bet you a tenner the neighbours never heard a thing.' The general public's capacity for not noticing crime was one of the inspector's favourite rants.

'The nearest house is a quarter of a mile up the road,' said Austin in defence of the neighbours. 'Nice place, this,' he mused as they passed a cast-iron table and chairs. 'Tea out on the lawn.'

'Bit too grand for me,' said McLusky dismissively. Passing the greenhouses, they could see ahead a group of people, most in blue scene suits. Only two of them wore white suits; one was Dr Coulthart, the bespectacled pathologist who was examining the body on the ground, the other Detective Superintendent Denkhaus, standing close by. As McLusky and Austin approached the group, the DSI looked up, then wordlessly checked his watch. Greetings all round.

The body lay crumpled on the immaculately trimmed grass of the circular lawn. The wound at the victim's neck looked messy; the dead man's mouth and eyes were wide open, his hands in front of him caked with dried blood. Beside him a large pool of blood had also dried, deeply staining the grass.

'Dr Coulthart thinks he bled to death,' said Denkhaus. McLusky wasn't sure whether this was an attempt at black humour. Rumour had it that the DSI was on a diet, but the oversized scene suit made him look like a loosely filled weather balloon. McLusky hoped the rumours were unfounded since the superintendent reacted badly to sugar cravings and low-fat foods.

'Who found him?' McLusky wanted to know.

'One of the gardeners,' said Denkhaus.

'There's our killer, then,' said McLusky distractedly as he squatted down to take a closer look.

'You'll find the gardener and his assistant in the kitchen,' said Denkhaus. 'You're in charge, McLusky.'

The DI looked up. 'DCI Gaunt is due back from leave tomorrow. Will he take over?'

'DCI Gaunt has been . . . erm . . . unavoidably detained. It's your investigation, McLusky. Report directly to me.' He nodded a goodbye towards the pathologist. 'Jon.'

McLusky waited until Denkhaus had swished out of earshot, then turned to his sergeant. 'Gaunt unavoidably detained? Things are looking up.'

Detective Chief Inspector Gaunt was almost universally disliked; McLusky was not sure whether Dr Coulthart shared this sentiment until the doctor said, 'Indeed, indeed. Long may it last. And I think it could.'

'Why, what have you heard?' McLusky prompted.

'DCI Gaunt bought a holiday home in Spain; he may have mentioned it . . .'

'Once or twice,' said Austin. Gaunt had talked of it incessantly.

'He somewhat overdid the celebrations at a restaurant in a nearby town, then drove home and on the way knocked a local girl off her scooter. Gaunt didn't stop. The Spanish police have arrested him for drink-driving, dangerous driving and leaving the scene of an accident.'

'Hit and run? Excellent,' said McLusky and meant it. 'And the girl?'

'In hospital. Broken leg, broken wrist.'

McLusky pulled a painful grimace. 'In that case "unavoidably detained" was an accurate description. OK, celebrations over; what have we got here, doctor?'

They were still closely surrounded by crime scene technicians making a fingertip search. One of them was trying to get a metal detector to work, calling forth pitiful squeals from the equipment and noisily complaining about it. 'This thing is utter crap. My nephew has a better one.'

'I'm pretty certain it's a gunshot wound,' said Coulthart.

'Handgun?'

'Most likely culprit. Fairly close range, by the looks of it. Bullet went through his neck, severed the carotid artery on that side. Game over. You can see there' – he gently moved the head to give the officers a better view – 'the exit wound.'

'Is that what it is?' All McLusky saw was a bloody mess as if a wild animal had taken a bite out of the man's neck. He hooked a thumb over his shoulder. 'So is he looking for our bullet?'

The SOCO had brought the metal detector under control and started sweeping the area. The detector indicated almost immediately with an unpleasant electronic squawk. The officer bent down, felt about in the grass with his latex-gloved hand and eventually held up a shiny ten pence piece. 'Bag it anyway,' McLusky told him.

'I was going to stick it in a bubblegum machine,' the SOCO grumbled as he dropped the coin into an evidence bag. He hated being told how to do his job by CID suits.

'Time of death?' McLusky wanted to know next.

'It was a very warm night,' mused Coulthart. 'I calculate late last night. Ten . . . eleven, around that time.'

McLusky waved away some of the numerous flies that the blood and gore had attracted. 'Out jogging, by the way he was dressed. Jogging in the dark. In his own back yard.' He straightened up. 'OK. Gardeners' Question Time.'

Austin nodded towards the house. 'In the kitchen, the super said.'

The kitchen at Woodlea House was nostalgically well equipped: earthenware storage jars, old-fashioned brass scales and bundles of dried herbs. The woman willing a kettle to boil on the cream-coloured Aga was in her late forties. Her shoulder-length hair was the colour of sand – probably dyed, McLusky thought. She wore a snow-white apron over a sober blue dress and gave the officers a red-eyed look as they entered. At the table, waiting for a mug of tea, sat a man in his fifties. He had been scratching at his salt-and-pepper beard and now belatedly removed his grey baseball cap, revealing short greying hair. Opposite him, with her arms folded in front of her chest, sat a woman in her mid-twenties, her blonde hair tied back and her blue eyes bored and resentful. Both man and woman wore identical green T-shirts and khaki trousers. A pair of well-worn gardening gloves curled on the table.

McLusky introduced Austin and himself, showing his ID. The woman by the Aga introduced herself as Mrs Mohr.

'You're Mr Mendenhall's housekeeper?' asked McLusky.

'Not quite. I come in three times a week to clean and do Charles's laundry,' she said, as though her employer did not lie still and bloodless on the lawn. She was pouring water from the kettle into three mugs. 'Would you like some tea? The kettle's just boiled.'

'Yes, please. Coffee would be even better.'

She sighed. 'As I said, I'm not really a housekeeper.' But she fetched a cafetière nonetheless.

McLusky and Austin sat down at the long kitchen table, leaving empty seats between themselves and the pair of gardeners, Tony Gotts and Emma Lucket. 'You found Mr Mendenhall's body?' McLusky asked.

'I did,' said Gotts. 'Emm was in the cold greenhouse. I had walked further up the path when I saw him lying there.'

'How close did you go to the body?'

'Quite close. I mean I walked right up – you can't just look at a thing like that from a distance.'

'Did you touch the body?'

'Didn't have to. I could see he was definitely dead.'

McLusky turned to the woman. 'What about you?'

She shook her head. 'Didn't look at him. Didn't want to.' Her voice was high, almost child-like, her accent, like Gotts', West Country. 'I took his word for it. Was he shot, though? Tony thought he was.'

'Yes, we believe he was,' supplied Austin. 'Did your employer keep a gun in the house?'

'No,' said Mrs Mohr as she set the cafetière firmly on the table. 'He didn't go in for shooting or hunting; he didn't like guns. Charles was an artistic soul.'

'You knew him well, Mrs Mohr?' asked McLusky. 'How long have you worked here?'

'Thirteen years. I used to come in twice a week when Yvonne – Mrs Mendenhall – was alive, three times a week since she died.'

'When was that?'

'Nearly three years ago now.'

'Any other immediate relatives?'

'His son, David,' Mrs Mohr said. McLusky noted that both gardeners shifted in their seats at this and reached for their mugs. 'I've already taken the liberty of informing him of his father's death. He lives in town, has an office there. He said he was coming over.'

'When you came here this morning, was everything else as you would expect it to be?'

'No,' said Mohr. 'The French windows from the drawing room to the veranda were unlocked. But I only noticed that after Tony found Charles's body.'

'As far as you know, is there anything missing in the house?'

'Not as far as I can tell.'

'Has anything been disturbed at all?' Mrs Mohr shook her head. 'Did Mr Mendenhall have enemies that any of you know of?' Shakes of the head all round. 'Any disputes, rows?' Again the gardeners reached for their mugs together. Mrs Mohr took the now empty cafetière to the Belfast sink. 'No, nothing like that.'

'How did Mr Mendenhall make his money?'

'He was a brewer. Well, used to be. He used to own one of the last big independent breweries in the West Country. But he sold out to one of the big players a few years ago and retired from business.'

'And the jogging?' Austin suggested. 'He did that regularly? Late in the evening?'

'Not during the day,' said Gotts without looking up. 'Never while we was here.'

'Charles took up jogging recently,' said Mrs Mohr. 'I think he didn't want to be seen doing it, so he jogged in the evenings. I knew he had taken it up but I never saw him do it. None of us are here that late in the evening.'

'And he jogged here in the garden?'

Nods from everyone. 'Nice and private.' It was the first and last sentence Emma Lucket volunteered before quick footsteps could be heard approaching. Seconds later a man pushed through the half-open door. 'Is it really true, Mrs M? Where is he?' Before Mrs Mohr could answer, he took in Austin and McLusky. 'Are you the police?' The man was in his mid- to late thirties, with short dark hair, noticeably small ears and an aquiline nose, both features he had inherited from his father. He looked flushed, harried. His grey suit was slightly crumpled and he wore a pale blue shirt without a tie. His black shoes, McLusky noticed, were very shiny.

Austin showed his ID. 'Are you David Mendenhall?' When David nodded, he gestured towards the door. 'Perhaps we could go somewhere private to talk—'

'Bollocks. I want to see him,' he said and walked out. 'Is he still in the garden?' Austin followed him out of the door.

'Please don't leave the premises for the time being,' McLusky said to the others. 'I may want to speak to you again.'

'Can we get on with our work?' asked Gotts.

'I'm afraid not. The gardens will remain out of bounds until further notice.'

'Great,' McLusky heard Emma say sarcastically as he left to go after Austin and Mendenhall's son.

He found both standing outside on the veranda. 'Because it is a crime scene, Mr Mendenhall,' Austin was saying. 'Until scene-of-crime officers have concluded their investigations, the gardens remain out of bounds. That could take all day.'

'Can't you at least tell me how he was killed, for Christ's sake?'

When McLusky nodded his permission, Austin told him. 'We believe he was shot.'

'Shot,' David echoed.

McLusky gestured at the door. 'Perhaps we could go inside, out of the sun?' It was another perfect summer's day with barely a cloud to be seen. Reluctantly, David led the way into the large drawing room, furnished like the rest of the house with a mix of antique furniture, art deco and Victoriana. It was a comfortable room but one that time had left behind sometime in the 1960s; there was a neat row of LPs and an old-fashioned record player that, even by McLusky's standards, looked ancient. Countless small paintings in dark frames adorned the walls, many of them executed in the same style, presumably by the same hand. On the mantelpiece stood a family photograph in an ornate silver frame, four people posing in the garden for the photographer. David stared at it intently for a moment, then laid it face down on the mantel and sat down, his expression grim. While Austin and David took an armchair each near the fireplace, McLusky remained standing, storing away the details of the room, picking up objects and setting them down again, never quite where they had been before.

David looked at him, annoyed and impatient. 'Would you mind sitting down, Inspector?'

McLusky ignored him. 'Are there any guns in the house, Mr Mendenhall?'

'No, no guns. Not even an air rifle. What kind of gun was my father shot with?'

McLusky ignored that too. 'Can you think of anyone who would want to harm your father?' he asked.

'No. It must have been an intruder. A burglar my father surprised.'

'Except, as far as we know, nothing was taken. Is there anything of great value at Woodlea House?'

David shrugged. 'Nothing more valuable than the furniture and carpets. Those *are* quite valuable.'

'What about all these paintings. Any of great value among those?'

'I doubt it. Half of them are by my father. He fancied himself a bit of a painter. The rest, I think, are all by friends of his. They are all semi-professional painters.'

McLusky took another look at the framed paintings. Most of them were landscapes or still lifes, some were portraits of women; most were oils, but there were watercolours, too. He quite liked them and thought they were well executed. McLusky's own spartan flat still remained unadorned by wall decorations. 'Did your father have a painting studio somewhere?'

'Right next door.' David led them through a connecting door into a room nearly as large as the drawing room. 'This used to be called the morning room, but even when I was a child my father painted in here.'

The place was bright, with two large sash windows and a half-glazed door to the outside. There were paintings and art materials everywhere, covering two tables. A plan chest was buried under rolls of paper, tins and boxes. A still life of bottles and bric-a-brac had been set up; on an easel nearby stood a small oil painting of the arrangement. To McLusky it looked finished. There was no shortage of objects with which to compose still lifes; the place was cluttered with pot plants, small bronzes, plaster casts, old china, glassware, silk scarves, oriental face masks, Japanese fans and candle lanterns. With the furniture covered in throws and scarves, the place looked like a bourgeois idea of the bohemian lifestyle. The studio smelled of turpentine, with a hint of overripe fruit coming from a bowl of peaches.

'Mrs Mohr must love dusting this lot,' said McLusky.

'Looks a very professional set-up,' Austin commented.

'My father took it quite seriously. He did exhibit here and there. Sometimes together with his friends.'

'Can you let us have the names of his close friends and fellow artists, please?' He continued his tour of the room, picking up things and setting them down again. 'And here nothing looks disturbed either?'

David looked around with a look of distaste. 'How could you tell in this mess?'

'Nothing else of value in the house? Sculptures maybe?'

'These little bronzes are worth a few bob but otherwise . . . There's Mrs Hebe in the garden but she's a copy, obviously. I suppose there's my mother's jewellery, but I think that's in the safe.'

'Where is the safe?'

David looked exasperated. 'Upstairs, in my father's study.'

McLusky made an inviting gesture towards the door. 'I'm sorry to have to put you through all this right now, but in a murder investigation it's important we gather as much information as possible early on.'

'I understand,' said David. 'It's just . . . not even having seen him.'

They climbed the stairs past more framed paintings. 'When was the last time you saw your father, by the way?'

'Let me see . . . must be two weeks ago. Yes, about that.'

'Tell me, who benefits from your father's death?'

'I beg your pardon?' David stopped on the stairs to give McLusky an offended look.

'Will you inherit?'

'Yes, I expect so. I hope you're not suggesting—'

'I'm not suggesting anything, sir.' McLusky walked on. 'It helps us get a picture of who may have had a motive and who may not.'

David paused on the stairs for a few more heartbeats, then followed McLusky up to the first floor. 'That's my father's study there, next to his bedroom.'

McLusky counted seven doors leading off the darkly carpeted corridor as well as a further, narrower door, which he presumed led to the attic. When David reached for the door handle of the first door, Austin held him back. 'Please don't touch anything at all up here.'

'Of course. I'm sorry.' He stood back while McLusky, wearing latex gloves, turned the black ceramic door knob and pushed the door wide.

In stark contrast to the bohemian studio downstairs, the study was tidy and efficiently organized, with no papers or letters lying on the spartan desk. It reminded McLusky of his own office on the day he had moved in, except here the furniture was solid and expensive and there were paintings, not city maps, on the walls. The dark wood wastepaper bin was empty; there was a whiff of furniture polish in the air. Files and ring binders on a shelf, some books. A floorboard creaked underfoot as McLusky stepped on the worn Persian rug. He opened and closed the drawers of the desk, saw nothing of immediate interest. 'Is it always this tidy in here?'

'Since my father retired from business, yes.'

'Where's the safe?'

'Erm, it's behind that painting, I believe.' David pointed to a painting of a seaside view to the right of the desk, held in a hefty wooden frame.

McLusky found it was hinged; he swung the painting back and revealed the small square safe behind it. 'Do you have the combination?' David shook his head. 'Who, apart from your father, would know it?' David shrugged his shoulder and shook his head again. 'OK, thank you. You can give your address and the names of your father's friends to my sergeant here.' He stepped to the window which overlooked the gardens. Below, the body was being carried across the large lawn by the coroner's men. 'I'd like you to come downstairs and formally identify the body before it is taken away – save you a trip to the mortuary.'

Downstairs, they arrived just as the men were closing the back of the van. McLusky made them slide out the body bag on its stretcher. 'Are you ready for this?' asked McLusky. 'I must warn you, there was a lot of blood.' When David took a deep breath and nodded, McLusky opened the body bag just far enough to reveal Charles Mendenhall's face. David stared down at him for an intense moment, then turned away.

McLusky had watched David's face closely but was not sure what his expression revealed. 'I need you to say it,' he said to his back.

'Yes, that's my father.' David took a few quick paces away from the van and buried his hands in his trouser pockets, hunching his shoulders.

McLusky allowed him no more than a minute before he walked up to him. 'I have to ask you this. Where were you last night? Let's say between nine and midnight?'

'I was in my office.' When McLusky raised both eyebrows inquiringly, he added, 'I run an online drinks business. There was a problem with our last import from California and I was trying to sort it out.'

'Can anyone confirm that?'

'No, I was alone. But I did speak to my secretary on the phone; I needed her help in finding something.'

'What time did you call her?'

'Look, you don't think I killed my own father?'

'We need to establish where everyone was. What time did you speak to your secretary?'

'It was late. After ten.'

McLusky nodded his thanks, looked around, took in the registration of David Mendenhall's BMW and filed it away in his memory. 'Get all the details off him,' McLusky said to Austin. He gave the nod to the coroner's men and went around the house and into the garden where he collared one of the forensics technicians and told him to fingerprint the safe in the office and David Mendenhall's car when the man wasn't looking.

Back in the quiet drawing room, McLusky stood very still. Sixty-four. Charles Mendenhall could – should – have lived another twenty years, but someone had obviously disagreed. Through the window he could see the blue-suited army of SOCOs combing the garden. Grey clouds were pushing in from the west, causing a change in the light and introducing an appropriate note of melancholy into the room. He took a last look around, then entered the studio next door. Now that the sky had darkened, it had taken on an air of sadness, too, or perhaps it was simply the knowledge that the painter who had worked here would not return that made him think so. A day's work clearing it out, a lick of paint, and this would once more be a cheerful morning room.

Who would be sitting in it? He had to get his hands on Charles Mendenhall's will if he had made one. Austin joined him just as McLusky was prodding one of the overripe peaches in the bowl, sending tiny fruit flies aloft. 'I've got all the details,' the DS said. 'His office is on a trading estate in St Philip's, off the Feeder Road. And he gave me the names of his old man's painting pals.'

The door to the drawing room was ajar and McLusky could hear the clink of crockery. 'Do you mind, Jane, while we're within earshot? You mean his father's artist friends.'

Austin lowered his voice. 'Sure, sorry.' He nodded his head at the easel. 'Do you think this stuff's any good?'

McLusky shrugged his shoulders. 'Don't know. Beats lights going on and off in an empty room. Let's talk to Mrs Mohr again.'

In the kitchen they found the gardeners sitting where they had left them. 'Did your employer mention anything out of the ordinary to you in recent days? Anything at all?' he asked them. Shakes of the head. 'Everything in the garden was as it always was?' Tony Gotts nodded, but his assistant said, 'The greenhouse door was left open a few days ago. That's the heated greenhouse. It's not a clever thing to do because we're trying to keep an even temperature in there. But otherwise no.'

'For the record, where were you both last night between nine and midnight?'

'I was at home,' said Gotts.

'Can anyone confirm that?'

'Nope,' he said, almost cheerfully.

Emma seemed less relaxed about the question. 'I was out with friends. At a pub. Then a club in town. You can ask them.'

'We will. Give their names to my sergeant here.'

McLusky told them they should go home since the garden remained out of bounds. They left the kitchen just as Mrs

Mohr returned. 'Mrs Mohr,' McLusky asked, 'the safe in the study . . .'

'Yes?'

'It has a combination lock. Is it worth asking his son for the combination?'

'I don't know,' she said, giving him a shrewd look. 'I certainly don't know it, Inspector. But Charles could not even remember his own phone number. He once told me he could never remember the combination, which is why he kept it somewhere in his study.'

'Thank you, Mrs Mohr.' McLusky turned towards the door.

'Aren't you going to ask me where I was last night, Inspector?'

McLusky turned back and raised his eyebrows at her.

'I was at home. And no one can vouch for me, either.'

In the hall he ran into the forensics technician. 'Not a thing on the safe or the picture frame. Both wiped clean.'

Back upstairs, McLusky and Austin once more donned gloves. 'It would save a lot of hassle if we could find the combination.'

'We could try his date of birth or something,' Austin suggested.

'Rubbish. No one's that daft.' He opened his notebook anyway and tried Mendenhall's date of birth in various combinations, without success. 'Told you.'

They opened and closed drawers, sifted through papers, looked in margins and front papers of books, even at the wall behind paintings. They got in each other's way and became irritable and short-tempered. McLusky recognized the signs of an underfed workforce and stopped. 'Forget it, Jane; we'll go and get lunch and come back to it.'

Austin gladly complied and slipped out into the corridor. McLusky stood in the door and gave the study one last scrutinizing look. 'If it were your safe, Jane, where would you put the combination?'

'Dunno. On a yellow Post-it note on the door of the safe, probably.'

McLusky closed the door. 'Not the clever thing to do.

Mendenhall, on the other hand, was clever . . . *and he was a painter.*' McLusky opened the door again.

Austin turned back too. 'Found something?'

'The painting that hides the safe. It looks as if it's one of his but it's painted in an odd way. Different. There's all those boats huddled together over here, the people on the beach are all in a row, there's a flock of seagulls . . . Let's hope they're in the right order.' He kept checking back with the painting as he entered the numbers. 'Six boats on the left . . . eleven sunbathers on the right . . . nine seagulls left . . . ten ice creams right.' A barely audible click came from the mechanism. 'Well, what do you know – a McLusky hunch that paid off.' He depressed the short steel handle and opened the door to the shallow interior of the safe. Bent into the space was a blue plastic-covered file. He liberated it carefully, holding it up. 'Copy of his will.'

'But nothing else. No jewellery. Weren't we expecting his wife's jewellery?'

'We were, Jane, and we are bitterly disappointed. Right. At least I feel we've earned our lunch now.'

THREE

'**M**issing person, sir? Surely that's a job for uniform, if it is a job at all.' DI Fairfield, sitting in front of the DSI's desk, tried and failed to meet Denkhaus's eyes. The superintendent swivelled away from her in his chair towards the window behind his desk and pretended to be interested in the shaft of light that had pierced the grey clouds and shimmered on the dark waters of the harbour, just visible between the buildings. 'Yes, of course, normally I'd agree with you.' The police had long given up investigating missing persons, unless the disappeared was a minor or otherwise at risk. With three hundred thousand people reported missing each year, there was really no alternative. 'This is different.'

Fairfield looked with disgust at the sheet of paper Denkhaus had pushed across at her. She was reluctant even to touch it. A badly printed photo of the girl was clipped to one corner of it. 'Says here she's nineteen. She can do as she pleases. There's no indication of foul play, is there?'

Denkhaus swivelled back to face her. 'Not as far as I know. Look, she's the daughter of an Italian government minister and we've been asked to look into it.'

'So he gets special treatment because he's a politician. If he was an Italian – I don't know – *car mechanic*, presumably we wouldn't bother.'

'Yes, DI Fairfield, that's precisely how the world works. Politicians have a lot of influence, car mechanics rather less. From an Italian politician via the Italian embassy, via the Foreign Office, the chief constable, the assistant chief constable, to this superintendent and finally it lands in your lap, DI Kat Fairfield. You are the bottom of this illustrious pile of buck-passers and you will please get on with it. I can't give it to anyone below the rank of inspector because if whatshername . . .'

'Fulvia Lamberti,' Fairfield read.

'If Fulvia does come to harm, we have to be able to demonstrate that we took it seriously.'

'She's an art student. It's summertime. Term's nearly finished. She's somewhere in Devon lying on the beach, surely.'

'Most likely, Fairfield. Stop fighting it and get going.'

DI Fairfield closed the door to the superintendent's office with great self-control, then stormed past Lynn Tiery, his secretary, and out into the corridor, where she stopped, tempted to scrunch up the info sheet on the missing girl and kick it down the stairwell. McLusky had just been put in charge of a murder investigation while she was told to find a bloody foreign student who couldn't be arsed to turn up at college. She trod heavily down the stairs. This would never have happened if DCI Gaunt was here. Most people disliked the chief inspector, but Fairfield found she could press Gaunt's buttons. With the superintendent she completely failed to do so; in fact, she was not sure if he had any buttons a lowly DI could reach. Missing bloody person's inquiry. She slammed into her office and made straight for her cappuccino machine.

*   *   *

'That's the problem with the bloody countryside: they allegedly grow all the food we buy but no one will let you have any.' After leaving Woodlea House, McLusky had driven around in search of lunch, wilfully ignoring anything that wasn't a chip shop, until they ended up in the small town of Keynsham. He had finally settled on the Keynsham Fish and Burger Bar in Temple Street, which Austin suspected he had been aiming for all the time. They found a window table with a view of the Iceland store opposite where, judging by the posters that were obscuring its windows, everything was priced at one pound.

Austin broke up the crisp batter coating of his portion of cod with a flimsy fork. 'I wonder why Denkhaus hasn't made you acting DCI while Gaunt is away?'

McLusky was concentrating on drowning his chips in ketchup, mustard and tartar sauce. 'Mmm? Because just saying the words would give him apoplexy.' He crammed his mouth with chips. 'I hope you realize that working with me doesn't do your prospects of promotion any good at all. If I were you, I'd get a transfer to Trinity Road and work with someone who is going places.'

Austin, who had shared many a meal with McLusky, understood most of it. 'I'm happy where I am. Are you trying to get rid of me?'

'Lord, no. Hate to lose you. I'm just saying.' McLusky attacked his portion of fish as though it were still alive and possibly dangerous. 'OK. David Mendenhall. Did he shoot his father?'

'Hard to say.'

'Working late by himself in the office. It's not much of an alibi. And he's got motive. According to his father's will, if the version we found is the most recent one, he gets the lot, apart from the paintings which go to one of his friends – I forget the name . . .'

'Longmaid,' supplied Austin who remembered names effortlessly.

'Him. And a few grand for the housekeeper – not enough for a motive unless she's got a marzipan habit. We'll do a check on all of them – gardeners, too.'

'Heavily armed gardeners? Unusual.'

'Yes, I can't see it myself. Rat poison or secateurs, surely. My money's on David "it's-behind-that-painting-I-believe". *I believe?* I'm sure he knew exactly where the safe was and how to get into it.'

'But why would he steal the jewellery if he's going to inherit it anyway? Oh, I see, he could have stolen the jewellery a while ago and flogged it or pawned it. Perhaps he killed his old man because he found out.'

'I don't know. It's a bit of a leap from theft to murder. But someone took the jewellery as well as any other valuables that may have been inside and then wiped the prints off the safe.'

'Which means they expected us to be dusting the thing for prints eventually.'

'Quite.' He watched with disinterest through the window as a traffic warden stuck a parking ticket on the windscreen of his car which was parked just outside on double yellow lines. McLusky's car attracted a lot of parking tickets, but he had not paid a single parking fine since joining CID.

A few minutes later they were once more on their way back to Woodlea House, the parking ticket crumpled on the back seat. 'Are we setting up an incident room at the house?' Austin asked.

'So that I can call all the suspects into the library and terrify the killer into revealing himself?'

'Yes. It's what you always wanted.'

'Told you: what I want is a vicar with a dark past battered to death in the vestry with a euphonium.'

'Ah, yes, that's the one.'

'No, we're close enough to town. Briefing back at Albany in two hours.'

The area in front of the house was still full of cars. McLusky parked on the grass so as not to block anyone in, then marched into the garden. The blue-suited army of technicians was now concentrating its efforts on the boundaries of the property, looking for signs of entry. The lily pond had been dredged in the search for the weapon; the three-foot-wide band of mud the SOCOs had deposited on the grass around it made it look like a giant bruised eye.

'Anything?' McLusky asked.

The team leader was sitting on a bench seat near the statue of Hebe, holding a sandwich. He had just opened his mouth to bite into it but closed it again. His walrus moustache almost completely hid his mouth, but McLusky thought he might be smiling. 'Found the bullet,' he said. He dropped the sandwich back into the lunchbox beside him and virtually skipped to his aluminium case on the lawn. 'But it won't tell you much, sir.' He handed it over inside an evidence bag. The bullet was barely recognizable as such. 'Flattened like a crashed cream cake. It's a ricochet, which is why it took us ages to find it. Went through his neck then bounced off that cast-iron arch-thing there. We found it near the greenhouse.'

'Oh, marvellous. See if ballistics can do something with it. How did the killer get in?'

The SOCO shrugged. 'Front door? No sign of forced entry anywhere. No sign of a ladder being used or anyone climbing the walls and jumping down, though we're still looking.'

'Would an intruder necessarily leave a trace?'

'Not if they're careful, no.'

The summer weather had disappeared under a dark bank of low cloud. Woodlea House now looked desolate to McLusky, as though its uncertain future had become visible in its grey façade. Would David Mendenhall keep the house? Would Mrs Mohr and the gardeners keep their jobs? As they crossed the lawn, he saw David behind the French window, holding a cup and saucer, watching them. 'Of the four people here, the son has the only convincing motive. And his alibi is vague.'

'He could have paid someone to do it, of course.'

'No, Jane. If he had done, he'd have found himself a cast-iron alibi for the time of the hit. That's the whole point. You have a strong motive but you were patently elsewhere.' McLusky stopped while still on the lawn near the edge of the veranda and looked directly at David who had not moved. After a few seconds David drained his cup, then turned away. 'I fancy him for it. We'll need to talk to his secretary and look into his business.' His phone chimed and he answered it.

Detective Constable Dearlove had been interviewing the nearest neighbours. 'None of them heard a shot but the couple living closest heard a car driving very fast along the lane around the time of the murder – about twenty to eleven. And they said it had an unusual sound. "Old-fashioned" was the closest they came to describing it.'

'What's that supposed to mean?'

'Dunno. That's all I got.'

'Thanks, Deedee.' He pocketed the mobile. 'Old-fashioned car engine heard bombing down the lane about ten forty,' he relayed to Austin.

In the kitchen they found Mrs Mohr sitting by herself at the empty kitchen table, straight-backed, her hands in her lap, scrunching up a piece of kitchen tissue she had been dabbing her eyes with. Only reluctantly did she look up at the officers with red-rimmed eyes.

'Mrs Mohr, did Mr Mendenhall have a computer? Only there doesn't seem to be one in his office.'

'Charles? A computer?' She steadied her voice. 'No. He had one when he was still in business but he got rid of it. Said it was a privilege to be able to give it away and never have to touch one again. Same with the telephone. He refused to have a mobile. He told me once that one of the things he enjoyed about being wealthy was that he could afford to have nothing to do with the whole digital thing. He thought he had been born into the wrong era.'

McLusky thought that explained much about Woodlea House.

There was a permanent incident room at Albany Road station, often referred to as the murder room. The windows faced the streets and the blinds were permanently at half mast. The room was well equipped with banks of computers, phones, printers and a whiteboard, next to which hung what McLusky called his storyboard; on to this he pinned two photographs of Charles Mendenhall – one supplied by Mrs Mohr, showing the man in life, the other a close-up of his face in death, courtesy of the SOCO team.

'We could be right back in the 1930s,' he told the assembled team. 'No mobile phone records, no browsing history, no digital photographs, no computer.'

A lanky detective constable in a polyester suit spoke up. 'I thought the guy was loaded?' DC Daniel Dearlove – Deedee to his friends and enemies alike – had been born into the age of computers and mobiles. In his world, electronic gadgets were minor status symbols and he refused to imagine life without them.

'He didn't have any *because* he was loaded.' McLusky could see that Dearlove did not quite follow him there, but he could not be bothered to elaborate. He turned to DC French instead. 'Frenchie, check out the two gardeners and the home help, Mrs Mohr, and anyone else who might go in and out of Woodlea House.' French nodded and took a sip of long-cold instant coffee; the legend on her mug read *I Should Be Out There Catching Murderers and Rapists*. 'I'm attending the autopsy at four.' He looked up at the wall clock; it showed twenty past two. 'That can't be right?' He checked the time on his wristwatch; it was a valuable 1940s Rolex which McLusky believed to be a cheap fake. It kept perfect time and said ten past three. 'That clock's wrong. Someone set it to the right time, please.'

'It's stopped, sir,' said French. 'Batteries run down; happens once a year.'

'OK, then call maintenance and tell them to put new batteries in the thing; we can't have a clock showing the wrong time in here.'

'Done that: no joy.'

'Eh? Oh, no, don't tell me. It's tea kettles all over again, isn't it?' Electric kettles had for a time been outlawed by Health and Safety as too dangerous for CID personnel to handle, but they had soon made a comeback.

'First thing they asked: how high was it off the ground? They're not allowed to use stepladders any more. Anything more than a foot off the ground now requires scaffolding or something.'

'Marvellous. Well, by my watch it's time I left; traffic is rubbish this time of day.'

*   *   *

The mortuary was situated in Flax Bourton, a village on the outskirts of Bristol. It was only a five-mile drive from Albany Road, but Bristol now officially had the slowest-moving traffic in the country and McLusky hated being late. As it was, it took him half an hour to cover the five miles, which meant he could have got there sooner by walking.

The body of Charles Mendenhall was already on the examination table when he entered the viewing suite. 'Perfect timing, Inspector.' Dr Coulthart seemed as eager as ever to get his hands on the victim's innards. 'Let us proceed without delay; I have a full diary.'

McLusky did not attend autopsies because he hoped to learn anything intriguing, as detectives on TV invariably did. He did it because it was a legal requirement. And he hated it. He maintained that he had never learnt anything at an autopsy he could not have gleaned from a well-written report. His eyes unfocused as the pathologist made the first Y-shaped incision. Most of the commentary that Coulthart was giving for the benefit of the microphone washed over him, until the pathologist said, 'There's absolutely nothing wrong with this chap. Apart from being dead, of course.'

'Fit and healthy?'

'Yes. He was in very good condition. Maybe could have done with losing a few pounds. But jogging might have taken care of that eventually.'

'Really? The man used to own a brewery.'

'He can't have drunk much of his own brew.'

'So, what's your prognosis? How long would he have lived had he not been shot?'

'There's no reason why he shouldn't have lived another twenty years. Perhaps more. He was a wealthy man – that usually puts another five years on someone's life span. Good food, warm house, early retirement, less stress.'

'So someone hoping to inherit might have had quite a wait.'

'Oh, yes. Decades. You think an heir helped matters along a bit?'

'It's possible. No proof as yet. Did I hear Denkhaus say this morning that you think he bled to death?'

'Oh, yes. He bled profusely from his neck wound.'

'How long did it take him to die, would you say?'

'Not long – a few minutes. And he would have been unconscious for most of the time.'

'But no one would have shot him in the neck on purpose, would they? I mean, they would have aimed at his head, surely? Or his chest? His heart?'

'Oh, yes. There is no good reason for *aiming* for the neck.'

'If he had been killed by a professional, then there would be further bullet wounds, to make sure of the hit.'

'Almost certainly.'

'We're definitely looking for an amateur, then. And an amateur who was no good with a gun. Perhaps never fired one before and might never again.'

'Possible. Quite possible. Did you find the weapon?'

'No. We have the bullet but it's a ricochet and probably not much use.'

'Pity. Do you have any suspects yet?'

'I quite fancy the son for it. I think he got tired of waiting for the old man to pop his clogs and bought himself a gun.'

Coulthart nodded. 'Wouldn't be the first time. But patricide is such an invidious crime, wouldn't you agree?'

'She's not been here for about three months, I should think. Well, I've not seen her.' Carol Clarke, the neighbour who rented the studio flat opposite Fulvia Lamberti's, leant against her door frame and looked down the stairs for inspiration. She was in her late twenties, had neatly cut short hair and wore minimal make-up. Also minimal clothes – a grey oversized T-shirt and electric-pink bunny-rabbit slippers. 'Yeah, at least three months. Although she must collect her mail because that disappears every so often.'

'Are you a student too?' Fairfield asked.

Carol gave a snort of amusement. 'Me? Not likely. I'm a cardiac nurse. You'd have to be quite a posh student to rent here – like Fulvia. Or a wage slave like me.' Even the rent on an attic studio flat in Clifton Village did not come cheap.

'Did she have a lot of friends round when she did stay here?'

'Once or twice just after she moved in, but after that, not that I noticed.'

'Did you have much to do with her?'

'Nothing at all. As soon as she realized I wasn't into art, she just nodded hello.'

Soon after Carol had closed the door behind her, the landlord's agent arrived with the keys. She wore a navy-blue business suit, white blouse and a silk cravat of sky-blue and lemon-yellow. 'She's not in trouble, is she?'

'Not that we know of.'

'The rent is being paid regularly.'

'Gone missing. Dad's worried,' Sorbie said. 'We'll take it from here, thanks.' He took the keys off her.

'Oh. Are you sure?' She checked her watch. 'Would you return the keys, please?' She clacked on kitten heels down the wooden stairs. The carpet ran out a floor below the bedsits.

The flat was tiny but in good repair. It had a small kitchen with a breakfast counter and a bed-sitting room with a two-seater sofa bed and a coffee table; the kitchen was blonde wood and brushed steel, the sofa shiny faux leather. The only toiletries in the claustrophobic bathroom were an empty bottle of Italian shampoo and a bar of soap in the shower cubicle.

'She didn't do much cooking,' said Fairfield, opening cupboards and looking in the oven. 'Not a stray lentil or a grain of spilled rice.'

'Washed her hair,' said Sorbie, holding up the empty bottle of Trivitt shampoo. 'When her Italian shampoo ran out, she couldn't bear it and went back to *Italia*. Case solved.'

'Why are you handling it like that, Jack? Without gloves?'

Sorbie swallowed, putting it down on the kitchen counter. 'It's not a crime scene, ma'am. Surely.' Sorbie only called Fairfield 'ma'am' when he knew he was in the wrong.

'We don't know that yet. Leave it there. No point in sending anything to forensics anyway until we know a bit more. Let's get out of here.'

'Gladly. I can't breathe in this pokey hole.'

McLusky checked his torch was working, switched it off again and set off down the lane. He had parked his car on the grass verge some fifty yards from the gate to Woodlea

House, just as an intruder might have done, but he was very aware that any mode of transport might have brought the killer here. He walked without the aid of a torch. Cloud hung low but there was just enough ambient light to walk by if you knew where you were going. He could hear distant thunder. It had been a sticky kind of day; McLusky hoped a thunderstorm might clear the air, preferably while he was indoors keeping dry. He stopped by the gate. No light was showing in the house and the gate was locked. Last night, when Charles Mendenhall went for the last jog of his life, it had probably been a little brighter, and there may have been light showing at the house somewhere.

He briefly considered climbing the gate but did not believe an intruder would have done so, not with hundreds of yards of wall to choose from and a smaller gate at the back of the gardens, completely out of sight from the house. He walked on to the end of the wall, a considerable distance, where he turned to the right off the lane. Immediately, he needed to use his torch to light the way. High grasses advertised the uncultivated status of the fields surrounding Woodlea. He had seen the place in daylight from the lane but had not realized just how uneven the ground was. He could see where the feet of SOCOs had flattened the grass in their effort to find where an intruder might have scaled the wall, which was barely more than eight feet high here; standing on tiptoe, he could finger the top of it, but he wasn't tempted. He scrambled along towards the dark line of trees that denoted the beginning of the wood after which the house was presumably named. Soon he found himself in the deeper darkness under the thick canopy. McLusky was no good at classifying trees but even he recognized some of them as oaks. Several grew close enough for their branches to overhang the wall which soon came to an end. Turning right, he struck a faint path which brought him to the back gate. It was narrow and fashioned from wrought iron, its lower half reinforced with fine chicken wire, to keep the rabbits out. But McLusky was no rabbit. Despite having to hold on to the torch, he had no problem climbing up and over the gate. He let himself drop to the ground on the other side.

His landing coincided with another growl of thunder, much closer now. 'Cue eerie string music,' he said out aloud.

The sound of his feet on the gravelled path grated noisily in his ears. He stepped off it and walked on the grass instead, aiming diagonally towards the site of Charles Mendenhall's murder. He walked slowly – prowled along, as the killer might have done.

You walked in the gathering dusk without a light, quietly, the gun in your hand, heavy, unfamiliar but reassuring. You knew Mendenhall's routine, knew he would come this way, every night. But it was getting late. Would he not come, tonight of all nights, tonight when you were ready for him?

McLusky swept the torch from side to side, trying to get his bearings. There was the group of trees. The shadow of a figure jumped across the grass to his left and McLusky pointed his torch at the movement like a gun, his heartbeat accelerating. It was the statue of Hebe, life-size, holding up some sort of dish. If he had held a gun, not a torch, he might have fired at it in surprise. The thought made him pause beside the statue; he laid one hand on her cool arm. *What if you did not come to kill him? What if you fired at him because he surprised you?* That might explain the awkward and inefficient wound. *But then why were you here? Why did you carry a gun around with you in the first place? Were you scared of him? Was he dangerous to you?*

The patch of grass where Mendenhall had died was almost black with dried blood. *Did you leave him to bleed into the lawn, convinced death had been dealt or else indifferent to the outcome? Or did you stand and watch until the man's last struggling breath, until the last drop and bubble of blood had drained from his fatal wound and all signs of life had extinguished? Did you stand in the dark and listen or did you watch the stream of blood turn to a trickle by the light of your torch?*

That would have been risky. The shot might have been heard. Yet shots were common in the countryside and the handgun would have sounded like the small calibre rifle of a man going after a rabbit.

The first drops of rain fell noisily in a heavy pattern around him, glittering in the concentric rings of torch light. He had a swift look about in all directions, then turned towards the back gate. Lightning flickered overhead, swiftly followed by thunder and a deluge of rain. By the time he reached the gate, he was drenched and his thoughts went to the virginal umbrella standing furled in his office. Climbing the gate was more effort in the rain and he splashed heavily on to the ground on the other side. Even before he had a chance to straighten up, he was grabbed from behind and pushed hard against the gate. His assailant tried to wrest the torch from him, but McLusky kicked out backwards and followed it up with a swing of the heavy rubberized torch at his opponent's face while both shouted a simultaneous 'Police!' at the other. It took another couple of seconds for the situation to sink in and the struggle to subside. McLusky shone his light at his assailant and saw that he was indeed a bareheaded PC wearing his stab vest.

The constable was now also shining a torch into his face and at the ID McLusky held up. PC Matthew Sharp, known as Sharpie to his colleagues, relaxed at last and rubbed the side of his face where McLusky's torch had made contact. 'Sorry, sir, we hadn't been told there would be an officer here. A neighbour on his way home spotted a man with a torch making his way along the wall and reported it. Understandably, considering what happened here.'

McLusky's shoulder ached from where he had been thrown against the gate and he was now in an uncharitable mood. 'You could have called out a challenge before wading in like that,' he growled at him. More lightning flashed above. 'Let's get the hell out of here before we both drown.' He directed his torch beam at the constable's face for a last look, as though to better remember him. That man, he decided, would have quite a bruise in the morning. Then he turned away.

'Yes, sir. Sorry about this.' Sharp didn't really know what he was apologizing for; it was all the inspector's fault for prowling around here after dark without telling anyone. *McLusky.* He had heard of him, of course. So that's what he looked like. Strange eyes, he thought. And he could definitely do with a haircut.

FOUR

McLusky's shoulder retained some memory of the event the next day as he drove down the A4 towards Bath to keep an appointment with – he glanced at the display on his mobile again – Nicholas Longmaid, one of Mendenhall's painting friends. He would go and see both of his painting buddies but he wanted to start with Longmaid because he was mentioned in Mendenhall's will and was about to inherit all of the dead man's paintings. Not that McLusky thought this enough of a motive since most of them were by the trio, but then, as Austin had pointed out, painters were usually a weird lot. And, he had added, talking of weird, did McLusky know that DI Fairfield went to art classes? It was news to him, but then Fairfield tended to keep her private life to herself, except when extremely drunk, an event McLusky had witnessed only once.

His mobile chimed just as he turned off the A4 towards the village of Corston where Longmaid lived. He pulled over, answered it and stepped out of the car to stretch his legs. 'Yes, Jane?'

'I've got the background checks on the staff at Woodlea.'

'Please tell me Mrs Mohr's last employer died in mysterious circumstances.'

'I'm afraid not. Pure as the driven. But you'll like the gardeners; we know both of them.'

'Marvellous. Let's have it.' He shook a cigarette from a packet and lit it, shielding the flame of his lighter from the fresh summer breeze.

'Anthony Gotts has form, mainly receiving stolen goods but also ABH and GBH. He was on parole during the last offence so did twenty-two months for the latter. Got out four years ago; nothing on file since.'

'What about the girl?'

'Emma Lucket is all drugs and theft. She got away with

community service even though she nutted the security guard who was trying to stop her from running from the shop with a CD player. Broke his nose. Nothing on the computer for the last two years.'

'That's gardening for you.'

'And we have a preliminary on the recovered bullet, they're pretty certain it was fired from a thirty-eight but nothing beyond that – too mangled.'

'Marvellous, ta.'

The Longmaids' house – or 'residence' as McLusky mentally corrected himself when he saw it – was a large Georgian villa on the outskirts of Corston, south of the A39. It sat in landscaped gardens of a similar size to those of Woodlea, but here no walls enclosed the property; instead, low wooden fences let the countryside bleed into the views across the garden. A herd of red Friesian cows grazed in the distance as though sketched in by a landscape artist to enliven the greenery.

McLusky parked his own car on the gravelled forecourt next to an even older black Mercedes in immaculate condition – circa 1960, he guessed. On the other side of it stood a small red two-seater Mazda, roof down, pointing towards the road as though impatient to get away. It was the owner of the sports car – Nicholas Longmaid's wife, Jennifer – who opened the door to him long before he had reached it. Jennifer Longmaid looked to be in her mid-forties; she had expertly dyed blonde hair and was as tall as McLusky. She wore a startlingly short black skirt, black tights and shoes and a shimmering charcoal-grey top. Inch-thick silver graced her earlobes, neck and wrist. 'You must be Inspector McLusky,' she said. She extended a manicured and beringed hand in greeting, which took McLusky by surprise; not many people offered to shake hands with police officers. He took it with only the smallest hesitation. She looked past him. 'My husband will approve of your car, I'm sure.' The tone of her voice strongly suggested that she herself had no interest in classic cars. 'Please come in.' She stood aside. There was plenty of room even had she not done so; everything at Stanmore House was large – large and antique.

Antiques were everywhere, yet Stanmore House was not

furnished with antiques like other venerable homes might be: it was stuffed, crammed and cluttered with antiques. Nicholas Longmaid was an antiques dealer and obviously took his work home with him. 'My husband is in his studio; I'll take you to him.' She led him swiftly through a drawing room dominated by a bulky if partially broken stone figure that looked vaguely Babylonian to McLusky – or was it Assyrian he meant? Other antiques stood, lay and hung everywhere; the closed grand piano was virtually buried under figurines, clocks, china and silverware. They were walking on old Persian carpets, some of which had smaller rugs lying on top of them. There was not a speck of dust in evidence. He followed Jennifer Longmaid's legs out into the garden. It was large but had a soulless air, designed to match the stark symmetrical grandeur of the Georgian architecture. McLusky was being led to a low timbered building with a large skylight in its low-pitched slate roof, forty yards from the main building among a group of beech trees. Jennifer entered without knocking. 'Darling, Inspector McLusky is here, and he is *on time*,' she said pointedly. To McLusky she said, 'Once in his studio, my husband would forget to eat if I did not remind him.'

The studio was spacious and bright. On the outside it looked as if it had been built in the early twentieth century; its interior, however, was even more fiercely nostalgic than Charles Mendenhall's. Everything in here looked authentically nineteenth century. There were many paintings, mostly still lifes and some landscapes. They too looked as if they would have felt more at home in the nineteenth century than the twenty-first.

Nicholas Longmaid was slim, tall and almost completely bald; what remained of his hair was trimmed to no more than a stubble. He had a deeply lined, intelligent face and wore delicate-looking round, rimless glasses. His blue painting smock, which he wore over a white shirt and tie, was covered in multicoloured streaks of oil paint. 'I'm so sorry, Inspector; once ensconced in here, I lose all sense of time.'

McLusky knew this to be a lie – no one forgot an appointment with a police inspector investigating a murder, let alone the murder of a friend. It was therefore a pose: Nicholas Longmaid wanted to be found deeply engrossed in the artistic side of his life. McLusky nodded understandingly.

'I won't shake hands,' said Longmaid, wiping his stained fingers on his painting smock. 'Excuse me for a moment while I get myself cleaned up.' He retreated to the back of the studio where he disappeared through a door.

'Charles being killed like that – I don't know what to say,' said Jennifer. 'Thank God Yvonne wasn't alive to witness this. It was so sad about his wife dying and now Charles is gone too.' She shook her head, looking bewildered and close to tears. 'It's so inexplicable! Who would want to kill him? And what for? Was there a robbery at the house?'

'Not as far as we could establish.'

'The officer who called to make the appointment would not say how Charles was killed.'

'He was shot, with a handgun. You don't keep any handguns at your house?'

'What are you suggesting?' she asked. 'That we shot him?'

'No, he's not, Jenny,' said Nicholas Longmaid. He had returned minus his painting gear and with clean hands, but he did not offer a handshake. His shirt was spotless. 'The police have to ask questions like that of everybody. Isn't that right, Inspector?'

'A lot of uncomfortable and intrusive questions have to be asked in investigations of this kind,' confirmed McLusky.

'I'm afraid we don't know anything about Mendy's murder,' said Longmaid. 'It came as a great shock, I can tell you.'

'Shall we go back to the house?' asked Jennifer. 'We'll be more comfortable there.'

McLusky looked around him; three armchairs and a nineteenth-century chaise longue were standing idle. 'By all means.'

Back at the house, McLusky was invited to sit in an antique armchair facing the bearded Assyrian statue. Jennifer Longmaid offered tea or coffee, both of which he declined, after which she prepared to dance from the room as though he could not possibly want to ask any questions of her.

McLusky stopped her. 'When did either of you last see Mr Mendenhall?'

Jennifer stopped and turned back. The Longmaids looked at each other. 'I last saw him about a month ago,' said Nicholas. 'I missed our last regular meeting. But Jenny saw him more recently. *Didn't* you.' It was not a question.

'I saw him only the other week,' she confirmed, settling herself on an armrest of the sofa, crossing her legs, then immediately uncrossing them again for better balance.

'My wife was very fond of Mendy, weren't you, Jenny?'

She stood up and smoothed down what there was of her skirt. 'Very.'

'But, unlike myself, my wife makes friends easily. She'll soon get over it. Won't you, darling?'

Jennifer gave McLusky the ghost of a smile and walked from the room.

'I'm afraid I have to ask you more impolite questions. Where were you the day before yesterday? In the evening?'

Longmaid nodded understandingly. 'I was here, Inspector.'

'And . . . can anyone confirm that?'

'No, I don't think so,' he said, unperturbed. 'My wife was out, I believe, at the cinema.'

'Do you own a handgun?'

'I do, as a matter of fact.'

McLusky knew from his routine background check that Longmaid held several firearms licences. 'Let me see your gun locker.'

'Sure. This way.' He led McLusky from the room and up the stairs, then along a short corridor to a mournful study overstuffed with old books in dark bookcases that reached to the ceiling. McLusky was willing to bet that none of them were ever touched by anyone except by whoever kept the house immaculately dust-free. 'I have a handgun licence that allows me to trade in antique and historic guns. Which I haven't done for a while now. It doesn't really interest me.' The tall gun safe was concealed inside a dark wood cabinet. Longmaid had no trouble remembering the combination which he keyed into the electronic lock. He opened the door wide, then stood aside, gesturing invitingly.

For someone who had no interest in guns, Longmaid was well equipped with them. McLusky also had no more than a professional interest in guns but recognized what he was looking at: a beautifully engraved over-and-under shotgun, a plain but antique-looking fowling piece, and wooden gun cases on several shelves. A double-barrelled Derringer was lying loose on top. 'Can we have the handguns out, please?' Longmaid made a show of being unconcerned. 'Of course, of course.' He opened the cases one by one: two sets of duelling pistols including all the accessories, a highly decorated Colt revolver and a .38 Webley service revolver. 'You'll find none of these have recently been fired.'

'To your knowledge,' qualified McLusky.

'To the best of my knowledge,' Longmaid admitted.

'Does anyone else have access to this safe?'

'I'm the only one who knows the combination.'

'But there is an override key.'

'There is.'

'And where is that kept?'

'Usually at the back of a little pencil drawer in my writing desk.' He indicated the gloomy antique under the window.

'Usually? Can I see it, please?'

'Well . . .' Longmaid looked uncomfortable for the first time. 'I have mislaid it. Quite a while ago. Simply can't find it.'

'That's not good enough. A mislaid key makes this safe no longer secure. I will have to take away the more modern handguns for forensic examination anyway, but you will find alternative secure accommodation for the remainder of the guns by the end of the week if you don't want your licences revoked. Understood?' McLusky hated cavalier attitudes to gun safety.

He tipped the small Derringer into an evidence bag, which he slipped into a jacket pocket, and carried the cases of the two revolvers under his arm like a couple of books. 'I saw a copy of Charles Mendenhall's will; unless a more recent version comes to light, you will inherit his paintings and the contents of his studio.'

Longmaid stopped for a moment in the corridor to consider it. 'Really? I had no idea. I wonder why he did that? Probably because his son and heir would make a bonfire of them.'

'The will states that you should "dispose of the paintings as you see fit". Any idea why he worded it like that? Why would he assume you would dispose of them?'

'That was Mendy being his modest bloody self. He always pretended to think nothing of his own talent. He was a good painter. Born entirely into the wrong century, of course.'

'Like yourself, perhaps?'

'Entirely so.'

Downstairs, Longmaid opened the front door for him and made a show of admiring McLusky's Mercedes. 'Oh, is that really yours? Bit unusual for a police officer. Not quite vintage enough for me but . . .' Longmaid had just launched himself on to the neutral waters of vintage car talk when his wife also exited the house, carrying a jacket and handbag which she dropped on to the passenger seat of her Mazda. Inside the house the phone rang. 'You must excuse me, Inspector.' He hurried back inside and closed the door behind him.

Jennifer Longmaid had already swung her legs inside her car. 'Mrs Longmaid—'

'I'd prefer it if you called me Jenny.'

'When you last saw Charles, how did he seem to you?'

'He was on good form. Charles and Leon – a mutual friend of ours – the three of us went to see an exhibition at the Arnolfini and had a meal afterwards. He was his usual self.'

'Your husband did not join you?'

'Not that time.'

'And where were you two days ago – say, between nine and midnight?'

'On a night out in Bath.'

'At the cinema.'

'Lord, no! That's just a euphemism for "Jenny going out and enjoying herself". I went to a pub, then a club, and afterwards went back for coffee with someone who turned out to be a disappointment.'

'How so?'

'He fell asleep.' She started her engine and raised her eyebrows to say, 'Is that all?'

McLusky drummed a short finger tattoo on the gun cases. 'Do you shoot, by any chance?'

'No, of course not. I don't shoot any more than I dig potatoes or milk cows.'

'And do you do any painting yourself, Mrs Longmaid?'

She waggled one hand at him while she put the car in gear
with the other. 'I don't even paint my own fingernails,
Inspector.' The Mazda's wheels spat gravel at the house as
she sped towards the main road.

'Naturally, we have no influence on what students get up to
outside the college but that doesn't mean we're not concerned.
Students do drop out each year but Fulvia appears to have
done more than that. No one knows what has happened to
her.' Carol West, the fine arts tutor whose tiny office Fairfield
and Sorbie were crowding, opened her hands in a helpless
gesture of surrender. She was in her forties, had very short
silver hair and one earlobe perforated with five silver studs
and rings. DI Fairfield, who abhorred piercings of any kind,
found her eyes drawn to them in fascinated disgust.

'Someone knows what has happened to her,' she corrected
the tutor.

'Yes, of course. But you know what I mean. And now we
are coming under considerable pressure from her father and,
would you believe it, some snooty voice at the Foreign Office.'

'Yes, I can well believe that.'

'I know Mr Lamberti is a politician, but is he an important
man?'

'I have no idea and I don't care,' said Fairfield. 'Fulvia is
nineteen and can do what she likes; we just need to satisfy
ourselves that nothing untoward has happened to her. We need
to speak to her contemporaries, any students she hung out
with – that sort of thing.'

Sorbie had remained standing behind his seated superior
due to a lack of chairs in the room. 'Did she have a boyfriend?'
he asked.

'Or girlfriend?' added Fairfield for the sake of political
correctness.

'Ah, now you're asking.' She glanced at the monitor on her
desk as though for inspiration. 'She did have a boyfriend.
Would have been a surprise if she hadn't. She's quite stunning,

even prettier than in your photograph – quite the Mediterranean beauty. She is also bright and has the sexy accent to go with it. She had to fight them off with a stick as soon as she walked through the door. But she did go out with one chap – another student in her own year – but not for long and there was a bit of trouble.'

'OK, I need his name. What kind of trouble?' asked Fairfield.

'His name is Marcus Catlin. She finished with him and he couldn't cope with it. Got quite upset.'

'That's par for the course. And the trouble?'

'He wouldn't take no for an answer. Kept trying to change her mind, and when she dumped him rather more forcefully, he lost it a bit. Tore up some of her drawings, vandalized one of her paintings. They're both painters.'

'How long ago was this?'

'That's six weeks ago now.'

'How did you deal with that?'

'Marcus is a very talented young man; we didn't want to lose him. He received an official warning: any repetition and he'd be out on his ear. We made him apologize, publicly, to Fulvia and to the rest of the students in his group. And there's been quiet ever since. But now Fulvia has disappeared and you say she hasn't been at her address?'

'Not for quite a while, which means she must have had other accommodation all along. Right, we'd like to speak to' – Fairfield consulted her notes – 'Mr Catlin.'

'He'll be in the painting studios today.'

Fairfield gestured towards the door. 'Which way?'

'Oh, the painting studios aren't here at Bower Ashton; they're at Spike Island.'

Having handed the gun cases to DC French for dispatch to ballistics, McLusky went downstairs into the windowless neon-lit dungeon that was the Albany Road station canteen. Down here, time seemed to stand still or at least move to a different beat. Only the type and amount of food on display hinted at the time of day, while there were almost no clues as to what century the food was cooked in; most of it – beige cauliflower bake, colourless fish pie, anaemic salads, wrinkled sausages in unfeasibly dark gravy – would all have felt at home in a 1950s school canteen. Plaice in bright orange breadcrumbs served with chips and peas was the most grown-up meal McLusky could find. He espied Austin sitting at a table by himself and carried his tray over.

Austin had completed half of the challenge of digging through the stringy gloop of his macaroni cheese. 'What did you make of the Longmaids?' he asked.

McLusky ripped open three sachets of ketchup for his chips, one of mayonnaise for his peas and one of tartar sauce for his fish. 'They've started charging for these; they're eight pence each now.' He indignantly jabbed at a few chips. 'I think Nicholas Longmaid lives in a fantasy world. No wonder he and Mendenhall were friends. You thought his place was a time capsule? You should see Longmaid's place. That's a time *machine*. He's an antique dealer and the whole place is kitted out in period stuff – not sure which, though. His studio looks like an illustration from a coffee-table book on the Impressionists. Even his car is an antique.'

'More antique than yours?'

McLusky ignored the dig at his choice of car. 'His wife – let's call her Jenny because she likes that – looks about twenty years younger than him and lives entirely in the present. When I talked to them together, there was a tiny bit of bickering that hinted that Jenny may have had a thing for Mendenhall. Or even *with*. She doesn't make a secret of looking for sex elsewhere.'

'There could be a motive right there.'

'Yes. Longmaid also has a gun safe full of the tools for the job. I sent them off to forensics just in case they can find a match but I doubt it very much.'

'He's got a licence?'

'Oh, yeah, all in order.'

'He wouldn't have returned the gun to his safe, would he?'

'Quite. He'd have faked a sale or even a burglary. Also, being a dealer he could easily have obtained another thirty-eight from the last war, undocumented, shot Mendenhall and dropped the gun in the river on his way home. Interestingly, though, he says he lost the override key for his safe.'

'Really? But that means his wife could have borrowed a gun. Or the cleaner or whoever else visits the house as long as they have the key to the thing.'

'Absolutely. I gave him a week to find a secure place for the rest of his guns. What about the gardener? Any hint of weapons use?'

'Gotts? Strictly fists. Threats, brawls, fistfights. Gave one bloke quite a kicking, but not even a baseball bat – all hands-on stuff. And by the looks of it, he's going straight.'

'We'll have a chat with him anyway.' McLusky did not trust criminals to reform any more than he trusted leopards to change their spots. 'About his choice of work mate, too. And we need to check her alibi – whatshername?'

'Emma Lucket. What about the Longmaids? Do they have alibis?'

'Not him. And she was out on the town.'

'What if it was a burglar after all?' Austin mused. 'Mendenhall runs into him in the garden, confronts him and gets more than he bargained for. Intruder flees in panic. Nothing nicked, no dabs, no DNA. We'll never find him.'

'That's what I love about working with you, Jane: your irrepressible optimism.'

'Just saying.'

'You're ruining my appetite. If that's how it went, then we're stuffed.'

'Well, I am stuffed already.' Austin pushed his unfinished food away from him. 'Are we checking out the gardeners?' McLusky nodded and grunted with one too many chips between his lips.

'In that case I'll go find out where they are.'

'No, I'll do that,' said McLusky. 'You chase up the people Emma Lucket says she was out with that night.'

Still air. Low cloud. Rooks on chimney pots. Woodlea House sat mournfully in its well-kept gardens, its colours subdued by the low light. More rain was forecast. McLusky had called ahead to find that nearly everyone he wanted to speak to was at the house.

'There's so much to think about,' said David as he ushered

McLusky into the sitting room. 'It's not like someone dying after a long illness. You know – then you'd expect it. At least the body has been released now and I can plan the funeral.' He let himself fall into an armchair. 'I don't suppose you're here to tell me you've identified my father's killer?'

'I'm afraid not. Early days yet. I have spoken to two of your father's friends – the Longmaids. Do you know them well?'

'No, but then why would I? They were my father's friends and all they ever talked about was art or antiques.'

'And what would you have preferred to talk about?'

David looked at him, puzzled. 'I don't know . . . stuff.'

'You're not married, are you, David? You don't mind if I call you David?'

'Suit yourself. No, divorced. Long time ago. What does that have to do with anything?'

'I just like to get a clear picture of everyone involved.'

'*Involved?*'

McLusky had taken a dislike to David Mendenhall the moment he had met him. He was the main beneficiary of his father's will, and since there was a great deal to inherit, in McLusky's book that made him number one suspect. He looked around the room and thought that a few things had changed since the last time he was here. The family photograph had disappeared from the mantelpiece and other items seemed to have been moved or removed. Already David was taking possession of the house, changing it to suit him. McLusky had checked on his address in Kingsdown and on his BMW 5 Series; the flat was rented, the car relatively new but second-hand, which might mean that his business was not going too well. He studied David's soft hands, his aquiline nose that looked as though it belonged to a leaner face, his small, almost insignificant ears. Did he kill his father? McLusky had met enough killers to know that looks did not give the slightest indication as to a man's criminal propensities, and yet a small part of him remained convinced that he should be able to see it, pick up on it, sense it, smell it. Looks were naturally deceiving, while words, trying to deceive, often failed to do so. Which is why police officers asked so many questions. 'So, *David*, how's the wine business?'

David looked as though he regretted having given McLusky permission to use his first name. 'Not so bad, not so bad. People don't give up boozing just because there's a recession; they simply look for cheaper booze and they find it online, which is where I am. I can sell you a case of drinkable wine at a price that would buy you nothing but cooking plonk at a supermarket. Of course . . . people are lazy and chuck any old rubbish into their shopping trolleys. But I believe more of them will catch on and change their shopping habits. Are you a wine drinker, Inspector?' He did not wait for an answer but droned on in a speech that McLusky felt David Mendenhall had given many times, perhaps to convince himself. 'People go to the supermarket and spend five pounds on a bottle of wine. Do you know what goes into a five-quid bottle of wine? I'll tell you: two pounds of that price is excise duty. Even more if it's from outside the EU. About sixty pence goes on the bottle, the label, handling, transport and filling the thing in the first place. Then the supermarket takes a third as profit. You know what's left over? Twenty pence. That's what the wine in your five-quid bottle is worth. That's not a bargain, Inspector . . .'

McLusky had the feeling that David was glad to be able to talk about a subject other than his father's violent death. He also thought that he was probably talking it up; he would be urgently looking into Mendenhall's business.

But not until he had talked to Gotts, whom he found in the garden, sitting on a rustic bench near the greenhouses, smoking. He was sitting hunched forward, studying the ground by his feet. At McLusky's approach, he briefly looked up, then returned his gaze to the ground. McLusky joined him on the bench. He crossed his legs, leant back against the backrest so that when he spoke he was addressing the back of Gotts' head. 'You didn't tell us you had form, Mr Gotts.'

Gotts took a while to answer. 'And why should I do that? I knew it wouldn't take you long to drag that up. I'm used to it. Anything happens anywhere near me, from petty theft to murder, sooner or later you lot knock on my door.'

'But you are going straight now, of course. After what? Four decades of crime?'

'Yup.'

'Don't tell me – you found Jesus while you were inside.'

'Nope, I found something better than him. Gardening. We did some with the Eden Project while I was inside. Then when I was moved to Sudbury, I got a chance to do some actual training and get a qualification. Never looked back. I used to be a right narky git but gardening has calmed me down.' He stretched out one hand in front of him, holding it steady. 'See that? I feel I want to smash your smug face in, but look: not a tremor. I'm grounded. Literally.' He tapped a short drum roll with the tips of his heavy work boots, then turned towards McLusky without meeting his eyes; instead, he held up the end of the cigarette he had been smoking. 'Look at this. That's how far it goes. I now smoke only filterless cigarettes because . . .' With a soil-blackened thumb, he eased out the glowing end then crumpled the remainder in his fingers, letting it scatter by McLusky's shoes. 'Before, I would have flicked a fag end, filter and all, just anywhere. Not anymore. Wouldn't dream of poisoning the ground with synthetic crap now.'

'Very commendable. The victims of your past crimes would be thrilled to know that, I'm sure.'

'You can't change the past, only the present.'

'How did you come by your assistant?'

'Emm? I got involved in a project with ex-drug users. They'd given them an allotment at St Werburgh's. The most hopeless bunch of waifs. Acting like they was tough as nails but couldn't do five minutes of digging without needing to stop and roll a fag. Half of them dropped out after the first day when they realized there was more involved than scattering seeds. But not Emm. She never wanted to stop. She went at it like her life depended on it. Which it did. I needed help with my work so I took her on.'

McLusky could see Emma pushing a loaded wheelbarrow on the far side of the gardens. 'How long has she worked for you?'

'Just over a couple of years now.'

'Stayed off the drugs?'

'It hasn't all been plain sailing,' said Gotts. 'But I've not regretted taking her on. Not once.'

McLusky walked off towards where he had last seen Emma and her wheelbarrow but stopped halfway there under a large oak and lit a cigarette. Night fell around him. Charles Mendenhall came jogging up from the house, breathing loudly. Emma Lucket stepped out from behind the tree. She was holding a revolver. Mendenhall stopped running. *Emma?*

Yes, it's me. I've had enough of gardening and have come to kill you for some strange reason.

McLusky shook his head and walked off towards the front of the house. Before he reached it, he had finished his cigarette. He pinched off the glowing end and put the remaining filter into the pocket of his leather jacket. As he did so, his knuckles hit something unexpected, hard and cold. He closed his hand around the object. He did not need to pull it out to know it was the black Derringer he had confiscated from Longmaid but forgotten to hand over with the rest of the guns.

For a while he sat behind the wheel of his car pondering this discovery, then he called the ballistics department. When he finally got to talk to the right man, he asked him about the guns he had sent in.

'We haven't even had time to look at them yet. I expect we'll examine them tomorrow and then do a test fire. But don't hold your breath.'

'I won't. Another question: what calibre is a Derringer? Is it a thirty-eight?'

'Could be, they come in all kinds of calibres.'

McLusky pulled out the gun and read the legend on its grip. 'How about a Bond Arms Snake Slayer?'

'Let me bring that info up for you, Inspector. That's a modern gun, and it's a forty-five. Fires two rounds, lower barrel fires first. Is there a connection with that case?'

'No, not at all. Just something I came across.'

In that case there was no point in handing it in to forensics. Was there? He idly cracked open the gun. The shiny brass ends of two bullets glared back at him. Longmaid had kept a loaded gun in his locker. McLusky slipped it back into his jacket pocket and started the engine.

FIVE

The place echoed too much. It was just too modern. For DI Fairfield, Spike Island was too contemporary, too bright, too industrial. Artists' studios ought to be cosier, more mysterious and should not have strip lighting. North-facing skylights, wood floors, Belfast sinks and wood burners for heat was how Fairfield imagined her perfect studio. Seeing the students at work made her yearn to be in her life drawing class where once a week she got to draw for two and a half hours. Every time she went to life drawing she felt she was entering a different, more exciting world, while in here these kids took it for granted. The many unattended painting spaces convinced her that some of them were wasting it. While she walked around looking for Fulvia Lamberti's disgruntled ex-boyfriend, DS Sorbie beside her gave a running commentary on this alien world, damping down her own ambiguous feelings.

He called into one room, 'Training hard for a life on the dole, kids?' Three girls with earphones ignored him while they stood in front of their paintings. 'I mean, look at this stuff,' he said to Fairfield. 'Would you pay money to have that on your wall? Any of it? I could do a better job than that. Is this Bristol's answer to Picasso?' He stuck his head into another work space. 'No, can't see the next Van Gogh in this lot, either.'

'Give it a rest, Jack,' said Fairfield, then asked a girl with a streak of sky-blue paint on her forehead where she might find Marcus Catlin.

'Cat? The door at the end of the corridor. Not sure he's there, though.'

Marcus Catlin was there, standing in front of a canvas taller than himself, a loaded brush in one hand, an e-cigarette in the other. He was working on an abstract painting in earth colours and greys that immediately made Fairfield think of autumn, wood smoke and freshly baked bread, though the predominant smell in the airy studio was of turpentine. There were two other painters working at the other end of the brightly lit room. 'Here.' She handed the list of first-year painting students she had been given to Sorbie. 'See if any of them have opinions on Fulvia. Or him,' she added more quietly.

At the mention of Fulvia, Marcus looked over his shoulder at the departing Sorbie and at Fairfield. 'Help you?'

'Are you Marcus Catlin?'

'I could be.'

'Your tutor described you well.' Marcus was tall, broad-shouldered and handsome. He had turned his hair into an ink-black mess with the help of dye and gel and had pierced his right eyebrow to counteract the extreme youthfulness of his face and the puppy-dog brown of his eyes. 'I'm Detective Inspector Fairfield, Bristol CID.' She offered up her ID for inspection.

'Oh, *what*?' Marcus lobbed his brush into the mess on his painting table where it spattered its load of dark paint over paint tubes and jars of white spirit.

'I'm here about Fulvia Lamberti, whom I believe you know well.'

'I can't believe they're sending the police after me. I *apologized*. Profusely. And sincerely. I was pissed and angry.'

'And in love. But that's not why I'm here. Fulvia has disappeared.'

'I know.'

'And we are trying to locate her.' Marcus sucked furiously on his e-cigarette. Fairfield had a ten-a-day small-cigar habit and watching Marcus smoke stirred her nicotine cravings. 'Are you allowed to smoke in here?' she asked.

He shook his head. 'No.'

'Perhaps we could find a place where we could both have a smoke and then have a chat?'

Armed with coffees from the Spike Café, they found a place to sit at one of the tables outside where Fairfield lit a small cigar from a tin of Café Crème. All the other tables were occupied. Not everyone looked like a student, but Fairfield thought that all of them looked more interesting than a group of CID types would.

'You don't look like a police officer,' Catlin said accusingly.

'Oh?' Fairfield blew a surprise cloud of smoke skywards.

'You're too good-looking, like American TV detectives.'

Fairfield knew what he meant. If TV series were to be believed, then the American police departments were recruiting almost exclusively from modelling agencies. 'I'll take that as a compliment, then. *I think.*' She was tempted to tell him that they shared nicknames, Cat and Kat, but stopped herself in time. 'Where is Fulvia?' she asked instead.

'I have no idea.'

'You must have. You went out with her.'

'She dumped me.'

Fairfield waited but no more was forthcoming. 'You didn't take kindly to that, did you?' Catlin lowered his eyes and sipped coffee. 'You wouldn't take no for an answer.'

'I couldn't.'

'In fact, you attacked her work and destroyed one of her paintings. You wanted to get back at her. You wanted to hurt her.'

'No! Not hurt her, never hurt her. You don't know her. You couldn't understand.'

'Try me. Explain it to me.'

Catlin broke eye contact and looked past her at the building. 'I can't really. She was too beautiful for me anyway. You haven't seen her.'

Fairfield patted her jacket. 'I have seen a picture of her.'

'You have a picture? Show me.' Catlin sat up straight, expectant. 'That's an ugly picture of her,' he said when Fairfield held the photograph up for him.

'Is it? She does look pretty, I grant you.'

'She's not *pretty*. Fulvia is beautiful. She's the kind of beautiful that makes you feel scared. Straight away. From the moment you first set eyes on her, you're scared to lose her, scared she would turn her back on you.'

'But she did just that. Why was that?'

Catlin fiddled with his e-cigarette for a moment before putting it down on the table and folding his hands, slouching forward. He suddenly looked much younger. 'She said it was all nonsense. Everything: my painting, her painting, us, the art course. She said I was only with her because of the way she looked and she was sick of me going on about how beautiful she was.'

'You adored her.'

'That's what she said: she didn't want to be adored. She was looking for something real. She wanted someone to look beyond her beauty. I *was* looking beyond it. I told her I did, but she didn't believe me.'

'When did you last see her?'

'Two weeks ago. They were going to throw me out of college for the vandalism thing. Then they said I could stay if I apologized to everybody. I did. I apologized to the whole group – we were at a lecture – and to her. That was wrong, too, apparently. She stormed out. That was the last I saw of her. I don't think she's been back to college since.'

'We went to her place in Clifton Village . . .'

'She hasn't lived there for ages. Her family got her that place, but she thought it was too bourgeois. And too boring. Almost straight away she moved into a shared place in St Pauls somewhere.'

'Somewhere? You must know where, surely.'

'She never told me. I was never allowed there, even when things were OK. She'd come to my place – I'm in a shared house in Bedminster – or I saw her here or we'd meet in town, but never at her place.'

'You never walked her home?'

'She wouldn't let me.'

'You weren't tempted to spy on her?'

'I didn't dare.'

'How did she get around? Did she drive?'

'When she first came here, she took a lot of taxis everywhere. Her parents send her a lot of money. But just before she disappeared she bought a scooter.'

'Very Italian. You wouldn't know the make and registration, by any chance?'

'No, but it was black and chrome – new but retro. She looked heroic on it.'

After getting a detailed, painter's-eye description of how Fulvia dressed, Fairfield asked to be shown to Fulvia's studio space. The studio was on the same floor as Catlin's. The room was deserted of students. Fulvia's painting space was a mess of paint tubes and tins, used brushes crammed into jars of white spirit, pencils and crayons, bits of paper and canvas. On the wall next to her table hung a three-foot square canvas, primed a brilliant white, across its pristine surface a single splash of bright cadmium yellow that looked accidental.

'This mess . . .' Fairfield begun.

'That's normal,' said Catlin. 'That's how she worked. She created beautiful chromatic wonders out of complete chaos.' He picked up one of a dozen small canvases that had been stacked facing the wall. He turned it around for her to examine, so she might agree with him.

It was a square of admittedly glowing colours, a pleasing abstract jumble, but it meant nothing to Fairfield. 'Very nice,' she said.

'Nice?' He returned it reverentially to the stack. 'It's as beautiful as she is.'

'Is anything missing here? Any of her painting equipment?'

Catlin pushed out his bottom lip as he searched her painting table with his eyes. 'I think it's all here.' He lightly touched the table with one finger as if to test for dust. 'It's just like the *Mary Celeste*.'

Downstairs, Fairfield collected Sorbie from inside the café where he had been talking to some of the first-years. 'She bought a scooter,' he announced.

'I know. Get on to DVLA and get us the index number.'

David Mendenhall's entire mail-order drinks business was run from a suspiciously small unit at a modern industrial park in St Philip's Marsh. McLusky parked outside the dispiriting place and fortified himself with a cigarette before walking up to the squat blue-and-grey unit, just as a woman let herself out of a scratched metal door which she pushed shut with her shoulder. She walked off briskly but he stopped her by waving his ID at her.

'Yes, I work for David. I'm his secretary. Well, girl Friday, really.' Sandra Lucas glanced at her watch before turning around and unlocking the door again. She was a plain-looking woman in her thirties, with a sensible haircut and sensible clothes. Every sentence she uttered had an undertone of disappointment. 'I was going to take the rest of the day off.'

'This won't take long,' McLusky promised.

The door led straight into a small office, carved out of the warehouse space with plasterboard and corrugated roofing material. A desk, a computer with a bulky old-fashioned monitor, two chairs and a filing cabinet. The door to the warehouse proper was made of raw chipboard and did not quite fit the frame.

'It's not very glamorous, I'm afraid.'

'It's bigger than my office,' he assured her.

'Then you must be a contortionist.'

'You were taking the rest of the day off?'

Sandra leant back against the desk and crossed her arms in front of her. 'Yeah, well, I only work twenty hours and really I go when I've run out of things to do. Is this about David's dad? Terrible that. Poor Mr Mendenhall. He was very polite to me. I quite liked *him*.'

McLusky noted the emphasis on 'him'. 'You met him, then? Mendenhall senior?'

'Yes. Came here a couple of times.'

'In order to do what?'

'In order to have flaming rows with his son. But he was very polite to me.'

'What were they rowing about?'

'Money, I think. It was around midday each time and David told me to go to lunch so I didn't hear the whole argument. I think Mr Mendenhall gave David money for the business and David spent it on other things, like a BMW. There was definitely a row about the car. He said he needed it to impress clients. I mean, he was right. His last car was quite old; it wouldn't have impressed anyone. But at the time we had irate suppliers on the phone who needed paying, so perhaps he didn't quite have his priorities straight.'

'How is his business going?' McLusky pushed open the door to the warehouse. It contained uneven rows of boxed wines, some standing on palettes, and a couple of tables full of packing materials, a franking machine and other paraphernalia. Six feet high and three feet in girth, a monolithic roll of bubble wrap stood some way apart on the concrete floor; it was ghoulishly illuminated by a shaft of light from a small skylight and looked as though it had materialized there from another planet.

Lucas became more diplomatic. 'It'll pick up towards Christmas, I suppose.'

McLusky closed the flimsy door. 'It must get a bit chilly here in winter.' There was no sign of a heater.

'I've not been here in the winter. He'll put a heater in when it gets colder, I expect. Well, he'll have to or I'm out of here.'

'On the night his father was shot, David called you at home – is that right?'

Sandra frowned. 'Yes, he did.'

'Do you remember what time that was?'

'Oh, it was after ten. Half past? Something like that.'

'What was the call about?'

'He wanted to find a list of our suppliers in California. It was filed correctly; he was just looking in the wrong place.'

'Is it normal for David to work that late?'

'No. But then there had been trouble with that supplier. Or rather with David paying them, and it would have been a good time to call them. The time difference . . .'

'And the file was found?'

'I suppose so. He said the next day he had. I mean, look around you – one desk, one filing cabinet, one wastepaper basket, empty. How can you lose something in here?'

'These rows David had with his father. Did you have the feeling they had been resolved at all?'

'I really couldn't say. David never talked about it and I never asked. I'd rather not get involved in things like that.'

McLusky thanked her and she followed him outside, shouldering the reluctant door shut. 'There was one thing, though.' She hesitated, her shoulder still against the now-closed door. 'I don't want to be disloyal or anything, but that night when he called me, I don't think it was from here at all. He was calling from his mobile and he can never get a signal down here. It sounded like he was outside. And while he spoke, there was suddenly some music and people talking in the background, just for a moment. I thought he was really calling from outside a pub.'

'Is there a pub around here?'

'None David would be seen dead in.'

'Are we calling him in?' Austin, sitting on a desk in the incident room, swung his dangling legs like a child. 'It was never much of an alibi to start with.'

McLusky conscientiously stirred his tea while thinking it over. To save a few calories, he now took neither milk nor sugar with his tea but he stirred it out of habit. 'I fancied him for it straight away. He has a strong motive. If his father got sick of bailing him out and told him "no more handouts", he may have decided to hasten his demise and retire on his inheritance.'

'And that must be a considerable lump. Mendenhall might even have threatened to change his will. But if he did, then he never got around to it. I spoke to his solicitor and there was no mention of changing his will. The copy we found was the latest version.'

Just as Austin began to wonder whether the inspector would ever stop stirring tea that didn't need stirring, McLusky dropped the spoon on the tea tray with a clatter. 'It's too thin. So what if he pretended to be in the office but was outside a pub? He'll wriggle out of that easily. He'll say, "I never said I was in the office; I said I *had been* at the office" or some such thing. It's only his word against hers.'

'Office or pub – what's the difference anyway?'

'The difference is that there's a pub five minutes' drive from his father's house, while his office is at least thirty-five minutes' drive away. But let's save it for later. We'll go and see his father's other painter friend in a minute. Mr Leonidas.'

'It's Mr Poulimenos. Leonidas is his first name.'

'I know. But Leonidas I can remember.' He checked his watch. 'We'd better leave now, actually. You can tell me about Emma Lucket's night out on the way.' He walked from the room, leaving his tea untouched on the desk. McLusky hated black tea.

He drove fast, but in his quiet Mercedes he felt insulated from the noise and wind rush and often needed to check his speed. In the past, Austin, who drove a minute Nissan, had often chauffeured the inspector since his ancient cars broke down so frequently; now that McLusky drove a five-litre Mercedes, it was he who frequently worked imaginary brake pedals on the passenger side. He was doing it now. 'Liam, that bend really tightens beyond those trees,' he warned. They were approaching another bend at an ambitious speed.

'Oh, yeah, so it does,' said McLusky as he struggled to keep the car on the road. Having scared himself, he drove on more sedately. 'What you're saying is that our gardening assistant has no alibi, either.'

Emma's story of being out with friends had been corroborated. It was quite a large group that had descended on the Basement 45 club on the night in question. Austin had spoken to three of them but two did not remember seeing her after ten thirty. He had examined the footage of the club's CCTV system. 'After about ten thirty there's no sign of her and all agree she was not there when they left. One friend' – Austin riffled the papers to find her name – 'has spoken to Emma since and, according to her, Emma said she got a headache and just went home.'

'What you're really saying, Jane, is that nobody has an alibi – not Mendenhall's son, not Emma, not Gotts and not the housekeeper. In fact, Mrs Mohr told me quite defiantly that no one could vouch for her and she seemed to be enjoying that fact.'

'Yeah, looks like they all had opportunity.'

'And there we are, back to square one, which is motive. David has the obvious motive: money.' McLusky had a mental list of reasons why the citizenry committed murder, and greed and stupidity ranked first and second. The third was fear. 'David's business looks shaky. His dad tells him "not a penny more". David's afraid to lose the lot. His dad has just taken up jogging, he's getting fit. Could live for another twenty years. The horror of it! So he goes and kills him.' They had reached the outskirts of Chew, a small town south-west of Bristol which gave its name to the valley and the lake therein – Chew Valley Lake. 'Well, we're here, but where is Bybrook View?' He fished a piece of paper from his jacket and handed it to Austin.

'It's got the postcode – just put it in your satnav.' He noticed McLusky hesitate. 'You do know how to use it?'

'Not got round to reading the instructions yet.' McLusky was not a Luddite by choice; it was just that technology often mystified him enough to make him steer clear of it.

'Instructions? You don't need instructions.'

Five minutes later a delighted McLusky had grasped the rudiments of programming his own satnav, guided by his patient sergeant, and was told by a mellow voice which way to drive. 'The nice lady says it's that way.' He sawed at the wheel and powered down a narrow lane.

Bybrook View was a converted farm complex at the edge of Chew Valley. It had a view not just of a brook but also the distant glitter of the lake.

'Nice. Very nice,' said Austin as they drove in. 'How did Poulimenos make his money?' They entered a large yard, entirely cobbled with ornamental stone in grey and terracotta. Several potted palms were doing well in the shelter between the main nineteenth-century house and the converted storage barns and other outbuildings. One of those had been turned into a slate-roofed garage, the doors of which stood open, revealing a dark-coloured Bentley Continental. 'Do you think he left the door open on purpose so he won't have to drop it *casually* into the conversation that he drives a Bentley?'

'Possible. But our man is in real estate and shipping. Perhaps he doesn't feel the need to impress a couple of coppers.' McLusky thought that the house did it quite well by itself.

Bybrook View, previously Bybrook Farm, had had a lot of money spent on it, and fairly recently too, it seemed. McLusky was well aware that appearances could be deceptive, a fact he was reminded of when Leonidas Poulimenos opened the front door of the main house. Poulimenos, who was in his early sixties, had long wispy hair and spoke without a hint of a

Greek accent. McLusky thought he looked more like an ageing hippy than a rich businessman.

'Come through, come through.' The interior of the house had been restored and furnished with an expensive mix of the modern and the traditional. All the floors were flagged in terracotta, with Persian rugs everywhere. All the walls were white, yet in the sitting room, which consisted of several rooms knocked into one, McLusky noted two tell-tale rectangles of brighter paint where paintings or wall hangings had been removed. The air smelled of cigar smoke. Somewhere in the depth of the house a vacuum cleaner was being pushed about.

Poulimenos let himself drop heavily on to one sofa and indicated the one opposite for them to sit on. He was a large man with an almost comically shaped pot belly which protruded above his black trousers and stretched his black shirt. His long hair, while mostly grey, still retained some colour. He breathed noisily as he moved.

On the blue-and-white mosaic table that divided the two camps stood a heavy Murano glass ashtray littered with cigar stubs and next to it a half-drunk glass of white wine. Poulimenos reached for it with a grunt, changed his mind and let himself slump back without touching it. 'Can I get you anything? Coffee perhaps? I'm afraid I have been drunk for most of the time since I heard Mendy had been shot.'

'You were close friends?'

'*That* close.' He tapped the sides of his extended index fingers against each other. 'What kind of bastard would want to kill Mendy?'

'That's what we're trying to find out.'

'Was anything taken?'

'What makes you say that?'

'I'm looking for an explanation, Inspector. People don't get shot for no reason.'

'Rarely,' McLusky agreed.

'Then what?'

'We have yet to establish a motive.'

Poulimenos once more stretched out a hand towards his glass of wine and changed his mind again. 'I'll make you some coffee,' he said abruptly. McLusky, who rarely turned down a chance to top up his caffeine levels, brightened up. 'I could do with some myself,' Poulimenos said and levered himself off the couch. 'Real coffee. *Greek* coffee. To the kitchen, gentlemen.'

The kitchen was luxuriously kitted out, yet Poulimenos made coffee on a tiny camping stove on the counter next to the wine-red Aga. While he did so, McLusky asked all the obvious questions. When did he last see Mendenhall? On the same day Jennifer Longmaid had, on their visit to the Arnolfini. Did he seem different? On good form. Was he in a dispute with anyone? Not that he knew of. All the while McLusky carefully watched the ritual of Greek coffee-making. Poulimenos appeared unperturbed by any of the questions. With his fleshy fingers he set tiny cups on a silver tray, spooned coffee into a long-handled little pot, then added a little sugar and three measures of water.

'His son, David. What's your opinion of him? You have met him, presumably?'

'What do I think of David?' He snorted dismissively. 'I don't think much of him at all. Altogether, I don't think I spent more than ten minutes in the same room with him. When he was younger, he wanted nothing to do with the brewery, purely out of opposition to his father, I think. Drifted along on an allowance, started some wishy-washy degree, dropped out of college, and then when Charles sold the business, he realized what a mistake he had made. Charles had wanted him to take over the business. When he sold it, David got upset because he had not been *consulted*. The little prick. There were huge rows and Charles stopped his allowance.' He had stirred the pot until the froth rose, then removed and returned it to the heat two more times before he whipped it off the stove and set it next to the cups on the tray. He led them back into the sitting room, carrying the tray like a sacramental offering at the head of the procession. 'That's when David started his so-called businesses – wheeler-dealing, buying and selling. But he wants to get rich quick. Hasn't managed it yet. He wants all the trappings but to do none of the work.' He divided the froth between the three little cups before filling them in turn with the fragrant coffee. 'He can have all the trappings now, I expect. I'm glad I don't have to watch him burn through his inheritance.' The cup looked even smaller in the man's large fleshy hands as he lifted it to his lips. They followed his example. McLusky had to suppress a groan of pleasure as the taste of the sweet and aromatic liquid hit his taste buds.

Poulimenos put down his cup and looked up. 'You don't think *David* killed his father?'

'I don't think anything at this stage,' McLusky lied. 'We need to get as complete a picture as possible of the people around him.'

Poulimenos contemplated this for a moment. 'And naturally that means you'll be asking other people about me the same way you asked me about him.'

'Naturally.'

'Then let me get in there first. I'm rich. I enjoy being rich and like people to know I'm rich. But I am not interested in making money. I've made a lot of it in the past and now I'm trying to enjoy what's left of my life.' He took another sip of coffee and grunted. 'My wife chose to betray me with a younger man and three weeks ago I threw her out. She took two paint-ings' – he nodded at the blank patches on the wall – 'her clothes and her Porsche.'

'Were these paintings you had done?'

He wrinkled his nose in displeasure. 'No. They were by David Bomberg.'

McLusky thought he had heard the name yet failed to bring an image to mind, but he rightly guessed the paintings had been expensive. He moved on to what he hoped was safer territory. 'Do you have children?'

Poulimenos pulled himself to his feet and walked off, beck-oning them to follow. 'No. I cannot have children.' McLusky and Austin exchanged a quick glance and followed. He led through a narrow door to the outside and under a covered walkway to a low building that had begun life as a milking shed but had, as McLusky rightly guessed, been converted into a luxurious painting studio. It was dominated by a long table full of art projects in progress. A mahogany easel with gleaming brass fittings stood at one end and a small hand-operated printing press at the other. A long skylight in the

open-beamed roof made it a bright and airy space, quite unlike
the Rembrandtian gloom of Mendenhall's studio.

'These are my children.' Poulimenos indicated a long line
of paintings propped up against the wall, all small enough to
fit comfortably above a fireplace. As with his two friends, his
favourite subjects were landscapes, but the treatment was less
dated. Some were coastal views but many were rural scenes,
perhaps from around the Chew Valley itself; McLusky couldn't
tell. He walked slowly along the line of paintings as though
studying them, but he was busy musing on other things. When
he spoke, it was from the opposite end of the room. 'Real
estate, brewery, antiques and *painting*. I assume it was the art
that brought you together?'

'You assume correctly, Inspector,' said Poulimenos, smiling
for the first time. 'The four of us met on a painting holiday.
In the Lake District.'

McLusky had walked back along the line of paintings. 'The
four of you?'

'Yes.' Poulimenos buried his hands in his pockets and
nodded lugubriously. 'In the beginning there were four of us.
Now there's only two of us left.'

'Who was the fourth of your painting group?'

'Ben. Ben Kahn. He was probably the most talented of us.
Actually, he was definitely more talented than the rest of
us. But then . . .' He shrugged and fell silent.

'What happened to him?'

'He died in a boating accident. Quite a while ago now –
summer of 1998. I don't know whom I'll miss more, Ben or
Charles. Time will tell.'

Austin's phone rang. The sergeant excused himself and went
outside to take the call. Poulimenos lifted his chin. 'Do you
appreciate the fine arts, Inspector?'

McLusky, making a note of the name Ben Kahn and the
date 1998 on his phone, hesitated before answering. 'I do,
though I don't know the first thing about them.'

'Please don't say it.'

'I won't,' McLusky promised. 'Primarily because I *don't*
really know what I like.'

'Do you like these?'

'Your children?'

Poulimenos snorted, but with delight. 'Precisely. You don't often hear an honest opinion about your own children. I mean, no one says, "Darling, your kids are quite ugly"; no, it's always "Aren't they gorgeous?" And it's the same with paintings, because who wants to strain a friendship with honesty? But you and I, Inspector, are never going to be friends. Go ahead, let me have your honest opinion.'

McLusky walked down the line of paintings, then back again. Eventually, he pointed at the third one in the row, a sunny seaside scene of a cove and lapping waves, with blue skies and a tiny figure swimming in the sea. 'I like that one. Better than the rest.'

'Then take it, Inspector.'

McLusky thanked him for the kind offer. 'But I couldn't possibly accept a gift from a member of the public; it could be considered a bribe. In fact, it would definitely be considered a bribe.'

'But that's nonsense! What would I be bribing you about?' Poulimenos asked.

Before McLusky could answer, the door opened and Austin came back into the room. He waggled his mobile. 'Something has come up. And it's quite urgent.'

'We were more or less finished here anyway,' McLusky said, 'but we might need to talk to you again. Oh, and thank you for the coffee; it was excellent. I'd never had Greek coffee before.' He told him they would find their own way out, but Poulimenos insisted on escorting them back to the front door.

'What's up?' McLusky asked as he slid behind the wheel of his car.

'Nicholas Longmaid has been found dead.' Austin slammed his door for emphasis.

'Shit. Where?'

'His place.'

Leonidas Poulimenos stood in the doorway to his house and wondered at the inspector's driving style as the Mercedes screeched away towards the road with tyre-smoking wheelspin.

SIX

'Gunshot?'

'Apparently.'

'Shit,' McLusky said for the fifth time and pressed harder on the accelerator. 'At least we're halfway there already.'

'So what's the hurry?' asked Austin, still grappling with his seat belt. 'We'll get there faster if we avoid a tour of the ditches.'

'You don't trust my driving at all, do you, Jane?' McLusky eased off the accelerator all the same.

'Do you want me to stick the satnav on?'

'No, I know the way to Longmaid's house. Anyway, I'm not keen on that woman's voice.'

'First Mendenhall, then his painting buddy. Are you thinking what I'm thinking?'

Just then the inspector had been recalling Mrs Longmaid's unusually short skirt. 'I doubt that. Although if you mean that the two deaths are connected, I can almost guarantee it.' McLusky, whose life was as littered with coincidences as everyone else's, stubbornly refused to believe in them. 'I'll bet you what's left of my pension that we are dealing with the same killer. And I don't bloody like it.'

The drive was already crammed with vehicles, among them the night-blue Jaguar of the pathologist. Superintendent Denkhaus was exiting the front door of Stanmore House just as McLusky got out of the car. 'Does Denkhaus teleport everywhere? I think I've yet to arrive at a locus before him. Afternoon, sir,' he called to Denkhaus. The superintendent was shedding his scene suit, meaning he would not re-enter the house, which immediately cheered McLusky up. 'What have we got, sir?'

'What we have is a dead man upstairs in his study and his self-possessed and extremely composed widow in the sitting room.' He checked over his shoulder that no one was close. 'And she'll catch a cold if she's not careful.'

'The body . . . another shooting?'

'Very much so, as you will see.'

McLusky realized what the DSI meant by that when they had pushed their way through the forensics team into the study. He already felt too hot and sweat pricked on his skin even before he took in the scene. Dr Coulthart was kneeling by the body and studying the bloody mess of Longmaid's head.

'Any sign of the weapon?' McLusky asked.

'No such luck,' said a SOCO.

Coulthart didn't even look up. 'Please don't ask me any questions, gentlemen. I have only this minute arrived myself.'

The crumpled figure of Nicholas Longmaid lay face down in front of his open gun locker. The locker was empty. The worn Persian rug in front of it had soaked up a large amount of blood that had both spattered and pooled. The pervading smells in the stifling room were the metallic smell of blood and the nauseating odour of warm plastic scene suits. McLusky turned to the team leader of the SOCOs. 'This how he was found?'

The man with the blonde walrus moustache confirmed it. 'We didn't move him. From the blood spatter, I would guess he was bending down in front of that empty safe when the bullet hit him.'

'That safe is a gun locker. It had two shotguns in it the last time I saw it.'

The SOCO shrugged. 'No sign of them.'

'What about this overturned chair?'

'Well, if you look carefully at the outside of the door, you can see it has been kicked. There's a partial boot print; it's faint but it's there. We're speculating, but it appears the door was wedged shut from inside. There's no key, see? If that is a gun locker, then my guess is that the victim came up here and wedged the door shut to keep the killer out while he armed himself with a shotgun.'

Austin stayed by the door where he could breathe more easily, but McLusky, despite his revulsion, leant in close enough to take in the wound at the back of the bald head and, when Coulthart gently moved it, the much larger exit wound at the front. Not much of Longmaid's upper face remained; the rest of it was stained with his blood. His gold-rimmed glasses had been crushed and deformed when, probably already dead, he fell to the ground. He was wearing his blue painting smock.

'Shot right here at close range, probably from the open door,' said the pathologist. 'DS Austin, would you extend one arm towards the victim?' Austin did so. 'From the hand that held the gun to the back of the unfortunate man's skull can't have been more than five feet.'

'Yes,' agreed the SOCO. 'If that's a gun locker, then my guess is he was just getting to his shotgun when the killer caught up with him. Bad luck.'

'Any sign of a struggle? That mess in the hall?' They had walked past the shards of a broken Chinese figurine on the hall floor when they came in.

'Inside the house, only that broken statue thing in the hall. That had stood on the little rococo table and had always been in danger of being knocked over, according to Mrs Longmaid. And she is glad it finally was. Her words, not mine. The studio out the back is a total mess, though.'

'The bullet?'

'We've recovered two bullets, one of them missed. But you won't like them, Inspector. One went right through the man's brain and hit the inside wall of the safe, then the back before it was spent. The other one missed the victim, caromed round the inside of the safe.' He held up the evidence bag with the projectiles inside. 'Both extremely deformed.'

McLusky managed not to swear as he glared at it. 'But we'll be able to tell if it came from the same gun?'

'I wouldn't bet on it.'

'Damn it.' McLusky would have bet that the SOCO enjoyed delivering bad news. His unglamorous job was to scrape stuff off floors and walls and pack it off to a forensic lab somewhere, and he didn't have to worry about apprehending criminals. In fact, the more crime there was, the more scenes of crime to visit and the safer his job. McLusky's career, what there was of it, depended on getting results. 'Who found the body?'

'Mrs Longmaid.'

'You spoke to her? How did she seem?'

'I only spoke to her about the statuette in the hall. She was drinking. I thought she was already quite plastered.'

'For want of a better word.'

'Sorry, sir.'

'No, no, plastered will do.' McLusky squeezed out of the room. 'No sign of forced entry anywhere,' he said as he descended the stairs with Austin.

'The killer charmed his or her way in or was known to him,' Austin speculated.

'Or married to him.'

'True.'

'And you don't have to charm your way in with a gun in your hand. You open the door to someone pointing a thirty-eight at you, what do you say?'

'Not today, thank you.'

'Exactly.'

They found Jennifer Longmaid in the sitting room, which had already been gone over by scene-of-crime officers who had now moved on to the painting studio. Looking at her, McLusky thought that both the superintendent and the SOCO team leader had a point. Mrs Longmaid had indeed been drinking, though probably not to drown her grief; she had drunk the better part of a bottle of vintage champagne. At first glance she seemed to be sprawled on a sofa in her underwear, but she was in fact wearing a very insubstantial black silk dress and a pair of patterned black tights. She had kicked off one high-heeled shoe and was balancing the other on one toe. She let it drop when the officers entered the room and pulled her legs under her.

'That outfit doesn't suit you, Inspector; it makes you look like a sanitation worker. And I loathe the sound it makes when you move. I don't suppose you'll join me in a glass of champagne? I opened a bottle of the good stuff.'

From the armchair in which he had sat down, all McLusky could read of the label was the name *Alfred Gratien*. He disliked champagne and the only champagne house he recognized was Bollinger. 'I realize this must be a difficult time for you and I'm sorry to have to bother you with questions . . .'

'No bother at all.' She lifted both glass and eyes towards the ceiling. 'I'm not grief-stricken. Shocked? Yes. Outraged at the violation of my home? Definitely. But not wracked with grief. Of course, it may hit me later but I doubt it somehow.' She drained her glass and leant forward to replenish it from the bottle on the coffee table, affording McLusky a look down her dress. Since he was clearly meant to look, he did so and confirmed to himself that Mrs Longmaid wore no bra.

'Was it you who found the body?'

'Yup.'

'Would you mind going through the events for me?'

Jennifer Longmaid's account was brief. She had been shopping for clothes in Bath. On her return to the house, she had found the broken statuette in the hall. She had called her husband's name and, when she received no answer, looked for him in the studio. It was a shambles. Back at the house, she had found her husband's body in his study.

'I couldn't even bring myself to go inside. It was obvious he was dead.'

'You did not call the police from up there? Didn't use the phone in the study?'

'No. I went into the garden. I went all the way down to the bottom and looked at the cows. I like watching the cows; it calms me. I needed a bit of time before calling the police. I knew the place would get busy with people and first I wanted a moment to rethink my life. I had to reimagine my future. Then I called Elaine to let her know.'

'Elaine?' Austin queried.

'Elaine Poulimenos. She lives not far down the road, now that she's left Leon. She always wanted me to leave Nick. I called to tell her she could stop going on about it.' She snorted into her glass.

McLusky rose. 'Thank you, Mrs Longmaid. We'll talk again later.'

They left the non-grieving widow and made their way to the painting studio. 'Fresh overshoes!' a SOCO warned as Austin held the door open for McLusky. 'You've just walked through the house and the bloody garden with those.'

Contrite, the officers exchanged theirs for the new ones

proffered by the man before entering. They were told to stay close to the entrance. 'This will take us a while,' the SOCO promised, 'as you can imagine.'

McLusky could. The place had been trashed. Easels and tables lay overturned. Houseplants, knocked to the ground and their pots shattered, radiated shards and compost across the floorboards. Brushes, pencils and multicoloured pastels were strewn across the floor, along with torn paper. Many canvases had been damaged. 'In your opinion, is this the result of a struggle?' he asked.

'Could be, but not all of it. See all those coloured pastels on the floor? Not one has been stepped on. Also, someone damaged a whole load of paintings, all in the same sort of area.' He pointed at a group of strewn canvases. 'Looks like someone kicked them. The canvas is dented but not broken. Tough stuff, canvas. Perhaps the killer hated still lifes? They're all paintings of pots and bottles and stuff. And right at the back there, someone burnt some paper in the wood burner. Quite a bit of paper.'

'Can you tell what it was?'

'Not offhand, no, but my guess is they were artworks done on paper. We'll empty out the ashes later but there were a couple of corners that hadn't burnt away and that was heavy paper, drawing paper, not the stuff you'd write on.'

'I don't suppose there's any way of telling whether it was burnt by Longmaid or a third party?'

'None at all, the ashes are stone cold. We might get a fingerprint off the bits of unburnt paper, but that would be a miracle.'

'I believe I'm due one of those.' McLusky turned to Austin. 'This was quite a cosy sort of place – creative chaos, romantic mess, that sort of thing.'

'Do you think anything is missing?' Austin asked. His inflection showed he had anticipated McLusky's answer.

'Are you taking the piss, DS Austin?' He gave the smashed-up studio one more disgusted look and walked out.

Austin followed him, thinking that he recognized the symptoms: McLusky's hypothesis that David Mendenhall was the killer now looked shaky. The inspector impatiently shed his scene suit by the door, then walked off through the garden to the wooden boundary fence beyond which grazed a herd of reddish-brown cows. Austin followed his example, despite a suspicion that McLusky would prefer to be alone. He watched him light a cigarette and noticed with satisfaction that it no longer made him want one himself, but he moved upwind from him all the same.

After a few furious drags on his cigarette, McLusky sighed and leant with both hands on the waist-high fence. 'Well, what do you know? Mrs Longlegs was right: cows calm you down.' He turned his back on them and folded his arms in front of his chest. 'Perhaps I should get a picture for my wallet.' He spoke without looking at him. 'What's going on here, Jane?'

'Buggered if I know. We don't have any proof that the two killings are connected. Could still be a hideous coincidence.' When McLusky snorted contemptuously, he added, 'I know, I'm just saying. We need to find the connection. Do you think it has somehow to do with painting?'

McLusky lit a fresh cigarette from the glow of the first one. He thought of Gotts the gardener and hesitated for a fraction of a second before flicking his cigarette end into the grass. 'Who knows? We don't even know the sequence of events. Longmaid was wearing his painting gear. Stands to reason he was painting or at least in his studio. Could be it was he who burnt the old drawings or whatever it was in the stove.'

'In comes the killer with his thirty-eight.'

'Then why isn't Longmaid's body lying by the stove?'

'They struggled, he got away and ran into the house.'

'He makes it upstairs but can't lock the door because there's no key. He wedges the chair under it and starts fumbling with the safe. Ammunition has to be kept in a separate place, of course; you're not allowed to keep loaded guns, even in a gun locker.' McLusky's hand slid into his jacket pocket and closed around the loaded Derringer pistol which had lain on top of the gun cases in Longmaid's safe.

'The killer got to him before he could load a weapon,' Austin completed for him. 'At least that tells us that he didn't believe he was in any danger, or else he'd have kept a gun ready loaded and to hell with the law.' He looked across at

McLusky who was staring up towards the house with a deep frown, keeping silent. When the inspector pushed himself off from the fence and walked briskly away, he called after him, 'Don't you think that's how it happened?'

McLusky did not slow down or look back. 'I'm sure you're right, Jane.'

Austin followed him. 'If you disagree, why don't you bloody say so?' he said quietly, not entirely caring whether the boss heard him or not.

Later that day they found themselves at the Clifton Antiques Emporium where Longmaid had been one of eleven antiques dealers who shared the rent of large Georgian buildings to sell to the general public. Much of buying and selling was now done online and they found every one of the dealers there staring at an iPad or other computer. They took names, asked questions and searched Nicholas Longmaid's stall. Most dealers had special areas of interest, like the man in the unit next to Longmaid's, who sold nothing but silver items.

'No, he was a boring sort of chap. Hated being here and knew nothing about silver. I think he was mostly interested in painting paraphernalia, nineteenth century and earlier, but he'd never sell any of it. It's really just general antiques that he has here. Don't get me wrong, he runs a successful business. All this is valuable but it isn't interesting. I hear he keeps all the interesting pieces at home.'

McLusky, who had a good mental picture of Stanmore House, agreed. The items Longmaid was offering for sale at the Emporium had little flair and were chosen for commercial value. McLusky looked around at the items in the rooms and all he could think of were the dead hands that had once bought them and used them when they were new. It was as though he could feel the weight of the dead that had left them behind dragging him down and all at once he felt tired enough to sleep. He gave up looking through Longmaid's desk and instead took a dozen photographs of the entire place on his mobile, then marched off. 'Let's get out of here, DS Austin, and rejoin the living.'

*   *   *

'Fulvia Lamberti. She has a scooter registered to her. Find it, Deedee.' Sorbie slapped a photocopy of Fulvia's photograph and name on DC Dearlove's keyboard and went to make himself a cup of instant coffee. Daniel Dearlove reluctantly put down his bag of Hula Hoops and pecked at his keyboard with his left hand while continuing to feed the cylindrical potato snack into his mouth with his right. Sorbie returned, blowing on his hot coffee, and eyed Dearlove with undisguised loathing. The man's suit was covered in cat hair, chicken soup stains and minute fragments of crisps. His thin hair was caked with gel. His work station was covered in empty crisp packets and Styrofoam cups that attested to his chicken-soup addiction. He was good with computers – he would give him that – but utterly unconvincing as a copper. 'Since she's driving around in town on a scooter, we'll just sit back and let traffic scoop her up for us.'

'You won't, you know,' said Dearlove, returning both hands to the Hula Hoop feed.

'And why the hell not?'

'Because she reported it nicked three weeks ago?'

'Oh, bloody hell. Where was it nicked from?'

'Corn Street.'

'Was it a Clifton address she gave?'

Dearlove fashioned two Hula Hoops into binoculars and peered through them at the screen. 'Erm . . . no, address in St Pauls.' Dearlove wrote it down.

'Bingo, found the bint.' Sorbie snatched the paper with the address from Dearlove's hand and went to see Fairfield in her office. 'She reported it stolen three weeks ago and gave a St Pauls address.'

Fairfield swiped her car keys off her desk. 'Three weeks is a long time in policing, Jack.'

A few minutes later she shoehorned her red Renault into a tight parking space in Albert Park. 'It's that one, with the purple door.'

Sorbie made a vague sound of disapproval. 'Look at this place. Why would anyone with a perfectly good place in Clifton Village prefer to live in some dump in St Pauls, with drugs and prostitution and muggings?'

'To be with other students? For the frisson? Anyway, we don't know that it's a dump yet,' she said. 'Could be nice inside.'

'You wanna bet?'

Broken glass crunched underfoot outside the front door which was deeply scored and gouged near a Yale lock too shiny to be more than a week old. There was an electric bell push dangling from a wire that protruded from a drill hole in the middle of the door. Sorbie pressed it and was rewarded with a mechanical snarl from the other side. They could hear voices but none approached and the door remained unanswered. He supplemented a second snarl with an open-handed policemen's knock. A moment later a girl with a mass of frizzy blonde hair wrenched the door open. 'Yeah?' Behind her could be heard confused voices, all talking at once.

Fairfield held her ID aloft. 'We're looking for Fulvia Lamberti.'

'She's not here. Sorry, we're having a bit of an emergency in the kitchen.' She made to close the door again.

'Perhaps we could be of assistance,' said Sorbie and pushed past her inside the narrow hall. The floorboards were bare and in need of repainting. There was a door immediately to the left giving on to a tiny front room. Next were the stairs curving up steeply; the battered banister was missing every other baluster and the newel post had come adrift from the handrail. Sorbie gave Fairfield a quick told-you-so glance and marched on into the kitchen which lay straight ahead. Some of the voices came from here.

The place smelled of stale washing-up water, cat food and burnt sausages. There were only two people in the kitchen, though Sorbie could have sworn he had heard more than two voices. Two blokes – studenty types, he noted – were wrestling with a washing machine. Nearly a third of the machine, which was still plugged in and in the middle of a wash cycle, had disappeared through the floor. An additional two voices came up from below the floorboards. All four swore and grunted.

The girl stood next to Sorbie. 'The floorboards are rotten underneath and it just kind of sank into the ground in front of my eyes. It had been leaning a bit for quite a while,' she admitted.

Fairfield waved the girl, who said her name was Anna, away from the wrestling students to quiz her about Fulvia. Anna was reluctant to move further than the door from where she could keep an eye on her sinking load of washing.

'What's she done, then?' she asked distractedly.

'Nothing as far as we know. But her parents are worried about her. She seems to have disappeared. When did you last see her?'

Anna pushed her bottom lip out and shrugged. 'Couple of weeks?'

'Can you be more specific?'

'Not really. She wasn't here that often even before that. And I'm not here all that often, either. I'm staying with my boyfriend; he lives closer to the uni. I only came to do my laundry. You think something's wrong? She's probably just got a new boyfriend.'

'Did you ever meet her old boyfriend? Marcus?'

'No, I don't think he came here.'

Fairfield got the distinct impression that Anna had not been Fulvia's biggest fan. 'How do you get on with Fulvia?'

She puffed up her cheeks and slowly expelled the air. 'She's a bit full of herself. And she doesn't mince words. Nothing's good enough. She tells everyone that their food's rubbish and how she can't believe no one she meets can cook. She did cook a meal once, for the whole house, like. I wasn't here but everyone went on about how brilliant it was. I think she just did it to show off. Mostly, she eats out, I think.'

'Does she? Where?'

'Search me. Italian restaurants, I presume. Why she came to England in the first place I've no idea.'

'Show me her room.' She turned to Sorbie, but the DS had got involved in trying to pull the washing machine, which had sunk yet lower, back into the kitchen, so she followed the girl without him up to Fulvia's attic room. The door was unlocked. She pushed it open and peered inside while pulling on latex gloves.

'Gloves! You really do think something's happened to her.'

'It's just routine,' Fairfield told her and let her go back down. The room contained a single bed, a canvas wardrobe behind the door and a long and narrow pasting table under the window. Rolls of charcoal-smudged papers inhabited the corners; a bulging leather portfolio was crammed with life drawings. The walls were covered with drawings, which she immediately acknowledged as being exceptionally good. Fulvia appeared to have drawn everything, from people to shoes to butterflies and dogs. There were many books, in a pile by the bed and stacked all over the pasting table which sagged in the centre under the weight. Fairfield thought she knew why Fulvia was in England. Almost all of the books were on British art and monographs on British artists, only some of whom she had heard of. The inside of the wardrobe told Fairfield two things: Fulvia liked browns, greys and blacks and she could not have taken many clothes with her. Fairfield methodically searched the room for anything that might throw light on the girl's fate and found none. Fulvia had rejected her small yet well-appointed attic bedsit on the other side of town to live in this tiny room on top of a cramped student house. As if to confirm her impression that the place was in urgent need of refurbishment, a loud crash shook the house. Two floors below her, the battle with the washing machine appeared to have been lost. She crouched down and pointed the beam from her pencil torch under the bed. A suitcase and a holdall took up most of the space. Both turned out to be empty. As she straightened up, her eyes fell on a blue-and-white object standing erect on its charger on the floor beside the bed: an electric toothbrush. She reached across and switched the charger off at the wall socket. On the table she picked up an empty clear plastic folder and held it against the light: plenty of fingerprints. She slid it into an evidence bag.

Sorbie was waiting for her at the bottom of the stairs. 'The floorboards gave way. Washing machine is now in the basement but I don't think it survived the fall.'

'How do you get down there?'

'Via the backyard.'

This consisted of a small concreted area surrounded by old

brick walls. Narrow steps led down into the basement which was dark, filthy and smelled of damp. Broken furniture lay in mouldering heaps. She found three of the students standing in a pool of grey water around the crashed washing machine. One of them was Anna who was kicking it half-heartedly. 'It won't open. I can't get my washing out.'

'Did Fulvia have a dressing gown?' Fairfield asked. All three shrugged their shoulders: not that they knew of. Fairfield could see Sorbie's face in the hole above, peering down at the mess from the kitchen above. 'OK, thanks,' Fairfield said. 'If you should hear anything about the girl, be sure to let us know.' They grunted their acknowledgement.

Anna watched her leave, then looked up through the hole and glared at the policeman staring down at her. She was almost a hundred per cent certain the officer had deliberately pushed the washing machine down rather than helped to pull it up.

Back in the car, Fairfield took out her tin of Café Crème cigars and lit one with a disposable lighter. She blew a smoke cloud at the windscreen. 'I'd appreciate it if in future you'd keep your mind on the job and not get side-tracked by domestic appliances.'

'Sorry, ma'am. Just wanted to help, that's all. Did you search her room?'

'I did,' she said and started the engine. She dropped the evidence bag in his lap. 'Her dabs for elimination. Her wardrobe is full and there's a suitcase and a holdall under her bed. Her electric toothbrush is sitting on a charger beside the bed. Wherever she is, she has very few clothes with her and no toothbrush. I don't like it, Jack. I think that girl's in trouble.'

He had made an effort. He had booked a table at what Laura had once told him was her favourite restaurant, shaved for the second time, put on a new shirt and freshly laundered clothes. McLusky had recognized the signs: he was nervous about meeting her. Having lived with her in Southampton for years, he was now nervous of just meeting her for dinner. They had carefully fluttered around the subject of getting back together like birds around a feeder that has a sleeping cat under it.

McLusky thought he had made progress in wooing her back; their last meeting had even ended in a lengthy kiss from which Laura had eventually extricated herself with what McLusky had hoped was difficulty. Yet the evening was not going well. They had met in a pub for drinks beforehand, but Laura was not drinking. She was on medication that did not mix well with alcohol but refused to say what the medication was for. When they had settled at their restaurant table, Laura opened the menu and found that it was completely different from what she remembered – the restaurant had a new chef who appeared to be a refugee from the 1990s and had bought shares in sun-dried tomatoes.

'We can always go somewhere else,' McLusky offered.

'Forget it. I'll find something.'

In the end they both went for the same dish: lamb chops accompanied by a quivering haystack of impossibly thin fries and a pyramid of roasted vegetables. McLusky knew he was drinking too quickly, especially as he was sitting opposite a stone-cold sober Laura, but he needed to drown out the image of Nicholas Longmaid reaching for a loaded gun that was no longer there, desperately fumbling with a shotgun and cartridge when the door burst open and his killer discharged his . . .

'You've stopped eating, Liam. Are you all right?'

'Fine, fine.' He emptied his glass of German lager and stabbed at his chips in an imitation of hearty appetite, then blurted it out. 'Do you think we could live together again?'

'*Live* together?' She clinked her knife against his empty beer bottle. 'How many of those did you have?'

'What are you saying?'

'You know what I'm saying. You're getting ahead of yourself. We've had dinner twice and you want us to move in together.'

'OK, but . . . it's not like we've only just met. We've lived together before.'

'Yes. Remind me how that went, Liam. Ah, no, don't bother; it's just come back to me.'

'We could give it a try. You could keep your room and just move in experimentally.'

'What, into your place? A rented flat over a grocer's, and with no central heating?'

'It's summer, Laura; what do you need central heating for?'

'You don't expect it to last until the autumn, then?'

McLusky left his food half eaten, demolishing the pretty arrangement just enough to make it look as if he had tried. His medical was coming up and he could do with losing weight anyway.

'Do you want to go somewhere else? Or perhaps we could . . .'

'Actually, Liam, I'm really tired tonight. I ordered a cab when you were in the loo. Perhaps I shouldn't have come out tonight.'

'No, no, I'm glad you did.'

'I thought about cancelling but I did want to see you, you know?'

When they stepped out on to the street, it was raining heavily. The taxi was waiting. 'I did buy an umbrella, honest. But it's still back at the office.'

Like sixty per cent of your mind, thought Laura. She gave him a quick peck on the cheek and ran to the cab.

Nicholas Longmaid's autopsy had been immediate and had revealed no surprises. The time of his death had now been pronounced by Dr Coulthart with reasonable confidence as being between eleven a.m. and one o'clock. Forensics, however, had not been nearly so obliging. They were happy to say with 'a degree of confidence' that he was killed with a .38, but refused to be drawn on whether it had been fired from the same gun used to kill Charles Mendenhall since both projectiles had been too deformed to reveal a match.

While listening to McLusky, DSI Denkhaus had been twirling his gold fountain pen between his fingers. Now he dropped it on to his diary in a gesture of disgust. 'Bloody typical. It's like it was planned that way. They couldn't have, could they?'

'I asked. They laughed.'

'No, I expect you can't predict ricochets.' His face brightened.

'I'm glad you asked them, though, because you have to wonder what the chances are. Have we checked alibis? What about David Mendenhall? You fancied him for his father's murder. Could he be involved in this? He knew him.'

'We'll have to talk to him again. Austin called him and he immediately said he would not talk to us again without a solicitor present.'

'Sounds promising. Why would he react that way to a simple inquiry?'

'He went off on one, to quote DS Austin, and shouted down the phone.'

'We can't pull him in without having anything on him at all, so go and get a statement from him, through his bloody solicitor if necessary. What about Longmaid's wife? Could she have killed her husband?'

'Oh, easily. By temperament, I mean. Not even a pretence of grief there. Forensics took swabs of her hands and clothing. No residue to say she fired a gun, but she could have worn different clothes and gloves and disposed of them somehow.'

'She doesn't have an alibi, then?'

'Said she went for a drive after going shopping – nice day and all that. She had at least two hours unaccounted for in which to do it.'

'You fancy her?' McLusky pulled a face. '*For the killing*,' Denkhaus added.

'I think she was fond of Mendenhall and may have had a fling with him. She has closer ties to *both* victims than David Mendenhall. When I spoke to Poulimenos, he suggested that David wanted nothing to do with the four painting friends.'

'Right.' Denkhaus frowned. 'Four?'

'Oh, yeah, Poulimenos mentioned a fourth friend. But he died some time ago.'

'Natural causes?'

'Accident, I believe. But I'll look into it.'

A few minutes later he was standing in a nearby supermarket, staring at the self-service salad bar. DSI Denkhaus had reminded him of his upcoming fitness test and dispelled any hopes McLusky might have had of postponing the evil day because of the ongoing investigation. 'There's always an ongoing investigation,' he had been told. This morning he had breakfasted on bran flakes with a splash of skimmed milk, which had instantly put him in a bad mood. Now he was looking at the salad bar with something akin to hatred. A sign invited him to squash as much stuff into plastic boxes of varying sizes. Anything that looked even remotely interesting was covered in high-calorie mayonnaisy gunk. With a sigh, he filled his container – he had sensibly opted for 'medium' – with slithering sliced cucumber, tomatoes as small and hard as marbles, mixed beans, mixed bean sprouts and shredded lettuce.

Back in his office, McLusky irritably made room on his desk by piling the clutter on it into a heap on the floor so that he could find a place to set down his box of salad. Never had he anticipated a meal with less enthusiasm. Still, it was only until the fitness test; anyway, it was a hot day and salad was supposed to be summery, wasn't it? He flicked on the little plastic fan which came reluctantly to life with a buzz and a squeak. He opened the salad box, peeled the foil off the little carton of French dressing he had bought at the same time and slam-dunked the lot into his salad. Attacking it with a plastic fork in one hand, he hammered out numbers on his desk phone with the other and ordered up a storm of background checks on all and sundry, as well as Elaine Poulimenos's new address. Then he called forensics. 'The boot print on Longmaid's office door . . .'

'Partial boot print,' the technician reminded him.

'Did you find any matches of it in the garden?'

'Didn't find any at all. Whoever it was probably stuck to the stone-flagged path and it was dry.'

'Did you try to match it to any prints at Woodlea House?' There was a pause at the other end. McLusky prompted irritably, 'In Charles Mendenhall's garden!'

'Did you want us to? No one suggested to us that the two deaths are connected. Anyway, it's only a partial and I haven't been there, but the gardens at Woodlea are quite big, aren't they? That would take a lot of man hours . . .'

McLusky grunted, dialled a different number and growled

down the phone until he was talking to the walrus-faced SOCO team leader who had attended at Woodlea House. 'There were many boot prints at Woodlea,' said the man on a crackly extension from his neon-lit basement lab. 'Both gardeners wear heavy boots. We only looked for dramatically different imprints, as from someone jumping heavily off the wall into the garden. It's a huge place, you know, it would take a lot of man hours . . .'

McLusky grunted some more and hung up, then went back to attacking the rest of his salad. He had nearly finished it when Austin knocked and entered. 'Looks nice,' the DS said experimentally and watched him chase the last few beans through the dregs of salad dressing in the bottom of the box. McLusky let the oily dressing run into one corner then poured it into the back of the six-inch fan. It stopped squeaking immediately and instead wafted *Herbes de Provence* smells at him. 'Making best use of police resources,' he commented. 'OK, Jane, astound me. What's the bloody connection between Mendenhall's death and Longmaid's?'

'The gardeners. Gotts and Lucket are doing the Longmaids' garden, too.'

SEVEN

'**N**othing.' McLusky had tried all the numbers for the gardeners he had, including the landlines at Woodlea and Stanmore House. 'Gotts' mobile went straight to voicemail. They're probably working somewhere else.'

'Or they've done a runner.'

McLusky dialled one more number and got no answer. 'Is it *National Just Let It Ring Day*, Jane?' He lifted his jacket off the back of his chair and shooed Austin out of his office. 'You keep trying to get hold of them.'

'Where will you be?'

'Poulimenos isn't answering his phone. I'm not taking any

chances. I'll pop round there. I'd quite like another chat with him anyway.'

'Ask him who does his gardening?'

'That, too.'

Without Austin pumping imaginary brake pedals and complaining about the speed, McLusky bombed south out of the city with a blue beacon flashing on his roof and no fear of speeding tickets. The twenty-five-year-old suspension on the heavy car was no match for McLusky's impatience, however, which meant that by the time he arrived at Bybrook View in record time, he had managed to give himself several good scares.

Through the bars he could see Poulimenos's Bentley in the garage, but the wrought-iron gate to the farm complex remained closed and ringing the bell under the intercom in the stone gatepost produced no answer. He called the number again, imagined he could hear it ring seven times across the expanse of the courtyard, then stowed his mobile in his jacket and climbed the stone wall beside the high gate. He dropped heavily on to the gravelled ground on the other side, hurting his left foot in the process. Every time he put weight on it, pain spread through the ball of his foot. He walked gingerly to the front door. There was an old-fashioned bell pull; McLusky yanked at it, which resulted in a loud chime just on the other side of the door but failed to rouse anyone. He walked around the side, paused to cup his hands and peer through the windows of the Bentley, then hobbled on to the back of the house. The door to the studio was closed; he knocked heavily, still hoping to get a response.

The door flew open with a red-faced Poulimenos filling the opening. 'What the fuck? How did you get in here?'

'I couldn't get an answer so I climbed the wall. I have bad news, I'm afraid. Nicholas Longmaid is dead.'

Poulimenos punched him hard in the face, knocking him to the ground. For a moment McLusky was stunned by the force of the blow, then he came to his senses and scrambled to his feet, ready to defend himself, but Poulimenos stood dumb-founded, rubbing the hand that had dealt the blow, looking almost as surprised as McLusky. 'Sorry. Don't know why I did that. You're bleeding. Come inside.' He turned and went in himself. McLusky gingerly dabbed at his nose and came away with blood. He didn't think it was broken, but it produced a lively pain and so did his left cheek. 'Marvellous.'

Once McLusky had followed him inside, Poulimenos fussed around him until he was seated in a chair at the long table with a damp cloth to wipe off the blood and a glass of single malt in front of him. 'Liquid inspiration. I always keep a bottle handy. Do you want me to get you some ice?'

'I take it straight.'

'For your face. It'll be quite a bruise, I'm afraid. I can't apologize enough. I don't know what made me do it. The shock. Not Nick too. What's going on? How was he killed?'

'He was shot. Shot in the back of the head while he was kneeling in front of his safe.' He should be withholding this information until Poulimenos had been eliminated as a suspect, but he felt a strange urge to share it with the man.

'That sounds like he was executed. But why? Why those two? Damn it, I thought I'd had enough to drink but I was wrong.' He fetched another glass and poured himself a large measure of Laphroaig from the bottle on the table. He took a generous swig and set the glass down heavily. 'What the fuck is going on, Inspector? Someone has killed off both my painting buddies. Does that mean I am to be next?'

McLusky sipped his whisky more cautiously. 'You might want to review your security arrangements and be careful who you open the door to. Did you know it was me?'

'No.'

'Then I could have been someone carrying a thirty-eight. Your freestone walls are climbed easily. I can arrange for police protection until we apprehend the killer.'

'No thanks, Inspector. I'm not going to barricade myself in. Do you really think someone will come after me as well?'

'Since I don't know why your friends were killed, I can't answer that. Do you perhaps have another place where you can stay? One not generally known? Relatives?'

'I have a sister. She married a Greek Australian and lives in Melbourne. And I do have a house in Cornwall. But I'm not running away, either. Anyway, whoever killed Nick and Mendy knew enough about them to get close to them. They probably know about Rosslyn Crag, too.'

'That's your place in Cornwall?'

He nodded. 'Port Isaac.'

McLusky leant back in his chair and swilled the oily liquid around his glass. 'Let's stay with the seaside for a moment. Tell me about Ben Kahn.'

For a moment the Greek's eyes widened as he stared past McLusky, then he swiped the glass from the table and drained it, refilled it and swigged some more before answering. 'Yes. We were a quartet of mad painters. And now there is one mad painter.'

'Ben Kahn drowned, isn't that right? Where?'

Poulimenos nodded. 'Cornwall,' he said hoarsely.

'How?'

'No one knows, though we were all there on that boat.'

'Whose boat was it?'

'Oh, we had hired it for the day, with a skipper, so we could paint the coast from the sea. Not a viewpoint you see very often. It was a warm day; we were all in shorts and swimming trunks. We had painted all morning, a view of Daymer Bay from seaward, had put in at Rock for lunch and painted some more in the afternoon. It was after seven when we decided to head back . . .'

'Back where?'

'Port Isaac. We were all staying at Rosslyn Crag that summer. On our way back up north, a wind sprang up. It was getting a little choppy but nothing out of the ordinary – by no means towering waves, you know; you could still have swum in it, near the boat. We were nearly home; I had put on more clothes because the wind made it a bit chilly. Then all of a sudden Ben was in the water. There was a lot of shouting and the skipper stopped the engine. I was on the starboard side with my things. I rushed to the port side and could just see Ben, already some thirty, forty yards off. The skipper turned the boat around, but Ben had vanished. He had simply slid under without a trace.'

'Did anyone go in after him?'

'We didn't. By then we had no idea where exactly he had

gone in; the boat was dancing about and there was no sign of him. We had thrown the lifesaver overboard but it was just bobbing uselessly on the water. We were panicking. It seemed to take forever to turn the boat about. The skipper informed the coastguard, but it took them a long time to get there, of course, and they turned up nothing.'

'The body?'

'His body was never found. There was some kind of investigation. The Cornish police interviewed all of us, but it was obvious it was some sort of freak accident. He'd fallen in or jumped in.'

'Had you been drinking? As a group, I mean.'

'We had had plenty of wine with our lunch – and it was a long lunch.' He gave a mirthless chuckle. 'We had another couple of bottles or so in the afternoon. Not the skipper – he was sober, as far as I know. He was devastated to lose a passenger. We were all devastated. Ben was . . . he was definitely the best painter of the four of us. Without him, it all changed. We were never the same again, us boys.'

'Just how boyish were you then?'

'It was seventeen years ago. Bloody middle-aged, but it looks like youthfulness from where I'm sitting now. Until then we took it all for granted – we were all well off, we had talent and we had friendship. His death changed everything. It became a time of legend, like someone else's past. I think that ever since that day all of us have been looking backwards, not forwards. Why your interest in Ben? It couldn't have anything to do with this.'

McLusky drummed his fingers on the table. 'I admit to a prejudice against people who disappear at sea and whose bodies don't turn up.'

'Ben didn't fake his own death! That's preposterous. Why? To what end? And we were all there.'

'But you came back without him. He was the first of you four to die. His death may have nothing to do with the two recent killings, but you can't expect me to ignore it. Do you remember the name of the investigating officer?'

Poulimenos pulled a face. 'It was seventeen bloody years ago.' He made a show of searching his mind. 'Wordsworth or Wandsworth or some such name.'

'I think it's time I had another look at Ben Kahn's death. It seems like too much of a coincidence.'

Poulimenos appeared to consider this for a moment and then he became more lively. 'Well, if you are going to Cornwall to look into it, you might as well stay right where it happened – at Rosslyn.' He reached for a bunch of keys and proceeded to twirl a Yale key with a red plastic cover off the split ring. When he slid it across the table, it clinked against McLusky's glass.

'I didn't say I was going to go down there myself,' McLusky said, not touching the key.

'Shame. You'd be doing me a favour.'

'How's that?'

'Haven't been there yet this year. You could give the place a good airing.'

'I see.'

'Look, I'm sorry I hit you. Why not allow me to make it up to you? Take the key, have a holiday at Rosslyn Crag. It's got great views of Port Isaac and the sea. There's a few bottles there I won't miss, I doubt I'll go down there this year. You're going to say that's bribery again, right?'

'You've answered your own question.' McLusky picked up the key and twirled it between his fingers until it escaped his grasp and clattered back on to the table. 'Where were you yesterday between ten and twelve midday?'

'Yesterday? You mean he was killed yesterday and you left it until today to tell me?'

'We get quite busy with hunting for killers when we find people shot in the head. Where were you yesterday between ten and twelve?'

'I was here. I didn't get up until after ten. I had a headache.'

'Did anyone see you?'

'No, I don't have an alibi for the time and I don't need one. Nick was one of my best friends. I did not kill him. Perhaps you should speak to his wife.'

'Meaning?'

'How did she take Nick's death?'

'Quite well, I believe.'

'I bet she did.'

McLusky dabbed his nose; it had stopped bleeding. He drained the last drop of whisky from his glass and got up. Poulimenos remained seated, looking down at the table, dull and deflated. When McLusky pocketed the key to Rosslyn Crag, he smiled briefly and, without looking up, said, 'Goodbye, Inspector. Thank you for coming in person to let me know.'

'I thought it best. Do I have to climb the wall again to get out?'

'Simple. Because you didn't bloody ask.' Gotts was on his hands and knees checking the connections on the automated watering system for the long border in the Mendenhall garden. He was talking to McLusky's legs beside him. 'I'm a gardener, not a bloody psychic. How was I to know that Mr Longmaid would be bumped off next? If you wanted to know who else we work for, you should have asked for my client list.'

'Are you by any chance working for a Mr Poulimenos too?'

'Who?'

McLusky, who had finally caught up with Gotts and Lucket at Woodlea House where Austin had tracked them down, felt angrier than he had for a long time. The urge to kick Gotts on the behind he was presenting to him was strong.

'There, found the bugger,' said Gotts and levered himself upright. 'Loose connection.'

'I'm happy for you.' McLusky stomped off towards the house, knowing that he was being unreasonable out of frustration but keeping his resentment well stoked for David Mendenhall, who was inside the house but had let it be known that he would not speak to the police without a solicitor. He squinted against the bright sunshine and thought he could see David watching him from behind one of the French windows; he made a beeline for it. He was right: David had been standing there, watching the inspector cross the lawn. McLusky walked up to the double doors so fast it looked as though he would walk straight through the glass without stopping. He practically threw himself against them, rattled the door knob, then cupped his hands against the glass to better see inside. 'Open up, Mendenhall, I need to talk to you.' He could just make David out standing by the door at the other end of the room, staring, not moving. He kicked the wooden frame of the French windows, making the glass rattle. 'Open the bloody door, David, or I'm taking you in for questioning.' David disappeared from view.

He jogged quickly to the front of the house in case Mendenhall tried to leave that way. Earlier, he had thoughtfully parked his car so close to David's that it would cause maximum inconvenience. Seeing no one, he thumbed his radio and requested transport for one prisoner. 'And make it a nice big van.' Then he worked the bell until the door opened a fraction and Mrs Mohr's frown appeared in the narrow gap. 'I need to speak to David, Mrs Mohr.'

She was trying to stand her ground. 'He won't speak to you, not without a lawyer. He said to tell you.'

McLusky, who was certain David was lurking just around the corner, allowed himself a malevolent smile and pushed the door wide open. 'Then would you kindly tell him that I am here to arrest him for the murders of Charles Mendenhall and Nicholas Longmaid?'

All the colour left her face and she looked uncertainly over her shoulder. David appeared in the hall behind the housekeeper. 'You're mental, McLusky. My lawyer is going to make mincemeat of you.'

'Know a good criminal lawyer, do you? That's very forward-thinking of you. David Mendenhall, I'm arresting you for . . .' He rattled off the caution and handcuffed the man who was swearing and threatening him. Mendenhall stared in disbelief at the handcuffs as though he had found someone else's hands at the end of his wrists.

Control had been as good as their word and had sent a malodorous van whose holding cage was still redolent of last night's puking public-order prisoners. David complained loudly and appeared to contemplate resisting, but McLusky had disappeared as soon as two muscular officers, utterly inured to threats and complaints, had taken charge of him. McLusky followed the van down the drive, watched from behind a window by Mrs Mohr. The van drove at a sedate pace, giving him plenty of time to mull over events and come to the conclusion that he had acted in anger and that arresting David had not been one of his better ideas.

DSI Denkhaus agreed. 'Could you not have waited until he came in to make a statement with his solicitor? You have to entertain the possibility that the son is completely innocent and therefore a victim in this crime. Have you looked at it from that side? Your father is murdered and the police arrest you for it.'

'He had no intention of coming in and making a statement, and when he said he wouldn't talk to us "without his solicitor present", he meant he wasn't going to talk to us at all.'

'How do you know that?'

'He doesn't have a solicitor. Nor did he make any effort to find one. We let him call his late father's and they were not at all keen to represent him, it seems. He's waiting for the duty solicitor now.'

The superintendent waved a hand, indicating he could go. 'OK, but go easy and by the book. If he's not involved in his father's death, he'll inherit enough money to make a nuisance of himself.'

'He's already threatened to sue me for wrongful arrest, make mincemeat out of me and promised me that my career is finished.'

'Not quite finished,' said Denkhaus when McLusky had left his office. 'More like stalled at the bottom of a steep hill, I'd say.'

In Interview Room One, McLusky soon admitted to himself that the interrogation had run on utterly predictable lines. It had taken two hours for the solicitor to turn up, nearly another hour while the solicitor, a short, blue-suited man called Green, had been closeted with his new client. By the time David, Green, McLusky and Austin sat down beside the rolling tape machine, it was late and McLusky was as irritable as David Mendenhall. He leant back on his chair, stared at David with undisguised loathing and let Austin do all the talking.

'You said in your statement that at the time of your father's death you were working and that you called your secretary from your office just after ten. Is that correct?'

'If you say so. I really can't remember. So much has happened since then.'

Austin tapped the file in front of him. 'It's here in your

statement. However, when we spoke to Sandra Lucas, your secretary, she told us that you told her in that phone call that you were at the office but she could hear noises that she described as a pub door opening and closing with music and voices.'

'Yes, I called her from outside the Red Lion; it's down the road from the office. I didn't say I *was* at the office; I said *I'd been* at the office. And I went back there, too. I only went for a swift pint because I was thirsty; we were out of teabags at the office.'

'So you weren't, for example, standing outside the Coach and Horses? Which is five minutes away from your father's house, calling your secretary, pretending you were at the office to give yourself an alibi, however feeble, for the time of your father's murder?'

'No.'

'Your secretary said the file you pretended not to be able to find was almost impossible to mislay in an office and, let's face it, a business of that size.'

'I'm not very good with paperwork.'

'What are you good with, Mr Mendenhall?'

'What kind of a question is that?'

'Moving on . . .'

Asked for his whereabouts during the most likely time of Nicholas Longmaid's murder, David said he was aimlessly driving around in the countryside, to help him think about recent events and how his life might change. 'How convenient. And naturally you didn't drive past a single CCTV camera. You didn't stop anywhere? Speak to anyone? Buy anything?' David Mendenhall hadn't.

It was nearly eight o'clock when McLusky left Albany Road station and drove home. He was irritable and hungry and needed a drink, but he would be sensible and eat before having a couple of pints at the Barge Inn, the pub opposite his flat in Northampton Street. When he reached his front door, he found a large package and some letters on the doormat where the Rossis often left his mail. Not remembering having ordered anything, he approached the package with caution. He was relieved to see that it appeared to have been delivered by Royal Mail, which meant it was unlikely to explode when picked up – McLusky had a certain expertise in packages that did. He dropped the letters on to the coffee table and turned the rectangular package round and round in his hands. It was relatively light for its size. There was no sign of the sender's name and the postmark was illegible. He fetched a knife and slid open the packaging and found copious amounts of bubble wrap. He soon guessed what he was unwrapping: a canvas by Leonidas Poulimenos. It was the painting he had pointed to when the painter had pressed him to express a preference – a sunny seascape, with parts of the coast visible and the tiny figure of a swimmer in the water. There was no note, just the painting. He propped the canvas up at one end of the sofa and sat in the opposite corner. He would have to give it back to him, naturally, or it would become a disciplinary matter should it be discovered, but why had Poulimenos, who knew this, sent it anyway?

He leant forward to examine the painting, nose close to the canvas, angling the surface so that maximum light fell on it. He thought the swimmer was a blonde-haired man, or else a broad-shouldered topless woman. There was no face; the whole figure was cleverly composed from just five or six brushstrokes. He really did like the painting. It would do his empty white wall good to have a splash of joyous colour on it. He turned the canvas around. Poulimenos had signed it on the back and dated it: 1998. McLusky swivelled it round again, looked at the lone figure. 'Hello, Ben,' he said aloud. 'Waving or drowning?'

In an effort to save some calories, McLusky had filled his freezer compartment with low-calorie ready meals, most of them curries. He ripped the packaging off a chicken jalfrezi and shoved it in the microwave, then went to check on the rest of his mail. Among the dross was a hand-delivered letter. He did not recognize the handwriting and ripped it open without any feeling of foreboding. It was written in an elegant script, and from the Rossis. They had decided to put his flat on the market and hoped it would not take him long to find somewhere else to live. He let the letter drop on to the table,

picked up his keys and left. He started on his first pint of
Guinness at the Barge Inn at the precise moment his microwave
across the street gave three forlorn bleeps to warn him that
his curry was done.

DI Fairfield had been lucky. Her airwave radio had mysteriously gone off air just seconds before control tried to call her
to say that a representative of the Italian embassy had flown
up from London to see what was being done to find Fulvia
Lamberti. Fairfield's phone also lost signal a moment after DS
Sorbie had warned her of the unexpected visit. 'Thanks, Jack,
I owe you one.' She had been on her way to Albany Road;
now she turned her car around and drove off towards
Bedminster. Fulvia's stolen scooter had just been discovered
there and carted off to Bishopsworth police station. There was
no good reason for her to go there except to keep out of the
way of the Italian diplomat. She wanted to see the scooter
only because it was a piece in the jigsaw, however insignificant.
So far it had been like trying to assemble the jigsaw puzzle
without knowing what the picture was meant to show. There
was Marcus Catlin, the ex-boyfriend, his attack on her painting
and, according to him, Fulvia's remark that everything,
including the course and her own work, was nonsense. To
Fairfield, Fulvia Lamberti sounded like a classic dropout.

The scooter was standing in the back of a van parked outside
the Bishopsworth police station. The station had been modelled
on the shoebox design popular in the 1970s and the sight of
it depressed her even more than that of Albany Road each
morning. The PC who opened the van doors for her and was
based at the station looked suitably dispirited. 'Do you want
us to do anything with it?' he asked without enthusiasm.

'Did you take fingerprints?'

'Yeah, we did. We'll let you know. I'm sure it was joyriders.
They ditched it when the tank was empty.'

The scooter had a desirable black-and-chrome retro look,
with wide handlebars and a shiny headlamp, and it was undam-
aged. Fairfield imagined Fulvia riding it, looking heroic, as
Catlin had described it, then imagined herself riding it: Kat,
the art student. She puffed up her cheeks and let out a long

breath and turned away. 'Do us a favour and send it to our gaff in Albany Road? It belongs to a misper and we're under pressure over it.'

'Sure.' The PC locked the van's doors.

'How difficult would a scooter like that be to ride?' she asked.

'That one? It's automatic, so if you can ride a bicycle then you can ride one of those.'

'Really? You know Compass Road?'

'Yeah, it's in Bedminster.'

'How far would you say it was from where the scooter was found?' Fairfield made a walking gesture with two fingers.

'What, on foot? Eight, ten minutes tops.'

'Interesting. Her ex-boyfriend lives in Compass Road.'

A few minutes later she parked her car outside the house where Marcus Catlin lived with three other students. It was a terraced house in the middle of the row in a street marginally more salubrious than Albert Park on the opposite side of the river, where Fulvia had chosen to rent a room. Just as she got ready to exit the car, the front door of the house opened and Catlin stepped outside, wheeling a mountain bike. Fairfield was there before he could swing himself in the saddle.

'What do you want here?' he asked in a whine. Then his tone changed and his hand gripping the handle bar whitened at the knuckles. 'It's not bad news, is it? You've found her?'

Fairfield made an unconcerned face. 'Do you have a driving licence, Mr Catlin?'

'Mr Catlin, is it now? I haven't. In a city, cars make no sense at all.' He patted the handlebar. 'I'm quicker on this.'

'You could get a motorbike. Or a scooter, like Fulvia. We found her scooter just a few minutes' walk from here, abandoned. Out of petrol.'

'Oh, I see. You're thinking I pinched it and rode it down here until the petrol ran out.'

'The thought had occurred to me.'

'Use your head. I go everywhere on my bike. I would have had to cycle there, then leave my bike to ride the scooter away. You're really wasting your time. And mine. I've a lecture to go to. 'Scuse me.' He wheeled the bike past her on to the road just as the door opened again and a girl emerged, also pushing a bicycle. She was clad in so many different colours that the pink bicycle appeared positively restrained. The girl frowned at her but in a friendly, inquiring way.

In the street Catlin hesitated, looking over his shoulder, suddenly reluctant to leave. 'Go on,' Fairfield called to him, 'you'll miss your lecture.' Catlin cycled off.

'He doesn't have a lecture,' the girl scoffed. 'He's just going to the shops; there's no milk as usual and it's his turn.' The girl, who had short multicoloured hair, wore a pink tie-dyed top, an orange-and-yellow skirt and Pippi Longstocking socks in white and blue stripes. Her scuffed Doc Marten boots were dark purple with a pattern of daisies.

Fairfield showed her ID and asked her name. 'I'm Bethany. It's about Fulvia? No news, then?'

'We found her scooter but that had been stolen before she disappeared. You have met her?'

'Yeah, she came out here a couple of times when they were still together.' She nodded her head in the direction Catlin had taken.

'Why do you think she finished with him?'

'She was out of his league, I think. I got the impression she wasn't sure why she was hanging out with him. And he was like a puppy dog, adoring everything she did and said and never taking his eyes off her. It would have driven me mad. Not something likely to happen to me, of course.'

Fairfield admired this honest assessment. 'What makes you say that?'

'I don't get many adoring looks.' Bethany's face was plain and pink from too much sun. 'Is it OK if I go? *I* really do have a lecture.'

'Are you on the same course as Marcus?'

A shake of the head. 'Sculpture, second year.'

Fairfield watched her cycle down the sunny road on her hand-painted boneshaker. When she turned on her mobile there was a text from Sorbie telling her that it was safe to return to the station. When she got behind the wheel of her Renault, she felt a new reluctance to return to the station as she visualized its echoing drabness. She slammed the car door shut and sat for a whole five minutes before starting the engine.

'Didn't you know you're not supposed to do that?' asked Austin.

'I thought that was takeaways.'

'It sat in your microwave for hours before you warmed it up. How are you feeling now?'

'Empty.' McLusky, sitting at the kitchen table, held the phone with one hand while miserably prodding a teaspoon at the peppermint teabag that was stubbornly floating on top of the hot water in his mug. He had been the last to leave the Barge Inn the previous night and on his return remembered the food in the microwave. After warming it up, he had wolfed it down and gone to sleep, only to be awoken two hours later by definite warning signs that his body was preparing to reject his latest food offering from all available orifices. He had spent half the night in the bathroom.

'At least you've lost weight.'

'Shut up, Jane.'

'Yes, sir. Hope you feel better tomorrow.'

'Ta. Don't mention warmed-up food to anyone.' McLusky let the mobile clatter on to the table.

By the afternoon, having eaten several slices of dry bread, McLusky felt less fragile, but his mood had not improved. So much for asking Laura to move in with him. At least he would make sure that the next flat he rented would have the central heating she required. He would be the first to admit that his living arrangements were on the primitive side – he still slept on a mattress on the floor, for instance – but memories of their life together in Southampton kept intruding into the blissful fantasies of their future life together. He had never been home long enough to really appreciate the domestic perfection of the home Laura had created for them, and he suspected that, deep down, domestic perfection bored him.

He was mulling it over while driving south to Bath, the picturesque city south-east of Bristol, with its eighteenth-century architecture and ostentatious gentility, and crime statistics Bristol could only dream of. Elaine Poulimenos, having walked out on Leonidas with two valuable paintings and her Porsche 911, had moved there. McLusky was surprised to find that it was less than ten minutes' drive from the Longmaid residence, and even less in a Porsche. Perhaps Elaine had wanted to keep close to her friend Jenny.

When he parked outside her new address in Newbridge, a northern suburb of Bath, he found that Elaine Poulimenos had exchanged life at Bybrook View for one in a small post-war end-of-terrace house with a view of hedges, brown DIY fencing, cars and a lot of other post-war terraces. There was no garage and no sign of the Porsche, but Elaine Poulimenos was in.

'Putting that up for sale was the first thing I did, Inspector,' she said with a certain pride. Elaine Poulimenos, McLusky knew, was fifty but looked a few years younger, dark and petite in bleached jeans, an amber-coloured top and leather sandals. McLusky thought that a Porsche 911 convertible would have suited Elaine perfectly; he was less sure about the IKEA furniture and the vinyl floor tiles in the square kitchen where she led him. McLusky saw with dismay that she was in the middle of preparing a meal and stifled a groan when she told him she was making a curry. 'My husband hated curry; now I make them all the time.'

'Do you?' McLusky seated himself at the bright pine kitchen table.

'And please don't call me Mrs Poulimenos; I've left that behind at last. I've gone back to my maiden name, Simmons. But you can call me Elaine,' she said, taking up her knife and dicing a shiny aubergine.

Where was she at the time of the murders? 'I was with Paul. Both times.'

'Your new partner?'

'Yes. But he won't be back for hours yet; he has some extra-curricular thing he's doing. He's a teacher.'

'I must warn you that alibis provided by husbands or partners don't count for much.'

The knife arrested an inch above a sacrificial carrot. 'I'm not a suspect, am I? Seriously? Why would I kill them both? If I had reason to kill anyone, it would have been my own husband. But I walked out instead. Ten years too late, I admit, but it's never too late to start again. Paul and I are happy. We may not want to stay here forever, of course.' She waved her knife at the window beyond which lay the drab corridor of a treeless garden. 'But I'm happier now than I can remember. And I can't say I will miss Nicholas Longmaid. I've been telling Jenny to leave him for ages. And Charles? I liked him, in a distant sort of way. I'm not a painter and that's all he ever wanted to talk about, which meant it was us girls mostly and the three boys off painting or looking at paintings or discussing paintings. Or, God forbid, discovering a new paint shop.'

'You yourself own a couple of . . . rather fine paintings, I hear.' He had already forgotten the name of the painter.

'At Christie's. The auction is next month. I'll be just as happy with a couple of reproductions.'

'There were four of the boys, as you call them. To begin with. Did you know Ben Kahn?'

'Oh, *Benjamin* . . .' She wistfully drew out the name and put down her knife as though she could not talk about him while slicing onions. 'Ben was . . . different. He was multi-dimensional and not boring at all. He could really paint. What was more, he could paint without boring the pants off everyone. It's a shame he died so young while . . .' She resumed her chopping, a little more vigorously than before.

'Did you know him well?'

'No, more's the pity. He died only a few years after they all met on that painting holiday. Drowned in Cornwall.'

'Yes, I heard. You weren't there?'

'No, just the four of them. Men doing their manly painting. It was terrible. They went out there to have a good time together in the cottage and only three of them came back. It was never the same after that. I think none of us were. It affected everything. The three who came back were not the same people that went out there.'

'Did it affect your marriage, too?'

Elaine put down the knife, faced McLusky and absent-mindedly wiped her hands on a tea towel. 'I think it did. There was a lasting sadness. Or perhaps it was guilt.'

'Why guilt?'

'For having been unable to save him. For having organized the trip in the first place. For coming back without him. Of course, it fell to us women to tell Ben's son. He had already lost his mother by then. Cancer,' she added when McLusky opened his mouth to ask.

'What happened to Ben's son?'

She reached over and flicked on the electric kettle. 'Elliot? He was brought up by Ben's sister, Hannah, in some place near Cardiff; I forget the name. I only saw him once after Ben's death, at the memorial service. But I think he moved back to Bristol and apparently he's a painter like his dad. Whether he makes a living of it I've no idea. I'm certain his dad could have, he was that good. I'm making coffee – would you like some? No? Are you sure?'

As he drove back towards Bristol, he was certain that coffee was not what he needed, but he felt dehydrated and only a couple of miles from Elaine's house he pulled into a lay-by behind a burger van and bought himself a large mug of black tea. For the first time ever, the smell of grilling bacon and stewing onions that pervaded the grassy verge failed to kindle his appetite. He stood by his car, sipped his tea and called Austin.

'Ben Kahn had a son, Elliot. After Ben's death he went to live with Ben's sister in Wales, near Cardiff, but apparently he's moved back to Bristol. Find me an address?'

McLusky almost enjoyed standing in the sun, sending tiny sips of tea down to his stomach. By the time Austin called him back, he felt a surprising eighty per cent human.

'Yes, Jane.'

'You sound a lot better.'

'I'm recovering.'

'I meant you sound a lot better than you did five minutes ago.'

'The restorative powers of a roadside mug of tea. Get on with it, Jane.'

'Found him. He's not in the city; he's in a village called Stanton Drew.'

'I know it. There's a stone circle nearby. Nice pub, too.'

'He lives at Primrose Cottage.' Austin gave the postcode.

'I found his website as well – artofbenkahn dot com, he's a painter.'

'There's a surprise.'

He pocketed his mobile and for a moment sat very still behind the wheel, then turned and felt around in the mess on the back seats until he laid his hands on his scuffed road atlas. He opened it at the appropriate page and with a biro marked off the places: Mendenhall's Woodlea House near Dundry, Poulimenos's Bybrook View near Chew Lake, Stanmore House where Longmaid had been shot. He connected them all with a heavy line. The places formed a near-perfect triangle around Elliot Kahn's Primrose Cottage. He entered his postcode into the satnav and drove to Stanton Drew.

He would easily have found the village without navigational aid. McLusky had been to the picturesque village before, on one of his rambling drives during his months-long suspension from duty. He fondly remembered the Druid's Arms, probably the only pub to have Neolithic standing stones in its beer garden. The satnav, however, urged him past the pub and the row of tiny cottages it abutted into narrow lanes on the outskirts of the village. Here, at the end of an unmade farm track between fenced-off pasture, he found Primrose Cottage, a utilitarian whitewashed house with a dark pantiled roof. The bright orange 1970s VW camper van parked in front would have barely enough room to turn around in the narrow concreted area in which the track dead-ended. As he got out of his car, McLusky could hear classical music, an orchestral piece he had heard before but could not place. Predictably, considering the volume of the music, there was no answer to his repeated knocking. The door was unlocked. With his warrant card ready to legitimize his intrusion, he entered into the tiny hall, which was made even smaller by having canvases stacked three-deep against the walls. Immediately to his left was the kitchen which smelled faintly of laundry though he saw no washing machine. He followed the music to a closed door at the back of the house and there knocked again forcefully. The door was wrenched open by a man of about thirty;

a blonde stubble of beard provided contrast to his deeply tanned narrow face. 'What the . . . oh.' His eyes fell on the proffered warrant card. The man nearly filled the narrow door but behind him McLusky could make out an easel and a nude female model sitting on a chair. The music was now loud enough to make communication challenging. Elliot Kahn wore jeans and T-shirt lightly spattered with paint and pushed a hand into his sun-bleached mop of hair, as an aid to thinking. 'Oh, yeah, of course, perhaps we should . . .' The young woman broke her pose to wrap herself into a dustsheet and turn the music down. 'Thanks, Berti,' said Kahn, and to McLusky he suggested, 'Talk in the kitchen?' McLusky walked to the kitchen, blinking away the after-image of the naked woman.

Kahn set a whistling kettle on the stove which was fed gas from a large butane bottle beside it. He turned the valve and lit the gas with a cook's match. 'You're here because of Charles Mendenhall, aren't you?'

'How did you hear about his death?'

'My auntie Hannah. She read it in the paper. A paper is another thing we don't get out here,' he said, nodding at the gas bottle.

'Did you hear about Nicholas Longmaid's death, too?'

The news made no visible impression on Kahn as he shook tea leaves from a tin into a brown teapot. 'No. He was another of my dad's painting colleagues. Was he also murdered?'

'He was. We're working on the assumption that they were killed by the same person.'

'And you came out here because you think I had something to do with it?'

'We're talking to anyone even remotely connected to the victims.'

'Remote is right. I haven't seen any of them since my father disappeared eighteen years ago and I can't say I've thought about them much recently. A lot back then, but not recently.'

'You're a painter, like them, and like your father.'

'No, not like them. My father was a doctor. Painting was a hobby for him. I'm a professional painter.'

'Do you make a living from it?'

'If you can call it that. If I didn't own this place outright, I'd be stacking shelves in a supermarket; as it is, I'm surviving.' He had poured out three mugs of tea while he spoke. 'I'll just take one of these through to Berti.' But the girl – McLusky revised down her age by a few years – saved him the trouble as she appeared in the doorway, expertly wrapped in her white cotton sheet. Kahn handed her the mug. 'I'll be back in a moment; have some tea.' The girl took the mug, said 'Ta' and padded back to the studio.

McLusky blew on his own tea. 'When you spoke about your father, you said "the day he disappeared", not "died".'

Kahn shrugged. 'Habit. His body never turned up. I was a kid. I didn't want my dad to be dead. No body, not dead. To me, he had mysteriously disappeared. As far as I was concerned, they were all wrong about him. It took me a while to accept that he wasn't coming back.'

'It must have been especially hard for you. You had already lost your mother.'

'I hardly remembered my mother; she died when I was three.'

'What do you think happened to your father?'

'You're asking me? I wasn't there.'

'Two of those who were are now dead.'

'I don't see any connection. Do you? After all this time?'

Back in the car, McLusky asked himself the same question, not for the first time, and answered himself that he had nothing else to go on. He started the engine and realized that with the old camper van in the yard there was no space to turn the big Mercedes around. He gave himself a crick in the neck reversing the two hundred and fifty yards back to the road. As he sat massaging his twisted muscles, he imagined himself inside the triangle of victims and suspects. Mrs Mohr lived in Dundry, which was part of the triangle, and David Mendenhall, who she now presumably worked for, had moved into his father's house. The gardeners, Gotts and Lucket, lived in Bristol, outside the triangle. To the only other place of possible significance not inside the triangle, McLusky had the key: Rosslyn Crag.

EIGHT

'*Cornwall*?' Laura sounded doubtful.

'Oh, come on,' McLusky coaxed, 'it's nearly the end of term anyway and it's only a long weekend.' He sensed Laura weakening in the pause that followed but barely dared breathe, holding his office phone very still. This could decide their whole future together. If Laura agreed to spend a whole weekend with him in romantic Cornwall in a windswept – or so he assumed – cottage by the sea *and it went well*, then he might have come a step further towards persuading her to move in with him. Once he had found somewhere to move into.

'I have an extended essay to write; I can't really afford to take time off now. Does it have to be now?'

McLusky had not been entirely frank about the provenance of the cottage nor about the fact that he himself would be working, at least for part of their stay. 'I only have the use of it for a while. Bring your books and laptop. What's wrong with writing your essay with a sea view between meals of excellent seafood?'

It was probably the mention of seafood that had swung it, McLusky thought as he steered his Mercedes through the narrow hedgerow-funnelled country lanes with the windows down and Laura lecturing on Neolithic Cornwall, burial sites, menhirs and quoits. She had been happily slouched in her seat with one foot up on the dashboard and only stopped her lecture when, at the end of their long drive, McLusky had found Rosslyn Crag, on the high ground overlooking the sea near Port Isaac. She sat up. 'Is this it? Are you sure?'

'That's what it says.'

'You said "cottage". This is huge. Look at it. The conservatory is as big as a cottage.'

McLusky had to admit that Rosslyn Crag did not correspond in any way to how he had described it to Laura. Had it been his own defective imagination or had it been Poulimenos who had led him to imagine a quaint little country cottage?

Rosslyn Crag turned out to be a substantial nineteenth-century house with a long conservatory constructed from decorative ironwork of the same period. The garden was surrounded by a waist-high dry-stone wall that carried on along the pasture to either side of the property until it disappeared out of sight around a bend in the road. The drive from the road to the house was washed-out gravel and narrow enough to demand caution in a large car like McLusky's Mercedes or the house owner's Bentley. It was when he had left the car on a patch of grass and stretched his aching limbs that he saw why the house was here; the spot commanded views of the sea and a stretch of rugged coastline, and provided a tiny glimpse of the little harbour town of Port Isaac. There were only two trees in the surrounding garden, both sheltering from the prevailing wind in the lee of the house.

'So let me get this right,' said Laura, dropping her holdall at his feet. '*Some chap* you know through work said, "I've a *little pad* in Cornwall. Go and spend the weekend", right? Who is he, the chief constable?'

'He's someone I interviewed about the case, and when I said I needed to go to Cornwall as part of the investigation, he gave me the keys to this.'

'We're here as *part of your investigation*?'

McLusky squirmed a little. 'I need to ask someone a couple of questions, that's all; it won't take more than a couple of hours – half an afternoon, tops. Anyway, you'll be too busy writing your essay on . . . on . . .'

'New evidence for changing burial practices in post-Roman Britain.'

'Yeah, that.'

The inside of the house had the faint smell of holiday homes everywhere – an empty, underused smell that can only be detected in the first half hour, after which it fades into memory. The house was simply furnished, almost stark, with many dark mahogany pieces that looked pre-war but utilitarian, as if all of them were rejects from Nicholas Longmaid's antiques business. 'Cheerful seaside cottage,' said Laura, but she passed a caressing arm around McLusky's waist as she said it. Upstairs they chose the master bedroom with the best sea views and the conservatory below the two windows. The kitchen was fully equipped but twenty years out of date. They found that all the downstairs windows had locks but the key could not be found. They managed to unlock the conservatory which was empty apart from a stack of striped deckchairs and some rusting iron garden furniture in one corner.

In the sitting room and dining room the walls were hung with many paintings, mostly unframed seascapes and coastal views. Laura ran a thoughtful finger over furniture and the top edges of paintings, then held it accusingly under McLusky's nose. 'Didn't you tell me your chap said you'd be doing him a favour using the place since no one had been out here this year? Someone was here – two days ago, I'd say. Maybe three, no more. And they gave the place a good dusting. This place has not been unvisited for six months. I know my dust.'

'I remember it. You're wasted as an archaeologist; you should go into forensics instead.'

'Much the same thing. I might become a forensic archaeologist – you never know.'

'He must have a cleaner. With a place this big, he'd have to or he'd spend all his holidays tidying.' McLusky didn't see anything mysterious in the lack of dust, but he realized it meant that someone else, probably a local, must have a key to the house.

They had brought with them supplies of milk and tea but nothing beyond that. 'I'll have to go out in a minute; I'll buy something for tonight on the way back,' McLusky promised.

'You'll do no such thing! You'll take me out and buy me dinner. Seafood, remember? Good for the brain. By all means get something for breakfast, though. You realize there's no phone here? No Wi-Fi and' – she held up her mobile accusingly – 'one flickering bar. How do people work out here?'

'In peace? It's a holiday cottage. House.'

'What if I break my leg?'

'Smoke signals. They'll see it in Port Isaac.'

*　　*　　*

Brian Wagstaff had been known to his friends in the Devon and Cornwall constabulary as 'Waggy' or simply 'the Wag'. He had retired a lowly detective inspector to a cheerless bungalow on the outskirts of Rock. There were no sea views, no flowerbeds in the windswept garden, and the car on the concrete hardstanding beside the house was a ten-year-old Ford with a dent in the bonnet. The net curtains on his windows had yellowed from cigarette smoke; when Waggy Wagstaff opened the door to McLusky, he had a hand-rolled cigarette in the corner of his mouth. It was short enough to threaten his moustache. Everything about him appeared grey, from his fragile comb-over to his shoes. 'DI McLusky?'

'Liam.'

'Call me Waggy – everyone does.' He led the way into the kitchen. 'Hope you don't mind, I'm in the middle of brewing more beer,' he said and coughed richly. He laid his cigarette, no more than an inch long, on the rim of a large and full ashtray on the kitchen table. He would later split the cigarette end open and save the tobacco in a tin to mix with fresh tobacco. There was a half-empty pint of dark beer on the table.

The electric kettle had clicked off as they entered and now Wagstaff emptied it into a large plastic brew bin and began stirring the sludge at the bottom with a long-handled spoon. There were four plastic beer barrels lined up by the door. McLusky rightly concluded that DI Wagstaff was systematically smoking and drinking himself to death. 'You've come about this Kahn business. After all this time. Did you know Kahn means "old boat" in German? I did German at school, see. Kahn. He fell from an old boat and drowned.'

'There was never any doubt about that?'

'Plenty of doubt, believe me. You go out on a boat and come back one short? Of course there'll be bloody doubt.'

'The body was never found and it worries me. Two of Ben Kahn's painting buddies have been killed.'

'How?' Wagstaff's interest was roused.

'Shot with a thirty-eight.'

'It's eighteen years later and they were shot. If they were both found drowned in the bath, I'd believe it. Any indication there's a connection other than that they once went on a boat trip together?'

'Not yet. You never suspected anyone in particular?'

'All of them. None of them. We couldn't find a motive and couldn't prove anything anyway. All the witnesses said they were a happy bunch. They had lunch here in Rock that day. Witnesses all said they were laughing and drinking, and there appeared to be no tensions. And without a body and all five sticking to the same story, it was death by misadventure, end of.'

'What do you mean "all five"? Who else was on board?'

'Apart from the painting party, just the skipper and his son.'

'His son? I didn't read anything about a son in the statements.'

'He was a boy. Fourteen? Fifteen? He didn't see anything; he was doing something in the wheelhouse when it happened. I think he may have been at the helm. Can't remember.'

McLusky had his notebook out. 'The name of the boat was . . .'

'*Destiny*. Which it was. For one of them, anyhow.'

'Is the owner still about? Tigur, was it?'

'John Tigur, known as Jonti. He's no longer with us.'

'Oh? How did he die?'

'Car accident.'

'Not suspicious?'

'Drunk as the proverbial. Drove into a wall. They all drink and drive round here. In Cornwall, who's to stop them?'

'Is the son running the boat now?'

'Boat broke its moorings in that big storm three years ago and smashed itself into driftwood.' Wagstaff was done stirring and was now noisily topping up the brew bin with cold water. 'But the son's still about. Mickey. Michael. Last thing I heard he was living or working in Port Isaac.'

'I'll look him up. In the meantime, I'll be looking for a good place to eat in Port Isaac. Any ideas?'

Wagstaff looked him up and down. 'Try the Mote; you'll be all right there.'

'You go there a lot?'

'Me? Not on my pension. And I don't eat seafood. But you'll be all right there,' he said again.

'Seafood, eh?' McLusky saw himself out while Wagstaff

sprinkled dried yeast over his frothy brew, paused to cough, then sprinkled some more.

Back at Rosslyn Crag, McLusky found Laura fast asleep in her bikini bottoms and T-shirt in one of the deckchairs outside the conservatory. It was late afternoon but still very warm. He woke her with a kiss and within minutes had persuaded her that, for health reasons alone, she'd be much better off upstairs in bed. Three hours later they screamed together under a cold shower when they realized they had no idea how to procure hot water from the groaning taps.

By the time they were ready to go out, the weather had changed and grey clouds had pushed in from the Atlantic, threatening rain. They left the Mercedes in the car park on the hill and walked down into Port Isaac; it was a warm evening and even McLusky managed to enjoy it, despite the fact that Laura had squirmed out of his arm to walk in her own step beside him as the first fine raindrops fell. They passed a bird-watcher on the way, kitted out in rainproof and hood, busy staring through binoculars, standing elbows akimbo right in their path; they passed around the figure on either side and giggled conspiratorially. The holiday season was not in full swing yet and the village, with its whitewashed houses, narrow alleys and slipway port, not yet stripped of all its romance by the brightly coloured hordes of high season. McLusky, knowing that he had to deliver a flawless performance if he wanted to impress Laura, had booked an upstairs table with a view of the harbour at the Mote, the restaurant closest to the water. As it was high tide, it was almost like dining in the harbour, with the waves below the window and the wind throwing moisture against the window pain. When Laura had ordered mussels to start and lobster to follow, McLusky happily said, 'Same for me.'

While they waited for their food to arrive, their conversation moved to holidays they had taken together. Their last one had been in Italy. 'But you're not really a museum person, are you?' Laura said. 'Me, I could spend days in a museum as long as it has *sculptures of aliens from the planet Zorg*. I get the feeling I don't have your full attention, DI Liam.'

'Look casually to your left. No, *your* left. Out the window,' said McLusky, himself not looking and returning to his food. 'See the figure on the edge of the slipway on the opposite side?'

'Looks like the birdwatcher we passed on the way down. Seems to be watching *us* at the moment or maybe there's a rare bird sitting on the roof. Should we wave?'

When McLusky looked up again, the figure was turning away. He had missed the opportunity to catch a glimpse of the face. 'Gone now,' he commented.

'Hey, Inspector. We're having a good time, the house is great, the views are to die for, this lobster is excellent. You don't have to lay on a mystery to make it complete. It's just a birdwatcher.'

Later that night Laura worked out how to procure hot water from the old-fashioned boiler, which meant the next day started well enough: McLusky had a very long shower and then, with hair still damp, cooked a cholesterol feast for their breakfast which they ate at the rusty table in the conservatory just as the sun broke through the clouds. Laura felt duty-bound to tease him about his recent weight gain. 'No wonder you've piled on the pounds, hon, if this is how you breakfast.'

'I don't normally. It's usually coffee and Danish.'

'It's Special K for you from now on.'

McLusky feared it might come to that.

He left her outside in a deckchair typing on her laptop with the wind noisily flicking the pages of her notebook in the grass beside her. Michael Tigur was not easily found. McLusky had imagined that the son of the *Destiny*'s skipper would be working on another tourist or fishing boat, but Michael Tigur had emphatically turned his back on boat life when he took a job as a driver for a fruit and vegetable wholesaler. After several phone calls McLusky managed to catch up with him at the Slipway Hotel where Tigur had dropped off crates of produce for the kitchen, his last delivery of the morning. They drank tall beakers of coffee outside on the terrace where Tigur could keep an eye on his delivery van in case it blocked the traffic through the narrow lane. Tigur was the same age as

McLusky but looked careworn; he had complex Celtic tattoos on his arms, pierced ears and a pierced nose, though his employer insisted he wear no studs or earrings while at work. His hair was dark and short and he looked as though he spent most of his life indoors.

'I was never happy on that boat. It was child labour, really. I had to help my dad run the bloody thing because it didn't make enough money to pay someone. I'm a lousy sailor, much happier on land. I mean, I don't even surf.'

'But back then you were crewing for your father. Did you often take people out?'

'Yeah, quite a bit. Around Daymer Bay, up the estuary, across to Padstow . . .'

'Tell me what happened on that day.'

Tigur puffed up his cheeks and let the air out slowly, then fortified himself with a sip of coffee. 'I'm not really sure, to be honest. I thought about it a lot. *Then*, I mean. And I never could make up my mind afterwards. But it was obvious something weird had happened because my dad told me not to say anything.'

'About what?'

'He said to say I hadn't seen anything or heard anything. When the police asked me, I said I was in the wheelhouse facing the other way. No one asked me a thing after that and I wasn't at the inquest, either.'

'So what did you see?'

'Well, that's the thing: it sort of doesn't make sense. My dad was at the helm. I was beside the wheelhouse and they were near the stern where they had set themselves up to paint. Their things were lying all over the place, their paint boxes and stuff – quite dangerous, if you ask me. You don't leave stuff lying about on a boat because you'll go arse over tit and you're overboard before you know it. The four of them were talking and I thought they were having an argument, but you couldn't hear anything with the engine and the wind. It had turned a bit choppy and I wasn't feeling great. But one thing I did hear, because it was shouted, twice. One of them shouted, "My daughter", like it was a question. Twice.'

'Which one?'

'I've no idea. Three of them had their backs to me; only Mr Kahn was facing my way, but I couldn't see his face. A moment later he was in the water, with all his clothes on.'

'With all his clothes on?'

'Yeah, because of the wind. Before they all had their tops off and just wore shorts, but it had cooled down a lot. So he was fully dressed.'

'Did he jump in?'

'That's what I can't make up my mind about. His son kept asking me that over and over, but I really can't say. There was a sudden—'

'Wait! What do you mean "his son"? When did he ask you that? Back then?'

'No, couple of weeks back. His name's Elliot. Came down here. Don't know how he found me – same way you did, I expect. Suddenly, he was there in the pub when I was trying to have a quiet drink, quizzing me about that day and about his dad.'

'And he'd come here especially to find you and ask you?'

'He said he was here for the weekend. He was with his girlfriend. I somehow had the feeling it was her who put him up to finding out more about his dad.'

'What did his girlfriend look like?'

Tigur's eyebrows rose and his eyes widened. 'Dark hair. Very pretty. *Very.*'

'OK, tell me what you told him.'

'As I said, they were all in the stern. There was a sudden movement. They all sort of moved but whether they were trying to stop him from jumping in or pushed him overboard I couldn't say. And my dad never talked to me about it – just told me to shut up about the whole thing.'

'What did everyone do next?'

'I went to look. Mr Kahn was in the water, already quite a way behind the stern. We had a following wind and we were doing quite a few knots. I called to my dad and he stopped the engine. That made the boat pitch even more; it does that when you have no way on – you just bob like a cork. He threw a lifesaver in the water – you know, one of those red-and-white rings that float, but Kahn wasn't going towards it.'

'Perhaps he didn't see it?'

'Oh, no, he was looking at us when it went in; with the swell he went out of sight, on and off, but he would have seen the boat.'

'He would have known which way to swim.'

'Oh, yeah, but that was just the thing. He was swimming the wrong way.'

'What, away from the boat?'

'Away from the boat but not just the boat. He was swimming away from the land, too. He was swimming out to sea.'

'Could he have lost his bearings?'

'How? We were a few hundred yards from the shore – you couldn't miss seeing the cliffs. No, he must have known which way he was swimming. Dad turned the boat around and gave it full revs to go after him, but we never saw him. He had gone. Called the coastguard and all that, but they never found him, either. His body didn't turn up – nothing. It bugged me for quite a while, that.'

'I can imagine. And now it'll bug me.'

'Sorry.'

'Why do you think your father wanted you not to talk to anyone about it?'

Tigur leant back in his chair, folded his arms across his chest and looked past McLusky towards the sea. 'The weirdness of it. I think he was mainly thinking about the business. You don't want a reputation that weird shit happens on your boat, especially with a stupid name like *Destiny*. Death by misadventure was the verdict. And it never did the business any harm.'

'Why was nobody wearing a life jacket? That would have saved his life, surely?'

'The *Destiny* was a big boat, which meant it wasn't compulsory. And it's not popular with passengers. But yeah, that might have saved him. If you're asking me, though, that bloke didn't want to be saved. Either that or he was trying to disappear.'

Tigur stuck an arm out of the window to give a wave as he drove off in his green-and-white VW van, relieved to see the detective inspector recede in his mirror. Until Elliot Kahn and his girlfriend had turned up, he had pushed the memory of that day away so that it had become like a tiny buoy, bobbing far out to sea, barely visible. He could never forget it entirely, with one of the men still owning the house above the village. Only last night he had seen lights at the house. Now it all felt again as though it had happened yesterday. Tigur left behind a pensive McLusky. He walked down the slipway on to the sands. The port at low tide looked messy. Cars were parked on the sand above the water line and fishing boats that had not gone out lay stranded on the sands further down. A couple of women were digging in the wet sand close to the water – for worms or cockles or something like that, he assumed. He looked up but could not see Rosslyn Crag from down here. Tigur had provided him with few answers and a lot of questions he had not asked before. He pulled out his mobile. 'Well, what do you know?' His mobile showed two bars. It also showed that it was almost flat; McLusky had forgotten to take his charger. He called Austin at Albany Road, let it ring a few times, remembered it was Saturday lunchtime and put his mobile away. All he really wanted was to run all he had just heard past the DS because it usually helped him make up his mind, but he would not bother him with it at the weekend. Perhaps he himself should not bother with it until Monday morning, either. He walked up to the water's edge. Tigur's account differed from that of Poulimenos. In Tigur's version, all four men had been standing together in the stern when Kahn went into the water. Poulimenos's version had him, not Tigur, beside the wheelhouse, unable to see what had happened. Was Poulimenos lying or had Tigur remembered it wrong? Or was Tigur lying even now? Did he know exactly what happened on the *Destiny* that day?

Kahn plunged into the water. It was choppy and he swallowed a mouthful of cold seawater immediately and coughed. He cringed as he realized that the propeller of the Destiny might easily have caught him, but already the boat was drawing away from him, fast. The three painters were gesticulating, but he could not hear what they were shouting and he did not want to. He wanted to swim away from them, as fast as possible, as far away as possible, until he could never make it back to shore, could no longer change his mind to end it all.

McLusky thought of the painting standing in his soon-to-be-sold flat – the lonesome swimmer in the empty bay. No boat, no lifesaver bobbing on the waves. Did Kahn swim away from the boat in order to kill himself or because he was afraid of staying on the boat? Did he swim away hoping to hide? Did he survive and come ashore somewhere? McLusky did not like dead people who did not leave their bodies behind. 'Bastard,' he said to the wind.

He realized that feeling resentful towards everyone he came in contact with in the course of his work, whether dead, alive or missing, had become a normal state of being for him. His conscious effort later that day of 'being in the moment', as Laura would put it, was rewarded with a cosy, intimate evening over a bottle of probably quite expensive wine from the ample store in the pantry. Even the choosing of the wine, however, had engaged his brain in forensic speculation. There were at least six dozen bottles, probably all of vintage quality, like this 2009 Château Pontet-Canet he had chosen, purely because it was the youngest bottle there. None of the bottles he had pulled from the racks in the hope of finding something cheap and familiar-looking had the slightest speck of dust on them.

'Would you dust bottles of wine?' he asked when he poured the last drops into her glass.

'Only if I felt more deranged than usual.' Laura's antisepticism, as he had termed it, had at times been irritating. 'Not that I have a lot of wine standing around these days, as you know.'

'If you were a cleaner – and I doubt Poulimenos came out here to dust in person – would you dust your employer's wine bottles?'

Laura shook her head. 'Not even sure dusting vintage wine bottles is the done thing.' With their limbs cosily intertwined in a corner of the sofa, they both sipped from the dark rich liquid. 'What's worrying you now, hon?'

'We shouldn't really be here.'

'I had wondered.'

'I have a sinking feeling that bringing you here was a mistake.'

'Oh, thank you.'

'I mean, for both of us to come here.'

Laura sat up straight and looked at him closely. 'Do you

mean you being here, us being here, could be seen as illegal in some way?'

McLusky sighed. 'It could be construed as corruption, I suppose. If they didn't know me and wanted to make something of it.'

'Or if they did know you but wanted to drop you in it. This is grand but I'd have been happy with bed and breakfast, you know.' She leant forward, rested her elbows on her knees and twirled her nearly empty glass between her fingers. 'Wasn't going to tell you. I didn't want to spoil things. But while we're busy spoiling things anyway, I might as well tell you. When I was out there sunbathing this afternoon, a gust of wind carried a sheet of notepaper off. I jumped up to catch it and there was the birdwatcher again. Definitely watching me this time.'

McLusky was alert and businesslike now. 'Where was he standing?'

'Behind the dry-stone wall, just at the end where it curves out of sight.'

'Can you describe him?'

'No, not really. Same waterproof, hood up – in the sunshine, mind – binoculars. I mean, she was further away than at the restaurant and disappeared as soon as I gave her the finger.'

'*Her*? You said "she" and "her".'

'Did I? Couldn't see the face. Could have been a woman. Something in the way she moved her body. Or her head.'

'You didn't see where he or she disappeared to?'

'You've seen my bikini; you don't go chasing after strangers in that.'

'Ah, yeah, probably not.' He paused, as if listening to the empty house. 'If I hadn't just drunk half a bottle of wine, I think I'd want to leave tonight.'

'Really? OK, we'll leave first thing. You don't have any more people to see, do you?'

Despite the wine he had consumed, he found it difficult to get to sleep. When he did, he found himself back at the window table at the Mote, alone, with the sea rapidly rising all the way to the windowsill. He could feel the house vibrating as the sea tore at its foundations. He woke to Laura shaking him and hissing in his ear.

'Liam, *Liam*, wake up.'

'What, what?'

'Burglars. Someone's breaking in.'

'Are you sure?'

'Someone smashed a window in downstairs. How could you have slept through that?'

McLusky swung himself out of bed and quickly slipped into his trousers. He found his pepper spray in his leather jacket and moved to the door. There were no more noises but he thought he could feel the intrusion, the changed atmosphere in the house as he opened the door a crack to listen again.

'Be careful, hon.' Laura had remained in bed under the doubtful protection of the duvet.

McLusky gave an ironic grunt and tiptoed down the stairs, bracing himself between wall and banister to lighten his footsteps on the wooden stairs. He thought he could see a dim light now, probably a torch being moved back and forth. If it was a lone burglar, his appearance and a shout of 'Police!' might get rid of him. He really had no intention of complicating his situation by apprehending the intruder. He had not quite reached the bottom of the stairs when he realized that his situation had turned more than complicated. He could smell smoke. He hit the light switch at the bottom of the stairs and saw grey smoke seep from under the sitting-room door which they had left open but was now closed.

Laura's voice from upstairs pre-empted his own call. 'Liam, I think the house is on fire, I can see it flickering on the lawn!'

At that moment the varnish on the sitting-room door shrouded itself in flame like a demonic apparition, so quick was the progress of the fire. 'Don't come down! Jump from the window! Do it now! I'm coming up!' Acrid smoke overtook him on his race up the stairs and he coughed his way across the bedroom. A splintering bang below his feet blew out the electrics and left him in near darkness.

Laura was crouching in the open window, in her underwear. 'I'm not sure I can do it. It's the conservatory roof. What if I break through?'

'Slide down carefully. The downstairs is on fire; we can't get out any other way!' He could feel the heat under his feet. Smoke rose from the floorboards. He ran back to where he knew his leather jacket lay. He stumbled over his boots, picked them up, grabbed blindly at clothes and, with a random selection, stumbled over to the window where Laura, with a small cry of dismay, let herself slide on to the sloped glass roof. He flung out of the window what he was holding and slid along the glass roof after her on to the fire-lit lawn.

The entire downstairs was on fire. The flames danced most brightly behind the sitting-room windows which had blown out or been smashed in. Black smoke and flames licked the outside of the house. Somewhere behind them a car engine revved and receded. Unseen, another window blew out. 'Let's get further away from the house!' McLusky scraped his belongings off the grass and stumbled away into the flickering darkness, with Laura beside him, moaning and muttering. He found his mobile phone. It had gone flat and was entirely unresponsive.

'Now what?' asked Laura. She had to speak loudly to make herself heard over the roar of the flames.

'Oh, someone's going to see the fire, surely. Probably already called the fire brigade out.' McLusky was pulling on what clothes he had managed to grab, which, by some miracle, appeared to be all of them, bar one sock.

'Well, I'm glad you're all right for clothes!' said Laura.

'I thought you'd chucked yours out before you jumped. Here, take my jacket.'

But Laura stood motionless on the lawn, her disconsolate face lit brightly by the fire. 'All my stuff. My favourite summer dress. And my laptop. I'd left it downstairs.'

McLusky hung his leather jacket over her shoulders but she shrugged it off.

'My essay! My funeral rites. *Cremated!*'

McLusky trod carefully. 'Did you back it up?'

'Yeah, but there's no broadband so I stuck it on a memory stick. *That's also cremated.* What the fuck happened, Liam? If this is your idea of a romantic weekend, I can do without it!'

Another window blew out, this time at the front of the house. 'The car!' McLusky sprinted across to his car. It was parked close enough to the house for the paint to blister in the furnace temperatures on the driver's side. Shielding his face from the ferocious heat, he climbed in, managed to get the overheated engine to start and reversed away on to the grass, leaving the path clear for the fire brigade.

By the time the two fire engines arrived, blue lights flashing and their enormous diesel engines growling, the house was completely alight, an enormous beacon on top of the cliff, visible for miles. While the firefighters rolled out hoses and began to dampen down the blaze, one fire officer questioned McLusky and Laura, who had gratefully climbed into a paper suit and shoes the man had offered her.

'Anyone left inside? Anyone hurt?'

'It's just us and we're fine,' said McLusky. Laura, who was standing two paces away from him with her arms folded across her chest, managed wordlessly to convey that *fine* was an unwise expression. 'We're unharmed, anyway,' McLusky modified.

'Any idea what started it?'

'I heard a window breaking downstairs,' said Laura in a flat voice. 'Two minutes later the house was on fire.'

'Did you see anyone?'

'No. But I did hear a car drive off after I landed on the grass.'

'What kind of car engine was it? Petrol, diesel?' McLusky asked.

'I'm not an expert on cars, but it actually sounded just like an old Beetle engine. I used to have one – my first car, in fact. It was terrible.'

'Possible Beetle engine – that's useful.' The fire officer made a note on his iPhone. 'You suspect anyone?'

McLusky shifted uncomfortably. 'Not offhand.'

'You're not the owners, are you?'

'No. Borrowed it from an acquaintance.'

The flashing blue beacons reflected off Laura's grey paper suit. 'He will be pleased,' she said, staring into what was now just the burnt-out shell of a house.

'We have the owner listed as a Leonidas Poulimenos.' He read the name slowly off his mobile. 'Have you informed him yet?'

'My phone's flat.'

'We'll contact him in the morning for you. Do you have anywhere else to stay?'

'Just get me home, Liam,' Laura said.

'That may not be possible,' said the fire officer, 'until the police have had a chance to talk to you. Especially if it turns out to be arson.'

Just then one of the firefighters came over to report just that. 'Strong smell of accelerant from one of the downstairs rooms – probably petrol, and plenty of it. We found the remains of a plastic petrol can.' He nodded at the civilians. 'Someone had it in for you, I'd say.'

'Or the owner,' said McLusky.

'Well, that settles it: you'll have to stay until the morning.'

'I don't think that'll be necessary.' McLusky produced his warrant card. 'I'll be in touch with my colleagues in Wadebridge first thing in the morning.'

The officer agreed, took their details and told them that they had been very lucky. Moments later McLusky manoeuvred his car past the fire engines and on to the road and, not feeling lucky, began the long drive back to Bristol with Laura pretending to be asleep beside him in the passenger seat.

NINE

In the margins of her page-a-day diary on her office desk DI Kat Fairfield drew the figure of a tiny naked woman, seated on a chair. The minute tremor that too many cappuccinos from her own little espresso machine had given her translated to quite a tremble at the end of her biro. She was drawing from memory while thinking of yesterday's life drawing class. Last night she had thought that despite the lopsided, not always well-proportioned drawings she ended up with, her drawing class was one of the few things she looked forward to each week. She already dreaded the summer break which now loomed close. A knock on the door made her quickly close her diary.

It was DS Sorbie. 'Prints came back from the scooter. The idiots who picked the thing up didn't think for one minute we might want the prints off it, even though they knew it was stolen, so their paws were all over it.'

'I despair,' Fairfield said matter-of-factly.

'But they got them eliminated and what's left is a lot of Lamberti's own prints and a lot of prints by one other person, possibly our thief's.'

'*Or* a friend's *or* a mechanic's. Right, go and take Marcus Catlin's prints. No, wait, I'll come with you, I want to see his face.'

In truth, Fairfield wanted to get out of the office, away from the endless bureaucratic tedium, and breathe some turpentine-laced art college air.

Spike Island studios were busy, perhaps due to the imminent end-of-term assessments. They made themselves known, then went in search of Catlin. Today every studio appeared to have its full complement of painters. 'It's probably like last-minute essays – last-minute paintings,' Sorbie scoffed. They found Catlin at work in front of a new painting, in the same pose as Fairfield had seen him before, e-cigarette in one hand, loaded brush in the other, staring intently at the few dark marks already on the canvas.

When he noticed the two officers close in on him, he turned to face them, arms by his side, legs slightly parted; like a gunslinger facing the sheriffs, Fairfield thought. 'Cue tumble-weed,' she murmured.

'*What*?' asked Catlin, whose hearing was excellent.

'Is there somewhere private we could go?' she asked.

'Not really.'

'Then perhaps your colleagues could leave us for a bit?' Sorbie said loudly.

'They're busy,' said Catlin, addressing himself to Fairfield. 'And I have nothing to hide. Do you have news about Fulvia?'

'Not for you,' said Sorbie. 'We've come to take your fingerprints.'

Catlin lobbed his brush on to the painting table and pressed his hand deep into the pool of paint on his palette. He advanced on Sorbie. 'Where d'you wannit?'

'Very funny, sir. Would you mind cleaning and drying your hands please?'

Catlin complied, slowly and thoroughly cleaning both his hands. He frowned at Sorbie's fingerprint device. 'What, no ink pads and stuff?'

'We went digital ages ago,' Sorbie bragged. 'Perhaps you should try it. Less messy. This will tell us instantly if you're worth arresting or not.' One by one, Sorbie scanned all ten of Catlin's fingers. The match was almost instant. 'Your fingerprints are all over Fulvia's scooter. Can you explain that?'

'Yeah,' said Catlin. 'I used to sit on it while having a smoke, when she'd park it here' – he hooked a thumb – 'outside the studios.'

Sorbie knew that this was entirely plausible since, according to his MobileID device, only four of Catlin's fingerprints matched, while eighteen further prints found on the scooter were by a person unknown.

Catlin picked up his brush again. 'That it?'

Sorbie was about to tell him that it wasn't when Carol West, the fine arts tutor, appeared in the door. 'Ah, I'm glad I caught you. Do you think I might have a word?' She retreated into the corridor.

'Don't go anywhere,' Fairfield told Catlin. 'We're not finished.'

In the corridor West beckoned them away from the door until they were out of earshot. 'I'm glad you're here,' she said quietly. 'I was just thinking of calling you. Another of our students has gone missing – Bethany Hall.'

'Hang on, I've met her,' said Fairfield. 'Wears really bright clothes, does sculpture.'

West looked surprised. 'Yes, that's her. She hasn't been seen for days and she's not answering her mobile. She's missed an important tutorial and her essay deadline.'

'She shares a house with Marcus Catlin.'

'Yes. I only realized that this morning when I was about to write to her about her absences.'

'Have you contacted the parents?' asked Sorbie. 'Perhaps she went home early.'

West gave him a puzzled look. 'This isn't a primary school. Our students are over eighteen. In fact, contacting the parents without the student's permission would be quite improper. Of course, you probably wouldn't worry about that.'

'Too right.'

Fairfield shot Sorbie an angry look. 'Did anything out of the ordinary happen? Do you have any explanation why she might not come to college?'

'None at all. She's one of our keenest students. Quite serious. Her work is good; it's engaged and well thought-out. She goes in for large, ambitious installations, all done from recycled materials. In her first year she made a piece out of tyres for the harbour festival; it was featured in the press.'

'What, the submarine made from old tyres? That was her?'

'That was Bethany. She's very inventive. All her things are so big we can't accommodate them at the college at all. She's always going around on her pink bicycle, scouring the city for empty spaces to place her work. And now I wonder if something has happened to her out there.'

'But you were going to call when you realized she lived at the same address as Mr Catlin. Why is that?'

West glanced towards the studio where Catlin was working. 'It's just . . . I don't know. I'm not accusing him of anything, you understand, but that's the second young woman who's disappeared, and Marcus was close to both of them, in one way or another.'

'Nothing other than that?'

West shook her head. 'Will you go and look for her?'

'Yes, I think I should. Leave it with us. But' – she handed West her card – 'you'll call me the moment you have news of Ms Hall. Or Ms Lamberti, of course.'

West took the card and stood awkwardly for a moment until she realized that it was she, not the two officers, who was leaving, then she walked off briskly, holding Fairfield's

business card by one corner as though it was something
unsavoury she had picked up off the floor.

Fairfield waited until she had turned out of the corridor.
'We'll have another chat with our Mr Catlin, but this time
somewhere private. We'll talk to him in the car.'

'Why not bring him in? Put a bit of pressure on the arrogant
little shit?'

'On what grounds, Jack? We've absolutely nothing on him
and no crime has been committed.'

'Wanna bet?'

'No, I don't. If we pull him, it'll be round the college and
in the papers in no time, and we're supposed to be discreet.
The super wouldn't be impressed.'

'Is he ever?'

'Not often, no,' Fairfield sighed.

Catlin was exasperated. 'This is police harassment. How am
I supposed to get any work done if you two pop in here unannounced every few seconds?'

Sorbie loved *police harassment*. In his book – and it was a
very large book – anyone complaining about harassment had
definitely something to hide. 'But you do want to be helpful
in any way you can, Mr Catlin, *surely.*'

The car was parked some distance from the college, and by
the time Catlin found himself in the back of Sorbie's Golf
with the child lock engaged, he was visibly angry. 'What did
you have to drag me all the way out here for?'

'Yes,' Fairfield said, 'it's not ideal, I admit. Of course, we
can do it more comfortably at the station if you prefer.' Catlin
subsided and looked out of the window into the traffic. 'Do
you have anything to add to what you told us about the
whereabouts of Ms Lamberti? Any idea how her scooter ended
up a few streets away from your house?'

'I've no idea who pinched the scooter. As for your first
question, don't you think I'd have told you if I had thought
of anything?'

'Oh, I don't know. Bethany Hall, a woman you share a
house with, goes missing and you completely fail to mention
it, so I must assume that there could be other things you failed

to mention. I could be tempted to arrest you and question you under caution. Do you know what that means?'

'Sort of.'

'It *sort of* means that if under caution you fail to mention something pertinent to this inquiry or you lie to us, we might consider that obstructing a police investigation. And that's a criminal offence. But you are happy to assist us in any way – isn't that right?'

Catlin suddenly looked and sounded much younger. 'Yes.'

'In that case, why did you fail to mention that someone close to you, someone you shared a house with, had disappeared?'

'Bethany? Bethany wasn't *close* to me. She lived in the same house, that's all. We hardly ever talked.'

'Why was that?'

'What would we talk about? I'm a painter. She takes junk and makes it look like some object or other. She made a sub out of tyres. And a car out of books. It's quite interesting but it has nothing to do with art; it's just novelty value, it's just entertainment.'

'OK, you didn't like her work. So if she disappears, it doesn't matter.'

'You don't know Bethany. Some of her stuff is so huge she needs a cathedral to show it in. She was forever running around on her bike looking for empty warehouses and buildings about to be demolished so she could stick her stuff in it and take pictures of it.'

'She's been gone for days. She has missed deadlines, we were told. But you weren't worried.'

'I didn't know she'd missed any deadlines; all I knew she wasn't there to complain about the fridge door standing open or someone using all the milk.'

'You're not worried about her, then,' said Sorbie. 'Or is it because you know exactly where Bethany is?'

'You don't know her. If Bethany thought there was an empty warehouse somewhere in Norfolk, she'd be cycling there to check it out. Look, I don't have anything to do with Fulvia disappearing *or* with Bethany. I don't know what you think I am – sodding Bluebeard? I'm trying to get over Fulvia dumping me and you're definitely not helping. Now, do you think I could get back to my painting?'

Sorbie let him out of the car and they watched him march down the road to the Spike Island studios. 'We got him a bit rattled,' Sorbie said with satisfaction in his voice.

'Yes, but that's about all. Two girls go missing. What do they have in common?'

'They're both art students and both know Marcus Catlin. One of them intimately.'

'Yes, one thing they have in common is Marcus Catlin. But the same could be said of thirty or forty other young women in that building. The other thing they have in common is art.'

'I don't see how that'll help us.'

'Neither do I, but it's the only other thing that seems to connect them. Fulvia is rich, Bethany is working class. One rides a trendy scooter, the other a boneshaker. Fulvia paints, Bethany does sculpture.'

'Of sorts.'

'Of sorts. She's constantly on the lookout for derelict houses and empty warehouses. You know what that means?'

Sorbie started the car. 'Yes, ma'am. We're looking for her in derelict houses and empty bloody warehouses.'

Leonidas Poulimenos gently set down the tray on the long table and began dividing the frothy coffee between the two tiny cups. He had brewed it on a little camping stove, identical to the one in his kitchen, on top of a plan chest at the back of the studio. 'I can't be bothered to walk all the way back to the house just to make coffee,' he had told McLusky. Now he sat down while exhaling noisily. He reached for a half-smoked cigar in the nearest ashtray but it had gone out and he did not relight it. He laid his elbows on the table and looked across at McLusky. 'You thought I'd be more upset.'

'You'd have every right to be.'

'I was a little surprised myself. When the fire service called to tell me about it, I almost felt relieved. Not immediately – I was too puzzled by it – but after a few hours, after thinking it through. Rosslyn Crag, the past, Port Isaac – it all seemed to be such a significant part of me at one time, but now . . .'

He looked away towards the bright windows. 'We never went back there afterwards, not together, not us painters. Elaine and I went occasionally; only very rarely did I go by myself. I would try to paint, but the house and the bay below always distracted me. It felt like a museum in a way; it was as though that day – the day Ben died – had been preserved inside it somehow. It was forever that same day in June as soon as you opened the door.'

McLusky let a pause develop to make sure Poulimenos had finished before he asked, 'Did you employ a cleaner or care-taker to look after the house?'

'Yes, why? Local woman – comes in once a month to blitz the house, more often when someone is actually staying. Why are you asking?'

'There was no dust anywhere and I had wondered.'

'Dust, yes. I should have shut it up and let it gather dust. No, I should have sold the house. Bought something else. Somewhere far away from Port Isaac.' His eyes snapped back to the here and now and he gave McLusky a benevolent, almost amused look. 'It was insured. It's gone and I'm glad neither you nor your lady was hurt.'

'You are a very generous man . . .'

'I can afford to be.'

'. . . but you shouldn't have sent me the painting. I will have to return it.'

'I was hoping you might change your mind. I realized you could not easily have walked out of here with a painting under your arm, but sending it to you was more discreet.'

'Is Ben the swimmer in the painting?'

'If you like.'

'So where's the boat?'

'I was on the boat. What I remember most, what I see in my mind, is Ben in the water, swimming out to sea.'

'I spoke to Michael Tigur.'

'The skipper's son? He was very young when it happened.'

'Not too young to remember that all of you were standing together in the stern when Ben Kahn went into the water.'

Poulimenos appeared unconcerned. 'Is that how he remembers it?'

'It is. Whereas you told me you were at the front of the boat by the wheelhouse. Which is why you did not see how he got to be in the water.'

Poulimenos shrugged. 'I only said that to make sure you knew I didn't drown him. He jumped. High spirits. Too much wine. You shouldn't swim if you've had too much to drink.'

'Michael Tigur heard one of you shout "my daughter". Twice.'

Poulimenos shook his head. 'I think someone may have shouted "my God, no" or something like that. He jumped in, like a complete ass, from right above the turning propeller. A stupid thing to do.' He picked up his cup. 'Your coffee is getting cold, Inspector.'

'Who would want to burn down your holiday home?'

'The Cornwall Liberation Front?'

'Whoever firebombed your house knew someone was in. Let me repeat what I said earlier: whether the arson attack is connected to the killing of your friends or not, I think your life might be in danger. I wish you'd reconsider our offer of police protection.'

'I'll be fine, Inspector. OK, OK,' he added when he saw McLusky did not like his light-hearted tone, 'I'll be *careful* to whom I open the door.'

Despite the fact that DSI Denkhaus was still in London at a two-day conference and that therefore the inevitable rocket from upstairs was still a day away, McLusky slunk towards his office like a man who at any moment expects to hear his name called in stentorian tones. But it was an unusually upbeat DS Austin who intercepted him in the corridor. 'Ballistics have come up with a possible match for the gun.'

McLusky, standing outside his office with one hand on the door handle, against his better judgement held his breath and waited motionless for the next sentence.

'They think they can match the projectiles to a gun that was used in three incidents over the last eighteen months. One in Knowle West, one in St Pauls, one in Easton.'

McLusky exhaled. It was something but not the break-through he had hoped for. He entered his office and sat down behind his messy desk. 'No names?'

Austin looked down at the piece of paper he was holding. 'None. The first one, in Easton, we know nothing about. People heard one shot fired in the night and the bullet was only discovered days later. It had gone through a wheelie bin and stuck in a fence post. The one in St Pauls was a robbery, of a corner shop, March last year.'

'Yeah, I remember it.'

'One shot fired when the shop owner refused to open the till.'

'Stupid man.'

'It was just a warning shot. Description was male Caucasian, six foot, blue eyes, masked, Polish accent. The gun was described as a "revolver that looked old". Then nearly six months later the same gun was used in Knowle West. That time it seems to have been some kind of argument over money. One shot fired at a cyclist. Bullet missed and hit a stationary car. This time the man was described as a skinny teenager wearing a hoodie; according to the witness statement, he had a Bristol accent.'

'What did he say?'

'Erm . . . that.' Austin turned the page and held it out for him to read.

McLusky's eyes widened as he read the string of swear words. 'Physically impossible, I should think, but imaginative. OK, three different incidents, at least two different gun users, possibly three.'

'Yes. Could be a loan.'

Even in twenty-first century Britain, guns were still relatively rare and handguns difficult to come by. Small-time criminals, often mere teenagers who wanted a gun for a day as protection, to intimidate a rival or for a one-off robbery like the one in St Pauls, rented the gun from the owner. It was almost always understood that the gun would not be fired unless in self-defence or to intimidate, since the owner might be charged with any woundings or killings should the gun ever be found in his possession. Often these guns were eventually found at the owner's place during house searches that were unrelated to gun crime, the weapon hidden in predictable locations such as toilet cisterns, in biscuit tins or desktop hard drives, hiding places that the criminals had thought fiendishly clever.

McLusky drummed his fingers on his desk in the tiny space that was not covered in empty mugs and papers. 'Loan guns don't get used for murder. Unintentionally sometimes, but not several killings. Either the gun has been sold on or whoever rented it has gone rogue with it. In which case he's probably not returned it.'

'Perhaps this is the scenario then: our man climbs into Mendenhall's garden with the aim to rob him at his home, runs into him unexpectedly and shoots him in panic.'

'Which might account for the badly aimed shot. So with Mendenhall shot, why doesn't he go and rob the place?'

'Because he's afraid the shot could have alerted someone. Because he's shocked. He didn't mean to do it.'

'Yes, Jane, he was so shocked that days later he kills Mendenhall's friend Longmaid in broad daylight, at his house which is full of valuable knick-knacks and leaves with only a shotgun and an old fowling piece.'

'Yeah, OK, unlikely,' Austin conceded.

'Whoever killed Mendenhall and Longmaid knew both of them. This isn't some chancer whose normal stomping ground is Knowle West or Easton.'

McLusky was surprised to have been asked to sit down, and DSI Denkhaus, his large shape sharply outlined against the brightness of his office window, looked annoyed that he had offered it. He was thumbing a report of the Cornish fire service with an expression of disgust. 'What the hell were you thinking? You went down there without telling anyone about it – not even DS Austin apparently, though I find that hard to believe – then mysteriously the house of one of the main suspects in the murder case you're investigating catches fire *with you in it!*'

'There was nothing mysterious about it. Someone broke a window, poured in a gallon or so of petrol and chucked a match after it.'

'What were you doing at the house in the middle of the night?'

'It had been a long day. I had at last tracked down Michael Tigur, the son of the skipper, and interviewed him about the events back in 1998. I had a last look around the house and had intended to drive back to Bristol that night but I thought I was too tired to drive. I know I shouldn't have but I went to sleep in an upstairs room and was woken by a noise and found the house was on fire. I had to jump from a window.'

'Their preliminary report describes you as "persons".'

'Must be a typo.'

'Someone set the house on fire with you in it. Could it have been a coincidence that they chose that night? Would they have been aware that it was occupied?'

'Most likely, since my car was parked in front of the house. They may have missed it, of course.'

Denkhaus leant back in his chair and thought for a brief moment. 'What car does Poulimenos drive?'

'Bentley Continental.'

'Colour?'

'A sort of midnight blue.'

'And yours is black. Was there any street lighting? Security lights?'

'None at all.'

'Which means someone might have mistaken your big Merc for the owner's Bentley. Either way, we'll need to treat it as attempted murder. We will give Mr Poulimenos police protection.'

McLusky threw up his hands. 'I offered it twice and he turned it down each time.'

'Even after someone burnt down his holiday home?'

'He lives in a big place in the Chew Valley with acres of land around him. I think it gives him a false sense of security.'

'Yes, I've come across it before. It's nonsense. The closer your neighbours, the safer you are.'

'Depends on your neighbours, sir.'

'Granted. I'll get a police patrol to swing by his house a few times. But if I was Poulimenos, I'd be worried.'

'Unless, of course, he knows he has nothing to worry about.'

*   *   *

This was a question that greatly exercised McLusky as he sat opposite Austin in the canteen and poked about in what was today's healthy option: a dull piece of smoked mackerel next to a pile of anaemic bits of lettuce, bean sprouts and grated carrot. It had been billed as 'low carb'.

'That's more like *no* carb,' observed Austin but got no answer from his superior who seemed miles away.

He was, his mind's eye full of flames. Was Poulimenos nonchalant about his own safety because he knew he had nothing to worry about since he himself was behind the killings? For some personal motive? Or did Poulimenos have something to worry about? Did he, McLusky, have something to worry about? Who had been the intended victim of the arson attack – he or Poulimenos? What he hadn't told the superintendent or anyone else was that he thought he and Laura had been spied on by someone posing as a birdwatcher. He put down his fork, pinched three chips from Austin's plate and told him about the stranger watching them in Cornwall.

'And you can't even say if it was a man or a woman?'

'No, though Laura thought it might be a woman, just from the way the birdwatcher moved.'

'But . . . if the birdwatcher is our arsonist, then you two were the intended victims. Or at least *you* were. And whoever set the fire didn't care if Laura died too.'

'Got it in one. Denkhaus, by the way, doesn't know about her being there.'

'How did Laura deal with it?'

'Not speaking to me. Her archaeology essay went up in smoke with her laptop, along with some library books and all her notes. She was ready to kill me herself. I said I'd pay for it all, but she never said a word to me all the way back.'

'It'll blow over.'

'Sure. Oh, and the Rossis want me to move out so they can sell the flat.' McLusky swiped the last chip off Austin's plate from right under his fork.

'Hey! Don't forget your fitness test.'

'Here, have my salad. I'm off to see a nasty man about a gun.'

*   *   *

'Ma'am? Body found on the railway line. Under Queen Anne Road. The description fits Bethany Hall.'

Fairfield moved so quickly from her office that Sorbie had trouble keeping up with her. 'A train driver coming the other way reported it and they stopped the trains on that line. Apparently, it's causing chaos. They want us to move the body pronto.'

Fairfield just nodded and drove, faster than an already dead Bethany warranted. Her humble missing person's inquiry had turned into something quite different. A mere twenty minutes after Sorbie had announced her death in her office, the inspector was standing next to Bethany Hall's body in the shadow of the four-lane flyover. A few hundred yards off in the direction of Temple Meads station and on the same line as the girl's body, she could see a stationary intercity express that had been halted there just in time. Bethany's body was fully dressed, for which Fairfield was grateful, in the clothes she remembered her wearing at their only meeting outside the house she had shared with Marcus Catlin. Her limbs were twisted in a way that only a fall from a certain height could arrange, one that involved multiple fractures. The site was guarded by two uniformed police officers, PCs Pym and Purkiss. No one else had arrived yet, apart from a second police unit who were busy closing one lane of the flyover above the site. 'Remind me what's up there, Jack. Can pedestrians use the bridge?'

'No. But there's a cycle lane.'

She turned to the tall constable called Pym. 'Did you find a bicycle up there? She used to ride one.'

He shook his head. 'I've not heard anything. Hang on. Who's up there? Is it Hanham?' he asked his colleague. The woman nodded. Pym called Hanham on his mobile; no bicycle had been found.

'Someone could have seen the bike,' Sorbie speculated, 'after she had jumped, and they stopped and took it away.'

'Jumped? She didn't jump, Jack. She didn't jump and she didn't fall.'

'You're quite certain already?'

'Tenner.'

'Done,' said Sorbie, despite a dismal record of losing bets with his superior.

One by one, the teams parked up in a nearby lane and went to work, erecting a tent over the body, taping off the area. As soon as DC French arrived, Fairfield nominated her the crime scene coordinator, something the constable was good at. When DCI Denkhaus arrived, he approved of the choice. He was immediately approached by a sergeant from the British Transport Police who looked unhappy. 'We need to get this stretch reopened as soon as possible, sir. With everyone wandering about here, we've had to close both lines.'

Denkhaus, who towered over the man, looked at him as though he had said something utterly absurd. 'My officers are not "wandering about", sergeant; they're working. We'll treat this scene as we would any other suspicious death. We'll be as thorough as with any other death. That train might as well go back where it came from; it won't pass through here for hours yet. Now, if you'll excuse me, I have an investigation to run.'

'Hours? But it'll be complete chaos!'

'Then organize some replacement bus services or something.' Denkhaus turned away and within a couple of seconds had forgotten the man.

The BTP sergeant, who was not used to being treated like a schoolboy, was about to protest when he thought better of it. He gave the superintendent a murderous look and walked off, talking urgently into his mobile. He now had several thousand stranded passengers to take care of.

Dr Coulthart was the last to arrive. He shook hands with Denkhaus, arranged to meet for a round of golf the following week, then walked towards the tent where Fairfield and Sorbie, now dressed in scene suits, were waiting. 'Ah, *la belle et la bête*,' he greeted them and dived inside the tent.

Sorbie rolled his eyes to heaven. 'I never know what that man is on about.' He stayed beside the track while Fairfield and a crime scene technician with a video camera followed the pathologist inside. Fairfield concentrated on a spot on the tent's side which moved with the soft breeze, until the pathologist had taken a rectal reading and noted the result on his mini tablet. She stayed quiet while the pathologist hummed and grunted as he uncomfortably knelt between the rails which, inside the tent, looked more out of place than the crumpled body. The face was dirty and scratched on the side that had hit the ground and was twisted further to one side than seemed possible, making Fairfield suspect that either her neck or her shoulder broke in the fall. Coulthart paid close attention to all the exposed areas of the body – face and neck and hands, especially the hands. Once he had scribbled some more notes on his mini tablet, he stood up with a groan and rubbed his knees.

Fairfield broke her silence. 'Did she die in the fall?'

'Pardon? No. No, she did fall but she was dead when she landed here. She's been dead for about twelve hours but she didn't die here.'

'Can you tell when she was thrown off the flyover?'

'My psychic powers are woefully underdeveloped, Inspector, but I think I can find you a man who can answer that question with preternatural precision.'

'Oh, who?'

'There's a sergeant from the BTP out there shouting into his mobile – I can hear him from here. Ask him to get his timetable out. She was obviously lobbed over the side between the last train going down the line and the one waiting out there arriving.'

'Of course,' murmured Fairfield, feeling foolish. Her next thought electrified her. 'But that means they dropped her on the line in broad daylight! There'll be witnesses. There might even be CCTV up there.' She rushed from the tent and squinted up against the sun at the flyover, looking for signs of traffic cameras. Sorbie stood beside her and followed her gaze. Fairfield snapped her fingers at him. 'Deposition site. Ten quid, Jack.'

'Erm, I haven't actually got any money on me.'

'Don't make bets you can't cover. I shan't forget.'

'So what was the cause of death?'

Fairfield gave him a brief wide-eyed stare; she had forgotten to ask. Looking around, she saw Coulthart walk off towards his night-blue Jaguar. 'He couldn't tell. We'll find out at the autopsy.'

'When's it scheduled for?'

She had forgotten to ask that too. 'He'll let us know. Go and find out if there's a traffic control camera that covers that stretch, because if it does, then we've as good as got our perpetrator.'

By the time he reported back to her, Fairfield had established that the body had to have been dropped between five past and a quarter past one, between a sprinter going through in the direction of Bath and the intercity that very nearly drove over her body. 'There's traffic cameras.'

'Brilliant.'

Sorbie shook his head. 'Not so brilliant. There's roadworks three hundred yards that way.' He pointed south. 'And they managed to cut through the cables. Someone's just arrived to try and fix them. They dug through the street lights too. Bloody idiots.'

'Thanks a bunch. That's great, Jack, that's just what was needed. Bloody typical.' She strode off, away from the forensics team and the uniformed officers searching the area, away from Sorbie, away from the dead girl, down the railway line towards the still stationary train. She paused briefly to light a small cigar from a tin of Café Crèmes, then marched on towards the train, letting out smoke from her nostrils like an angry cartoon bull about to charge. The intercity train revved up its diesel-electric engines and moved slowly away from her to return to Temple Meads station. Fairfield stopped and called after it. 'Coward!'

McLusky let his seatbelt slip to get out of the car so he could use the intercom set into the ancient sandstone gatepost, but the electric wrought-iron two-leaf gate was already opening, each leaf at its own sedate pace. The motion detector and CCTV camera mounted on the ten-foot wall that surrounded the property were obviously well monitored. He was exactly on time. His appointment with Roy Hotchkiss had been surprisingly easy to procure, considering that Hotchkiss was a known career criminal who had been investigated a number of times. Yet not since early in his criminal career, back in the 1980s, had he been convicted. McLusky had met and even interrogated the man in the past, but Hotchkiss was too well protected behind the legitimate parts of his business to be directly connected to the criminal operations he was controlling. Most of his sphere of influence lay in Bristol, although for a long time now he had preferred to live in the more genteel surroundings of Cold Ashton, a small village near the Georgian city of Bath. 'Who says crime doesn't pay?' McLusky asked his car as he steered the Mercedes up the drive towards the big house.

Ashton View stood in several acres of grounds, much of it woodland, at the top of the valley. It was a gothic pile built in the mid-nineteenth century by a merchant with more money than taste. There was a self-important portico in the centre of the façade, mock turrets and a tower at the corners and decorative crenellations above. The coach house to the side of the main building had room for five cars, two of which were taken up by Rolls Royces. Groups of cedars and other trees shaded the area in front of the house. McLusky parked with a crunch of tyres in the oval of gravel. The coach house was shut up; his was the only car parked on the gravel. Once more, the house gave no clues to the era he found himself in. Just as at Mendenhall's house, he had the eerie feeling that he might have slipped backwards into the past, a past romanticized with the aid of considerable amounts of money.

Nearly two minutes elapsed between McLusky working the old-fashioned bell pull, which set off a raucous bell inside the house, and the door opening and Hotchkiss's PA appearing. Frank Alvis – chauffeur, strongman, bodyguard and cook – was fifty, six foot four and bald; he was an ex-boxer with an angelic smile and a criminal record that stretched back thirty years. McLusky had come across him before. Since then Alvis had found the need to wear glasses, he noted: delicate gold-rimmed spectacles which looked precariously out of place on his large face. Alvis closed the door gently behind McLusky. 'Allow me.' He walked in front of him and opened a door in the enormous hall. 'The inspector is here, sir,' he announced and let McLusky enter the room. The door closed so quietly behind him that McLusky checked over his shoulder to see whether the PA was still there or not.

Roy Hotchkiss was sitting in a white armchair, lighting a cigar with a table lighter set in a lump of rose quartz. He was in his late sixties. His once-muscle-bound body still lent him a menacing presence and his eyes were still bright and blue and cold. What remained of his once-blonde hair had turned the colour of dirty snow. The fireplace to his left was flanked by two life-size china Moors. The gilt of their turbans was picked up again by the gold flecks in the maroon wallpaper; little of it showed between the gilt-framed paintings that covered the walls. An oily seascape dominated the chimney breast. The room was well proportioned and luxurious, and the French windows looked out on to a long terrace with large urns planted with garish flowers.

'The wages of sin, DI McLusky. I can tell you're impressed.' His cigar had gone out again and he lit it once more, puffing between words. 'Do . . . grab . . . a seat . . . Inspector.' Having managed to relight his cigar, he waved it invitingly at the other armchair. Beside it sat a very large black dog. 'Don't mind George. He has finally crapped his last into my flower beds; I had him stuffed.'

McLusky, who did not care for dogs, felt relieved but tried not to show it as he sat down in the other armchair, an unsociable twelve feet away from Hotchkiss. 'Good of you to see me.'

'Not at all, not at all. I like to show an interest in young, up-and-coming police officers. Of course, I am also curious to learn in what way I can be, erm, *of assistance* to a detective inspector hunting a killer.'

When he had made the appointment, McLusky had been at pains to avoid the phrase 'helping with our inquiries', the stock police euphemism for 'being interrogated'. Before he could answer, Alvis appeared with a tray of refreshments, coffee in an ornate silver pot, fine china cups and a large box of dark chocolates. While Alvis poured, McLusky took out his cigarettes. 'I'm sure you don't mind . . .'

'Put that filthy stuff away, McLusky, and smoke something decent. Alvis? Get the man a cigar. A Don Ramos, I think – one of the Petit Coronas.'

Alvis obliged by walking across to a tall mahogany humidor that reminded McLusky of a gun locker and returning to offer him a cigar from a box of twenty-five. When McLusky had managed to get it lit, he tried not to cough as he enveloped himself in a blue cloud of Honduran tobacco smoke.

'Yes,' Hotchkiss continued, 'always happy to *assist* in any way I can. I know young DIs are always under pressure to perform and get results, and, of course, the pay is quite appalling – wouldn't you agree?'

McLusky would and did but wasn't prepared to admit it. 'I assure you it's quite adequate.'

'Nonsense.' He pointed an accusing finger at him. 'I know what you earn. And let me tell you, this year alone I spent more money on a new car than you will earn over the next ten years of slogging police work. So I'm always glad to help out hard-up police officers.'

'And how many police officers are . . . receiving your assistance?'

'Over the years I have been able to ease a lot of hardship.' He smiled benignly. 'At the moment only three or four of your colleagues are receiving *regular* assistance to make ends meet.'

The candid admission that Hotchkiss was bribing officers on his own force was irking McLusky, but he treated it as mere conversation, smoked his cigar and drank the excellent coffee. It was pointless to antagonize the man when he was here to enlist his help.

'So how can I help, Liam? You don't mind if I call you Liam? You can call me Roy.'

'I'm here because we two have something in common.'

'You and I? I didn't get that impression the last time we met.'

'That's because we were talking about an extortion racket that had left two Indian restaurants in ruins and one Bangladeshi cook with ten broken fingers.'

'Which you never managed to connect me to, however hard you tried.'

'We'll have better luck next time.'

'I doubt it. And what is it that you and I supposedly have in common?'

'I hate guns. You hate guns.' McLusky knew that Hotchkiss had a passionate dislike of firearms, never used them and never allowed his men to use them, relying instead on old-fashioned muscle and cricket bats.

'That is true. I've always hated them, though *I* hate them for entirely different reasons. You think only you lot should be allowed to run around with guns. I believe *nobody* should be allowed guns. Using guns is against nature.'

'Against nature?' McLusky leant forward with interest. This brought him within striking distance of the chocolates. He picked one, then read the legend on the box. 'Hotel Chocolat. Did you pinch these?'

'Don't be daft; it's the name of the brand.'

McLusky popped one in his mouth. 'Why have I never heard of them?'

'Because you couldn't afford them.'

'Mmm, very nice. You were saying? Guns are against nature? How?'

'Guns are counter-evolutionary, a fudge. Evolution is based on the survival of the fittest – am I right? So the strong get all the best stuff, the best food, the best shags and hence the best chances for their offspring, and eventually only the strong and healthy go forward. Right? In comes a moron with a gun. He's a weedy little scrote and not very bright, but the gun gives him power over those brighter and stronger and *more deserving* than him. The gun stopped evolution.'

'Interesting theory.'

'It's not a theory, McLusky. If a five-year-old came through that door and pointed a loaded gun at your head, you would do exactly as he told you, no matter how crazy his demands. Such is the power of the things.' He blew a large, satisfied plume of smoke towards the ceiling. 'All over the world, decrepit, demented, psychotic dictators oppress billions of people through the power of the gun. Without the gun they would long have been hacked to death and fed to the crows.'

'We can't turn the clock back. You can't uninvent the gun.'

'But you can clean up your own house. You can keep them out of your sphere of influence. Which is what I have done.'

'And it hasn't put you at a disadvantage?'

'Not very often. Guns are used by morons, and morons I can deal with. If not today, then some other day, if you know what I mean. I don't deal in drugs; you know that. That's where you find guns.'

'I need to find a gun.'

Hotchkiss smiled. 'Not for personal use.'

McLusky, the Snake Slayer heavy in his pocket, ignored the question. 'I need to find the thirty-eight that killed both victims. I believe it's a rented gun.' He told him about the two incidents at which it had previously been fired.

Hotchkiss had listened with interest. 'Leave it with me, Liam. I'll get my boys to show an interest. Naturally, I expect a favour to be repaid in kind. I suggest you get your boys to show less of an interest.'

'Naturally,' McLusky said neutrally. 'I shan't forget.' He scrabbled another chocolate from the box in front of him and quickly popped it in his mouth.

'Make sure you don't.' Hotchkiss levered himself off the chair and went to the humidor. He slid three Petit Coronas into a leather cigar case and handed them to McLusky who took them reluctantly. 'Take it, take it, Liam. They suit you. And they will remind you of all that was said in this room,' Hotchkiss said pointedly.

As he drove back towards the front gate which opened for him as he approached, he was no longer sure that going to Hotchkiss had been such a good idea. He had, of course, expected that Hotchkiss would have his man record the conversation, just as he himself had recorded it on his mobile. He played it to himself on his way back to Bristol, checking that nothing he had said could be used to blackmail him.

'All of them?'

'All of them,' said Coulthart, waving a scalpel at the computer screens on the wall which showed two groups of X-rays of Bethany Hall's body. 'All the injuries you see are post-mortem, Inspector.'

'But there are so many of them,' said Fairfield. She was surprised by the number of breaks and cracks in the victim's bones and the general state of her body, which now lay grey and bloodless on the table in front of Coulthart.

'Whoever manhandled her body treated her like a sack of potatoes. No, that is not true; you would not treat a sack of potatoes this badly. This body has been dragged about, bumped over things, probably flung into the boot of a car or the floor of a van, then heaved over the parapet of the flyover. It hit the railway line with all the force of its dead weight and that broke the larger bones, but someone stood on her left hand at some stage and that broke three of her fingers.'

'And what killed her?'

'Almost certainly heart failure.'

'What? She had a heart attack? Natural causes?'

'Heart attack brought on by electrocution.'

'*Electrocution*,' Fairfield echoed.

'Yes. Both palms of her hands show signs that they grasped something with a high current running through it.'

'Like what?'

'That I can't say. But it was a substantial object, perhaps an inch or more in diameter. Not a thin cable. And she grasped it with both hands. Whether voluntarily, I can't say, of course; neither can I pronounce on whether her killing was unlawful or accidental.'

'One does not necessarily exclude the other.'

'I can safely leave that for your legal mind to ponder. But there are no signs that she had been restrained. Her clothes went off to forensics first thing; perhaps they can tell us something about where she might have been. You never know, you might get lucky.'

Kat Fairfield did not think of herself as the lucky type – not lucky in love or at cards. Did she have a murder case or not? Here was her chance to shine; with DCI Gaunt still being delayed in Spain and McLusky busy with two shootings, the super had given the case to her. Standing in the car park at Flax Bourton mortuary, she lit a small cigar and squinted into the sunshine. Was it unethical of her to stand here and hope that Bethany Hall had been murdered, that Fulvia Lamberti was not just a missing person, so she might head up her own murder investigation?

Back at Albany Road, Sorbie displayed no such qualms. 'Let's hope it's murder,' he said simply. 'We could do with something decent to do around here while McLusky vacuums up all the interesting stuff. But electrocution? I don't know. If she was clambering all over derelict places and into empty houses, she could have electrocuted herself, touching stuff she shouldn't have.'

'And then presumably threw herself on the railway line afterwards.'

'Yeah, you're right.'

'I know. Where's my tenner?'

Sorbie reluctantly handed over two limp and sweaty-looking fivers which Fairfield stuffed into a pocket of her charcoal-grey business suit. She had worn it to attend the post-mortem, now regretting the impracticality of it. The answers to Bethany Hall's death might well lie somewhere in the rubble of a derelict house.

'Are we going for lunch?'

Fairfield would use her lunch break to drive home and change. 'You can. I have got things to do.'

Sorbie looked after her as she marched down the corridor. 'Not a diet,' he muttered. 'Please don't let her be on a fucking diet.'

Having spent his lunch break shopping for cigarettes and drinking cappuccino in Park Street, McLusky made a decision. It was as sudden an impulse as the one that had resulted in him buying the huge and hugely impractical Mercedes. Instead of looking for a new place to live, he would buy the one he already lived in. He liked the area. He liked living above the Rossis' grocer's shop, where herbs stood in buckets of water and olives of all shades lived in old washing-up bowls where you served yourself. He liked the sign telling customers not to spit olive stones on to the floor. Anyway, it was high time he sorted out some of his finances with his building society and he'd make an appointment with a mortgage advisor while he was there.

Every time he went into the branch for any reason, staff pointed out to him that his savings account was very old-fashioned and earned him practically no interest. The compensation payment for the 'incident' – as he referred to the attempt made on his life two years earlier – had swelled his already healthy finances to the extent that a deposit on his flat would leave him with plenty of money to spare for improving it. His branch was a few minutes' walk from the station, which gave him time to smoke one cigarette and eat one of the sticky Danish pastries he had bought to get him through the afternoon. McLusky did not walk much, and never for pleasure, which meant he felt virtuous at the end of his twelve-hundred-yard stroll. The building society was a small branch in a narrow building. Only one counter was open and there was one customer in front of him. When McLusky looked up from the papers he had extracted from his jacket, he noticed that, unusually, the man was wearing a balaclava.

'You! Stand against the counter.' The robber waved a black semi-automatic at him. McLusky obliged, staring into the eyes of the gunman. Pale blue, almost grey. Accent local. A stray blonde hair protruding from the balaclava. Synthetic material. Hands not gloved, nails longer on one hand than the other: probably played the guitar. The details barely penetrated McLusky's consciousness, but all of it would be there later. The man's voice sounded firm but his eyes were panicked. The woman behind the counter also looked terrified when the muzzle was once more pointed at her. Was it a real gun? That was the important question here. Still not a foregone conclusion, even today. Several replica guns had been confiscated in the city only last week.

'And you!' the man shouted at the woman who had frozen. 'Stop fucking me about and open the till!'

'I can't!' she pleaded.

McLusky thought of the Derringer in his pocket, then of being thrown off the force for illegally carrying a weapon, and decided to try another tack. He tried to sound casual, despite his heart hammering in his chest. 'She's right, you know?'

'And who asked you, fuckwit?' The gun now pointed at him once more.

'It's new regulations. She is not allowed to hand over money unless you can prove it's a real gun. You're supposed to shoot at the ceiling.' McLusky pointed upwards. The gun hand of the robber seemed to sag a little. He pointed it at the woman behind the counter. The woman nodded. She also pointed at the ceiling, playing McLusky's game. The door opened and a middle-aged woman walked in, one hand rummaging in her handbag for her credit cards. She saw the balaclava and the gun, froze and let out a strangled cry.

'Out of the fucking way!' The irate bank robber shouldered past her and stormed out of the door, pulling his balaclava off as he disappeared from view. McLusky caught a glimpse of blonde hair, thought for a split second about giving chase, then decided against it. The woman behind the counter, whose name badge said S. Lovelace, sat, hand on heart, breathing heavily but managing a wan smile. 'I've been scared of that happening for years and now it's happened!' she said, getting some of her colour back. 'I pressed the panic button earlier; the police should be here soon. I wasn't sure if it was a real gun, either. That was a great idea, telling him to prove it.' Relief made her gush. 'Just as well it wasn't a real one; there's people upstairs and it's a wooden ceiling.'

McLusky swallowed hard. He had never thought of that; a nine-millimetre bullet would easily have gone through it. 'Well done for playing along,' he said on his way to the door. 'I think I'll come back some other time, though; you'll be busy, I expect.' He nodded as he passed the other customer and left, walking swiftly away once outside. Seconds later, first one and then two more police cars sped past him. He knew he would have been tied up for hours giving statements had he hung around. Of course, if he hadn't left his pepper spray, speed cuffs and airwave radio at the station, the suspect might now be in custody. As his colleagues would be quick to point out. He had been stupid, of course; you had to give guns the same respect whether you thought they were real or not, because it was hard to tell the difference. What the morons who used fake guns didn't realize was that using a replica in a robbery would get them a mandatory custodial sentence, even if they had carved it out of a banana.

TEN

Adeadly car accident on the A4, a simultaneous robbery at a jeweller's and a break-in at a pharmacy slowed services down to a crawl. Police and forensics had always been thin on the ground; now the thin blue line was broken in many places and investigations crawled along. Unlike in TV imaginings, real forensic investigation was notoriously slow. It took weeks for results to come back to the investigating officers. Fingerprinting was now done 'in-house', by police officers themselves, but anything more than that involved the slow and costly services of the privatized forensics industry.

Investigations were even slower, Fairfield thought resentfully, when they weren't started at all. She was standing on the upstairs landing in the house Bethany Hall had shared with Marcus Catlin. The girl's room had been sealed up until a forensics team was available. Now it was being opened and two technicians entered, with Fairfield, also wearing a blue scene suit, following hard on their heels. Not very far, however, since the room was small and cramped. One of the technicians stepped outside again to let her have a look around. 'Could you live like that, Inspector? What's all this stuff supposed to be?'

The eight-by-ten-foot room housed only a narrow bed and small child's desk, yet there was virtually nowhere for her to set her feet without treading on something. The bed was covered in piles of multicoloured clothes, some of them knitted and crocheted, much of it dyed in pinks and purples. More clothes lived in sagging bin liners against the wall. The floor was littered with more clothes, papers, drawings, books, pizza cartons and assorted junk, tangles of galvanized wire, tins of all sizes, defunct-looking electrical items: a toaster, a blender without a goblet, three electric kettles and a microwave with a damaged door.

The technician at the back of the room followed tangles of

cable to see what, if any of it, was plugged into the mains. 'Did you say she electrocuted herself?'

'I said nothing about her doing it herself.'

'None of this is plugged in. In fact, the only socket I can see is by the head of the bed. We'll bag all this up and test it, see if any of it was capable of electrocuting her. What do you think she wanted with all of this stuff?'

'She was studying sculpture.'

'Really.'

Fairfield squeezed out of the room and knocked on the door opposite. A pale girl opened it and gave her a doubtful look. She was slight, neatly dressed, kept her hair in a ponytail and wore a silver crucifix at her neck. Her name, Fairfield knew, was Lauren, the only resident of the house not studying art. She kept her thumb in the book she had been reading, entitled *Problems in Ancient History*. 'Could you have a look in Bethany's room for us? But don't go inside, please.' The girl shrugged and, without putting down her book, crossed the landing. 'Do you see anything unusual here?'

Lauren looked left and right. 'Mmm, no. That's Bethany.'

'Do you have any idea what she meant to do with all the electrical equipment?'

'One of her projects. She wanted to build an automatic kitchen that did lots of stuff by itself but without ever achieving anything.'

'Why?'

'Art. Don't ask me; I'm studying classics.'

Fairfield and Sorbie had now interviewed all of Bethany's housemates and several students she had shared workspace with at Spike Island, but none of them admitted to knowing where Bethany had planned her next installation. Despite every police unit in the city looking out for it, her distinctive bicycle had not been found.

Back in her office, Fairfield spent an hour going through all the papers and sketchbooks she had taken away from Bethany's room. She had to admit that to her untrained eye it all looked like the scribblings and drawings of a mentally unstable person, yet she had been assured by the course leader herself that they were perfectly good working drawings of a sculpture student, albeit a messy one.

The council clerk on the other end of the phone told Fairfield irritably that a colleague of hers – 'a Mr Sortie or something' – had already called about a pink bike and none had been found. 'We'll let you know if one is handed in or found abandoned; I already told that to your chap. If it was nicked, then they'd have long resprayed it anyway,' he added helpfully. 'I don't think you'll see that bike again.'

Fairfield dropped the receiver heavily on the cradle, then went to wash her hands. Some of the sketches had been in charcoal and had left a residue. Here she was heading up an investigation into a suspicious death and at the same time wishing she was at her life drawing class instead. Yesterday she had spoken to Bethany's parents, who were beside themselves with grief, bewildered and full of anger. They needed someone to blame and they needed explanations, none of which she had been able to provide. The hour-long ordeal had left her feeling useless and bleak. For the first time since joining the force, Fairfield had doubts that becoming a police officer had been the right decision.

Flames filled the entire doorway. McLusky forced the door shut against the ferocious heat. He had not realized the place was on fire until he opened the door. He could not get out that way. There was only the window but he knew a jump from a second-floor flat could be lethal. What could he save? What should he leave? People got killed that way, dithering about what to take with them. In the event of fire, get out and stay out. He knew it, he knew it, and yet . . . He frantically searched through the mess in his bedroom, looking for the umbrella, but he could not find it. He found a whistling kettle – it would have to do. He ran back to the sitting room and, with flying fingers, scrabbled open the sash window and looked down. The entire Rossi family were standing in the street, in their Sunday best.

Mrs Rossi called up to him. 'You did not want to move out, Mr Clusky, so we had to make fire under you.'

'I wanted to stay with the vegetables,' he called back. He

*could hear the old-fashioned alarm bell of a fire engine,
ringing, ringing, never coming nearer.*

McLusky sat bolt upright in bed and took a deep breath,
then scrabbled around for the ringing phone in the early-
morning light that fell through the uncurtained window. His
alarm clock told him it was five in the morning.

'Erm, yeah, Mc–McLusky.'

'Are you sure, Liam?'

'Eighty per cent certain. What's happened?'

'Poulimenos. Shot dead at his house near the lake. Do you
want to meet there or shall I come round to yours first? I'm
driving already.'

'Is Denkhaus on his way?'

'They haven't managed to contact him yet.'

'I wonder what he's up to. OK, come round here, I'll put
the kettle on. If I can find it. I'll need half an hour to turn
back into human form.'

Ten minutes later he opened his door to a wide-awake Austin
holding a paper bag of poppy-seeded rolls.

'Where'd you get those in the middle of the night?' he
grumped at him.

'Real bakery up my way. You can get them round the back
– self-service.'

They had a hurried breakfast of coffee and rolls, sharing
the last scrapings of McLusky's low-fat margarine, and then
set off in the Mercedes.

During their hurried breakfast McLusky had barely spoken
a word; now he was driving at ambitious speeds through the
early morning, with the roads still virtually empty. Austin
stole a look at his superior and found the expression on his
face frightening; he looked as though he was about to explode.
'It's difficult to see how it all . . .' he began, but McLusky
talked across him.

'We've failed, Jane, we've bloody failed. We should have
protected Poulimenos whether he wanted us to or not. Instead,
I let Denkhaus talk me down. "Have the locals from Chew
Magna drive by every so often." I knew it was useless then,
but I gave in. I should have pressured Poulimenos and I should

never have settled for the wait-and-see. It's one huge fuck-up.'

'You can't blame yourself for this; you didn't kill the man.'

'As good as. And you know why? I suspected him. He sent me a painting I had admired. I thought that perhaps it was meant as a bribe. Or even to mock me in some way, because I think the painting is supposed to show Ben Kahn swimming in the sea. Disappearing in front of our eyes. Then he offered me the keys to Rosslyn Crag. I suspected that was meant as a bribe, but it suited me since it gave me an opportunity to look around and put myself into the painting boys' shoes. But when it went up in flames, I have to admit I wondered whether Poulimenos hadn't torched it with me in it, to stop me from finding out what really happened on that boat.'

'I had wondered that, too,' Jane admitted. 'Of course, just because Poulimenos got shot doesn't mean he didn't torch his own place.'

McLusky's foot went light on the accelerator and the car slowed a little. He looked at his passenger with wide eyes. 'Shit, Jane, I hadn't thought of that. I must still be asleep.'

'Look out!' Austin shouted and braced himself against the dashboard. Their car had slowed but was still travelling at over forty miles per hour when they caught up with the back of a tractor and trailer that had joined the road from a side track, going at walking speed. McLusky never even touched the brake pedal. He swerved right, then back to the left. The car fishtailed once then settled down as McLusky accelerated again, leaving the tractor behind.

'You know you don't have any airbags in this barge, don't you?' Austin said accusingly, a little louder than he had intended.

'Haven't I? Now he tells me.'

They arrived at Bybrook View without further incident. The approach to the property was crowded with police vehicles from Bristol and Chew Magna. A forensics van was just arriving. A fire engine was parked beside the gate. As soon as they left the car, they both noticed the characteristic smell of a burnt-out vehicle.

DC Dearlove had arrived at Bybrook View before them, not having had the luxury of breakfast or even a cup of tea. He yawned expansively, then pointed. 'Whoever topped the old geezer torched his Bentley, too.'

'You know that for a fact, do you, Deedee?' McLusky stomped past the DC without looking at him.

'What's up with him?' Dearlove muttered to no one in particular, then followed the two detectives warily into the main building.

McLusky found a uniformed police officer from Chew Magna waiting for him in the hall. This was Sergeant James Bond's first murder scene and he was torn between the excitement of the occasion and his impatience at the late arrival of the CID officers. He was a man in his late twenties with a pleasant, eager face. It was his burning ambition to be promoted through the ranks until his colleagues stopped making fun of his name, at least to his face. 'We sent a patrol past the house every few hours,' said Bond. 'When the last one came up to the house, they found the owner's car on fire.'

'You didn't see it yourself?'

'No, the fire was out when I arrived.'

'Then find me the chaps who did.'

'Yes, sir. But their shift ended over an hour ago.'

'Mine doesn't start until two hours from now. Go and find them.'

'Yes, sir. The body is through there.'

There is never an ideal time for an encounter with a corpse, but on the whole McLusky preferred the afternoon. This morning he couldn't decide whether he was glad he had breakfasted or if he would have preferred to face the scene on an empty stomach, with no chance of adding his breakfast to the DNA at the scene. That kind of thing sometimes happened and was not popular with forensics. Once they had donned scene suits, McLusky and Austin entered the sitting room where, not long ago, they had drunk Greek coffee with Leonidas Poulimenos. The Greek man's large body lay across one of the two sofas. At the time of his death he had been wearing blue jeans and a dark blue shirt. He had been shot through the head. There was a lot of blood. His face was covered in it but a spectacular amount of it had ended up on the wall above the sofa, most of it inside the pale rectangle where one of the two David Bomberg paintings had once hung. Blood had also made artistic spray patterns sideways, becoming more delicate at the outer fringes. Austin looked away, pretending to study the room, but McLusky moved in closely. He felt he owed it to the victim to become closely acquainted with his death. Bloody tissue, hair, bone fragments and brain matter had also hit the wall. Under the blood, McLusky thought he could see where the bullet had entered, just above the nose, and he knew from experience that there would be an exit wound, ten times the size or more at the back of the dead man's skull, the source of the brain tissue on the wall. The smell of death was strong in the room: not of decay, but the reek of blood, of emptied bowel and bladder.

On the table stood a carafe with a few inches of what looked like red wine; a large wine goblet had been overturned, its content spilled over coffee table and floor. Austin, hoping to find a second glass under the table, was on all fours; he found none. He remembered the way to the kitchen and left the room to return a moment later. 'There's an identical wine glass sitting on the draining board, washed up.'

'Someone could have washed their DNA off it. Get them to bag it anyway.'

Sergeant Bond stood just outside the door. 'The two officers who called the fire brigade and found the body are outside.'

'Fine, I'll talk to them in a minute. Is there any sign of forced entry?'

'None that we found, but we haven't been over the whole place yet – it's a large property.'

Several forensics technicians were now entering the house, just as the pathologist arrived. Dr Coulthart looked fresh and even-tempered, showing no sign that he resented having been woken early and made to drive out to the Chew Valley; McLusky had seen the doctor at all hours of the day and night and always found him looking awake, eager, interested and impeccably groomed. He wouldn't be surprised if Coulthart slept in a scene suit and with his gold-rimmed glasses on his nose in case he was called out.

'A beautiful morning out there, Inspector.'

'You love the smell of burning Bentley in the morning?'

'Is that what it was? Pity. And what have we here?' The question was rhetorical and McLusky did not answer it. All would hang on ballistics matching the bullet to the previous shootings, but McLusky had little doubt that the same gun would prove to have killed all three men. 'You do have your hands full, McLusky, I must say.'

'So do you.'

'Ah, but after the post-mortem I wash my hands of the matter, so to speak, write a report and that's it. I rarely even get called to give evidence these days. *That's* how thorough my reports are.' He gave McLusky a look over the top of his glasses. McLusky knew for a fact that it was purely theatrical since he had it on good authority that the pathologist could see virtually nothing without his spectacles. Coulthart started with a rectal reading and then went methodically over the body. The scene-of-crime officers entered and for once their presence was less than oppressive due to the generous proportions of the room. They photographed and filmed every square inch of the place while Coulthart worked. Austin had left the room. 'Shot from almost point-blank range, I'd say. Large exit wound; can't see the projectile at this stage. Looks like the bullet went straight through his skull and then hit the wall.' Gently, he let the head sink back.

Austin came back into the room. 'Sir? There's something you should see.'

'Will it wait?'

'Oh, aye.'

McLusky turned back to the pathologist. 'You think the killer came quite close? Almost point-blank, you said. Could it have been fired across the table? Could the killer have been sitting opposite?'

'It's possible. But the victim was standing or in the process of standing up. We can try to establish an angle during the autopsy. And there's a second bullet wound in his shoulder and, you'll be glad to know, no exit wound.'

'Is there? I completely missed that.'

'Easily done with all that blood on him. This one didn't

bleed so much so it's probably the second shot. You will at last get a bullet that hasn't been deformed by hitting a solid object.' Coulthart gave McLusky a sideways look. 'So you can compare it when the next killing happens.'

'Don't say that. Three friends, three bodies. The fourth died last century. This ought to be the last.' Even if he never caught the killer, McLusky thought, this had to be the last. Because who else? 'When did he die?'

'I'd say between ten o'clock and midnight.'

'That far back? But hang on – the Bentley was torched early this morning, wasn't it?' He went to the door and called for Bond. 'Sergeant? Your officers – the ones who reported the fire?' They were duly produced and looked every bit as tired as they were. 'What time did you see the fire?'

The older one of them had his notebook ready. 'It was four thirty-five. We called the fire brigade, then climbed over the wall with our fire extinguisher, but the car was burning fiercely and the garage roof had caught fire; our little car extinguisher had no impact. In the end, Neil here just threw the thing at it and we retreated. The firefighters were here quickly, but the garage was practically gone by then.'

'And you didn't see anyone.'

'See – no,' said the younger officer. 'But we could hear a car engine moving away fast. We couldn't give chase, not while people and property were in danger. We asked for backup, but at this time of night in the valley we were the only available unit.'

'What kind of a car engine was it?'

'Well, my colleague here thought it was an old VW, like a Beetle?'

The man confirmed it. 'Sounded a bit like that. It's the image I had in my mind, anyway.'

'In which direction did it go?'

'It went that way.' He gestured the way Austin and McLusky had come. 'Away from Chew Magna.'

'And was it you who found the body?'

'It was. We couldn't rouse anyone despite there being lights on, and the front door was ajar. We called, got no answer, and since we knew the homeowner was at risk, we entered the premises. It was obvious that . . . erm – sorry, I can never remember his name correctly – the victim, shall we say, was quite dead.'

McLusky sent the officers home and turned to the nearest forensics technician. 'There's security cameras out there: find the recorder for me.' Then he went to look for Austin. When he found him, the sergeant was standing in the sunshine with his eyes closed. 'This time next month Eve and I will be basking in proper Mediterranean sunshine in Spain.'

'It's warm enough for me here,' said McLusky. 'God, that burnt car stinks. What was it you wanted me to see?'

'It's in his studio.'

'Why doesn't that surprise me?'

'It still might,' said Austin and led the way.

Two forensics technicians were standing in the studio, surveying the debris of broken crockery, smashed jars and damaged paintings. Several of the canvases had been slashed in dramatic fashion, as though a large cat had raked them with its claws. McLusky ran his fingers across a series of slashes as though they were harp strings. 'This is pure theatre. Look at it. It's so systematic. If you're in a rage, you don't cut neat slashes next to each other; you lash out. This is either pretend rage or very old, very cold rage. D'you remember Mendenhall's studio?' McLusky asked.

'Yes. Overripe peaches,' said Austin.

'Anything else?'

'Erm, yeah, it wasn't messed up. But then the killer didn't get into the house.'

'Perhaps. Or else the killer didn't want to mess up their own inheritance. So what am I supposed to be looking at?'

'Through the door at the back.'

The narrow door at the end of the studio was ajar; Austin used one finger to push it open with a flourish.

McLusky stood in the open door. His face fell. 'Oh, *God*. That's all I bloody need. And he seemed such a civilized guy.'

'You were looking for a pink bicycle, I believe?'

Fairfield sat up straight at her desk. 'I still am, yes.'

'Well, this could be something – mind you, not a lot left

of it. It's just the frame of a bicycle. Just had a call from a maintenance crew repairing street lighting. There's a pink bicycle frame chained to a street lamp and they want us to cut it off. What do you want us to do with it?'

'Nothing until I get there. What's the location?'

It turned out to be not a million miles away from the place where Bethany's body had been found, at the outer edge of an industrial area near the Feeder Canal. While she kicked her heels, leaning against her car, Fairfield watched the workmen who were servicing the tall street lamp, working on its innards through a narrow hatch. The bicycle frame lay flat at the base of the post, chained to it by a nearly matching pink bike chain. The workmen, who had not been told anything about the bike, noticed their audience. One of them called across. 'Anything we can do for you, love?'

'I doubt that very much.'

His colleague found this hilarious, but the first man was not so happy. He muttered something to the effect that she was probably a dyke. For once in his life, Fairfield thought, he was probably right, though her relationship record with women was every bit as fraught as that with men. Was there a third thing she had missed? She had no time to pursue the thought as at that moment the council van arrived. She met up with the young council worker and his bolt cutter by the lamp post.

'Are you the police officer I'm meeting?' he asked.

Police officer, one of the workmen mimed to the other.

'Yes, just cut the chain for me and I'll take it away.'

The workmen stood back in head-scratching silence while the man cut the bicycle chain with ease and Fairfield, wearing latex gloves, took it away to her car and stowed it in the boot. She knew it would have countless prints on it anyway, but she had not wanted to add her own. She threw the gloves after it and slammed the boot shut, then lit a small cigar, blew a satisfying cloud of smoke towards the blue sky and walked away past the staring workers. 'As you were, chaps.'

Naturally, the area around the deposition site had been searched for possible places where Bethany might have met her death, but without a result. Since she could have been killed anywhere in the city before being dropped off the flyover, not a lot of man hours had been allocated to it. She called Sorbie and told him to drop everything and come and join her. Sorbie, who knew the area his superior was talking about, was less than enthusiastic, but Fairfield insisted. Yes, it would make sense to go back to Denkhaus and ask for a new search in the light of the new find, but first they would have to establish that the bicycle frame had really belonged to the victim. Personally, she had no doubt about it – after all, how many pink adult-sized bicycles could there be in this town? – but it would take time and Fairfield had never felt more impatient to get a result, to conclude an investigation successfully. And she felt lucky as she stood in the sunshine, wearing black from head to toe, light on her feet in her trainers despite the weight of the airwave radio in her shoulder bag; no, even the weight of the radio felt good to her today. With the press of one button she could summon a small army of officers to her side, armed to the teeth if necessary. She was walking on the other side of an invisible but definite divide: she was not a civilian. Kat Fairfield was walking on the right side of the tracks wherever she walked, and right now the sun shone on it.

Sorbie made good time and joined her soon after she had flicked the butt of her small cigar on to a patch of concrete rubble. Sorbie noted the transformation in Fairfield's mood but did not share it as he took in his surroundings with a look of distaste. He knew every city had places like this, *needed* places like this, but he would rather spend his time sitting behind his computer, no more than ten feet away from the tea kettle. He already felt too hot in the sun and now the inspector suggested they themselves should look for the place of Bethany Hall's electrocution. This wasn't intelligence work; it was foot slog. That's what uniform were for.

None of it, however – not even this drab and rundown area of Bristol – could depress Fairfield today. She crossed strips of concrete, passed rows of parked articulated trucks, climbed through the odd no-man's-land created between car parks, streets and buildings. 'This is exactly the type of place where a young sculpture student would expect to strike gold,' she informed Sorbie, who wrinkled his nose at the smell of dog's piss and nests of wind-blown fast-food litter. They found themselves at the fringes of the industrial units, a mix of recent and very old developments. Some of the older flat-roofed buildings were clearly waiting for demolition, but there were still signs of life even here. At the end of a row of closed-up units, a garage was still doing business. The car repair shop did not attract the glamorous end of automotive failures; in fact, most of the cars outside and inside the garage looked more than ten years old. At least they were in business, and the mood of the mechanic at whom they waved their ID seemed unaffected by the realization that he was in the unexpected company of CID officers. He was either a good actor or had nothing to hide or – in DS Sorbie's opinion – had whatever he did have to hide well hidden.

'Pink?' the mechanic echoed Fairfield's question. 'Nah, I'd have remembered that. Is that the girl who jumped off the bridge, you mean?'

Fairfield gave Sorbie a pointed look. 'We don't believe she jumped.'

'And you think she came through here? On her bike?'

'Or on foot. She was very colourfully dressed and had her hair dyed all sorts of colours, too.'

He shook his head again. 'I'd have remembered that.'

Sorbie briefly stuck his head under the raised bonnet of the car the man had been working on, as though he understood car mechanics, and emerged with a knowing look. 'What about your colleague back there?' Behind a scratched and grimy Perspex window sat a middle-aged sandy-haired man who had been talking animatedly on the phone and just then slammed the receiver on to the cradle.

'That's Terry, my boss; you can ask him.'

Terry came steaming out of his cubbyhole office. 'Bloody useless w—' He swallowed the expletive when he saw Fairfield. She repeated her question.

The man, while talking to Fairfield, kept one eye on Sorbie who was wandering about the place. 'No, not seen her. Or anyone on a bicycle, not for ages. Here, you wanna investigate summat criminal, investigate the bloody leccy company. They sent us an outrageous bill – it's nearly twice what it should be. I just told them there's no way we used that much – we could have tig-welded the QE2 with that – but the bastards aren't having any of it.'

'Seen anything unusual in the area recently? Anyone who shouldn't be here?'

He shrugged. 'None of us should be here – look at this dump. But finding new premises is a nightmare. I might pack it in for good if it goes on like this.'

Sorbie returned from his wanderings. 'All these motors are legit, are they?'

'I thought you was here for the girl on the bicycle.'

'We are,' Fairfield assured him and turned away. 'Thank you, sir.'

Sorbie made a show of reluctance, peering into car windows as though he were an expert on car crime, before joining Fairfield in the sunshine.

'Now, if I were a sculpture student and needed a place to plonk my stuff, I'd try those buildings over there.' She indicated three low, red-brick industrial units that once could have housed anything from potteries to metalworks. The one furthest from them had a squat round chimney, some thirty feet high.

'What, the ones with "Keep Out" and "Unsafe Structure" plastered all over them? If you were an idiot sort of student, yes.'

Fairfield had found a rent in the chicken-wire fence that surrounded the buildings and the rubble-strewn areas between them.

'We're not, are we?' Sorbie complained.

His superior had already squeezed through the gap and was picking her way through broken bricks and other debris towards the closest building. There were more signs telling potential trespassers to keep out and even warning stickers that the place was patrolled by apparently fearsome Alsatians, if the drawings of a snarling dog could be believed. Sorbie's shirt snagged on a protruding piece of wire and he scratched his forearm freeing himself. He swore as he followed the inspector who was already probing doors and boarded-up windows. 'If you want the damn place searched, why not get the foot soldiers in and wait in the car, for fuck's sake?'

'Are you saying something, Jack?'

'I scratched my arm on some wire.'

'Will you make an injury claim for compensation?'

'It could go septic.'

'See if any of the boarded-up windows have loose panels. Squatters sometimes loosen them and then put them back in place afterwards to make it look like no one's at home.'

They inspected the entire building, walking in opposite directions. Sorbie gave every chipboard panel a perfunctory tug and met with his superior at the far corner. 'We'll try the other two; won't take us long.'

There was plenty of evidence that the place had long been used as a dumping ground before it had been surrounded by wire fencing: the usual supermarket trolleys far from home, mouldering mattresses, their rusty springs protruding from the ticking, a couple of burnt-out scooters and not a few car parts, possibly the overflow from the garage. The second building also appeared secure.

'It's that one.' Fairfield pointed a confident finger at the grimy structure. She contemplated the building for a moment, wondering why she was so sure. Then she noticed that some of the rubble had been moved aside to create the semblance of a path leading up to the wooden double doors on the narrow side of the building they were facing. It was not methodical, but it looked as if someone had kicked aside a few bricks here, a lump of concrete there. It was faint but it looked like a path to her. There was a different smell around here too. The breeze was wafting it away from her nostrils before she could identify it. 'Can you smell anything, Jack?'

Sorbie closed his eyes and smiled angelically. 'Piss, mould, burnt plastic.'

'Let's get in there.'

The double doors were wooden and locked. The paint had been scorched off at the bottom where it looked as though someone had unsuccessfully tried to burn the doors away. Windows at the ground floor had again been blocked off with chipboard. Here, too, it had been professionally done by one of the many security companies providing that kind of service – in this case, Secure Somerset; every panel carried a sticker with their website and phone number. A side door had also been boarded up. Here, however, the sticker was missing and Fairfield noticed immediately that the chipboard was of a slightly different colour and even thicker than that used on the windows. Sorbie had moved on to examine the board over the windows beyond the door, but Fairfield hadn't moved. He noticed and looked over his shoulder. 'What?'

'Through here.' Fairfield ran a hand along the edge of the chipboard cover. It had all the usual bolts at fifteen-inch intervals, but they were fake and merely stuck on with too much glue. When she felt something cold underneath the board, she gave it a good tug and the board came loose. 'Held on with magnets. Not seen that before.'

Sorbie was now by her side, helping her to remove the board completely. It covered a grey and battered metal door that had its lock drilled out and opened easily.

Fairfield sniffed. There was a strong smell of mould and damp on the other side of the wall. They found themselves in a small concrete foyer with pitted floors. To their right a scuffed and litter-strewn stair climbed to an upper floor; to their left an open doorway led into a dark cavernous space. Fairfield stood in the opening. Rays of sunlight pierced the large space which was littered with dark shapes, debris, remnants of machinery, dangling chains and cables. Fairfield found her Maglite and snapped it on, but its beam was swallowed up by the size of the emptiness in front of her. 'Can you hear anything?'

'Yeah.' Sorbie stood very still. 'Coming from upstairs. It's some sort of humming sound.'

'And now can you smell anything?'

'Yes, something pongs. Let's have a shufti upstairs. I'm pretty sure I know what we'll find.'

'Be careful: there might be people up there.' She followed close on the sergeant's heels, lighting the way for him. At the top of the stairs they came to a double wooden door, painted an ancient brown, its two square windows painted black. The two-hooped iron door handles were black and battered. The humming had become a loud chugging.

All of a sudden Sorbie was keen to get on with the job. 'Let's see if anyone's at home, shall we?' He reached for the iron hoops.

Fairfield yelled, 'No! Don't!'

It was too late. He had laid both hands on the iron hoops just as Bethany Hall had done. He let out a scream. The electric shock that ran through him was enough to throw him backwards into Fairfield's arms. Slowly, he sank to the ground against Fairfield's knees, shaking all over and groaning quietly. His breath came in jerks and he could feel his heartbeat doing somersaults in his chest. 'What the fuck?' he said weakly. 'What the . . .' Fairfield pressed the panic button on her airwave radio.

'Oh, marvellous; thanks, Jane. You've just turned my headache into a migraine.'

'Perhaps Doctor Coulthart has some painkillers,' Austin suggested.

'This'll need more than painkillers. It'll need surgery.' While the SOCOs went about their business in the studio behind him, McLusky remained standing in the narrow doorway and took it all in. The room before him was small, no more than eight by ten feet, but it was crammed full with all the paraphernalia a neo-Nazi could wish for. There were no fewer than three portraits of Hitler on the wall, all framed. Two were photographs, one a print of a painting that tried to make the man look heroic. Swastikas were everywhere; there was one at the base of the lamp on the writing desk which also sported a small bronze bust of the corporal as a paperweight; there was a standard in a corner and a Third Reich flag displayed under glass. But the flag above the desk belonged to a different organization. 'That's a Golden Dawn flag, I'm sure. The Greek neo-Nazis who did so well in the last elections.'

'But didn't the Nazis commit all sorts of atrocities in Greece during the war?'

'Yes. Turkeys voting for Christmas.' An election poster behind the door confirmed the connection. All the writing on it was in Greek, but McLusky recognized the face of the current leader. 'Isn't he in jail at the moment for belonging to a criminal organization?'

Austin scratched the tip of his nose. 'Not sure. Greek politics isn't exactly my forte.'

'So old Leonidas here was a fan. Or a member. Golden Dawn may pretend otherwise, but he certainly made no bones about being a Nazi.' He stepped into the middle of the room. 'It's a bloody shrine, this. But someone's been through it.'

'Oh, for sure. That glass case is all messed up.'

Between two shelves crammed with books about the fascist movement, the Weimar Republic, Third Reich and the Second World War stood a small display case. The content of it was disturbed and there seemed not to be enough of it to warrant a display case in the first place: a signed photograph of the Nazi leader, a cigarette holder adorned with swastika carvings and a Hitler Youth wimple.

'Whatever else was in here, someone's had it away. But what?' He stuck his head out of the door and spoke to the closest scene-of-crime officer. 'Are you done with this room?'

'Yeah, we started with that; you're welcome to paw the stuff.'

'Everything been photographed? Because I'm going to turn it upside down.'

'Be our guest.'

For the next hour he went through the Nazi shrine with a methodical rage, cautiously assisted by Austin. Not only did McLusky find the glorification of the Nazi crimes distasteful but the sudden complication of the case aggravated his already smouldering anger. As he riffled the pages of another book in the search for anything hidden, he suddenly stopped, dropped the book on the now messy desk and stepped outside. 'This door isn't concealed or anything, is it?'

'No, not at all. The door wasn't forced either, which means the intruder had a key or found a key or it had never been locked.'

'That means other people must have known about this. I don't know if the other two painters ever came here, but his wife must have known.'

'Perhaps that's why she left him?'

'If she had any bloody sense.' He walked out, through the studio and into the sunny courtyard. Greedily sucking on a cigarette, he sat down in dappled shade on the edge of one of the enormous planters in which the palms grew.

Austin joined him. Not having a cigarette to play with, he drummed his fingertips on the side of the planter for a while until he felt it was safe to address McLusky without having his head bitten off. 'I can't see how this connects with the other two deaths at all.'

'The Nazi shit?' McLusky squinted against the sun. 'Perhaps it doesn't. We've no evidence that the other two shared Poulimenos's politics. Or even knew about it.'

'Could you ignore this kind of thing?' Austin asked. 'I mean, if you found that someone close to you was a neo-Nazi. Would you just think "each to their own"?'

'Are you trying to tell me something, Jane?'

'Hardly. But it's not illegal in England to be a neo-Nazi.'

'A lot of people would be in trouble if it was. No, I couldn't ignore it. I wish we knew what was missing from that display case. It would be a start. I'll be asking Elaine Poulimenos about it, or Elaine Simmons as she now prefers.'

A forensics technician carrying a large evidence bag entered the courtyard from the house. 'Ah, there you are. Inspector?'

'Yes. What?' McLusky never expected good news from a forensics technician and he didn't get any.

'You asked me to find the CCTV recorder.' He held up the evidence bag. It contained a vaguely rectangular blackened object that had been in an intense fire. 'Found it. Inside the burnt-out Bentley.' He offered it to him.

'Take it away, man; what do you expect *me* to do with it?'

'No pleasing some people,' said the techie and walked back to the house.

Superintendent Denkhaus arrived soon after that, making light of the fact that he had omitted to tell anyone that he was staying the night with friends where his mobile had gone flat, as well as having forgotten to turn on his airwave radio, an omission he frequently berated junior officers for. McLusky reported to him at length about what they had found so far. Denkhaus was not happy about the neo-Nazi complication, either.

'The press are going to be all over that. We'll keep it quiet for as long as possible. There's already a camp of the vultures outside the gates. What do you make of it, then?'

'Nothing so far. We'll know more when we've been through the phone and internet records. There was no indication that the other two victims had far-right connections. I'll be interviewing the victim's wife again; she should be able to throw some light on it.'

While McLusky had been talking, the superintendent had reached for his freshly charged mobile to check the text message that had just arrived. 'DS Sorbie injured in the line of duty,' he read out loud and walked quickly away to his car.

Four hours later McLusky repeated the message to the CID officers assembled for his briefing in the incident room. 'Nothing trivial, I hope,' someone said. There were one or two chuckles in response to the remark.

McLusky thought of challenging this but could not bring himself to do it. He found Sorbie a constant source of gloom and he suspected that the man drank while on duty. 'I am sure that most of us – or at least some of us – wish him a speedy recovery.' Laughter all round. He tapped the eight-by-twelve photographs of the latest victim pinned to the board behind him and the room went quiet. One grainy black-and-white picture, an enlarged passport photo, showed him unsmiling yet alive, the other one dead on his sofa. 'Leonidas Poulimenos was the last remaining member of the painting quartet consisting of Ben Kahn, who disappeared, presumed drowned, Charles Mendenhall, shot with a thirty-eight' – he pointed to the relevant pictures – 'Nicholas Longmaid, ditto. We have found one of the two bullets that killed Poulimenos; it had hit the back wall and – you guessed it – deformed on impact. It lodged in the sofa. But a second bullet is safely inside the victim and might tell us once and for all if we are dealing with the same gun that killed the others.' He pointed to a column of writing on the whiteboard. 'Nothing so far connects any of the other victims to the neo-Nazi crap we found at Poulimenos's place. What does connect them is that they were friends. That they all painted in their spare time – which Poulimenos had a lot of. And all three were present when Ben Kahn jumped, fell, was pushed overboard – take your pick – from a boat called *Destiny* in 1998. Now . . .' McLusky looked for his mug of coffee and found he had already emptied it. He felt very tired all of a sudden. 'We are working on the assumption that all three were killed by the same person. Poulimenos was shot sometime during the two hours preceding midnight. The fire that destroyed the Bentley could not have been started long before four thirty this morning when a patrol spotted it. They thought they heard a car drive off, possibly a Beetle. Not one of the new Beetles – they sound different – but an old one from the sixties or seventies. They are rare in Britain, so find the damn thing. I want the car history of everyone connected with these killings, dead or alive. Someone might have one stashed away for sentimental reasons.'

French raised her biro in the air. 'Could have been stolen for the occasion.'

'Possible but doubtful. A similar engine was heard when Poulimenos's holiday home was torched. Whoever killed Poulimenos either came back in the early morning or – and that's much more likely – stayed for hours afterwards. They destroyed a lot of paintings and rummaged around in the man's shrine to fascism. We also think they removed at least one item from a display case in there, but we can't yet tell what it was. We have the approximate time of death. Everyone has to be reinterviewed. I want the whereabouts at the time of the murder of everybody, including Mendenhall's gardeners, all the wives, the housekeeper Mrs Whatshername and David Mendenhall. In fact, I'll tackle him myself, and you can also leave Elaine Poulimenos and Mrs Longmaid to me and Austin. Dearlove? Internet history and phone records for Poulimenos, when we get them. French? Bank details, suspicious money movements, unusual payments.' He dealt out several more orders to various officers and civilian operatives and then waved his arms around in an exasperated gesture. 'Get on with it!' People moved smartly away to their workstations, computers and phones.

Only Austin remained. 'Whoever is behind it isn't stupid,' he said. 'They knew there was CCTV; they chucked the hard drive into the Bentley and then set fire to it.'

'Quite. But they are also utterly cold and ruthless. They spent at least five hours in the house with the dead man lying there.'

'It means they're either sociopathic and don't care or they hated Poulimenos so much that the sight of him pleased them.'

'The only thing that'll please me today will be my head hitting the pillow,' McLusky said with conviction.

It was another eight hours before it did as he let himself fall on to his crumpled bed. He checked his messages and emails on his phone for the last time; there was nothing from Laura. He had sent her a few apologetic texts but had not heard from her since she slammed the car door on him on their return from Port Isaac. At the foot of the bed, leaning against the wall, stood the painting Poulimenos had sent him.

Elliot Kahn's father Ben was swimming, forever swimming out to sea.

ELEVEN

'Fuck, fuck, I'm gonna . . . I'm gonna die. Shit. My heart.'

'You're not going to die, Jack.' Fairfield, squatting on the filthy concrete landing, had her left arm around the shoulder of the crumpled Sorbie. 'Take deep breaths. The ambulance is on its way.'

'My heart is–is–is not right, it's not slowing down. My elbows are hurting, everything's gone dark.'

'That's because it *is* dark. Here, you take the torch. Sit up a bit. Can you lean against the wall?' Sorbie, scared to move, fearing his heart might burst at any moment, didn't answer. 'Come on, Jack, you're a tough old bastard. Takes more than that to kill you.' She pulled and pushed the panting DS until his back rested against the wall.' The persistent humming on the other side of the door, the musty smells, Sorbie's panting fear, the ache in her legs from squatting beside her colleague had wiped away her elation but could not tarnish the bright conviction that for once she was in the right place. 'I can hear a siren. I'll go down and guide them in.'

Fifteen minutes later Sorbie was being carried away in a

sitting position – he was too panicked to lie down – and slotted into the back of the ambulance. 'Tachycardia – it's not uncommon,' one of the paramedics assured her. 'Will you go with him?'

'I'll have to stay here.' She called to Sorbie as the door closed. 'I'll come and see you as soon as I'm done here.' The ambulance pulled away unhurriedly, without sirens or beacon.

The first police vehicles had also appeared and the arrivals took their cues from her, waited for her to give instructions, issue orders. It did not last long enough for her to get used to the sensation; a large black Audi arrived and stopped with a crunch of tyres.

The car matched the dark-suited man who swung himself out of the driver's seat and marched purposefully towards the gap in the fence which had been widened by the paramedics and was now guarded by PC Hanham who was sweating in the heat. As the man ducked past him through the fence, Hanham thought he could feel the nimbus of air-conditioned coolness still clinging to the officer who didn't as much as look at him.

As soon as Fairfield saw him arrive, she knew she had been reduced to a bystander. She had never personally met DI Wheeler but had sat through a self-important lecture by the man during a training day. Keith Wheeler was one of the leading lights of the Bristol drug squad, an officer who had distinguished himself in the ongoing Operation Atrium, with several high-profile arrests and successful prosecutions under his belt. Fairfield thought he was probably five minutes away from making detective chief inspector, and he looked younger than she felt.

Wheeler marched towards her, his crew-cut head advancing like a bullet. 'You Fairfield? I'm Wheeler.' He shook her hand, but just the once. 'What have we got?'

Fairfield pointed. 'Cannabis factory. I'm sure of it.'

'How'd you find it?'

'Dead girl. Got electrocuted. Probably happened here.' Fairfield found herself talking in the same short machine-gun bursts as Wheeler, who was already marching on towards the building. She kept pace with him. 'The door handles to the factory are electrified.'

'Yes, that's not uncommon.'

'It put my sergeant in hospital. He touched both handles.'

Wheeler stopped and looked at her. 'Will he be all right?'

'I think so.'

'Good, good.' He set off again. At the ground-floor entrance, also now guarded, he no more than stuck his head inside the door. 'Can smell it from here.' He looked up. 'Place hasn't been connected to the grid for years.' He walked off along the side of the building. 'First gotta find their leccy source.'

Fairfield, who hadn't moved, called after him. 'I might be able to help you with that.'

Wheeler stopped, turned on his heels and returned as though pulled by a bungee cord. 'You can?'

'I'm willing to bet they're stealing it from the garage on Dulcote Row.'

The drug squad now descended in large numbers on the site and soon established that indeed a short tunnel had been dug to access the electricity supply of the car repair shop. A thick cable had been laid, partly dug into the ground, partly covered with debris, from there to the back of the building where it was fed inside through a hole in the brickwork, disguised under rubble. As soon as the electricity supply was cut at the garage, the engineer at the door upstairs reported that the charge had disappeared. The humming subsided, too. 'That's the extractor and cooling fans off,' Wheeler explained. Fairfield, who had a good idea of how cannabis factories worked, did not get a chance to say so. 'After you, Kat. You found the place.' They had by now moved on to first names.

Despite the engineer's assurance that the electricity was off, she cringed all over as she pulled back the double door. Immediately on the other side hung sheets of grimy plastic. They pushed through those and found themselves in a subtropically warm plantation of cannabis plants. All were grown in black pots in neat blocks. Suspended on pulleys above them hung grow lamps, three strips per block. Here and there, thick silver hoses connected to extractor fans snaked between them. The smell was very strong but not unpleasant, Fairfield noted.

'Guys, it's Typhoo! Damn it,' Wheeler called to the forensics

technicians and members of his entourage who now flooded
into the place, filming, photographing, taking samples of soil
and plants. He made his way through it all, with Fairfield
following close behind.

'Typhoo?' she asked.

Wheeler did not answer straight away. Right at the back
they found a kind of office space with a mattress on the floor,
some dirty clothes, a tea kettle and a half-collapsed box of
two hundred and forty Typhoo teabags. He flicked a finger
against it. 'I recognized the set-up. Whoever looks after the
place likes Typhoo tea and drinks it black. Shame you had to
call in the cavalry, Kat, crying shame. We could have staked
out the place and nabbed them at harvest time. In about three
weeks by the looks of it. But they'll not be back now.'

'My sergeant had just been electrocuted—' Fairfield started.

'Yes, yes, don't fret. It's just that they get harder and harder
to find and I really wanted these guys. Been at it for years all
over the south-west. They're now running out of urban spaces
like these – every square inch is being developed. Some gangs
move into the countryside, but there everyone knows everyone
and people get suspicious, and the costs are much higher. The
latest trend is to move into the suburbs and rent a large family
home, nice bit of garden around so the neighbours don't get
too close, and then stuff the house with plants and equipment.
They get a man and a woman to look after the plants and they
pose as a married couple. It's more elaborate for them to set
up, but much harder to find for us.'

'Well, I'm sorry I loused it up for you,' Fairfield said with
a tinge of bitterness.

'Don't be too hard on yourself, Kat; you found the place
– that's the main thing.' He made a sweeping arm gesture.
'Look at it. There must be, what, twelve hundred plants? If
not more. Good to take that much herbal off the street. We'll
get Typhoo some other time.'

'Is it really worth it, us expending so many resources on
this sort of operation? I mean, it's only weed. Isn't it time it
was decriminalized?'

'How? You can decriminalize the use of it, but if you do,
you just get more of this kind of stuff going on. That girl has

died. Your sergeant nearly copped it. The electricity for all this was stolen from the chaps in the garage. And these gangs are often involved in people trafficking, smuggling, violent crimes of all sorts – and other drugs, of course. They siphon millions of pounds out of the economy and don't pay taxes. I mean, OK, if you want to grow a bit of pot on your window-sill to alleviate the boredom of your little life, you've nothing to fear from DI Wheeler – but this lot? You can't be serious.'

'All right, you've convinced me,' she admitted reluctantly.

'Wait a second, Kat. Tell me you don't smoke this stuff yourself.'

'Me? Café Crèmes is as strong as it gets with me.'

'I'm glad to hear that.' He made an arm gesture which Fairfield rightly interpreted as an invitation for her to leave. 'I hope your sergeant makes a full recovery.'

An hour later she found herself in the Royal Infirmary at DS Sorbie's bedside. He had recovered but looked more miserable than usual, sitting up in bed and complaining with a bitter, querulous voice Fairfield had not heard before.

'A bit of arrhythmia, but it's all completely gone. I feel all right, but now they want to keep me in overnight – "for obser-vation", they said. Look around. Do you see anyone observing? Nope. Does anyone come when I press this button? Nope. Can I get a bloody cup of coffee? Nope.'

'I'm glad to find you so cheerful, Jack.'

'It was a cannabis factory, right?'

'Massive thing – the whole upper floor. Very professional. Remember DI Wheeler?'

'Drug squaddie? Talks like he'd rather be in the army blowing stuff up?'

'Turned up and took charge. He'll get all the glory, if there's any to be had. He recognized the set-up by the teabag habit of the caretaker. Said he was disappointed I had called ambu-lance and backup. He'd have liked to have staked out the place. And I got a whole lecture about the importance of busting cannabis factories and the sterling work the drug squaddies do.'

'Glad I was out of it, then. But this means Bethany Hall

had nothing to do with it. She probably found the cannabis factory the same way we did, only she died from the electric shock. The bastards found her dead on their doorstep and drove her down the road and dumped her, hoping we'd think it was suicide.'

'Yes, they can't be terribly bright if they thought that might fool anyone for more than five minutes. Poor Bethany probably had nothing to do with anything – not with the cannabis, not with Marcus Catlin, and nothing at all with Fulvia bloody Lamberti. We're basically back to square one. Forget Bethany. If Wheeler gets his Typhoo man, then we'll stake a claim on the bastard for manslaughter. In the meantime, we're no nearer to finding Fulvia.'

A nursing assistant entered the room with a tea trolley. 'Ah, here's the tea lady at last,' said Sorbie. 'Coffee for me, love.'

The girl gave Sorbie a less-than-impressed look and consulted the patient notes at the foot of the bed. 'A nice cup of camomile tea for you, sir.'

Sorbie fell back on his pillow with the expression of a Renaissance martyr, while Fairfield walked from the room, suddenly feeling cheerful again.

McLusky had no idea whether a Petit Corona cigar suited him, as Hotchkiss had said, but they probably suited his car. He had pulled over within sight of Jennifer Longmaid's house on an impulse, telling Austin that he felt the need to fortify himself with a smoke before questioning her.

'I don't blame you. But what am *I* supposed to do?' Austin complained.

'You just sit and breathe deeply.' After sliding one of the cigars out of the leather case and lighting it, McLusky sat back and blew large clouds of fragrant smoke out of the open window.

Beside him, Austin practically had his head out of his window, busily avoiding passive smoking. 'Cigars? Not you as well! Fairfield is smoking cigars – did you know that?'

'Of course.'

'Why is she smoking cigars if she doesn't want people to know she's a lesbian?'

'She's bi.'

'Same thing. I don't think most of Albany Road station can wrap their head around the concept of a bisexual police officer. Some are old enough to have arrested people for it.'

'I'm not sure I'll take up the habit myself. I'm talking about cigars here.' McLusky had quite enjoyed the cigar he had smoked at Hotchkiss's house. He looked at his own hand holding the cigar, blew on the glowing end, trying to decide how he liked it. It was such an old-fashioned thing to do, smoking cigars, but so was smoking, it appeared.

How much of a bribe had it been to accept the cigars in their leather case from Hotchkiss? He had looked it up: the little cigars alone cost six pounds each. If he had wanted to make a habit of smoking these, he would need to accept regular bribes from the man. He coughed and flung the cigar out of the window – at least five quid's worth, he thought. He had no intention of sticking to any bargains made with Hotchkiss, so perhaps smoking his cigars was an unhealthy thing to do. He slid the other two cigars from the leather case and dropped those out of the window too. After a moment's hesitation he threw the leather case after it into the grass on the verge.

'I feel I should arrest you for littering,' Austin said. 'Changed your mind about cigars, then?'

McLusky grunted. 'These cigars have a bitter aftertaste.'

'Look, it's her.' Jennifer Longmaid's little sports car emerged from the drive of Stanmore House and accelerated past them with her at the wheel. If she had spotted them, she did not show it, not giving their car a second glance.

'Think we should follow her?' Austin asked.

'Can't just follow her for the heck of it; we have nothing on her. Can't follow her covertly without permission from on high and can't follow her overtly because that's harassment. No matter; we'll start with the other grieving widow.'

'I've been wondering about Elaine Poulimenos's Porsche. How old is it?'

'Dunno, not seen it. Why?'

'The older models sound surprisingly like a Beetle. A noisy Beetle. Especially from a distance.'

'Do they? Interesting.'

'Basically made by the same people. A Porsche is just a squashed Beetle, isn't it?'

'Not sure Porsche owners would see it that way. But we'll have a look at it.' He turned the car around and pointed it south towards Bath.

'Will she inherit her husband's fortune?'

'We don't know yet. *She* left *him.* He did have time to change his will and leave it all to a home for decrepit Sunday painters. She could probably challenge that in court and so on and so on. People do change their minds where money is involved. Last time I spoke to her, it was "poor but happy, starting a new life with nothing but my little Porsche and a couple of David Bomberg paintings". We'll see what the mood is, shall we?'

The mood at Elaine Poulimenos's house was, if not sombre, then at least less ebullient than the last time McLusky had been there. He made the appropriate noises. 'I'm sorry for your loss, Mrs Poulimenos.' This time Elaine did not insist he call her Simmons. 'But we will have to ask you a few routine questions.'

It was her new partner, Paul Chappell, who had opened the door to them and admitted them with a show of reluctance.

They followed the couple into the sitting room which, despite the bright sunlight that streamed in through the UPVC windows, looked sad. Elaine, a nervous hand plucking at her T-shirt, looked lost in the room, as though she still wasn't used to the positioning of the furniture. All four found places to sit around the coffee table, Elaine and Paul sitting close together. McLusky realized what made the room so depressing, despite being larger and much better furnished than his own: it was the relative grandeur of all those drawing rooms he had been in lately, from the Victorian stuffiness of Mendenhall's Woodlea House to the tasteless opulence of Hotchkiss's Ashton View.

'We need to know exactly where you were two days ago in the evening – let's say between nine and six in the morning. Both of you.'

'Well, I was here,' said Elaine, looking up at her partner, who nodded.

'I was at my mother's house; she was feeling unwell. She lives in Wells.'

'I hope she is feeling better now,' McLusky offered.

'She is,' said Elaine. 'But she really needs someone to look after her. And that'll be us, I expect,' she added with a marked lack of enthusiasm.

'Can anyone confirm that you were here, Mrs Poulimenos?'

'I spoke to her on the phone, twice,' Paul said eagerly.

'I'm afraid partners giving each other alibis counts for very little in the eyes of the law, but thank you.'

When Austin spoke, the couple looked at him as though they had previously thought he was mute. 'Can you tell us who will benefit, financially, from your husband's death, Mrs Poulimenos?'

'Yes, I expect that'll be me, unless Leon changed his will recently. If he did, then he didn't tell me. I don't think he would have done. He wanted me back. He wanted me there, even though I was seeing Paul.'

'This may sound like an idiotic question,' McLusky said, 'but do you have any idea who might have wanted your husband dead?'

'It's only idiotic because naturally I'd have told you if I did, but no, I have thought about it ever since the woman police officer came to tell me. She was very good by the way – made me a cup of tea in my own kitchen so I could sit and have a cry.'

Austin left a few heartbeats of a pause before he asked, 'What were your husband's politics like, would you say?'

The ghost of a smile. 'I expect you found his little Nazi theme park at the back of his studio. Yes? Oh dear. It started off quite gently, almost like a hobby. An interest in history, German history, World War Two history. He was reading books about it. Of course, he had the money to buy more than just books, so he started collecting bits of World War Two and Nazi memorabilia, and that's where it got strange. He started talking about it differently. I told him what I thought about it and he never pushed me to share his convictions after that. After all, I was only the little woman with no head for politics. It was as though the stuff he bought – that flag and other things – it was as if they were infectious. As though he caught something off them. It turned from a hobby into a philosophy. And when Golden Dawn became more prominent in Greece, he was convinced it was the right answer for the old country. He thought at the next election they might be victorious and sweep away all the old parties, and he didn't seem to mind that they murdered the odd opponent here and there.' Her face brightened up. 'Looks like Greece went quite the other way now, doesn't it?'

'Did he have any political associates in this country?'

'I don't think so. It was all done over the internet. He Skyped with Golden Dawn types sometimes.'

'Can you tell us what was discussed?'

'No idea. He always chatted to them in his fascist cubbyhole; anyway, they would have spoken in Greek. I don't speak it. I tried but I couldn't even master the alphabet.'

McLusky pulled a couple of large photographs from a folder. 'When we entered Bybrook View, we found that things in your husband's cubbyhole, as you call it, had been disturbed. There was a display case.' He held up the pictures. 'Would you be able to tell us what is missing from it?'

'No idea. Not the foggiest. It's all yucky Nazi stuff and I never went inside that place. It felt like a dustbin to me.'

McLusky still held up the photographs. 'Are you sure you don't remember anything about this display, Mrs Poulimenos? If the items turn up somewhere, we might be able to trace them back to your husband's killer.'

'No idea. For the last two years I've never been over the threshold of that room. I was afraid I might find something – not just something distasteful but something really horrible, you know?'

McLusky thought he did and put the photos away. 'I know what you are saying. We found nothing more distasteful than memorabilia – objects with Nazi logos, a few postcards, that sort of thing.'

'Thank you,' she said simply.

'I think that is all for the moment. We'll keep you informed of any developments.'

They all rose and made for the hall. 'Just one more thing. Your Porsche. Have you sold it yet?'

'No. And I've changed my mind about it; I'm not going to sell it after all.'

'Oh?'

'It's quite an old model and I wouldn't get that much for it, I expect. So I'm holding on to it.'

'Perhaps wise.'

McLusky and Austin sat in the car outside Elaine Poulimenos's house while the inspector made a phone call. As he waited for him to finish, Austin thought he could see Elaine's silhouette behind the net curtains. McLusky put his mobile away. 'Yup. The two Bomberg paintings have been withdrawn from auction by the owner. Looks like "poor but happy" has been cancelled.'

They did not catch up with Jennifer Longmaid until the next day. In front of Stanmore House, beside the little Mazda, stood a large white box van, back doors open; it contained several tea chests. The door to the house stood wide open too. McLusky walked right in without ringing the bell or knocking and Austin followed behind. 'Perhaps we came none too soon,' he suggested.

In the drawing room they found a lot of empty boxes and three men: two workmen in jeans and T-shirts carefully wrapping antique items in copious amounts of bubble wrap and a chubby man in a white shirt and pink bow tie writing in a notebook. The bow tie looked challengingly at the newcomers but relaxed when IDs were proffered.

'Where would we find the lady of the house?' McLusky asked.

'In the garden. I'll tell her you're here.'

'Thank you, but we know the way.' They squeezed past the workmen and went out into the garden. Jennifer Longmaid was sunbathing on a lounger some way from the house. Beside her on the grass stood a tray with a wine bottle and a glass; a paperback lay open beside it. McLusky stopped and squinted against the bright sunshine. 'Is she wearing anything at all?'

Austin squinted too. 'Erm . . . yes, two slices of cucumber, I believe. She knew we were coming.'

'She knew we were coming yesterday but went out anyway.' McLusky cupped his hands and called from where he was standing. 'Mrs Longmaid? Can we have a moment?'

Jennifer Longmaid lifted the slices of cucumber from her eyelids, looked across and sat up, temporarily mesmerizing the two police officers with the seductive movements of her breasts. She stood up and slid into a black, red and gold kimono and changed the lounger into a sitting position. By the time McLusky and Austin stood at a polite ten-foot distance, she had poured herself another glass of wine and sat, with her long legs crossed and on view, smiling ironically. 'And then there were none,' she announced. 'Isn't it all terribly Agatha Christie? Three country houses, three murders, lots of suspects. What you need is a Miss Marple, Inspector, or a little Belgian.' She looked at Austin. 'You're not Belgian, by any chance? No? You're not little, either.' Austin remained impassive.

'Can you please tell me,' McLusky asked, 'where you were three nights ago? Between, say, nine in the evening and five in the morning.'

'Three days ago? I can hardly remember last night.' She drained her glass of red and reached for the bottle. Only a mouthful remained, which she attempted to pour, half of it arcing over the top of the glass. 'Bugger. Another one bites the dust. Three nights ago . . . three nights . . . I was probably here, pissed. Or in Bath, pissed. Or first in Bath, pissed, and later here, more pissed. I have been drinking rather a lot lately. Enjoying the weather.'

'We'd like you to be a bit more specific, Mrs Longmaid. That was the night your friend Elaine's husband was killed.'

'I know. Bang bang. Just like mine.'

McLusky noted the double 'bang'. 'I'd be grateful if you contacted us should you remember where you were – and with whom, if applicable. Is there a regular bus service from here to Bath and Bristol?'

'Eh? Bus service? What d'you want with a bus? There used to be, but the service has been withdrawn.'

'Then may I suggest you don't give us reason to withdraw your driving licence – for drink-driving, say? Life in the country can be tricky without a car.'

Jennifer wrinkled her nose. 'Yeah, all right, all right. Don't go all prissy on me.'

McLusky pointed over his shoulder. 'Or are you perhaps in the process of moving house?'

'That? No, I'm just getting rid of some of the old crap. I never did take to antiques; I found I prefer younger things on the whole. I'm selling the lot and doing up the house in contemporary style. No more fusty old nonsense. Room to breathe is what I need now. Isn't the twenty-first century wonderful?' She stood up and returned the lounger to its lying position. 'If that is all, gentlemen, I'd like to resume my sunbathing. They said it'll rain tomorrow, so make the most of it.' She let her kimono fall to the ground and resumed her sunbathing as McLusky and Austin turned away. They returned to the house.

The man with tie and notebook was busy talking on his mobile. 'Astounding, astounding. Yes, that too. Peculiar chap.' He noticed the officers. 'Actually, can I call you back?' He put away his mobile. 'You found her all right?'

'Yes, thanks.' McLusky waved an arm at the room which was still full of countless antiques. 'All this stuff, for want of a better word – is it as valuable as it looks?'

'Absolutely. Worth a small fortune. Longmaid had a brilliant eye, but . . .' He shrugged.

'But what?'

'He loved antiques too much. He liked living among them more than selling them. There is more and better stock in here than in his Clifton outlet. I think the man was more antique than dealer. If you gave him a thousand-year-old piece of china, he'd probably eat his porridge out of it.'

'Did you know him quite well?'

'Not really. I have a stall in the Emporium too, but, to tell you the truth, I don't think he liked me. Or anyone, for that matter. And I think he hated selling antiques.'

'I got that impression. He loved antiques but hated selling them. Mrs Longmaid feels quite the opposite.'

As McLusky checked his watch, the antique dealer looked at him with sudden professional interest. 'That's a fine time-piece you have there. Mind if I have a quick look at it?'

McLusky held out his wrist. 'Cheap fake, I'm afraid.' The Rolex had been part of a whole box of worthless tat recovered from the house of a habitual burglar, and when McLusky found he had absent-mindedly pocketed it, he had kept it to replace his own broken one.

'I disagree,' said the dealer. 'I know my timepieces and that is a genuine 1948 or 1949 Oyster perpetual date Rolex. I'd offer you five grand for it. But I'd probably sell it for eight.'

McLusky stared at it, then at the dealer, then at Austin who – thankfully – was having a conversation with one of the workmen at the other end of the room. 'Thanks for telling me. I'll sleep with my arm in a safe tonight.' He buried his hands deep in his jacket pockets and left the room quickly, signalling Austin to follow him. 'I have to get a move on,' he told him, 'if I want to get to Poulimenos's PM on time. I'll drop you off at the station.'

At Flax Bourton, Dr Coulthart greeted him like a long-lost friend when he appeared in the viewing suite. 'Inspector, what a pleasant surprise. I had expected DS Austin.' In the past McLusky had sent his sergeant to attend whenever possible, but DSI Denkhaus had put an end to it, insisting that he be present if he was leading the investigation. McLusky loathed autopsies almost as much as Austin did. 'Then let us begin.'

Leonidas Poulimenos had been a large man who had indulged his earthly passions without much restraint. His naked grey body on the steel table evoked no pity in McLusky, only revulsion, and he felt uneasy about that. He was a police officer and he owed it to the dead man – all three dead men – to find the killer and to avenge their deaths, or rather to allow society to exact revenge within the framework of the law. All too often society felt let down by the law; yet perhaps no section of society felt more disillusioned about the efficacy of the legal system than the police force. McLusky had now worked on a good number of murder cases and led quite a few investigations himself, but he felt more impatient than usual. He put it down to the way the murders were committed, close together, almost with impunity, wiping out an entire group of friends. His early conviction that David Mendenhall had killed his father for the inheritance had crumbled when his friends were murdered. All murder was strange, firmly outside people's normal experiences, and what led up to murder was sometimes complex, but mostly it was bloody obvious and depressing. He could cope with that; policing the obvious and depressing was what they were here for. It was mostly stupidity or greed. Often it was stupidity combined with greed, sometimes intelligence and greed. But what McLusky hated – loathed with every fibre of his being, in fact – was the *weird*. He couldn't abide weird. People who picked up a bottle in anger and bashed someone's head in, he could understand; turf wars between drug gangs – obvious; morons with knives and low self-esteem – par for the course. But the killings of the three painter friends in their luxurious houses was different. Jennifer Longmaid had put her finger on it: it was like walking around in a bloody Miss Marple story, only the busybody spinster never had to watch dead bodies being eviscerated. Now, without its covering of clothes, the second bullet wound on the right side of his chest was only too obvious. It was the deliberateness of the killings, the cold-hearted point-blank shooting, that got McLusky's goat, and, as Laura had frequently pointed out, he had a lot of goat to get.

The pathologist cut, lifted, drained and weighed while McLusky unfocussed his eyes and let them drift over the immaculate inhumane surfaces of the operating theatre. 'You asked me a while back about the first victim,' Coulthart said. 'How much longer he might have lived had he not been shot. I can tell you categorically that Mr Poulimenos was killing himself quite effectively already. I suspect a heart attack would have done for him within a couple of years anyway. Some of his arteries are in a shocking state and so is his liver. Now, from the way we found him and the spray patterns of blood above the sofa, I'd say the victim was standing or perhaps in the process of standing up when he was shot. The trajectory of the bullets as they hit suggest the gun was fired from below. The killer was either sitting opposite him or lying on the floor, or you're looking for a midget, about three feet in height. I can also confirm that the gun was a thirty-eight.' He held up the projectile he had recovered from the body. 'Even I can tell that from looking at it. It'll go off to forensics within the hour, I'm sure you'll be glad to hear.'

'Oh, ecstatic.' McLusky slammed out of the viewing suite.

'No pleasing some people,' said Coulthart and dropped the bullet into an evidence bag.

TWELVE

'Y ou already made an offer on it?' Laura pulled away from him in order to give him an inquisitive look from her corner of the sofa.

He had hoped he might feed it into the conversation, but all through the meal that Laura had cooked for him at her place – most of her fellow students were at a music gig – he had failed to find an opportunity. In the end he had just blurted it out. 'I *like* the place. And I like the neighbourhood.'

'You mean the pub opposite.'

'Not just that.' McLusky had always known how Laura would interpret the purchase of the Northampton Street flat: as a confirmation of his status as a bachelor and of her status as a convenient add-on. But he really did like his flat; it had a quirky charm, just like the Rossis themselves. He enjoyed their Italian voices as they chatted under his window while setting up the vegetable display outside the shop, and he did not even mind the voices of the pub's patrons leaving at closing time. He wasn't sure he really wanted triple glazing to shut out the world or to live among easy-to-wipe surfaces.

'A week ago you wanted me to move in with you; now that you're buying the flat, you didn't even think to mention it.'

'I just did.'

'After you've already made an offer on it.'

'You didn't answer any of my texts, remember?'

'I'd have answered them if they'd been about the flat. I can tell you one thing: I'm not setting foot in the place until you have central heating fitted.'

'It's seventy-five degrees Fahrenheit out there, even though it's' – he checked his watch – 'half past nine in the evening. What do you want heating for?'

'Yeah, like that's going to last. Half past nine? It's *Sherlock!*'

'*What?*'

She fetched the remote from the coffee table and pointed it at the prominently positioned TV set. 'It's a Sherlock Holmes series but it's done tongue-in-cheek and quite funny. You'll like it. And you never know,' she said, settling into her corner of the sofa with her glass of wine, 'you might pick up some tips.'

McLusky found it hard to keep his eyes open. He had had an afternoon of interviews, phone calls, report writing and a case conference, after which he had found more forms to fill in on his desk. Sherlock Holmes, it appeared, never had to deal with those. And if he felt that everything was getting him down, he simply took some cocaine and got his violin out. McLusky was just glad it wasn't a Miss Marple movie and dozed through most of it.

Eventually, he drifted off into a dream where DS Austin, sunbathing fully clothed next to a naked Jennifer Longmaid, was using Sherlock's voice from the soundtrack to tell him: 'And where is the best place to hide a letter, Watson? Why, in a letter rack, of course!' McLusky started awake to see the credits rolling on the screen and hear Laura calling from the kitchen, 'We haven't had our dessert yet; do you fancy it now?'

McLusky grabbed his jacket and made for the front door. *In a bloody letter rack.* He stuck his head in at the kitchen. 'Sorry, hon, got to go. Loved the meal. I'll call you.'

'Yeah, right.' She waited for the front door to close then ripped the lid off the family-sized tub of tiramisu and, armed with a tablespoon, returned to her corner on the sofa just as the next programme started.

McLusky drove with the windows open through the sticky, humid night. The town centre was full of young people in summer clothes, girls in shorts and skimpy dresses, young men without their tops, showing off tattoos and sunburn, moving noisily between drinking venues around the harbour area.

McLusky saw them and saw through them as he drove south out of the city.

Once again, he parked out of earshot of Woodlea House, just as the killer might have done. After the brightness of the car's headlights, the countryside felt very dark. Heavy rain clouds had crawled across the sky all evening and not a single star lit his way down the lane. He used his mobile phone for illumination, but having little charge left on it, he used it intermittently, like a giant firefly. He flicked the light off when he came to the tall wrought-iron gate. There were lights showing at the house and silhouetted against the ground-floor windows he could make out David Mendenhall's BMW. He saw no movement. He stood for an hour, staring at the house in the cricket-chirping darkness, before walking back to his car and driving out to Chew Valley.

He left his car in front of the gate of Bybrook View. He was carrying the keys to the house but the gate had been secured with a D-lock by the Chew Valley police. He climbed the wall and let himself drop into the courtyard. The smell of the burnt-out car and garage was still strong as he crossed to the house. At the front door he pulled down some of the *Crime Scene Do Not Enter* tape that warned unauthorized persons to stay out, found the right key and let himself in. The main fuse had been tripped. He restored electricity to the property by throwing the main switch in a cubbyhole in the utility room, then flicked on the lights in the kitchen. A quick search produced a long-handled coffee pot, cup, coffee and sugar, and, remembering with bitter clarity how Poulimenos had done it, he brewed Greek coffee on the camping stove in the dead man's kitchen. He poured it carefully into the little cup and carried it on its saucer to the sitting room, flicking on lights as he went. In the sitting room, the aroma of his coffee competed with the chemical smells of reagents and other chemicals used by the forensics technicians. McLusky was not sure whether the smells were really there or whether they were just a memory. He brought the little cup to his lips, took a sip of its sweet froth and the smells disappeared and did not return. He stood very still.

Leonidas Poulimenos was sitting on the sofa under the pale patch left by the missing Bomberg painting. He was smoking, sharing a bottle of wine with his visitor. One by one McLusky conjured them into the armchair opposite: Elaine Poulimenos – having left him for a younger man, she had come back carrying a gun to make sure she would inherit her husband's wealth; Jennifer Longmaid – having killed her own husband, she thought she would make sure her friend Elaine stayed rich by shooting Leonidas; Ben Kahn – dripping wet from the sea, come back to avenge himself; his son Elliot – covered in paint spatters, come to avenge his father's death; and finally David Mendenhall – holding a thirty-eight and a petrol can. David had a sound alibi for the time of the torching of Rosslyn Crag: he had been watching a football game at a pub near his home. The petrol can disappeared from David's hand. McLusky drained his cup too far and ended up with a mouthful of coffee grounds. He washed up in the kitchen and dried and returned the cup to its rightful place.

The presence of his car at the gate had triggered the outside lights, illuminating the courtyard and part of the garden. McLusky locked the front door and turned his attention to the studio. It pained him to see so many of the paintings damaged. He had almost liked the man. It was clear that the disappearance of Ben Kahn on that sunny Cornish day had blighted his life, but had it also brought about his death? McLusky stared into the office at the back of the studio. Many of the articles had been taken away for forensic examination, but the framed Nazi flag remained on the wall. What had been taken from the display case by the intruder? Had it been valuable? There were many valuable things at the house that had remained untouched. Had the killing been about that object and been unconnected with the other deaths after all? McLusky dismissed it and turned away. *The best place to hide a sodding letter.*

When he stepped outside, rain began to fall and a cool wind drove it across the lake at him. He climbed out of the place and returned to his car. As he drove off, the security light turned itself off and Bybrook View fell into sepulchral darkness in his mirrors. Just over half an hour later he let his car crawl slowly past Stanmore House. Jennifer Longmaid's little sports car stood in the rain with the roof down. There was no

light showing at the house. McLusky drove back to Bristol
with his headlights on full beam and a squeaking windscreen
wiper, occasionally swearing out loud at the night. 'Bloody
Sherlock! Bloody Sherlock bleedin' Holmes!'

Having found that none of the available ingredients in his
house amounted to the kind of breakfast he felt he deserved,
McLusky made sure he was the first customer through the
door at the Bristolian in Picton Street. He ordered English
breakfast and took a cup of black coffee with him to one of
the tables outside. Every sip produced a small rebellion in his
stomach but he persevered. When the waitress put his breakfast
in front of him with a flourish, he was no longer sure he could
eat it: eggs, bacon, a sausage, beans, black pudding, tomatoes
and fried potatoes, arranged around a dollop of spinach leaves.
McLusky eyed spinach at breakfast with suspicion and warily
began to work his way through the cholesterol feast that
surrounded it.

There are two kinds of drivers who can afford to park their
cars on double yellow lines: police officers and the rich.
McLusky did not register the blue Rolls Royce Silver Shadow
that had crept up on the bumper of his car until Roy Hotchkiss
left the driver's seat and walked towards him. He was wearing
a dark suit, black T-shirt and very shiny black shoes. Hotchkiss
inserted himself into the bench opposite McLusky. 'Yes, I do
hear the canteen food at Albany Road isn't up to much.'
McLusky speared a roundel of black pudding and stuffed it
in his mouth. 'Fortifying yourself before another round of
wrangling with red tape and the complexities of the Police
and Criminal Evidence Act? Can't say I blame you.'

'How did you know I was here?'

'Didn't. I was driving past and saw your motor. Came round
for another look and there you were, stuffing your face.'

'What do you want?' McLusky said through a mouth full
of beans.

'*Want*? Me? Nothing. It was you who wanted something,
remember? You're not eating your greens. You must eat your
greens, Inspector.'

'Not for breakfast.'

'Then I'm having them; they're cooked with sesame oil.'

'You'll have to wait until I'm finished.'

Hotchkiss swiped the teaspoon from McLusky's saucer and dug into the spinach leaves in the centre of the plate. 'I'm not good at waiting; that's one thing you should know about me.'

'Attacking another man's breakfast ought to be an arrestable offence.'

Hotchkiss scraped around in the middle of the plate until the last bit of spinach had disappeared, flicked the spoon back on to the saucer and took a gold biro from an inside pocket of his jacket. He scrawled a name and address on to McLusky's napkin. 'Just an educated guess. And, naturally, at your own risk.' Hotchkiss slid from the bench. 'Stay healthy. It's your annual fitness test soon.'

McLusky watched as Hotchkiss walked to his car and drove off. He resented the man's insinuations that he knew all about his affairs, from the state of the canteen breakfasts to his upcoming fitness test. He waited until the car had disappeared down the street before he turned the napkin around. He was not familiar with the name: Jamie Fife. It was a St Pauls address. He called Austin about it. 'See if he's known to us.'

'How did you get the name?'

'Never mind that. We'll check him out later, when I get back.'

'Is it allowed to ask where you'll be this morning? In case Denkhaus is prowling around.'

'If Denkhaus is asking, you've never heard of me, OK? I'm going out to Stanton Drew again to have another chat with Elliot Kahn. You know what sounds a lot more like a Beetle engine than a Porsche? An old VW camper van, which is what Elliot drives. Or it could have belonged to the girl he was painting.'

'Do you want me to do a quick DVLA check?' Austin offered.

'Nah, I can ask him myself when I get there. Elliot has recently shown interest in the circumstances of his father's death. He quizzed the skipper's son about it. And when I was at his place, something seemed odd, though I couldn't have said what it was. It's been nagging at me.'

*   *   *

Halfway to Stanton Drew, McLusky's stomach began to rebel. A sharp pain developed under his solar plexus and it came and went even while he bumped along the unmade track to the house. Why on earth had he opted for the giant plate of fried food when his usual breakfast consisted of toast and marmalade or a Danish pastry from Rossi's? It was frustration with the investigation, he decided, rather than greed, that made him eat, drink and smoke like this, just when his AFT was coming up. He wondered how Hotchkiss knew that his annual fitness test was due? Who was feeding him gossip from inside Albany Road station?

He had made no appointment to see Kahn. If possible, he liked to turn up out of the blue when quizzing suspects, since their reaction to the intrusion could be telling: unreasonable anger and complaining often hid a guilty conscience, but over-friendly eagerness to cooperate was also sometimes employed. Often criminals believed that most police officers were a bit thick and could therefore be deceived; in McLusky's experience the ratio of thick to bright in the police force broadly matched that of the general population.

The orange camper van was parked in front of the house and there was again loud music, only this time it was pop, not classical music that was playing. The loud music and open door meant that he was able to surprise Kahn in his kitchen; he was on his knees using a large chef's knife to attack the ice that completely encased the door to the freezer compartment in his fridge. 'The damn thing is frozen shut,' Kahn said as casually as though McLusky was a neighbour who had just wandered through the door. 'I suddenly had the idea that there might be a pack of lamb chops inside it and I thought I'd test that theory.' He resumed his stabbing and scraping. All around him on the floor, shards of ice were quickly melting into puddles. 'You've not found the killer yet?'

'You're aware that now all three of your father's painter friends have been shot dead?'

'Yes, very. Are you suggesting this painter could be next or do you have some notion it might have been me?' McLusky asked him where he had been on the night in question. 'I was here. All night. You can ask Berti.'

'Your model? Presumably more than just a model, then.'

'Much more. She is a lover first, model second.'

'Then your alibi would not carry much weight in the eyes of the court.'

'The *court*? What court?'

McLusky shrugged his shoulders as though it didn't matter. 'Your camper van – use it much?'

'As little as possible. It's a thirsty old thing and I prefer to spend my money on my own thirst. I have an electric bicycle for most journeys. Why? Do camper vans come into it somehow?'

'Just an engine noise. Probably from a Beetle.'

'Ah, yes, same stupid engine.' A large piece of ice broke loose. 'Now we're getting somewhere.' He lobbed the frozen lump into the empty sink where it shattered.

'What happened to your father's paintings after his death?'

'I have quite a few of them. My aunt kept some, but a few of them were lost. I inherited most of my father's things. Still have a whole trunk of them.' He pointed towards the ceiling with the knife. 'Can't bring myself to throw them out, even though I never look at them.'

'Would it be possible for me to have a look through them?'

Kahn worked on for a moment before answering. 'What are you hoping to find? Yeah, OK, just let me do this; I'm nearly there.' He managed to prise open the door to the narrow compartment and hacked at the insides for a bit before inserting his hands into the icy cavern and freeing a battered carton. 'Ah. Not lamb chops. Economy fish fingers. Best before . . . today! They must have been calling to me.'

McLusky followed Kahn up a narrow wooden staircase to the upper floor and a room at the end of the corridor. It had once been a small bedroom; now, besides a wardrobe and an old dressing table, it housed mainly paintings – a lot of them, all turned to the wall – boxes of books and sketchbooks. There was a school trunk which Kahn freed of the boxes that stood on top. He swung open the lid and stared morosely into it. 'Look at it. If it wasn't for his paintings, that would be all that's left of him. There's not much to a life, is there?' The trunk was filled with an assortment of objects: an alarm clock, a stack of LPs, shoeboxes, a few books, an old SLR camera, bundles of oil painting brushes, boxes of charcoal, tins of pencils. The music now thumped under their feet, muffled by distance.

'Many of us feel like that when loved ones are gone. Most people's possessions can be bundled up in a day or so. But it is the more intangible things they leave behind that really matter.'

'Yes.' Kahn sighed as though he had been told this a million times and was tired of it.

'These are your father's brushes and things? You being a painter as well, I'd have thought you would use them. Carrying on the tradition.'

There were two bundles, a large one consisting of two dozen or so brushes of all sizes, and a smaller one. Both bundles were tied together with string. Kahn bent down and picked them up, one in each hand. Downstairs, the music stopped abruptly. 'I'm a bit superstitious about that sort of thing. Very superstitious, if I'm honest.' He lifted them up and scrutinized them, held the hog-hair bristles to his nose and sniffed. 'Still smell of turps.' He turned the smaller bundle round and round, held it up to the light coming through the narrow window. 'These are the brushes he used on the boat the day he disappeared. I'd be scared to paint with them.' He let them fall back into the trunk. 'I'm quite superstitious about my own painting too. I don't know where it comes from; it just happens.'

'Surely it comes from your father. You inherited his artistic talent.'

'Oh, that – yes, probably.' He stuffed the larger bundle under his arm. 'But that leaves inspiration. Being able to draw and paint – you can learn all that, pick it up. The inspiration that fires it up into a work of art on the canvas rather than some well-painted cliché is the difference. Not many have it. I know I do have it. But I'm scared to interfere with it by scrutinizing it, analyzing it, naming it. It's like that fairy tale of the poor shoemaker and the elves. You know the one: he only has leather for one pair of shoes left. Overnight, elves come and turn them into exquisite shoes which he sells for a lot of money. He buys more leather and next day there are more shoes. All wonderfully made. And so on. Then one night he and his wife decide to spy on whoever makes them. But the elves notice them and never come back.'

'And you think your inspiration is a bunch of elves that could let you down.'

'Yes, like Cornish piskies. They could disappear like my father did.'

'And yet you went to Port Isaac and asked the skipper's son about that day.'

Downstairs, the music started up again, at a lesser volume. It was a classical piece this time. Kahn smiled briefly, looking at his shoes, then up at McLusky. He wasn't sure whether the question or the change of musical genre had prompted the smile, but it was short-lived. 'You know about that, do you? That's impressive. Berti and I were down in Cornwall for a few days. It was Berti's idea to find Tigur. She thought it was important to know the truth. But it was a mistake. We only found the son and he didn't really know anything. I don't want to poke around in it any further; it makes me feel anxious. For myself and for my work.'

'Would you mind if I had a look through the things in the trunk?'

'That's what we're here for.'

McLusky proceeded gently, watched by Kahn. Without disturbing things too much, he lifted and inspected items and let them sink back into the dim past. He lifted the lid of a scuffed shoebox. It was full of letters.

'They're from my mother,' Kahn commented. 'Most from before they were married.'

McLusky ignored them. Tucked into the space beside them were two rolls of thirty-five-millimetre film. He teased them out with one finger and held them up.

'Yes, my father took a lot of photographs as well. Black and white; he printed them himself. I have a lot of them downstairs.'

'Did he take photographs the day he disappeared?'

'No, he didn't take the camera on the boat.'

'These two rolls have been exposed – you can tell. The end bit's not sticking out. But they haven't been developed.'

'They've probably gone off by now.'

'That's possible. Would you mind if I had them developed?' Kahn shrugged uncomfortably. 'It might help us,' McLusky said.

'Yeah, OK. Most of his photography was landscapes and trees and stuff.'

'Could I see some of your father's paintings?'

'Yes, sure. It's just . . . I don't like looking at them. I know them all, of course, but they don't have a good influence on me. I'll be downstairs. Just be careful with them and don't make dents or scratch them or anything.'

'I'll be very careful.' McLusky started turning paintings, which were stacked six-deep against the wall, inspecting them with a criminal rather than artistic eye and returning them gently in the right order. Many were landscapes. Unlike those of the other painters he had seen, however, these did not look back towards the nineteenth century. There were portraits of people he did not know, and these also had an edge that took them far beyond the search for likeness. McLusky could tell because among them were portraits of Charles Mendenhall and of Leonidas Poulimenos. In both they looked much younger. The canvases were painted, according to the dates on the back, in 1993. The longer he stayed in the claustrophobic little room, the more uncomfortable he became, until a squirming irritability made him rush out of the door and down the stairs. He had the distinct feeling that he had been wasting his time and a strong sensation that he was in the wrong place. He thanked Kahn, who was now deicing the freezer compartment with a hairdrier, and left the house to reverse along the track to the road.

Austin drummed his fingers on top of the steering wheel and peered along the narrow road at the small Edwardian house. They had come in his Micra, which they hoped would look less conspicuous in a street in St Pauls than McLusky's car. They had checked out James Fife on the computer and found he had a string of convictions, some for drugs, many violent, but none involving firearms. 'If Jamie Fife is the owner of the gun, should we not have got armed response out?'

McLusky had thought about it and decided against it. 'If he's renting out the gun, it'll be either out or hidden under the bathtub. He won't be sitting around with it strapped to his arse. Anyway, we're only acting on a tip-off.'

'How reliable is your source?' Austin had asked who had supplied the information but had received no answer.

'We may be about to find out.' McLusky believed that it was entirely possible that James Fife was making a nuisance of himself on the big man's patch and Hotchkiss was only using McLusky to harass or arrest him. If that was so, he would find a way to harass Hotchkiss. 'Well, there's no movement. The longer we sit here, the more likely he'll get wind of it. Let's knock on doors. You take the back. Give me a buzz when you're in position.'

These were back-to-back working-class houses with tiny backyards separated by the narrowest of alleys. Austin found the entrance to the alley smelling sharply of urine, but the alley itself surprisingly free of the usual rubbish. He found the back of Fife's address: an eight-foot wooden fence and narrow door that had once been painted white, now peeling and overgrown with ivy and half swallowed by some kind of shrub on the other side. Austin often complained that he was always given the door-kicking and fence-climbing duties, but he didn't actually mind it; it made for better memories at the end of the shift than keyboard tapping and form filling. 'I'm at the back. A fence needs climbing. Give it thirty seconds.' He pocketed his mobile and pulled himself over the fence which swayed precariously under his weight. Apart from recycling boxes, the concrete yard was completely empty. He was at the back door in four strides.

McLusky reached the front door at the same moment and immediately started ringing the bell and hammering open-handed on the door. After half a minute of that he stopped to listen. The door remained unanswered, the net curtains untwitched. He bent down and lifted the aluminium letterbox flap to look into the hall. 'Shit.' He thumbed the emergency button on his airwave. 'Alpha Nine to control, requesting backup at my position, ambulance and the full works. Possible homicide.' He called Austin. 'I have a possible body right behind the door. Can you get in there?'

'Yeah, half-glazed kitchen door. No problem.' He tried the door, found it locked. A loose lump of algae-covered concrete did for the glass. The key was in the lock; Austin reached through and pushed open the door which crunched reluctantly over broken glass. He rushed across the kitchen and into the hall. 'Jeez.'

At this moment he only had eyes for the body in the hall. A woman was lying crumpled on her side on the vinyl floor in a pool of blood. Her hands were clutching at her midriff. He squeezed past her in the narrow hall to open the door for McLusky. There was not much room. McLusky half inserted himself into the hall and looked down. 'Is she dead?'

'Just checking.' Austin bent down and felt for a pulse at the neck. The body felt warm. He thought he could feel a faint pulsing but couldn't be sure. 'I think she's alive.'

'Got a first-aid kit in the car?'

Austin lobbed the car keys at him. 'In the boot.'

McLusky disappeared. Austin could hear him run down the road. He could smell nothing but blood. The woman was young, perhaps twenty-five, and she was dying, dying in front of his eyes. He had seen dead bodies before but never anyone whose life was trickling away while he looked on. Half of his mind was here, scrutinizing the woman, half outside following McLusky's footsteps. Her face was pale, her mouth and eyes closed; she wore blue eye shadow. He could hear McLusky slam the boot of his car. Some of her eyelashes were caked together with excessive mascara. There were many silver rings on her hands; blood still trickled through her clasped fingers. Her blue denim shorts were turning purple with blood. Her white top was wicking up blood, a line of it creeping like a slow tide towards her breasts. McLusky's footsteps pounded outside and then he was there, first-aid kit open. He held it out to Austin who was close to tears.

Austin scrabbled for anything that could be used to stem the tide of blood – gauze, bandages, cotton pads – and slid them under and around the victim's hands. It was impossible to make out what the wound consisted of and whether he was making it better or worse. His hands were slick with her blood.

'I'm not sure I'm doing it right.' His voice was verging on tearful.

'You're doing something. Press down on it. Best we can do.' They stood, a tableau of frozen helplessness, in the dingy blood-spattered hall, waiting, straining their ears for a siren, willing the ambulance to arrive. Austin thought it would never happen. He felt himself fuse to the centre of the woman's body as though he had grown into it. His nose itched and he let it; he was grateful for it, for the tiny bit of distance it gave him from the life trickling away under his hands. McLusky shut the lid of the kit and withdrew through the door. 'Going round the back.' Austin wanted him to stay, did not want to be alone. His knees were beginning to scream at him but he did not dare shift to relieve the pain. *It's just pain, just a bit of pain*, he thought. *It's the least you can do, the very least, having a bit of pain.*

McLusky scrambled into the backyard with a little more difficulty and more swearing than the athletic Austin had done. He crunched across the kitchen and pulled on latex gloves as he went. The kitchen looked cold, functional and tidy. 'It's me,' he said to the back of the crouching Austin as he entered the hall. 'How's it going?' When he got no answer, he added, 'Can't be long now.' He was right. The single squawk from an ambulance siren nearby announced the imminent arrival of the paramedics. As the first one inserted himself into the hall, a bright yellow energetic bundle of medical efficiency, McLusky breathed a sigh of relief and pushed open the door to the front room to give everyone more space.

He didn't make it far into the room. Slumped over the blue sofa under the window lay the body of James Fife, dressed in tracksuit bottoms and faded blue T-shirt. His skin was very pale, turning to grey. His hair was almost black, his eyebrows bushy and his face unshaven. McLusky had seen enough murder victims to know that Jamie Fife would not need to be seen by the paramedics who were working feverishly in the hall. The victim's lower body had slid off the sofa on to the floor. There was less blood here and most of that soaked into the T-shirt from around the knife that was still stuck in the region of his solar plexus. Not a knife,

McLusky mentally corrected himself, but a dagger of some sort, its hilt and guard smeared with blood. He did not want to approach the victim without first donning a scene suit. The slumping body had pushed the flimsy coffee table into an angle to the sofa without upsetting the half-drunk mug of tea and half-eaten fried egg, sausages and beans on toast. Knife and fork lay neatly crossed on the plate. The rest of the room looked undisturbed and tidy – no ash trays, no drugs paraphernalia, nothing disturbed. A face appeared at the window, nudging McLusky away from the acute observation of every detail. It was the face of PC Hanham. The officer cupped his hands around his eyes, trying to peer through the net curtains, then his face disappeared only to be replaced by DC Dearlove doing the same.

'Round the back!' McLusky called. Dearlove gave a thumbs-up and disappeared.

In the hall the body of the woman had been stabilized on a stretcher and was receiving plasma and oxygen. Austin stood ashen-faced, apart from a smear of blood where he had finally scratched the itch on his nose. He held his bloody hands away from his body. 'Got to wash,' he said dully and started towards the kitchen.

McLusky stopped him. 'Not in here, Jane; it's a crime scene. Go outside.'

Mutely, Austin turned and followed the stretcher to the front of the house where PC Hanham found him some mineral water and tissues from his vehicle. The narrow road soon filled up with cars and personnel. Some of the neighbours, having been questioned, were persuaded to move their cars elsewhere so that forensics vans, police cars and the coroner's van could take their place. A large command vehicle turned up and was promptly sent home again by McLusky for being impractical. Both ends of the road were sealed off.

Austin, now with his hands cleaned with the aid of water, wet wipes and other tissues, still held them as though he did not trust their cleanliness. 'Do you think we could have saved the other one had we known he was there? We should have looked, shouldn't we?'

'Not a chance.' They were standing outside beside a police

van. McLusky was pulling on a scene suit. 'Are you OK to go back in there? It's all right if you want to stay out here.'

'I'll be fine.' Austin tore open a scene-suit pack. 'I can handle the dead. It's dying girls I'm not keen on.'

The little house was now crowded and the synthetic sound of scene suits swishing past each other was everywhere. McLusky knelt next to the body with Austin standing behind him. Flash photography glittered around them, a strong light on top of the video camera made shadows sway. 'The handle is very ornate.'

'It's called a hilt when it's a dagger,' said a forensics technician.

'Ah, thank you,' said McLusky.

'And the curved crossbar below it is called the guard.'

'Thank you again. Now shut up.' McLusky shifted to get a better all-round look at the weapon. 'Oh, shit.'

'What?' Austin leant closer.

McLusky stood up to give him a chance to scrutinize what was visible of the weapon. Austin peered at the other side of it. 'A swastika. Two swastikas even. It's a bloody Nazi dagger.'

'You said it.'

A scene-of-crime officer clattered down the stairs and waved McLusky over. 'There's a couple of blood stains on the way up and plenty of blood residue in the bathroom. Someone went upstairs to wash blood off themselves and then tried to rinse it all away – not very well, though.'

'Anything disturbed up there?'

'The lid's off the cistern and there's wet plastic bags lying on the floor.'

'I have a fair idea of what that's about.' McLusky waved Austin to follow him and they stepped outside into the back-yard where a SOCO was examining the fence and locked gate.

'I'll need fibre samples of your clothing in a minute,' said the SOCO, 'for elimination. You both went over this, didn't you?'

McLusky just nodded and lit a cigarette. 'All right, Jane, what happened here?'

'Fuck knows. Can I have a cigarette?'

'No, you can't; you gave up, remember?'

Austin gave his hands one more scrutinizing look before he stuffed them into his trouser pockets. 'Someone comes to the house, carrying a Nazi dagger. The girl opens the door and is knifed in the hall. Fife is in the front room having his tea. In comes killer with dagger . . .'

'Now dripping with blood.'

'Walks up to Fife and kills him with it.'

'Not until Fife has politely crossed his cutlery on his unfinished plate of grub.' McLusky took a luxurious drag from his cigarette and blew smoke skywards.

'What are you saying?'

'Nothing. I'm thinking. Killer goes upstairs, washes hands and takes something out of the toilet cistern. Told you it's always in obvious places. Killer leaves, without blood stains, by the front door.'

'Tight squeeze with the girl lying there.'

'He doesn't mind banging the door into the body because he thinks she's dead. He wouldn't leave a live witness behind.' He took a hasty drag on his cigarette, then dropped it on the concrete and walked to the back door. 'Deedee?'

Dearlove appeared, scene-suited and armed with his notebook. 'Where did they take the woman?'

'Hospital.'

'Which damn hospital? Find out. And then arrange twenty-four-hour protection for her until further notice; I'll clear it with the super. I want an officer with her from the moment she comes out of the operating theatre.' Dearlove turned on his heels.

'If she survives,' said Austin gloomily.

'If she doesn't, you have my permission to blame yourself for the rest of your life. Can't say fairer than that.'

When eventually they left the crime scene in his car, Austin remained gloomy. 'The killer came out of the front door. And we were watching it for ten minutes, while she was lying there. We must have missed the killer leaving the house by a whisker.'

'I know. But did we just miss Jamie Fife's killer or was Fife killed by the same person as the others?'

'OK, the dagger could have come from Poulimenos's

collection, but the MO is totally different. Shooting someone with a thirty-eight is one thing but stabbing is very close up and personal.'

'Think about it, though,' McLusky objected. 'All the other victims lived in their bloody Agatha Christie villas in the country. Who cares about gunshots out there? But a shot in Fife's pokey hovel would bring the neighbours out on the street.' When Austin locked his Micra in the station car park, McLusky dug around in his jacket and produced two rolls of thirty-five-millimetre film. He dropped them into Austin's hand. 'Before you sign out, send these to be developed. I want them pronto.' He walked away towards his car.

'Where will you be?'

McLusky kept walking. 'I'm going to see a man about a cigar.'

McLusky drove fast. Distracted, thinking intensely about the recent deaths, he triggered every speed camera between Bristol and Cold Ashton. He did not slow down until he had a near head-on collision with an ancient Citroën on the narrow road to Ashton View. It was dusk by the time he stopped in front of the gates. Working the bell had no effect and produced no answer. McLusky reached in through the car window and worked his horn a few times, then went back to the gate and stared through the bars. Now he could see the dark silhouette of a figure in the garden to the left of the house, simply standing in the gloom. McLusky parped his horn a few more times. Eventually, the silhouette moved towards him, slowly and carrying, McLusky now saw, a garden fork. He stared at the approaching figure with murderous impatience. 'Take your time, I've got all night.' The silhouette sharpened into a man wearing blue trousers stuffed into black Wellingtons and a faded checked shirt. McLusky noted with relief that it was not Tony Gotts who looked after Mendenhall's garden.

The man, fortyish, fair-haired and tanned, stopped fifteen paces away from the gate. 'What do you want? There's no one here.'

McLusky stuck his hand through the bars and held out his ID. 'Where's Hotchkiss?'

'Mr Hotchkiss has flown out to Turkey. For a holiday. He has a house there.'

'Do you have a contact address or number?'

'Nah, he doesn't tell me stuff like that. Sorry.' The man turned around and walked leisurely back towards the house, cradling his fork on the crook of his arm.

THIRTEEN

Fairfield already regretted having agreed to come. There were only two women on the squad DI Wheeler had assembled for the raid and both of them had to be spending all their spare time in the gym lifting weights and downing protein shakes, and had now disappeared under forty pounds of protective Kevlar and helmets. Fairfield herself was only wearing her stab vest which was enough to make her feel large and ugly.

From the moment she had joined the operation as an observer, she had felt faintly patronized. DI Wheeler let no opportunity pass to point out that the anti-drug Operation Atrium was the most crucial thing Avon and Somerset did in the city, how it impacted on all other aspects of policing and frankly was the only department worth being in. He could rattle off the statistics of how many convictions they had procured, how much crack and how many guns they had taken off the street and how many cannabis factories they had closed down faster than a press officer with seven cups of coffee inside him. 'Shame your sergeant isn't here; he'd have enjoyed this, I'm sure.'

'Still off sick, though I suspect he's milking it.' The moment she had said it she regretted the disloyalty and recognized that she had been trying to impress Wheeler all along. They were sitting in Wheeler's BMW in a leafy street on the edge of Redcliff. It was raining. The weather had broken the night before. The summer temperatures had been replaced by a cool north wind and it had not stopped raining for nearly twenty-four hours. Two units of drug squad, including an armed response unit, were getting into position. DI Wheeler talked in his airline-pilot voice as though drug raids were nothing but tedious routine for him. 'It's typical of the premises they're using more and more now: large suburban houses that no one would suspect. We wouldn't normally raid a place in the early evening – we prefer the dawn – but we've had good intelligence on this and it looks as though a large number of people are on the premises. Initially, we had a tip-off from a neighbour who noted that as soon as the new tenant moved in he installed blinds on every window and they are permanently closed. That's a good indicator. Last night we sent a car past with infrared equipment and they registered a huge heat plume. On infrared, that house is pulsing with heat, which is a sure sign that they're running banks of grow lamps in there. We've a good chance of scooping up a few people too; we've had reports of at least a dozen people arriving over the last hour, in dribs and drabs, hiding under their umbrellas. The door was opened only just wide enough to let them slip inside. I think we can be pretty certain . . .' Wheeler's walkie-talkie crackled. '*Unit three in position, sir.*' Wheeler turned to Fairfield. 'Let's do it, shall we?' Into the walkie-talkie he said decisively, 'Go go go!'

Immediately, the street filled with blue. Officers in protective gear and wearing helmets were approaching the front door in two lines, one burly officer carrying his 'door knocker', a heavy ram designed to break down locked doors. When he had reached the door, Fairfield and Wheeler left the car and rushed down the road to the house. Fairfield liked the house and thought it was sacrilege to turn it into a drug factory. After only the second stroke of the ram, the front door splintered open and the officer stood aside to let the press of officers trample across the threshold. Wheeler and Fairfield were last in. The heat inside was remarkable. Officers were bellowing contradictory commands. 'Armed police! This is a raid!' 'Stay where you are!' 'Show yourselves!' There were screams and then sudden silence.

Fairfield entered the large sitting room, illuminated by the warm glow of oscillating heat lamps. Apart from the overdressed officers, she counted ten people in the room, all middle-aged men and women, holding wine and sherry glasses, sitting or standing in complete astonishment. All of them were completely naked. An unnaturally pink and balding man with a perfectly round pot belly and genitals that made Fairfield think of tinned hotdogs set his wine glass down on the mantelpiece with an audible click. Rightly assuming that the man in the suit was in charge of the fiasco, he marched up to Wheeler, his penis swinging from side to side like the trunk of a charging elephant. He stood very close to the officer and bellowed at him. '*What* is the meaning of this?' Wheeler blushed to the roots of his hair.

Operation Atrium, it transpired in the overheated discussion that followed, had raided a meeting of the BBNS, the Bristol and Bath Nudist Society, at the house of its chairman, Julian Pinchbeck. Wheeler's troops shuffled from the house while Wheeler remained to explain on whose authority he had invaded his house and who his superiors were – to whom, on behalf of the entire membership, Pinchbeck would complain in the strongest terms.

By the time DI Wheeler, now covered in sweat from the sauna-like temperatures, stepped back into the rain, he was in time to see Fairfield climb into a cab. She gave a cheerful wave. 'Thanks for the experience, Keith; I shall cherish it.'

'I texted you several times and never got an answer.' As soon as he had said it, McLusky knew it was the wrong opening gambit. He could hear Laura's sharp intake of breath on the other end of the line.

'I was busy buying a new laptop, setting it up, restoring all my files on it and rewriting an essay that went up in smoke in a house in Cornwall!'

'I know, I'm sorry, but the invitation still stands. Let me take you out for dinner. I'll bring the umbrella.'

'That's why I'm calling. You can stop asking me out for dinner for a bit because I'm going on another dig.'

'I could lend you my umbrella.'

'I won't need your umbrella where I'm going.'

'Where's the dig?'

'Israel. Six of us wheedled our way on to a Tel Aviv university dig in northern Israel. It'll be brilliant, it'll be sunny and the food will be spectacular.'

'Have a good time. When are you back?'

'In three months. Good luck with your case.'

For a moment he sat frowning at his mobile, then he checked his watch. 'Bugger.'

McLusky burst from his office and moved so fast along the corridor on the CID floor that DC Dearlove had to sprint to catch up with him. 'Sir?'

'What is it, Deedee? I'm late for the autopsy.'

'Pictures you asked for. Been printed.' He proffered a Manila envelope.

'Ta.' McLusky stuffed it into a jacket pocket and clattered down the stairs, strode across the foyer and jogged to his car. It wasn't just that he was late but he was also hoping to burn a handful of calories for his imminent fitness ordeal. The rush hour was over, traffic lights were on his side and he turned into the mortuary car park with a minute to spare. Contrary to custom and despite the drizzle, he parked as far away from the entrance as possible and jogged across the car park, feeling silly and hoping no one he knew was watching.

In the theatre, Coulthart, his long-suffering assistant and the body of James Fife were all waiting for him. 'Still raining, Inspector? You should invest in an umbrella.'

'I'll think about it.' McLusky was not in the mood for banter. He sat down and almost immediately stood up again. Impatience and irritability were getting the better of him. All the cures he knew for it – chocolate, smoking, beer and sex – were out of his reach.

On one of the two screens on the wall behind Coulthart was a photograph of the Nazi dagger, next to an enhanced image of a piece of red cotton. Forensics had found the very faint outline of the dagger on the piece of fabric that had lined the display case at Poulimenos's office. While exposure to light had bleached the colour of the fabric, where objects had lain on it, it had remained a shade darker. 'No doubt about the cause of death,' Coulthart continued. He pointed over his shoulder at the screen. 'Very little doubt about the provenance of the weapon, either.'

'Yes, we now think it was stolen by the killer.'

'No fingerprints or useful DNA at all on the weapon. Let's see if I can be of help.' Coulthart began his examination with the first Y-shaped incision. 'This man was in dubious shape.'

McLusky could see the flabby stomach, the pale skin, the thin legs. 'Couch potato?'

'Yes. And I don't think much of his diet. His internal organs are covered in fat deposits. His liver is borderline. His last meal appears to have been . . .'

'Eggs, sausages and beans.'

'Correct. The condemned man ate a hearty breakfast. He must have eaten a lot of hearty breakfasts in his time. Ah, now we're getting to the interesting bit.' Coulthart was examining the area of the wound from the inside as though he was merely sorting through a kitchen drawer. 'I saw the photographs taken at the scene – you found the body with the dagger still inside it?'

'Yes, like some film noir murder scene. I'm surprised we haven't had candlesticks yet. The whole investigation has been a bit like that. Who leaves murder weapons at the scene and knives inside bodies? It's theatrical stuff.'

'I agree. And whoever delivered this piece of *theatrical stuff*, as you so eloquently put it, was particularly keen on it. A deliberate display of histrionics.'

'And you can tell this how?'

'The victim was killed with a single upwards stab to the heart. But the weapon was then withdrawn and later – I'd say a good half hour later – was returned into the wound, but not quite at the same angle. The second internal injuries are clearly post-mortem.'

'That explains the sequence of events. We thought the woman opened the door and was attacked first. But this looks like the woman arrived while the killer was still there, possibly in the sitting room. He withdrew the dagger, stabbed the woman and returned the dagger to the body of the intended victim. And left the dagger there presumably to cloud the issue. I think our killer went there for one reason only, and that was to get more ammunition for the thirty-eight.'

The rain had stopped. On the way back to his car his mobile chimed. The text message read: *You have missed your 10.30 appointment for your Annual Fitness Test. Please reply to this message to re-schedule. Non-attendance may be a disciplinary matter.* For a while he sat in his car, thinking. The thirty-eight was obviously a revolver and new ammunition would be needed after killing Mendenhall, Longmaid and Poulimenos. It suggested only one thing: that the killing was not over yet. He started the engine, pulled at his seat belt, then let go again as he felt the envelope of photographs inside his jacket. He slit open the flap and withdrew the fifty-odd photographs which were held inside a sheet of notepaper. The handwritten sentence on it read: *For the attention of DI McLusky.* Elliot Kahn had been right: the film stock had had enough time to decay. The images were sharp but the colours were faded like early colour prints from the war years, which gave them an additional nostalgic atmosphere. The first roll of film, twenty-three exposures, was taken in Cornwall; McLusky recognized Rosslyn Crag – how it had looked in happier days. In front of the conservatory, all facing the camera with various degrees of ironic smiles, were Poulimenos, Mendenhall and Longmaid. They were sprawled in deck chairs, all wearing shorts and holding long drinks. There was a female shape behind them inside the conservatory but the figure was out of focus. More pictures of the trio were taken at restaurant tables with the faded blue of a twenty-year-old summer sky behind. There was one photo of Ben Kahn himself, holding a wine glass, looking seriously into the lens. Other pictures were of the Cornish scenery, usually with a sliver of sea showing.

The second roll of film was of a very different character. All the pictures were taken in interiors, mostly inside a painting studio that he did not recognize. Without exception they were of a blonde girl and she was naked in all of them. Some looked like nude painting poses but many were a great deal more intimate, probably post-coital. McLusky put the age of the girl at no more than fourteen. He stuffed the pictures into the envelope and screeched out of the car park.

An hour later outside Stanton Drew he bumped his car up the track to Elliot Kahn's house, tyres splashing mud and rainwater from the potholes. This time the front door was closed but he could hear music inside. Seeing movement behind the kitchen window, he walked over and tapped on a pane. It was Berti who looked up, nodded and pointed towards the front door. She opened it a moment later. This time she was dressed in jeans and T-shirt but McLusky was once more struck by the troubling beauty of the girl. She stepped back to let him in. From somewhere Elliot called, 'Who is it, Berti?' and a moment later stepped into the hall himself. 'It's you again. Do you have any news?'

The girl withdrew to somewhere else in the house and McLusky followed Elliot into the kitchen. The kettle was sitting on the stove, singing gently. The music coming from another room was turned low. 'I have questions.'

'OK.' He picked up a ceramic coffee pot from beside the stove and looked inside. 'Looks like coffee in the making – are you having some?'

McLusky nodded, wondering how best to broach what could turn out to be a traumatic subject for a son who had adored his father and still suffered from not knowing what exactly happened to him and why. Or did Elliot have suspicions he had kept to himself? 'There's something I want you to look at.'

The kettle began to whistle. 'Oh, yeah? Hang on a sec.' He busied himself with making coffee, straining it the old-fashioned way into three mugs and adding milk and sugar to one of them. 'I'll just take the lamb her coffee.' While Elliot was out, McLusky searched through the prints for an inoffensive photograph and returned the others to his jacket. Elliot returned. 'Right, what do you want me to look at? Oh, did you develop the films?'

McLusky held out the photograph. 'Seen this girl before?'

Elliot took it and held it into the light. 'Not like that, I haven't. That's Vicky, but—'

'Who's Vicky?'

'Vics – Victoria Mendenhall. David's sister. She's a bit younger than him.'

McLusky set down his mug of coffee so hard on to the counter that some coffee spilled out. 'Charles Mendenhall had a daughter? *Has* a daughter? Is she alive?'

'*I* don't know. I've not heard . . . Wait.' Elliot frowned at the picture, then at McLusky. 'This photograph. Is this one of my father's? From the rolls you took away?'

McLusky nodded. 'Yes.'

'He took pictures of her in the nude. When she was a kid.'

'Some of the pictures also show paintings of her in progress. Judging by these pictures, your father painted several nudes of her.'

'Can I see the other photographs?'

'No.'

'Not for any prurient interest . . .'

'I wasn't suggesting that. Tell me about Victoria Mendenhall. Nobody involved in this case mentioned the existence of a daughter.'

'She was pretty wild.' McLusky did not know whether Elliot was offering it as a kind of explanation. A pause developed during which Elliot nervously flicked at the photo in his hand. 'Did he sleep with her?'

'I don't know.' McLusky took the photograph back and returned it to the envelope. 'I'll have to go, but I'll keep you informed of any developments. But first I need a word with your girlfriend.'

'What? Why?' Elliot's voice was sharp. 'Are you going to ask her *how old* she is?'

McLusky took no notice. He flicked through files on his mobile while he wandered through the hall towards the softly playing classical music. The young woman was standing by the window cradling her coffee mug against her chest. McLusky, closely shadowed by Elliot, walked up to her. 'Is your name Lamberti? Is this you?' He held out his phone with a picture of Fulvia Lamberti from the missing person's file.

'Yes. So?'

'We have people looking for you.'

She shrugged. 'Then you can stop looking,' she said. Her Italian accent was soft and seductive.

'Your parents don't know where you have got to. They are worried about you.'

'I don't mind that.'

'You stopped going to college. Have you dropped out for good?'

'I am learning more here.'

'Can I inform your father that we have found you?'

'Yes, but don't give him my address; he'll only turn up or send people to make trouble.'

McLusky looked around the room; it was crammed with paintings, sketchbooks, books on artists and art movements. 'Fair enough. Nice to have met you.'

On his way back to Bristol he called Elaine Poulimenos, Jennifer Longmaid and Mrs Mohr. While he spoke to them, he struggled not to litter his speech with the swear words that came so readily to his mind.

In the corridor on the CID floor he stopped DI Fairfield from disappearing into her office. 'Kat?'

Fairfield looked at him impatiently, her hand on the door handle. 'Yeah, what?'

'Your student – Fulvia Lamberti? Alive and well. And safe.'

Fairfield walked towards him like a drunk looking for a fight. 'How the hell do you know? You've seen her?'

'I have, and she's fine.' McLusky turned away.

'Wait! Where is she?'

McLusky stopped. 'Sorry. She doesn't want anyone to know.'

'I don't give a shit what the spoilt brat wants. Where is she? Why has she stopped coming to college? What is she up to?'

'She's painting. And she's in love, I guess. Look, she's over eighteen, she can do what she likes.'

'Great. In love and painting. It's all right for some. I hope you told her what she's putting her parents through and what lengths we went to in order to check that she's alive and safe.'

'Yes, I told her all of that,' McLusky lied, 'and she's very contrite.'

'I bloody well hope so.' Fairfield turned away towards her office. Her homicide case had evaporated into thin air but she felt none the lighter for it.

McLusky shrugged and continued down the corridor; a moment later he heard Fairfield's door being slammed so hard he could feel the draught of air at his back.

In the murder room at Albany Road he fumed at everyone in the room and Austin in particular. 'Everybody knew about Victoria Mendenhall, everybody knew David Mendenhall had a sister. Why the hell didn't we?'

'No one mentioned a daughter,' Austin said. 'And there was no mention of a daughter in the will—'

'I spoke to Elaine Poulimenos. According to her, Vicky went feral as a teenager, got into drugs and started stealing from her father. He threw her out. Mrs Longmaid said she'd forgotten all about her. I spoke to Mendenhall's housekeeper woman, Mohr. She said her employer had disowned the daughter and forbidden anyone from ever mentioning her in his presence. When I objected that Mendenhall was dead and not *present*, she said, "You never asked." And she was bloody right. How come a background check on the family did not dig her up?'

Dearlove had been busy hammering on his keyboard. 'Found her, sir; born 1985.'

McLusky tapped the envelope of photographs. 'That means she was about thirteen when Ben Kahn had her naked in his studio.'

'No Victoria Mendenhall on the electoral register . . .'

'If she's a drug addict, she's unlikely to bother to vote. Does she have a VW registered to her?'

Deedee accessed the DVLA files. 'No. She doesn't have a licence for a car and no vehicles registered to her.'

'Details like that never stopped people with chaotic life styles. Find her!' He stormed out of the incident room to his office, Austin following at a safe distance. In his office he scrabbled around on his desk for a scribbled number and called it. Austin was amazed at the happy politeness in the inspector's voice. 'Good afternoon, McLusky here. Is Mr Mendenhall there, please? Oh, not to worry, thank you.' He hung up. 'David's secretary. He's not been at his drinks empire today.' He snatched up his car keys. 'We'll see if he's home, shall we, Jane?'

As they strode across the Albany Road car park towards his car, his phone went; it was DC Dearlove. 'Hospital just called.

Jamie Fife's girlfriend briefly regained consciousness. Her name is Nicola Bacham. She was awake just long enough to say her attacker was a woman.'

'Ta, Deedee. Nice to have one's suspicions confirmed.'

McLusky drove fast. In his mind, the murder of Jamie Fife for the sake of a few bullets suggested that Victoria Mendenhall, if she was behind the killings, was about to strike again. 'And who is left apart from the women? Only David.'

'But why would David not have mentioned her?' Austin objected as he clung to the door handle for support through the corners.

'Because he knew it was her? Because he was in on the killings from the start? I thought he was behind it right from the start. He is the one to benefit from his father's death. And the moment I saw the photographs of the naked Victoria I realized I had seen the face before. It was in a family photograph on the mantelpiece at the house. When David turned it around, I thought it was a gesture of grief, but he wanted to make sure I did not see the girl in the picture. It had barely registered at the time.'

'But the next two murders . . .?'

'She killed them to suggest a different motive for the first murder. It's Sherlock bloody Holmes's bloody letter rack. Where to hide a letter? Among a lot of other letters. By the time Poulimenos was dead I was convinced David had nothing to do with it.' On the dashboard McLusky's airwave radio, which had been sliding back and forth during cornering, came to life. 'Answer that for me, Jane.'

'Alpha nine.'

'We have just received a nine-nine-nine call from a Mr Mendenhall at Woodlea House. Request for an ambulance.'

McLusky called loudly, 'Thanks, control. DS Austin and I are nearly there.' He speeded up even more, fishtailing around the turn-off towards Woodlea House with a tense and wide-eyed DS Austin beside him. One leaf of the double gate stood open. It was not quite wide enough for the Mercedes, as McLusky found out as he barged though it, crumpling the left wing against the second leaf, pushing it wide.

He raced up to the house. David's BMW was the only vehicle in front of it. Its windscreen was shattered, now a blind cobweb of broken glass; both headlights had been staved in and the driver window shattered. A red brick lay on the bonnet.

Austin ran to it. 'No one in the car.'

'Front door locked. Round the back.' Austin was already running around the house, but McLusky turned back, picked up the brick from the bonnet and followed. He caught up with him at the French windows.

'Locked,' said Austin.

'Open,' said McLusky and threw the brick through the glass. Once inside, they started searching the rooms, calling David's name. They found him upstairs, slumped against the wall in his father's office next to a blood-smeared phone. He was conscious. He held a seat cushion pressed against his side. Blood had soaked into his pale pink shirt.

'Ambulance is on its way,' said Austin.

McLusky nodded his head at the door. 'You're an expert at this now, Jane; see if there's a first-aid kit in the BMW and leave the front door open for the ambulance.' He turned to David who was looking straight at him, alert but in obvious pain. 'Your sister?' David nodded. 'All the killings?'

He nodded again, then made an effort to speak. 'She was cut out of the will. We were going to share it.'

'But the other two murders?

'To lay a false trail. I had nothing to do with that. Vicky is quite mental. I had no idea. I threatened to give myself up. She shot me. I think she knows I'm not dead. I think she couldn't bring herself to shoot me again. That means she can't be all bad, doesn't it?'

'Where is she?'

'She's been living in a derelict pub down by the canal near Limpley Stoke. The Moon.'

'I'll find it.'

Austin returned with a first-aid kit and began to rip open packs of gauze and bandages.

McLusky was already by the door. 'What does she drive? A VW?'

David spoke with difficulty now. 'She rides a trike. Beetle engine.'

On his way downstairs McLusky called control, told them the victim was being looked after by a trained first-aider and ordered an armed response unit to Victoria Mendenhall's address.

The Moon Inn by the Kennet and Avon canal had closed three years previously and had stood empty and unloved. The few boaters who tied up on the short mooring and the sparse walkers at this overgrown bit of the towpath had not been enough trade to keep it going. The Moon had always suffered from the fact that access from the road was along a narrow potholed track and the complete absence of any parking spaces by the building which was hemmed in by the canal on one side and large trees and water meadow on the others. Now it was also in danger of being swallowed up by brambles which had grown right up to it. A few slender self-sown trees grew close to the hundred-year-old building.

McLusky had left the car on the road and taken to the narrow lane. The verges were overgrown with high grasses, and the trees to either side had deposited three autumns' worth of leaves on to the perished tarmac where they had formed an incomplete layer of leaf mould. Three lines of marks were clearly visible where a heavy trike had moved back and forth. Moving from tree to tree for cover, he did not see the trike until he had nearly reached the building. Although the blue-and-yellow pub sign was missing, faded ancient writing on the sandstone above the door still proclaimed this to be the *Moon Inn, Free House*. The windows were boarded up but the front door had its board removed and stood ajar. The trike was parked to the left of the frontage, pointing towards the track. It was a large machine, nearly as broad as a car at the back, with the single front wheel on long raked-out forks, surmounted by cow-horn handlebars. The trike had a single seat at the front and a two-seat bench at the back, which had disappeared under a large overstuffed holdall and two bin liners tied on with bungee cord. The logical and operationally sound procedure would be to wait for armed response to make the arrest, but the bike looked as if departure was imminent. McLusky approached the machine cautiously, keeping half an eye on the front door. The ignition was next to the speedometer on the handle bars and the keys were in it. He had taken three quick steps towards it, his hand outstretched towards the keys, when Victoria Mendenhall's voice stopped him.

'Keep your filthy paws off my bike.' She emerged from the front door gun hand first, pointing the muzzle of an old Webley army revolver at him with her right while carrying a brown tasselled leather bag in her left. She was wearing jeans and black trainers and a zipped-up black biker jacket. 'He told you, then? The stupid coward. David was always useless. And you're a fucking nuisance.' She slammed the bag on top of the bin liners and snapped the bungee cords across it.

'Yes. He told us about the killings. That you killed your father for the inheritance. A bit tacky, if you don't mind me saying.'

Her hand tensed on the heavy revolver that she kept pointed at his chest. 'What the fuck do you know? I had plenty of reasons for killing my dear daddy.'

'Because he threw you out?'

'Bullshit! Because he threw Ben into the Atlantic.'

'You think so?'

'How else do you think it happened? All three of them.' She swung herself into the saddle. 'Dad found out he had been sleeping with me. The fat Greek had seen the paintings and drawings he had done of me. So they pushed him over-board, I'm sure of it. I never believed any of that accident crap – not then, not now. And poor, poor Elliot. They were all so sorry for poor little Elliot who had lost his dad. What about me?' She was shouting now, spit flying. 'I had lost a lover! I was thirteen and my whole world had disappeared! My father treated me like I had an infectious disease after that. And he didn't chuck me out – I left. Then he disinherited me because having been seduced by one of his bloody friends was my fucking fault, of course!' She started the engine which rattled into life with the distinctive Beetle sound. 'I know I should shoot you, but I only have five rounds left and I have a feeling I'll need them when I get to the end of the track. Because you wouldn't be stupid enough to turn up here all by yourself.' McLusky made no answer. 'Would you?' A brief smile flickered on her face, then she stuffed the gun into the top of her jacket and opened the throttle. The trike noisily clattered past McLusky to the head of the track where Victoria lined it up and accelerated. McLusky ran to the track, pulled out the Derringer and cocked it. He shouted over the engine noise, 'Stop or I'll shoot!'

Whether she had heard the actual words or not he could not tell, but he saw her look into her mirror. He aimed to miss, but not by much, and fired. The bullet whisked past her close enough for her to look over her shoulder. Her expression was more of surprise than fear. She opened the throttle wide, accelerating away. Only one bullet remained. Was he going to waste it too on a warning shot? He closed his eyes and fired the second and last bullet. It too missed yet it whisked so closely past Victoria's left ear that she jinked violently to the right. The front wheel of the trike slid into a pothole, she overcorrected and the trike shot at a violent angle to the left. Its front hit the tree as it overturned, burying its rider underneath. The engine raced for an instance, then stalled in a puff of smoke.

McLusky ran towards it, then slowed, then stopped and stood in the sudden silence twenty paces away from the twisted, ticking wreck. He could see one arm moving, pushing ineffectually against the weight of the heavy trike. He stared at it as though he were watching a reptilian movement; he could not find in himself the slightest impulse to help. With a soft coughing sound the trike caught fire. Victoria, trapped underneath with one arm and ankle broken, her clothes soaked with petrol from a severed fuel line, was enveloped in flame. For a moment McLusky saw her struggle, then the flames and smoke obscured his view.

He turned his back on it and walked back to the pub. On the left hand side was an overgrown area bordering the towpath, where once the beer garden had been. He made his way through the high grass to the edge of the canal. There were no boats or walkers in sight. He waited until a family of ducks had passed before lobbing the Derringer into the middle of the canal.